THE LION AND THE ROSE, BOOK TWO: THE GATHERING STORM

HILARY RHODES

For friends
old and new

The Lion and the Rose, Book Two: The Gathering Storm.
Original electronic version published 2014. Print version © 2016 by
Hilary Marie Rhodes. All rights reserved.

ISBN: 9781519097163

PROLOGUE

Winchester, England
November 1050

THE CLOUDS LAY OVER the river bottom like a heavy iron mantle, bare trees creaking in the autumn gale and the wind whistling forlornly through the chinks. The thatch of the cottars' cottages had been strewn in all directions, and from his solar window, Godwin of Wessex could watch a swineherd struggling in the mud with his recalcitrant charges, holding up his hood against the rain slashing sideways. *Their lives are nasty and short.* There was a great and tangible cost in this dark and grim earthly realm, for failing to seize power when it was there to be taken. He regretted none of the choices he'd made when it was to conquer or to collapse, whether it was accepting the earldom of Wessex from the Viking usurper Canute, serving him his life long, then double-crossing and betraying Alfred Aetheling, son of the last true king, in support of Canute's son. Well, that last. . . it *would* have behooved him to have done somewhat differently. It was Alfred's elder brother Edward who had finally become king of the English, seven years ago, and he made no attempt to disguise his rancid, rotting acrimony toward the man responsible for doing away with his last living relation. Wessex might still be the most powerful earldom of the four beneath the crown, but that meant nothing. A king's enmity was never to be underestimated. And with Edward or without him, Godwin meant to keep what was his.

He turned back to the letter he was writing, pausing to consider his words. He did not at all like the news his spies had brought, though he should have been expecting it. Edward, despite being wed to Godwin's eldest daughter, had continued to fall down

5

on the kingly duty of getting an heir on her, and hence had been sniffing around in unwelcome quarters for a possible replacement. Hence, he had sent Robert Champart, Bishop of London, to Normandy earlier this year. The place had been embroiled in a vicious, chaotic, and draining civil war for over a decade, which had only recently ended. It had done so thanks to the offices of its new Duke – well, old one truthfully, the lad had held the title in name since he was seven, and his father died on pilgrimage. But as he was a bastard-born babe, the powerful and ruthless Norman barons had decided he could much more profitably be deprived of life, land, and holdings, leaving them to enjoy fief of the place instead. One unarmed, penniless child, guarded only by a small group of devoted men whittled thinner every year with poison or ambush or assassination. How difficult could it be?

Apparently, quite. The boy's entire minority had been nothing but one long and gruesome attempt to kill him, and yet they had not succeeded. And he was no longer a boy. Two-and-twenty, a man who had crushed his opponents at the Battle of Val-ès-Dunes three years ago with the help of the French king, who had become the most feared young warrior on the Continent, who was now, if the rumours were true, betrothed to the Count of Flanders' daughter Matilda – a match that would firmly reinforce him as a dangerous player in the games of politics and power. Oh yes indeed. A wolf not to be overlooked, William of Normandy. And even worse, he was Edward's cousin. Once removed or something of the sort, but in the present climate, with a childless king searching for an heir, especially a childless king who had spent almost all of his life in Norman exile and had a decided temperament for their language and culture. . .

Godwin's mouth tightened. No, this could not be allowed. Especially with Champart off to make a report on the man, something which Edward still thought he did not know. He had a plot of his own in mind, but –

Just then, a knock on the door wakened him from his reverie, and he glanced up to see a servant hovering on the threshold. 'My lord? A messenger's come. Urgent news.'

'Is that so?' Godwin put his quill back in its pot, and shoved away the hound that was drooling on his knee. 'Show him in before he melts away, this weather has been horrendous.'

The servant hurried off. Godwin cast another stick of wood on the fire, prodded it back to a roar, and made sure he hadn't got any ink on his hands. Then he seated himself again and waited for his visitor to be shown in: a bedraggled, dripping, shivering monk, who continued to shiver as he bowed. 'M-my lord.'

Godwin inclined his head. 'Whom do I have the pleasure of addressing?'

'B-Brother Théomund, m-my lord. Of C-Canterbury.'

'Very good.' Godwin presented his hand for the monk to kiss. 'Urgent news?'

'Aye, my lord.' Brother Théomund crossed himself. 'Archbishop Eadsige is dead.'

There was a long pause. 'Indeed,' said Godwin.

'Aye. It wasn't unexpected. . . he so old, and this poor weather. God rest his soul.'

'God rest his soul,' Godwin agreed. Inside, his mind was already whirring. Eadsige had been his creature, and had incurred considerable criticism for his habit of persistently siphoning off land and money to the earldom of Wessex. The archbishop of Canterbury was a useful ally, and Godwin felt that he should have anticipated this development, but he had not. Nonetheless, he had a long and well-practised ability to land on his feet. 'How long ago?'

'Just a few days past, before All Hallows.'

'And the monks will soon place their nominations for a new archbishop?'

'Aye, my lord.'

'Whenever they do, I hope they remember my kinsman Æthelric, who has served there for some time. Quite ably too, I understand.' Godwin smiled at the monk. 'You look cold, Brother Théomund. Would you care for a goblet of mulled wine?'

'Th-thank you, my lord, but I really must be getting back.'

Godwin shrugged. 'If you insist. At least allow me to provide you with a dry cloak.'

Brother Théomund was induced to accept this liberty, and departed into the dusk. Godwin watched him go, considering, then turned to the servant. 'Fetch my son Harold.'

The servant scuttled out again, leaving Godwin to prepare the mulled wine for himself instead. He sat to wait, sipping, until the servant and Harold returned. Godwin dismissed the former and indicated the latter to take a seat, which he did. Stretching out his long legs, Harold accepted the goblet that Godwin handed him, fair skin ruddy from the wind and hair tousled with sleet. 'It's colder than blazes out there.'

'Indeed. No doubt you are wondering why I dragged you out of a warm hall. Well, I have a few pieces of news.'

'Aye?'

'Aye. First, Edward sent that creeping Champart off to visit Duke William of Normandy, earlier this year. My source swears up and down that it was only a diplomatic courtesy, but I think that as likely as me growing wings from my arse. Secondly, Archbishop Eadsige of Canterbury is dead, and I did my best – not too delicately, I fear – to plant the notion that the monks should support your cousin Æthelric for the succession.'

Godwin took a drink, watching his son's face. At the moment, it showed polite interest coupled with complete confusion. 'I am sorry to hear it,' Harold said. 'I am sure that Eadsige will rest in peace, he was a good man.'

'Indeed,' said Godwin again.

Harold raised an eyebrow. 'No doubt there is another motive here which you wish me to discover, but I fear I lack your subtlety, Father, so I'll ask straight out. What do you mean?'

'I mean that Edward is sending secret envoys to France! The last thing we need is for him to name the Bastard his heir!'

'The last I looked, Edward *was* King of England. He does have that prerogative.'

Godwin frowned. 'Who are you loyal to? Edward or me?'

'I was not aware that was a choice which had to be made.' Harold's clear blue eyes had gone flinty. 'If you're trying to recruit me into your intrigues, you'll have to do better. I won't betray my king, and I won't betray my country.'

Godwin considered that Harold's propensity for gallantry was really rather tiresome. 'That is precisely why you should be concerned. Aren't there enough Frenchmen already? Next he *will* name the Norman his heir, and we'll be but a province of France!'

'Are you suggesting I sue for him to name me instead?'

'Something to that effect, yes.'

'Sweyn – '

'Come, lad, do better than that. Any man wagering on Sweyn to do anything aside from cause trouble will lose his money. He's a *niðing*, after all.'

'He is my elder brother.'

'And drastically unpopular. I did everything I could for him, but he could hang himself with a handspan of rope. When Sweyn careers over the cliff and into happy oblivion, you will stand as heir to my title, lands, and wealth.'

'Sound any sadder, Father, and you'll be weeping.'

'Why are you pretending affection for Sweyn?' Godwin regarded his son with a cool green gaze. 'He has had his chances. He is out of my hands. You're much better fitted.'

'If that was a compliment, thank you.'

'It was. From this moment on, you will be groomed as my heir. Why not ask Edward to name you heir to England as well? Not out loud of course, but carefully, slowly. Elegantly. Get him to trust you, share the burden. He keeps running into difficulties with the witan. Help smooth them over. If we can get Æthelric into Canterbury, why, there's the first step to securing it. You are my son, Harold. You'll never be anything else.'

'Just like Edith will never be anything but your daughter,' Harold mumbled.

'What was that?'

'Nothing, Father.'

'This is for England.' Godwin refused to let Harold off the hook. 'To keep it guarded against the French. If it means going against your king's will at the moment, we'll all be better served in the future.'

Harold was quiet, and Godwin knew he'd struck a vein. Then Harold said, 'No doubt you are right. May I have your leave to go, my lord?'

Godwin waved it. Harold rose from his chair, bowed, and was gone into the darkness.

PART ONE

The Lion and the Wyvern

1051 – 1060

CHAPTER ONE

London, England
August 1051

'WELCOME TO ENGLAND, my lord. I pray you'll overlook the smudges.' The king of the English descended the dais to clasp his visitor's arm. 'It's good to see you, Eustace.'

'And you, Your Grace.' Count Eustace of Boulogne, a thin, angular man whose face looked perpetually pinched, was Edward's former brother-in-law, the second husband of his late sister Goda, and the two of them remained close allies. 'Though I must say, I see no smudges.'

'These aren't the sort you would,' Edward said dryly. 'Just a way to say that all is not. . . ah. . . internally tidy at the moment. I fear Earl Godwin is sulking.'

'Why?'

'Because he made a brazen attempt to install his lackey to the archbishopric of Canterbury, and I stopped him, that's why.' Edward smiled. 'I made sure Robert Champart was appointed instead. He recently returned from Rome with the pallium, and Godwin was obligated to watch him be enthroned.' This more or less qualified as the truth, but notably failed to mention that the monks of Canterbury, who actually *had* chosen Æthelric, had been less than pleased at the king interfering with their ancient right to select their own archbishop. Edward, however, thought it had been justified in this instance. He knew quite well what was at stake, and he flatly refused to give Godwin virtual command of the Church.

Eustace made a shocked noise. 'Who does this Saxon think he is, to defy you like that? Unless it is a habit – yes, it must be. I seem to recall he was the shining example who butchered all my men with your brother Alfred.'

Edward cast a furtive look over his shoulder. Some of the courtiers, noting his preference for French, had learnt it, and it would do him no good to have them overhearing that. 'It can be trying. The English have a stubbornly patriotic streak, and anyone I appoint with a French name must be resisted on that alone.'

Eustace shook his head. 'Even more difficult, I collect, is the fact that you are married to Godwin's daughter?'

'My queen is not to blame,' Edward said gruffly. 'I have been advised several times to set her aside, but I will not.'

'She has not given you an heir, however.' Eustace shrugged. 'You may be interested to hear that I have brought my stepson with me – your nephew Ralph. A good lad, courtly and mannered, if perhaps a touch too chary at times. I hope your barbarians will stiffen his mettle.'

'Is that so,' Edward said neutrally. He could hear, of course, what Eustace was truly saying, and indeed as his sister's son, Ralph had the strongest claim by blood. The last thing he needed, however, was to throw a meek, waffling young Frenchman to the English wolves. If Godwin wasn't de facto king within a fortnight of Ralph's coronation, Edward would be disappointed in him. *I need someone who can hold these madmen.*

Nonetheless, Edward succeeded in getting his hopes up that the visit would go well. The banquet that night was even accomplished without a single derogatory remark about pet Frenchmen – at least, none that he heard. Ralph proved a charming young man, whom Edward took a liking to at once, and Eustace refrained from insulting his lords to their faces.

The only hint that all might not be copasetic came, as usual, from the Godwinsons. Five of them – the earl of Wessex was the patriarch of a damnably fertile family. Sweyn, Harold, Tostig, Gyrth, and Leofwine. Sweyn's hawk glare was fixed on Ralph, which Ralph was attempting to pretend he had not noticed. Harold looked troubled, Tostig drank too much, and Gyrth and Leofwine were playing a game that required them to shout some sort of colourful word, clash their tankards, and arm-wrestle furiously, whereupon the loser had to chug the victor's ale at one go. The rest of the hall started getting into it, and trouble developed when Gyrth beat one of Eustace's knights three times running. 'Ah, you French piglet,' he said. 'You can't match against a real man.'

Either the soldier had a better grasp of Saxon than expected, or he took the meaning admirably from the tone of voice, because he launched himself at Gyrth – a decision doubtless facilitated by the three tankards he'd had to imbibe. Gyrth, as Viking-tall, broad, and strong as the rest of his brothers, got his assailant in a headlock and danced him in a circle, making oinking noises, to the uproarious amusement of his fellows. The rest of Eustace's men sat looking very tight-lipped, something Edward noted with a sinking heart. Then, deciding that he had damned well better remember he was king, and do something about it, he shot to his feet. 'GYRTH GODWINSON!'

Gyrth dropped the sputtering Boulonnais into the rushes. 'Your Grace?'

'Leave off this childish foolery at once,' Edward ordered. 'The man did you no insult.'

Gyrth blinked incredulously. 'He jumped me.'

'Because you insulted him. I will not have you shaming me like this before our honoured guests. Apologise at once.'

Gyrth looked at the snivelling Frenchman, then back at his brothers, who were in transports of mirth; even Harold was biting a smile. 'Sorry,' he said lazily.

Leofwine got up and sauntered over to Gyrth, slinging a companionable arm over his shoulders. 'Don't worry, milord, we were just finished here. Weren't we, lads?'

'Aye,' Sweyn grated, eyes still fixed on Ralph. 'Harold, help me with Tostig.'

Harold glanced at Edward briefly, but obeyed Sweyn. The two of them hauled the giggling Tostig upright and suspended him between them, his boots dragging like a puppet's. It was in a suddenly complete silence that the five Godwinsons vanished through the heavy doors at the end of the hall. They closed with a boom that must have been heard in Hell.

'The ingrates!' Eustace fumed, later. 'They insulted us on purpose! They walked out – any man tells me there was no disrespect meant, and I will tell him he is a liar!'

Edward said nothing, mainly because he could not deny it. Eustace was, of course, right – it was a slap in the face of the first order. He was angry as well, furious that the Godwinsons had to always complicate everything. Christ, they *were* barbarians, and worse, there was a sixth – young Wulfnoth, only ten years old, but sure to grow up another head of the snake. He disliked blaming children for their fathers' sins, as it reminded him too much of his cousin William and how he had left the boy in a vulnerable position, to pursue his own inheritance in England. But every day Godwin and his ilk ran unchecked, the more dangerous they grew.

Eustace was still ranting. Hoping to distract him, Edward said, 'On the morrow, I'll show you the site where I am building a splendid church, on Thorney Island. Dedicated to St Peter.'

'St Peter? Any reason?'

'Aye. I swore that if I became king, I would undertake a pilgrimage to St Peter's Basilica in Rome, to make up for the sin of abjuring my vows as a monk. But it would be worse than foolish to leave my kingdom for a day, let alone for months, so I decided to build a church instead.' Edward had spent much of his time in Normandy as a monk in Fécamp Abbey, a temperament and a vocation that he oftentimes felt he had been vastly more suited for. Tilling the fields and singing the hours was scant preparation for the realities of ruling a kingdom.

'In the style of the Continent, I am sure?'

'But of course. The Saxons do not have much skill in architecture.'

'Do they have skill in anything apart from bashing one another's brains out, my lord?' Eustace asked sourly. 'I have already lost quite enough thanks to this lawless gang of wastrels.'

Edward hastily attempted to steer them off this dangerous topic. 'Also, you may wish to spend a few days in Dover. It is beautiful in this high summer.'

'Dover. I shall consider it.' Eustace got up. 'I'd best go see that Ralph hasn't gotten into any more fights with that horrid Sweyn character. Good night, my lord.'

It wasn't until after Eustace had gone that Edward had time to think on what he had said, at which his heart sank still further. *I wish there was a way to rid myself of Godwin and his spawn all at once. One clean bolt from heaven. I do not pray often for violence. It frightens me that I am doing so now. I fear that I am losing my path, O God. My torch is flickering out, and soon I will be alone here in my darkness, a small and bitter old man, waiting for an echo.*

The next morning, Eustace departed for Dover in a puff of dignified outrage, removing himself, Ralph, and the rest of his muttering Boulonnais for what Edward desperately hoped would be a relaxing outing. Not that it seemed exceedingly likely. Nobody had been sorry to see them go, and more than one comment was made to the order that if m'lord decided to carry on right back across the Channel, he would be doing the whole of England a favour. Edward was grimly aware that public sentiment was overwhelmingly on the side of the Godwinsons, who were cheered for having the nerve to thumb their noses at the latest incursion of meddlesome Frenchmen. Gyrth in particular was strutting around like a victorious pugilist, escorted by crowds of admirers. *Aye, and now it's the fashion to defy your king.*

Edward woke often that night, and had disturbing dreams when he did slip off. He finally gave up near dawn and rose, going to his small chapel. It was early enough that even his chaplain – Osbern fitz Osbern, one of the many Normans who had come to England with him at his accession – was still abed, and the castle had not yet roused to life. Yet he breathed the cool morning air, and managed, for an entire hour, to feel at peace.

This apparently impermissible state of affairs was remedied late that afternoon, while Edward was occupied with business. The financial situation had been retrieved enough that he was considering abolishing the *heregild*, a measure introduced in his father's day to keep the treasury stocked in the all-too-likely event of a Viking attack. But he had not been required to pay off armed invaders yet, and he took leave to hope that this would continue. Like most taxes ever invented by mankind, the *heregild* had been the cause of heated displeasure since its inception, and without marauding Danes to require it, he might just –

'Your Grace?' A harried voice interrupted him.

Edward jumped, nearly overturning his inkwell, and looked up to see a servant hovering in the doorway. At once his hackles went up. *Oh Christ, now what?* He arrested the inkwell before it ruined his work, resisting the urge to rub his tired eyes. 'Aye?'

'My lord. There has been a. . . small disturbance. At Dover.'

And by small, doubtless you mean colossal. 'What?'

'Your kinsman Eustace and his men. . . ran into a difference of opinion with the Dover townsfolk,' said the servant evasively.

'They demanded to be fed and sheltered for the night. The townsfolk refused. The matter escalated. There was a brawl. . .'

Oh, bloody hellfire. 'Was anyone wounded?'

'Aye, and . . .' The servant hesitated. 'My lord, I fear there are several dead.'

'Where is my kinsman?' Edward asked, far more levelly than he felt.

'But recently arrived back in London.'

God almighty, if they see him, they'll start another riot. Edward turned away, vying in vain for calm and control. The dragon in his chest was breathing a firestorm. 'Fetch him.'

The servant bowed and scampered. Upon his re-entrance some moments later with the grubby Count of Boulogne in tow, he immediately made himself scarce, a decision for which Edward could not fault him. Eustace was sooty, breathless, and almost incoherent with fury.

'They are savages!' he gibbered, pouring a cup of wine and splashing it everywhere. 'All we asked for was decent lodging and a good supper, hardly unreasonable! And what do they do but fall on us like the witless beasts they are! By the love you bear me, my lord, punish them!'

'I shall.' Edward noticed his brother-in-law was still wearing his armour – itself a harbinger of trouble, as no man would ride in full chainmail unless expecting an imminent attack. 'I swear.'

This promise of justice was far from enough to placate Eustace, who subsided into a chair, wiping his forehead and gulping his wine. He was so thoroughly overwrought that it took close on three goblets to bring him back under control, and Edward stood gazing out the window, as the light faded. Finally he said, 'Go to bed. I will have double the guard on your chambers.'

Eustace hauled himself to his feet and nodded jerkily. He departed in a sullen silence, and Edward turned to a page. 'Fetch me,' he said, even more grimly, 'my lord of Wessex.'

The page's jaw dropped. 'G-Godwin?'

'None other. And his sons. All of them. Saving only the youngest, Wulfnoth.'

'The sons are here, but the earl is in Winchester, Your Grace.'

'Send a messenger. I want him here by morning.'

'With respect, Your Grace, it is – '

'*Now.*'

Edward had never heard that coldness in his own voice before. He fancied that he was standing on the brink of a lightless abyss, as if his kingship, and indeed his life, hinged on his next move. And it was not cowardice he felt, for he had never been less afraid. But all there was in its place was a hot, hard wall of iron. *I am hating,* he realised. *It is even easier than I thought.*

He lay awake all that night, boiling himself dry with it. When the morning came, he rose, and went out to meet his match.

'I must have misheard, Your Grace.' Godwin's face showed the weariness of a long ride to London, but his voice remained as urbane as ever. 'Surely a man as renowned for wisdom as you would not ask such a thing of me.'

'Surely a man as renowned for brutality as you would not shrink from it.' Edward whirled to stare down the earl. 'Dover is under your jurisdiction. The townsfolk damn near started a war for the most vanishing of causes, insulted Eustace and killed several of his men. I would be fool indeed to let them think they can expect no reprisal. I will not wear a puppet crown. Punish them.'

Godwin's green eyes were flint. His sons stood at his back like stormclouds, Sweyn and Tostig shoulder to shoulder, Gyrth and Leofwine grinning, Harold with that same troubled look. Godwin himself spoke two words. 'I refuse.'

'You wish to join them in their treason?'

'I fail to see how punishing my own countrymen counts as service to the crown.'

'*I* fail to see how permitting anarchy is in the service of the crown!' Edward snarled. 'Because you speak the same language, that makes you all one? Mayhaps next you won't hang a murderer who has green eyes, is that just as defensible?'

Godwin laughed. 'Perhaps all that fame for your wisdom is quite in error, my lord. You sad little would-be Norman, with your pet archbishops and your shoving and your grasping and your French. You've never wanted to be an *English* king. You've gone so long in exile that it would have been better if you'd never returned.'

'God rot you! You brand yourself more a traitor with every word you speak!'

'My lord.' Harold's voice was so quiet that Edward almost did not hear. 'My father speaks without tact, but he strikes at the heart of the matter. We long for you to be our king. *Our* king. You were turned out from England when very young. It is reasonable that you seek to reshape it as the only place you found solace. But it is more than a language. It is who we are.'

'Oh,' said Edward. 'Aye. Speaks the half-Dane.'

Harold held his gaze. 'Why do you shun the Danes, and not the Normans?'

'The Normans never assailed this country constantly for the last three centuries.'

'Nor ruled it twenty years with good purpose and fairness, encouraged settlement and intermarriage. The Normans do not attack us with swords, nay. But they attack something deeper: our very soul. Not on purpose, mayhaps. But it happens nonetheless.'

Edward remained pale. 'I will give you one more chance, Godwin. Punish the burghers of Dover, and I will forget even this. Or else you are in defiance of your king.'

The look Godwin gave him might have withered the Tree of Knowledge. '*My* king?'

'Aye. Perhaps you recall an oath you made at my coronation, when you knelt in the sight of God and man to do me your homage? *I acknowledge my most grievous transgressions. You need never doubt my loyalty. I am your man now, in life or in death.*'

Godwin's lips curled in an even more alarming smile. 'Pardon. That was when I still thought you something you are not.'

'Do you stand as an oathbreaker?'

'Does an oath sworn to a lie have any power to hold a man?'

'Then get out,' Edward said. 'Go, and think on your own lies. And then, my lord Godwin, we shall judge who is in the greater wrong here.'

Godwin bowed. He turned, escorted by his sons. It was only Harold who looked back. 'My lord. Do not do this.'

Edward's lips peeled back. 'I shall stand for no more,' he said. 'I will.'

The rumours were about by Vespers. Godwin was summoning the might of Wessex: ships, housecarls, fyrdmen. He was about to raise his banners in open defiance of the crown.

Edward stood in the chapel and did not hear a word of the service. Afterward, he returned to his chamber and wrote two more summons. He stamped them with his ring, gave them to a messenger, and sat staring out the window. It was some hours later that he was roused by the arrival of the first man he had sent for: the earl of Mercia. Old and stout and strong as a weathered oak, Leofric had counselled Edward sagely in previous times of trouble. 'Your Grace,' he said. 'You have my oath in life or death, I meant it. If Godwin is gathering an army, I will stand for my king.'

Edward let out a breath. 'I know what this is. If I break, it is the end of me. I will not.'

'Godwin has broken many stronger men, my lord. And over worse causes.'

Edward glanced at him sharply. He had heard both things said: firstly, that he, Edward, was far from the most worthy foe Godwin had faced, and secondly, that Leofric himself thought Godwin's sentiments at least somewhat justified. 'Well, I thank you. If I may ask a question?'

'Of course, Your Grace.'

'If I ordered you to fight Godwin, would you do it?'

Leofric paused. 'Godwin is the Earl of Wessex – the strongest and wealthiest of us all, but Goliath falls the harder for being hit with a small stone. Yet since you ask, Your Grace, no. I do not wish to be the one to fling it. You swore to me once that you would not tear the country apart for the sake of your own grudges.'

'I am king. Anointed by God, set in my place by the rightness of heaven.'

'Kings are held to higher standards than other men.'

Edward clenched his fists. 'Will you muster your levies?'

'I will, my lord.'

'Godwin is your rival. Will you attack him for that?'

'If he should happen to stumble into his own downfall over this matter – why then, how fortunate. But while Godwin and I have never liked each other, I do not feel the need to place my rivalry with him over the good of the country.' Leofric paused again. 'However, I fear my son Ælfgar may not feel likewise.'

Wonderful, Edward thought. *So there's that to look forward to as well.*

'Your Grace,' said Siward of Northumbria. His eyes shone beneath craggy brows, like dark pools in the gauntness of his face. 'I will stand against this traitorous southerner, have no doubt.'

Edward kept his own gaze on the earl's. 'You will.'

'Aye.' Siward's laugh was like a distant avalanche. 'Long the North was under the rule of the Vikings, in the days of the Danelaw. That was an older time, colder, stronger. The southerners are not like us. They know nothing of honour, as Godwin proves.'

'My lord?'

'Aye?'

'If I told you to attack Wessex on the morrow, would you?'

'If you ordered, my lord, I would see it done with my whole soul. I can hate the southerners, for I am born and bred of the north. Yet are you king of all England, or part?'

'What I am not,' said Edward, low and vehement, 'is a coward. Muster your levies.'

The next three weeks passed at an excruciating peak of tension. It was not quite a war, yet it stood at the very precipice of one, the breath before a storm. Godwin was threatening to unloose his lightning at any moment, but Leofric and Siward's combined thunder was set against him – resulting in them all, for the nonce, holding in check. *And here I was thinking that I would not have to pay off armed invaders again. That is half-true – they are not invaders. No. The enemies are inside the walls.* Edward *could* order Leofric and Siward to attack Godwin and make an end of it. He could bring the war. He could. He was King. Oh God Almighty, he was King.

Yet there was one last chance. Never had he known less where the line between cowardice and prudence lay. *All I have been doing is running from it, doing anything so long as it cannot be used to call me craven.* Under the shadow of rebellion and war, he called together the feuding parties: himself, the earls, and the witanagemot, to meet at Gloucester on the Welsh marches. A last chance to resolve the conflict by diplomacy, and not by blood. But considering all that was weighing on it, it could have started out better. To say the very barest least.

'My lord Godwin could not have made his intentions clearer!' The archbishop of Canterbury's face was flushed with ugly colour. 'He is plotting to kill our gracious liege King Edward and install himself to the throne, by violent and unlawful usurpation! He stands in arms as a traitor and forsworn before God!'

Godwin rose to his feet. He had refused to come to the moot without his army, and as such was surrounded by a sea of soldiers. 'My lord Champart thinks himself well informed, I see. It is in this England alone that I can be adjudged treasonous for standing up for my country. Truly, my lords, our grandsires pitch in their graves.'

'What would you know of that?' one of the Mercian ealdormen sneered. 'Or no, I suppose you know a great deal. Aren't you attempting to send us to join them?'

Godwin swung on him, but Robert Champart interrupted. 'The realm can never be safe so long as these madmen are permitted to defy the king so freely. Wessex is but a pale and tawdry shadow of itself, led by an earl whose hands are stained with blood.'

'Surely you know a great deal about the lore of Wessex, my Norman friend,' Godwin snapped. 'You've had nothing else to do ever since the king helped you to buy Canterbury. So ironic that you refused to consecrate your successor to the bishopric of London on grounds of simony. I *do* find it amusing when clergymen preach morals only when it suits them.'

There was an incendiary uproar. Every delegation began to shout at once, some actual fistfights breaking out in the benches. It was Leofric who bellowed, 'STOP THIS MADNESS!'

Fraught silence fell, awaiting any stray spark to ignite the inferno. Old anger and deep grudges carved the air like wounds, and the archbishop of Canterbury took a moment to compose himself. Then he said, 'It is clear that this situation cannot be mended so long as the rebels remain. And so I advise the witanagemot, Earls Leofric and Siward, and His Grace the King, to sentence Godwin of Wessex and all his progeny to anathema and exile. Cast him from the country. Never let him return.'

Edward saw Harold close his eyes briefly. He said something in an undertone to Tostig, who brushed him off, then to his father, who growled, '*I* suggest the archbishop overreaches himself. Despite the outrages I have been subjected to, I do not wish to start a war against my own countrymen. I love England.'

'You cannot love England without loving its king,' Champart snapped.

'Godwin,' said Leofric coolly, 'you're not a man known for dependable loyalty.'

Godwin barely glanced at either the earl or the archbishop. His attention was fixed on Edward, teeth bared. 'My king values peace. If he means it, let us make it.'

Every face turned to Edward. Waiting for his move.

Edward rose to his feet. 'There will be peace between you and I, Godwin Wulfnothsson, when you bring my brother Alfred home. Home and alive from the cold grave where you laid him, blinded and violated, in service of a Viking bastard. Henceforth, you and all your sons are exiled from the kingdom of England, on pain of death. Leofric. Siward.'

The earls stepped forward. They bowed.

'See them to the shore,' Edward said. 'And see them gone.'

Leofric and Siward obeyed. Their men seized Godwin and his sons, marched them off. Shouts rang after them. The moot disbanded in total disorder.

Edward, later, went to the chapel. Knelt, and prayed harder than ever before. *What have I done? Who am I? Oh God, I am your servant, but I am more afraid than ever that it is the devil I am listening to. Speak. Speak so that I know it is you. It is easy to have faith in a monastery, when you are touched by nothing else. It is easy to forgive. And now, here in the world, I can do neither. God Above, be near me. I beg you.*

God Above, as it pleased Him, was silent.

CHAPTER TWO

Caen, Normandy
February 1052

'I've A QUESTION for you, sweetling.' William crumpled the parchment in his hand and turned to his wife. 'Is your aunt Judith anywhere near you in terms of causing trouble? In short, is she someone I need fear aligned against me?'

'Judith is sweet, sophisticated, and could not summon a drop of guile to wet her throat in Hell,' Matilda said dismissively. 'And certainly it would never occur to her to have an opinion, much less to voice it. Why do you ask?'

'I've just had curious tidings from Flanders. Your father decided it was a stroke of genius to marry her off to Tostig Godwinson, this past November. The Earl of Wessex and all his family are in exile there, save for his daughter Edith – she was a queen, but that did not stop her from being packed off to a nunnery. Oh, and his son Harold, who went to Ireland.'

'You hardly appear to be shedding tears.'

'I'm not,' William said bluntly. 'Godwin and his brood are a dangerous nuisance, and the longer they are in exile, the better. I *could* wish that your bloody father had not chosen to shelter them.'

'He is a practical man.' Matilda said with a shrug. 'Besides, Tostig is the third son, isn't he? Hardly about to inherit anything. The chief reason to recommend the match is the fact that Flanders and Boulogne have been at loggerheads for years. Doubtless Earl Godwin wished to spite Eustace. Again.'

'I mislike it, even so.' William lobbed the letter into the fire. 'But your father's troublesomely pliable loyalties aside, I'm glad of this news – Earl Godwin's exile, that is. It may indeed make Robert Champart's visit loom even larger.'

'I tremble to ask what you mean. Normandy is not in such an outstanding state as to give you leave to occupy yourself elsewhere.'

All that won her was a sour look. 'Heaven forfend I plan for the moment when that might not be the case. But I *am* suspicious; I've heard too many rumours of Geoffrey Martel sticking his ugly face in. I'm sure that Angevin whoreson is up to something.' The count of Anjou, regardless of who he might be, was the interminable and implacable rival of the dukes of Normandy, and Geoffrey Martel was the worst of a bad lot. He had, in the nine years of his tenure, accomplished the nearly impossible feat of making folk yearn for his father, Fulk the Black, who most certainly had not been called that for the colour of his hair.

'I am certain as well the sky was blue when we woke this morning,' Matilda shot back.

William grunted. 'Could barely tell, with all this rain. Maine *will* be mine, I promise.'

Matilda said nothing. She knew there were a number of rough edges that her vigorous application of manners and culture would never buffer away, but she flattered herself that William could now do a passable imitation of a lordling. Though there were some things he had not needed to be taught. The two of them were eerily well matched, and it manifested the most in the marriage bed. He was astonishingly strong, but he bridled it with her; even with his wife, there was a wall he did not always let down, a guard he did not necessarily drop. But when he did. . . it was like grasping lightning with her hands, swept into a storm, where he would take her so deep she thought they had changed skins. If it was a sin to enjoy making love with one's spouse so much, Matilda welcomed it the more. The Church, after all, was quite convinced that she and William were *not* married (largely thanks to the arm-twisting of her uncle Henry, King of France) and their fornication could be chalked up as further black marks on their uncanonical union. They had received a number of threatening letters from Rome, maintaining that a fresh interdict would be slapped on Normandy unless William separated from her. William himself had announced that the Church could bloviate all it wished, he had no intention of complying.

Matilda was grateful, of course, but she did rather think that William could do without adding the Church to his still-sizeable list of enemies. Abbot Lanfranc, head of the influential religious Norman house of Bec and William's envoy on their behalf, remained posted in Rome, doing his best to talk the curia into compliance, but his efforts went backward as often as forward. Gold, greed, opportunity, and self-interest turned the wheels of the great papal beast, only incidentally tempered with a genuine pastoral care for the souls of the Christian faithful. The Holy See had been vigorously criticised by the clerical reformers for its worldliness and venality, but yet somehow this was never sufficient to mend its service to mammon before God.

Matilda put a hand on her belly, thoughtful. Conceiving an heir would be both advantageous and furtherly difficult, as any children would be regarded as illegitimate. She had thought the spectre of fathering a bastard might dampen William's spirited opposition somewhat – after his own nightmarish childhood, tormented and bedevilled and nearly killed for his base birth, he had sworn never to inflict the same on any offspring of his – but he of course did not see their relation as anything other than lawful matrimony. That was the other thing she knew she'd never touch – the sheer stubbornness and indomitable will that nothing short of an act of God (and possibly not even that) could derail.

'Well,' she said. 'I doubt you need to march to Bruges and ask my father to explain himself – yet. But do you truly think there is opportunity here?'

'Aye.' William finished his wine, crossed the solar, and linked his arms around her waist. 'Let us just say,' he murmured, 'that I would lay good coin on Robert Champart suddenly finding an excuse to make another errand to Normandy. And soon.'

Either William had second sight, or his instinct was even keener than she thought. Robert Champart did indeed arrive in Caen not two weeks later, and this time with a trail to quite dwarf his previous escort. This could have been due to his improved status as Archbishop of Canterbury, as they had heard about that fiasco. But it was also plain that William's cousin Edward was a good deal more comfortable on his throne than he had been the last time, and thus felt entitled to such a spectacle. *False spring and a wet summer*, Matilda thought. Edward might be enjoying his kingly prerogatives without the earl Godwin to clip his wings, but the earl Godwin was not doing the same. He was thinking of one thing and one only: how to get back into power, and to the devil with the hindmost. Her father's letters, whether or not they intended to be, were most revealing on this accord.

Robert Champart, however, did not share this opinion; he brimmed with the confidence of the world restored to rightness. 'My lord. My lady. I offer the greetings of the King of England.'

'They are returned.' William was seated in his lion chair, Matilda standing at his side. 'Such a surprise to see you again, my lord. I was not expecting this in the least.'

If Champart suspected he was being lied to, he did not let on. 'I bear a letter from your cousin Edward. If I may. . .'

William waved an acquiescence. Champart stepped just close enough to pass him the letter, then moved back quickly. Matilda offered him a sweet smile. She had no idea if this particular churchman subscribed to the opinion that they were living in heresy, but even if so, he was far too timid to remark on it.

William carelessly broke the royal seal and unfolded the letter. Matilda cast an eye at the crisp uncial script – written, she noted, in the king's own hand. Reading over her husband's shoulder, she finished it before him, and bit back a gasp of surprise. Her reaction, however, was positively demonstrative beside William's. His eyes flicked once, and then he negligently cast it into the rushes as if it were a useless scrip. 'My cousin wishes me to come to London?'

'He does, my lord.' Champart looked pleased. 'I have told him only good things of you.'

'Then you'll have lied somewhere. But it would be a pity to do otherwise, when the Godwins are out of the way at last.'

'No one misses them,' Champart hastened to assure him.

'And there you're lying again. The kingdom always misses men like that, if only since they make life interesting.' William stood up, towering to his full height. 'So then. Bear word to the King that I will pay court on him in London, before the end of Lent.'

'You mean to go?' Matilda asked later, in bed. 'Certainly?'

'Certainly.' She could see the devious smile on his face.

'Who will be the regent of Normandy?'

'You, sweetling.' He draped an arm over her waist and pulled her against him, kissing her neck. 'Your first chance to prove why in God's name I should trust you.'

'What if Geoffrey Martel attacks while you're gone?'

William bit her nipple, making her gasp. 'Fight him off.'

London, England
March 1052

If anything could have improved Edward's morning, it was the news he received just as he was splashing out of Prime, and the windswept messenger came hurrying to kneel before him. 'Your Grace! Your cousin William has agreed to your generous proposition. He has taken ship from Fécamp with the archbishop of Canterbury, and they will be arriving in London within the week.'

'Very good,' Edward said in approval. 'What else?'

'My lord. . . this may come as great sadness, but. . .'

'Aye?'

'Your mother Emma is dead, Your Grace. Just two days past, in Winchester.'

Silence, a searing moment. Without Edward's volition, a broad smile broke out across his face. 'Well, well. God has blessed England at last, ridding it of her.'

'Your Grace. . .'

'May she rest in peace, I suppose.' Edward turned away, pulling his hood up. 'Not, God knows, that she ever gave me any.'

At breakfast afterward, listening to the rain patter on the damp-darkened thatch, Edward supposed that perhaps his response had been a touch ungracious. But he could not help it. He was feeling as if he had come up for air for the first time in his kingship – which was far from saying that everything was perfect, as there were unsettling whispers from Flanders. Godwin did not mean to take his exile sanguinely, and was pulling every string in sight to secure his re-admittance. If Edward had his druthers, this would be some time between the Tribulation and the trumpets, but he was canny enough to realise that Godwin's absence was all too likely to be temporary. Thus, he had to get his affairs in order while he could.

To his surprise, he missed Edith. He hadn't wanted to send her to the convent, but she was Godwin's daughter. She would never escape it, not even through marriage, consecration, and coronation, and it was the nunnery or divorce, as Robert Champart had been continually attempting to persuade him. Edward had to admit to the dubious wisdom of retaining a barren wife whose fortunes were intimately tied with those of his greatest enemy. Yet he must consider the witanagemot, the earls, the bishops, the people, the fabric of England itself – and him, and the odd, shy love he had developed for his wife despite all. He had also taken considerable pleasure in endowing Leofric's son Ælfgar with Harold Godwinson's old earldom of East Anglia, hoping to head off any lurking disenchantment, and in creating his nephew Ralph as Earl of Herefordshire. But the greatest appointment he meant to make still lay, as yet, unfinished.

Edward passed the day in his usual work, and after Compline, he retired to his empty bed. Lying in the darkness, he tried fervently to forgive his mother, to know that the ability was even in him. She was dead, he lived, she wore a shroud and he a crown. Surely he could be the better person that he had always supposed himself. He had to forgive her, or he would only be her.

And perhaps God was still silent, but Edward, for what felt like the first time in years, knew that He had heard. A depth of gratitude flooded him.

'Pax,' he whispered, and slept.

'Your Grace,' the herald announced. 'Duke William of Normandy is in the antechamber, with the lord archbishop of Canterbury. They arrived in London just this morn.'

Edward resisted, as always, the urge to adjust his crown. 'Show them in.'

The herald bowed and vanished through the hall doors. Edward waited, unaccountably apprehensive, until his visitors entered. Robert Champart seemed wearied by his errand-running, but William did not, and Edward felt a jolt like a blow to the gut. For some reason, he had an image of the child he had left. He really should have remembered that sixteen years of blood and madness would have wrought a stunning transformation.

To say that this young man drew the eye was an understatement. He was indeed most handsome – his golden head burned in the sunlight, and his height, strength, and the fine bones of his face all bespoke his Viking heritage, bold and clean as a brand – but that was not it. This was something else, a cold majesty and a cool confidence, an utter self-possession. He walked with a measured, loping stride, grey eyes taking in everything.

Edward swallowed, then regained his self-possession. 'Be welcome to my kingdom and court, cousin,' he said, descending the steps and offering his hand. 'It is good to see you again.'

William knelt briefly to kiss his ring, but rose again at once. His eyes crinkled. *'Vinco,'* he said. *'Vincere, vici, victum.'*

Surprised, pleased, and unsettled all at once – he had once taught a small boy his Latin grammar and despaired of him remembering any of it – Edward laughed. Then he turned to Robert Champart. 'My lord, I will attend you privately after Vespers.'

Champart bowed and excused himself. Edward turned back to his cousin, wondering if he dared something so familiar as clapping him on the shoulder. He decided, for the moment, that he did not. 'Come,' he said. 'Walk with me.'

'It would be my pleasure.' William followed Edward out into the corridor beyond. When they had passed into the cloisters, the smell of wet earth rising from the gardens, he spoke again. 'My lord. I suspect I know your purpose.'

'I suspect you do,' Edward agreed. 'You seem the sort of man that it would be difficult to keep anything from for long.'

A faint smile pulled at that hard mouth. 'I hope I have not made a mistake in coming. No doubt Champart has kept you informed of the madness in Normandy.'

'He has. But more than that. I. . . was generally pleased by what he told me about you.'

'Generally?'

'It was favourable, aye.'

'Favourable enough to decide you?' William halted in his tracks. 'I will not tolerate sweet promises and vague distractions. If this is only to natter on about "circumstances" – why, you should have continued to employ the estimable archbishop as your messenger-boy. I will not thank you for wasting my time, and giving my enemies a chance to act while I am gone.'

He spoke so coolly and flatly, with such a total lack of conciliation, that a shiver crept down Edward's back. For the first time, a seed of doubt entered his mind. William was outstandingly qualified, there was no question, but it was plain to the most casual of observers that there was not an ounce of mercy or compromise in him. Knowing as he did the fiendishly delicate balancing act that being King of England entailed, Edward had to wonder if it was indeed wise to install a man like this to the position. *Not even he can beat every challenger, single-handedly bend them to his will – and they shall resent him bitterly, if he tries.* Unless he *could*, which was somehow more terrifying. *Who is this man? A force of nature, or more?*

'Well?' said William, clearly waiting on a response.

'After his visit two years ago, Champart was under the impression that your reaction to the prospect was. . . mixed, at best.'

'It's a fool that tips his hand before he makes his move.' William's wolfish smile was unpleasantly reminiscent of Godwin's. 'Surely you do not imagine that I would reveal my thoughts or inclinations to an envoy who had just turned up for uncertain purposes? How was I to know that he'd not go pour them into the ear of, say, the Earl of Wessex and his sons?'

'You needn't have feared. Robert was the one who pushed hardest for their exile.'

'Now I know that. Then I did not.' William shrugged. 'He could have a use for me, true, but never my confidence. I doubt you realise how rare it is that I gave it to you.'

'Why did you?'

'You have something I want. Do you recall where, and when, I first met you? When I was old enough to remember?'

'In Falaise, my lord. You were only five.'

'Aye, and much less cynical, though wholly as much a bastard.' William's teeth flashed again. 'I was worried about not becoming duke, so you offered me a crown instead.'

'That was almost ten years before I wore it myself. I was a monk and you were very young. And you *are* the Duke now, so all was achieved as it should be.' Edward smiled.

William did not. His eyes had narrowed into cold slits. 'Were you lying, then?'

'No, but – '

'Did you intend to break it later?'

'My lord, I had no way of knowing what the future held.'

'Pity. I could use that skill.' William leaned casually on a pillar. 'I have been preoccupied with idiots ever since, aye. But God has happily placed us both in a position where you can keep your word. You are, I am sure, no oathbreaker?'

'I do not know if that qualified as an oath.'

'I hear distractions and excuses, my lord.' William took a step forward. 'I left my wife to rule in Normandy. She will do, I am certain, an exemplary job. But if Geoffrey Martel, or any of my barons, takes the idea into his head to attack, she can scarce ride out to meet them on the field.' *I can. I will fight, and I will win. Do you really wish to do this the hard way, my lord?*

'Well,' Edward said at last. 'It's quite chill out here. Let us retire to my solar, cousin, and then we can talk more.'

'Think, if you must,' said William. 'But not too long.'

Considering the dubious precedent established the *last* time he held a feast for a visiting Frenchman, Edward was strongly tempted not to make the same mistake twice – the last thing he needed was an incident along the order of Eustace's. But there was nothing for it. If he had the nerve to make William his heir – which he had not decided if he did or not – he could certainly have the nerve to inform his nobles. It was not without severe misgivings, however, that he swept into his hall that night, William at his side.

The guests obligingly rose to their feet and removed their hoods, but their eyes were on this exotic commodity. While throwing Godwin and sons out of the country had toned down some of the anti-French sentiment, it to no degree had been eradicated. It was all too easy for the earl to be viewed as the wronged English patriot, done a bad turn by the gang of Norman courtiers and churchmen who had usurped his rightful position. *That is not the case, of course, but since when do people want complicated answers? It is better for it to be black and white.*

Edward cleared his throat. 'My lords, thegns, ceorls, and fyrdmen. It is my pleasure to present my kinsman, Duke William. He shall be treated with honour for the duration of his visit, and will, of course, return the favour.'

William, not understanding the Saxon in which this speech was delivered, nonetheless was attending intently, as if he would wring out meaning by watching their faces. Doubtless he could, as he was extraordinarily sensitive to the mood of a mob. There was still an undercurrent of suspicion, but the sheer force of William's presence muffled any overt expression. He stood there, young and hale and dazzling – and hard as iron, utterly unlike the weedy Eustace or the mild Ralph. It was plain that he would not be challenged or crossed without the most grievous of consequences, and the Englishmen were all too aware of it.

The feast managed to proceed without egregious incident. William made pleasant conversation with a few of Edward's favourites, but he was still watching everyone in the hall, assessing who understood French, who understood Saxon, and who understood both. At the end, he announced that he was weary, and asked Edward's leave to retire. Edward granted it. Then he himself went to his quarters, and sat with a cup of hippocras, wondering.

'My lords,' said Edward, the next morning. 'At the moment we are scarcely spoilt for choice, and I will put the matter plainly. It must be either William or Ralph.'

'Why must we have them at all?' Earl Ælfgar complained. 'Your Grace, no one understands why you cling to your barren, traitor queen. Remarry at once, and you could still have a son of your own blood. Anything but this damnable cabal of Frenchmen.'

Leofric shot his son a warning look, but did not seem to disagree with his general sentiment. The rest of the witan, gathered in London for Easter, clearly felt likewise.

'If you are going to banish Godwin and his family,' Siward rasped, 'at least do it fully. Otherwise you merely languish about waiting for their next move, in a game that goes on and on without end. Divorce the queen.'

Edward did not answer. He knew they were right; only a few years ago, he would have taken inordinate pleasure at how thoroughly Godwin's schemes had exploded in his face. Now. . . it struck him as blackly amusing, but that was not about to solve this mess. So, with nothing else to do, he lied. 'My lords, the fault does not rest with the queen. My devotion to Christ our Lord means that I cannot muddy my soul with the sin of fleshly intercourse.'

'With your wife? When you are king, and need a son above all?' Leofric sounded incredulous. 'How is that a sin, my lord?'

'Chastity may be admired in a monk,' Ælfgar added. 'Rather less in a king.'

'I was a monk.'

'But you are a king now.'

'I do not need reminding of that.'

The witan exchanged black looks, furious with his obstinacy, when it was entirely within his power to solve the problem. 'A monk, a Frenchman, and a coward. This is too much.'

The dragon reared its head in Edward's chest. 'Remember who you are speaking to.'

'Exactly who I just said.'

'My lord,' said Leofric. 'Do not do this. For our life, we cannot see why you would foist a choice of Frenchmen on us, save to suit your own selfish whimsy.'

Edward had to admit to trepidation – if he was losing Leofric, he was losing them all. *Maybe it is selfish.* He wondered if that would stop him.

'Think on it, my lords,' he said stubbornly. 'But not too long.'

'Did they agree?' William asked calmly.

'No. I did not think they would, but hoped they'd surprise me.' Edward did his best to consider the sunlit solar, rather than the look on his cousin's face. 'That does not mean it is impossible, merely that the matter is far from clear.'

'Sand in my eyes.' William moved closer, the lines of his body sharp as a knife. 'If you will not give me an answer, my lord, must I consider this a massive waste of time?'

'No.' Edward had to tread with great care. 'My nephew Ralph is. . . unsuitable, and they know it. I love him dearly, for he reminds me of what I myself could have been, and am – flaws and all. But he is kind and pliable and indecisive. Managing only Herefordshire may prove a trial.'

'And so that is that? If you mean it, my lord, then say it.'

Edward took a breath. 'Very well. You will be king after me.'

'Swear it.'

'I swear it.'

'I hope you do not mean to break this one as well.'

'I do not.'

'Good.' Rather than lessening the tension in William's shoulders, this drew it tighter. 'Then I will take my leave on Easter Monday, in a fortnight's time. In the meanwhile, I will do my best to ensure that when my hour comes, there will be. . . compliance.'

And even with that, Edward did not feel markedly better.

He knew William would be a strong ruler – too strong, he feared. It seemed there were only two halves of the fulcrum: Ralph on one end, and William on the other. He wished there was another choice, that there was someone. . . someone, he hated to admit, like Harold Godwinson. Who had courage and mercy both, conscience and kindness, but was capable of being terrible to his enemies, who understood honour and the meaning of pride, the scion of a traitor yet not one himself. Harold was the best of them, and Edward, if he was being honest, knew that he would be a better king – at least, for England – than William. Proof that no matter what they thought, he was not intentionally plaguing them with Frenchmen.

William stayed through Easter, as planned, but he made himself scarce and scrupulously avoided further inflaming sentiments against the Normans. He did nothing but watch, filing away everything into a mind that seemed to retain every scrap of information, judge it coolly for its use or value to him. But Easter Monday arrived at last, and with it the duke's departure. He was seen aboard his ship with due honour, and Edward bid him safe journey. William nodded, touched two fingers to his brow, and took a long look at London, imprinting it into his memory. The wind was steady, and he was into the Channel by early afternoon.

William returned to Caen with minimal fanfare. He was glad to see the season ripening to summer, and he was even gladder at the thought of seeing his wife. Yet when he dismounted in the bailey, the faces that greeted him were tight and drawn with worry, which he did not at all understand. 'I'm alive. The Saxons didn't murder me, see?'

'My lord. . . we had word just a few days ago, we sent a letter, but it must not have. . .'

William repressed a sensation as if his stomach had just fallen into his foot. 'What?'

'While you were gone, my lord. . . King Henry and Geoffrey Martel. They've invaded. They've taken the castle of Domfront. And soon the town of Alençon as well.'

Domfront. The most massive castle in Normandy, rumoured to be unbreakable, and Alençon, heart of its merchandising and trade. If his dolts of yeomen had merely stood aside and let the invaders rape their own mothers and daughters, the insult could not have been more stinging. 'And so why in God's name,' said William, quite calmly, 'did you not *go to meet them?*'

'Will fitz Osbern has already left, my lord – the instant the news came. Duchess Matilda saw to it. He rode to Talou, to claim the support of your uncle Guy. If all went well, they'll be marching on Domfront this very moment.'

'Will fitz Osbern is my only loyal man, it seems.' William's face was a remote, icy white. 'And I give thanks to God that my wife has more wits than you. You *idiot.*'

To say the least, the duke was utterly incensed by this development, and everything breakable that was present to be grasped and thrown suffered accordingly. Even so, he had been too well schooled in betrayal to remain unprofitably angry for long, and the rage froze overnight into grim resolve. He simply did not lose. And if anyone had not learnt that by now, more fool they.

However, William did not race to the battlefield – although indeed every particle of him was screaming to do so. He actually took Matilda's advice that he try diplomacy first, and bundled off to Vitry-aux-Loges with extreme dispatch, to do his best to wrench apart the devil's collaboration between France and Anjou. Henry and Geoffrey had retreated there to refresh their stores and plot their next move, having successfully taken Alençon. To say the least, they were extremely surprised when the object of their insults turned up in person, having bellowed and bluffed and beaten his way past every guard, hanger-on, gatekeeper, seneschal, castellan, or other assorted unfortunate who attempted to bar his way, and stormed into the royal solar, where the stout, black-haired king of France and the thin, languid, flame-haired count of Anjou were enjoying the spoils of treason. William threw the door against the jamb and leaned against it, arms crossed, waiting for them to recover enough wits to speak.

'My – my lord of Normandy,' said Henry at last, rising gamely to the challenge. 'We – we had heard you were in England.'

'Doubtless you did.' William would not sit, only stood there, towering over them like a grim menhir. 'Leave my lands now.'

Henry feigned surprise. 'What is this about?'

'You know bloody damned well what it's about. Idiocy ill becomes you. You were my ally. Must someone prime your memory on what that word actually means?'

'He was mine as well,' said Geoffrey Martel with a smile. 'Before he was yours. I told you, my lord. You should have left Maine to me.'

'Fuck you, Martel.'

'Is this what you consider negotiations?'

'Fuck you, Martel.' The two of them had been scuffling over the lordship of the county of Maine, the reason for their continued bad blood. 'Devil's spawn you are.'

'You aren't one to talk.' Geoffrey rose to his feet. He was almost of a height with William, and their gazes, green and grey, met and snarled. 'If you prance off to consort with your Saxon friends, you'll pay the price. When was it safe to turn your back?'

William, livid, surged forward – and stopped abruptly. 'Ah-ah-ah,' said Geoffrey, twisting the misericordia that had appeared in his hand, its long thin blade poised at the hollow of his adversary's throat. 'That's close enough.'

'Would you like to make a wager?' William asked through his teeth, ignoring the fat drop of blood trickling from the wound. 'On who will win this engagement? Maine to the victor.'

'Done. I wonder how I'll redecorate the castle at Le Mans.'

'With orchids and a shroud.' William stepped away, wiping the blood off. 'And the stench of brimstone.'

Geoffrey laughed. 'See if you can catch me first. I'm leaving for Domfront this very afternoon. You might have taken it back alone, you might have taken back Alençon alone, but you'll never overcome both. Surrender now, it'll spare you some humiliation.'

'When hell freezes over.'

Geoffrey laughed again, turned, and vanished through the tent flaps. Yet his mocking voice drifted back. 'You'll have to send me a letter, when you get there.'

CHAPTER THREE

London, England
August 1052

T HEY WERE COMING. The news was everywhere. They had
landed with an armed force and were marching for London,
returned from Flanders (and Ireland, in Harold's case) to
force a final reckoning. It was defiance on an unprecedented scale,
but anyone who knew Godwin and his sons had to own that it was
entirely in their character. Edward had tried his best to keep them
out, to be sure, but after a few scuffles with the Wessex ships, the
sailors of the royal fleet – the lithesmen – had more or less deserted,
unwilling to perpetuate anything that looked so much like civil war
as the previous autumn. Edward attempted to find replacements,
but could not. This second defeat inflicted, he realised he had very
little chance of success, and prepared to negotiate.

These sentiments were far from universal. When he heard
the king's decision, Robert Champart went an ugly white, fists
clenched. 'Your Grace,' he said at last. 'You cannot be serious.'

'My opinion does not seem to count overmuch, Robert.'
Edward smiled bleakly.

'You are *king*, my lord! Enforce it!'

'How? With the blood of my people? Throw them into war?'

'Better than letting the Godwins return. If you permit them
back into this kingdom, you'll never be respected again. No one will
believe you able to stand behind an order.'

'I thank you, Robert. Yet I can start a war in truth, or I can
attempt to make peace.'

Champart stared at him. 'Peace? How can you think that?
Did you not say it would be so when Godwin brought back Alfred?
The blood that would be spilled is that of the Saxon peasants who
defied you in Dover, and gave rise to this in the first place!'

Edward turned to the wall. 'Am I king of the whole of England, or part?'

'You are *king*. When God gives you rightness of a cause, the Church will endorse war.'

'Against my own countrymen?' Edward felt unfathomably tired. 'I can push no further.'

'Then I will have to go.'

'I was unaware that you were the irreplaceable one, Robert.'

'My king! I cannot believe that I am hearing this from your own lips!' Rather than backing down, Champart drew up. 'The English – '

'Robert.' Edward turned to face him. 'I hear echoes of them in you. If anything is Norman, they must oppose it, discussion ended. If anything is English, you must oppose it, discussion ended. You are as blind as them, I fear.'

Champart flinched. 'If I have given offence – '

'You have not. But, in this case at least, no wise counsel.'

'My lord, I am your *friend*. And you have few enough of those, it seems.'

'My friend. Indeed you are. But you were also the one who told me I was learning to be a politician. Well, I have taken your tutelage to heart. The two do not always go hand in glove.'

'Will you really cast me out of England? For the sake of the kin-slaying, treasonous murderer and his devil's brood?'

'I was also unaware that I must offer the whole of it as a sacrificial lamb, for you. You are much concerned with affairs in Normandy. Well then, go. You have my leave. Return to Jumièges and take up your post as abbot.'

Champart tried one last tactic. 'My lord, without the Normans, who will you have? We have no love for Godwin and thus will never betray you. But if you put faith in the English, there's always the earl lurking to buy them off, plant rebellious sentiments in their heads.'

'Perhaps I am fiendishly over-optimistic, Robert. Or perhaps I am as blind and weak as everyone likes to think. But I prefer to believe that in all of England, there is such thing as a man who is not about to follow Godwin's every word, no matter how much he pays him. And may I add, Normans scarce have much leeway at present to declare other folk faithless.'

'Next you'll name an Englishman your heir!'

'A terrible fate indeed, for England. You asked a question. Who I would have if the Normans were gone. I will have myself, Robert. That is who.'

'You cannot turn me out. God will judge you for this.'

'I expect He will. He will judge me for a number of things. But I am not in heaven yet. So you have a choice, Robert. You may leave now, or you may wait until the Godwins return – and they will. In recognition of your loyal service, I shall not force you. I shall, however, no longer come close to starting wars on your behalf. I wish you well in Normandy.'

The silence this time lasted even longer. Then Robert Champart bowed. 'My lord,' he said woodenly. 'As you command.'

Edward was woken the next morning with the news that the archbishop of Canterbury had fled the country, taking with him the Norman bishops of Dorchester and London – and Godwin's youngest son, twelve-year-old Wulfnoth, who had no part in the treasons of his kinsmen and thus had been spared their exile. Apparently thinking to make a clean sweep, Champart had also removed Hakon, Sweyn Godwinson's firstborn. Sweyn himself had been exiled for life, and there was no rumour that he was with the party forcing their attentions on the capital. Nonetheless, Edward was furious. Wulfnoth and Hakon were no more than boys, his own subjects, and he had had more than enough of punishing sons for the sins of their fathers. The idea that his friend could so undercut him had, strangely, the effect of firming his resolve to come to terms with his enemies. That, as it happened, would be soon.

Godwin and his sons had seized the town of Steyning which had caused so much trouble before, driven out the Normans, and set themselves up as its beneficiaries. Godwin needed the tide to come in for him at London Bridge. It had. Now they had reached the city itself, attracting crowds of sympathisers drawn to the romance of exile and their fair English faces, fighting for their country when it was in danger of losing itself. They were, they announced, prepared to forgive past grievances and hammer out a peace-accord – so long as everyone else was.

Edward listened calmly. He then deputed Stigand, the Bishop of Winchester, as a go-between; Stigand juggled a constant stream of offers and counter-offers, rushing from the Godwins' camp outside the walls of London to Edward's hall within. At first, it appeared to be nothing more than furious tail-chasing, but at last, a fortnight later, the whole messy imbroglio actually looked to be resolved. Yet when he did reach the moment of ceremonially welcoming the Godwins back, Edward could not help but wonder if they were destined to repeat this for all time, one pulling at the other like a balky mule, one winning at the expense of the other, but only briefly. If this was merely some farce staged by a melancholy player, and if kingship mattered in the slightest. If anything did.

The next few weeks were occupied with a flurry of reparations. The erstwhile exiles were reinstalled to their positions and honours, a succession of banquets were thrown, and England let go a breath of deep relief. But merely administering the kiss of peace did not mean that everything had been mended.

Ironically, the Godwins got their wish. A council held in late September, almost a year precisely after the one that had outlawed them, settled on a fairly foreseeable resolution: blaming the French. Robert Champart was named the outlaw instead, and hordes of his fellow countrymen were obliged to take the fall with him. The lot of them were fingered as wholly responsible for England's internal strife, accused of making helpfully vague 'bad laws.' While this exculpated Edward himself from blame, he resented it. As well, the great part of the Normans that had come over with him had been of low status and no account, and had interest in genuine service, not politicking and plotting. But they all had to go.

With an English archbishop of Canterbury – Edward had appointed Stigand to the newly vacant see as a reward for his help in negotiating the peace – the Frenchmen thrown out on their arses, and the situation with Godwin mended, England's temper was very high. Edward further raised it by repealing the *heregild,* acquiring in popularity what he lost in cash, and to prove that England's power would not be again turned against itself, he ordered a decrease in the ranks of the lithesmen (as well a small piece of revenge for their abandonment of him). Yet the greater reward came near Michaelmas. For that was, at long last, when his wife came home.

Domfront, Normandy
January 1053

Domfront Castle was a massive, glowering stone edifice, strategically situated on a bluff, guarded by a double curtain wall and a formidable portcullis. The icy rain slashed at it, but even it did not seem able to penetrate the defences. The castle was half a phantom, dissolving in the mist, making it even more maddeningly out of reach than it already was. In theory, it was not the strength of the fortress William objected to, though he did rather wish that his ancestors had not been so fastidious at securing its reputation as unbreakable. But still, that wasn't the precise source of his aggravation. That would be the sight of Geoffrey Martel's banners fluttering insouciantly atop the towers, bright smears in the clouds.

William eyed Domfront balefully, riding his grey back and forth at a prudent distance from the archer-lined ramparts. He found it insulting in the extreme to have to put his own castle under siege, but he did not have the brute strength, at present, to smash it into submission. *Bloody Angevins.* Part of him would have liked to be back in Caen, sitting in front of a hot fire with Matilda – she was expecting their first child near Easter, a development which enthused both of them considerably. Yet it was partly for that reason that he was out here, freezing his balls off and trading skulduggeries with Geoffrey twice-damned Martel. He was not only fighting for himself now, but for the future of his line, and if he was honest, he did not mind it. Not in the least. No matter that he had to sleep under a pile of furs with Will fitz Osbern, next to a constantly stoked fire, to have any hope of keeping warm. Each skirmish gave him a thrill of joy, each enemy he killed allowed him to breathe, each time he drew his longbow was the very blood in his veins. *Feast, you whoreson. Feast away. I'll wait.*

'My lord.' As if summoned by his thoughts, Will rode up next to him. 'Your uncle Guy has news.'

'Does he?' William had been astounded by the fact that Guy had agreed to bestir himself and march a force to Domfront. He was pushing forty, but his guile had only matured with age, and William had never forgotten how slippery and untrustworthy his uncles had been during his chaotic minority. Nonetheless, late help was better than none. Winter sieges were exquisitely unpleasant, but he'd endured it in Brionne and he would now.

'Sorry,' he said, realising Will was trying to get his attention again. 'What news?'

'Poor, naturally. Henry has sent reinforcements to Alençon.'

William's mouth tightened. He had not yet developed the helpful ability to be in two places at once, and Domfront was the more crucial of the two, the one he must win, but this could not be overlooked. 'Damn. I can't let them get away with it, can I?'

'Nay.' Will spurred alongside William. 'Some bloody uncle-in-law Henry is, eh?'

William snorted a bitter laugh. 'Every man in creation has betrayed me by now, Henry merely thought to get his fingers in the pie. I wonder which baron it was this time, welcoming the twin prongs of Lucifer's pitchfork as a better lord than me.'

'Your marriage to Matilda – '

'Has caused me no end of trouble, I know.' William's rare smile showed hard as granite. 'But opposing me on those grounds is all a pretext. The Pope doesn't like that I'm a bastard, Henry doesn't like that I won, the barons don't like that I'm still alive.'

'Well,' Will said with an answering smile. 'Bugger them all.'

William's even rarer laughter cracked the sky as they rode back into camp.

'My lord.' Guy of Arques and Talou had not changed much over the years, except to grow thinner and more choleric than ever, his tangled pale hair showing grey and his scraggly beard hiding scars instead of whelks. Although they did not mismatch like his brother Mauger, the Archbishop of Rouen, his eyes still had a vaguely unsettling quality, colourless as the fog. 'Did Will bring you the news from Alençon?'

'He did.' William blew on his hands, accepted the bowl of stew his uncle handed him, and began to spoon the gristly meat into his mouth. 'Do you have something to suggest?'

'If you'd wish, yes. Considering you have had no success in taking Domfront, you cannot be seen to wallow here, doing nothing. You must move more decisively on Alençon.'

'And how shall I do that?' William's voice was sharp; he disliked the reminder of failure. 'Exactly?'

A smile turned up Guy's mouth. 'There is something else I have not told you, my lord. Alençon has employed. . . unusual measures. Well-nigh demanding your attention.'

'Stop speaking in riddles, Talou.'

That strange smile widened. 'It was most unwise. But it is this. The citizens of Alençon have hung skins from the city walls.'

'Skins – '

'To mock you, my lord. To make sport of the fact you were born of a tanner's daughter.'

There was a long, tenuous pause. Then William slammed his bowl of stew into the ground and stood up. 'Did they?' he growled.

'My lord,' said Will fitz Osbern. 'This stinks of a calculated insult. It's Henry Capet's work, he's trying to draw you off. Geoffrey Martel is here, after all. He's the one we must – '

'Don't tell me what to do. If they have not learned to take me as their lord, to fear me, then it is time their errors were corrected once and for all. It seems we are in need of a new plan. Guy, you stay here. I'm leaving you in charge of the siege of Domfront.' William did not like the idea of letting his uncle out of his sight, but he had no other commanders that he trusted any more, and Guy had after all supplied a good part of the men. 'Will, you take a company and ride to Alençon. Give the whoresons a taste of holy wrath. I'll go to the Cotentin to find reinforcements. I'll meet you back at Alençon, and then we'll break them.'

'Are you sure about that, my lord?' Will said with a frown. 'The last time – '

'I need no reminding of Valognes, thank you. And this time I'll certainly not be going with only you at my back.' William stood up. He was a tall, looming shadow in the gathering dusk, the fire catching on his impassive face. 'Are we in accord?'

'Aye, my lord,' said Will, sounding resigned.

'Of course.' Guy of Talou never raised his voice, yet it carried in the icy evening. 'I will do my best to persuade Martel to see sense. With mangonels and pikes, forsooth.'

'Aye?' William said. 'Why, and here I thought you'd do it with sweetmeats and songs.'

Coutances, Normandy
February 1053

'It is a great surprise, though of course always an honour, to receive you, Your Grace.' Geoffrey de Montbray, Bishop of Coutances, descended the steps in perfect order, a marked contrast to the unwashed, dripping, scruffy duke standing at the foot. 'We were not expecting to see you in the Cotentin. We had heard you were occupied with traitors in Domfront.'

'I was.' William had made the fifteen-league ride to Coutances in record time, even with the damp, freezing wind in his face the whole way. 'And I've come to claim my tithe of men.'

Montbray smiled. A stocky, vigorous man, he was not wearing the usual vesture expected of a bishop, and instead was clad in a knight's gambeson and tabard, a stout truncheon – churchmen were not permitted to carry swords – hanging from his belt. 'I shall be delighted to spread the word.'

'Do so. And fetch mulled wine before my fingers fall off.'

Later, installed before a sooty fire, William thawed his hands and mulled his options. He had a mind to take Montbray with him when he left, not least because this fresh bout of contumacy had made it more vital than ever that he trust no one. By God, how could he love the act of warfare so much, yet be furious that there was no end to it? He knew very well he would be bored witless if he had nothing to do but sit on his arse at home, but sometimes he thought he'd sell his soul for one damned night in which he did not have to sleep with one eye open. *Why should I think it makes any bloody sense?* William did not know if he was making progress, if this was an endless cycle in which loss and triumph followed inexorably. If there would ever be an end, or only a reprieve.

But no matter how commonplace they were in his life, betrayals never rankled any the less. As was proved yet again, not three days later, by the panicked arrival of an unwelcome visitor. Not in who he was, but what he bore. 'Your Grace! Your Grace! My lord William!'

'I'm here.' William had left young William de Warenne and Walter Giffard at Domfront to keep an eye on Guy, and he was troubled by the former's abrupt materialisation. 'What is it?'

Warenne flung himself to his knees. 'My lord. I beg that you permit me to atone for this.'

'What now? Are you about to announce your perfidy too?'

'No, my lord. But another man has.' Warenne swallowed. 'Your uncle Guy of Talou has abandoned the siege of Domfront, and raised his own banners in rebellion.'

William wished that the ensuing silence would really be more obliging about ending. Finding that it refused to do so, he opened his mouth to take the initiative. But what emerged was a barking, scraping, yet genuinely mirthful laugh. 'Why, who in the world would have expected any different? And I did give him a golden opportunity. Have you more information?'

'No, my lord. All my man heard Guy say was that he had waited for this chance ever since Aubrey de Hauteville.'

'Aubrey de Hauteville?' William couldn't say the name was familiar, but for some reason he thought it should be. 'Well, it seems we have our new destination.'

'Domfront, isn't it?' Montbray interrupted. 'Your Grace, we must go at once! We cannot afford to lose the siege – '

'No. We ride for Arques at once.'

'Arques?' said Montbray, frowning. *'Arques?'*

'Is there any other man who does not see the sense in riding to my enemy's principal city to cut off his supplies, prevent him from gathering reinforcements, and ensure that I do not have to deal with a hostile fortress in the middle of my lands when I am attempting to do likewise?'

Everybody did.

Alençon, Normandy
March 1053

Will fitz Osbern had expected his lord's furious appearance for at least the last fortnight, and he grew increasingly concerned with each day it failed to be effected. He didn't *think* Coutances had turned into another Valognes, but there was no way William would tolerate unnecessary delays when it came to trouncing Alençon – raw animal skins had indeed been hung from the city walls, reeking with old blood and fresh defiance. Attempting to fulfil William's order for holy wrath, Will's men had mounted several raids on the city, but these had been abortive and inconclusive. Every time they held against an assault, the citizens grew bolder, and now they were a regular sight on the wallwalks, spitting and jeering.

Will was fairly sure that the citizens thought he himself was William, to judge from the way they energetically flapped the skins whenever they caught sight of him. But when he turned in response to a shout of his name, saw a page running for him, heard the thunder of approaching riders, he knew for a fact that they were about to be enlightened on *that* sad misapprehension.

'My lord.' Will strode into the tent. 'I was worried. I was expecting you much sooner.'

'So was I.' William was standing by the brazier, still clad in his grimy armour. 'Then again, I was not anticipating having to make a detour to Arques first.'

'Arques?' Will repeated, confused.

'Why is that everyone's reaction?' William asked wryly.

'The citizens of Alençon have been most vigorous in their insubordination, my lord,' one of the captains put in. 'Doubtless they think themselves justified by God. You could not have arrived at a more opportune time, Your Grace. We must show them the – '

William gave the man a hard stare. 'They will be schooled, I assure you. Even as Henry Capet and Geoffrey Martel will be.'

'My lord. . . is Martel not still squatting in Domfront?'

'Likely,' said William grimly, 'but not certain. My gracious uncle has betrayed me, and left the siege. That was the reason for my delay, as I was obliged to ride to Arques and cut it off. Thus leaving Domfront to whatever evil devices Martel has in mind.'

'Surely not – '

'I sent Warenne and Giffard back to do their best to hold it.' William shrugged. 'Or at least be sure that the Angevin supply lines are cut. They wanted to attempt storming the siege itself, but I felt that to be foolish.'

Will had been conscious through the entire conversation of a vague feeling that something was amiss, but it was the peculiarly offhand way in which William said this that sharpened it to a pitch. Guy of Talou's treachery was a major if sadly not unprecedented blow, and the potential loss of Domfront loomed like a spectre, tugging at all the fragile threads by which William maintained both dukedom and life. Surely he should have been there himself, and even if he was not, he should be storming with fury. William was standing there so *calmly.*

And so, Will had to ask. 'My lord. . . why are you not at Domfront?'

William turned his head, and Will caught a glimpse of something in his eyes, something the glow of the brazier smelted into iron. Something wild, harsh, coldly cunning. The smile that took its place was not discernibly more comforting. 'I had an idea.'

The assault began at dusk, and carried on well into darkness. Fire strafed the night, cracks of burning wood or the thunder of falling stone, the shouts of men or William's unmistakable roar. He seemed to be everywhere at once, and he drew his longbow relentlessly, sending volleys at the scurrying shadows atop the walls. As for Will, he was in command of the faction at the gate, which was employing both force (a battering ram) and guile (a team that had wriggled through the grates and into the sewers) in their attempts to break into Alençon. This latter innovation had been William's idea, and he'd had no trouble at all finding volunteers. That was the effect he had on men: galvanising them to do the unthinkable, and gladly.

The scent of blood was thick in the spring night. Most of the skins hanging off the walls had caught fire, and the Normans helpfully torched the rest. The destruction continued apace, and by dawn Alençon was theirs. A man waved a white flag from one of the slagged towers, the charred remnants of the skins still writhing. Not long later, the broken gate yawed open, and William, at the head of his army, rode into the city. It was beaten and burnt, men watching them with gaunt faces and empty eyes, but Will felt no sympathy. They were traitors, and they had refused to simply surrender. Instead they had opted for defiance, and salt in William's most gaping wound. No one, however, had entirely expected the scale of the vengeance that was taken.

'Find every man in the city,' William instructed them calmly. 'Drag them out from beneath their beds, if you have to. Then cut off his right hand and foot.'

The soldiers blinked, but did not demur. It was finally left to Will to raise the question – not out of personal compassion, but professional thoroughness. 'My lord, should we attempt to find out which of them hung the skins from the walls? Surely it was not every man in Alençon.'

'I could care less.' In the dawn light, William's eyes looked shut off, soulless and ghostly as a frozen lake. 'I have no interest in their excuses. I said, every man.'

Will nodded crisply, put two fingers in his mouth, and whistled his detachment to his side, cantering off through the narrow, muddy streets. He did feel a brief pity, but he put it from his mind. *You did ask for it, you know. I really could have told you.*

The methodical, merciless dismantling took two days. Baskets heaped with bloody limbs were festering in the marketplace, and the screams of the dying cut colder than the March chill. When at last the carnage was through, Alençon resembled an abattoir more than a city. Flies hummed in the streets and crows croaked from the sooty stones. William refused to allow the dead to be buried, and the scent was pervasive, as clinging as despair. But this was only half of what remained to be done, and when they amassed for council, everyone thought they knew what the rest was. 'It is Arques, is it not? To show your uncle the same?'

William let them talk, though his smile was harder and more wolfish than ever. At last, he spoke. 'No,' he said. 'Now we go to Domfront.'

CHAPTER FOUR

Winchester, England
April 1053

EDWARD RECEIVED the news of his cousin's triumph with mixed emotions. On one hand, any lord was justified in punishing disobedient vassals, and it was largely William's absence in England – just as he'd warned – which had impelled said vassals to try again. Edward of all men knew the disruptive force they could exert, and he was glad that William had recovered his position with a quick, efficient masterstroke. In addition to Alençon, the Duke had speedily retaken Domfront; news had travelled quickly, and the latter, terrified that William would do the same to them, promptly opened its gates. (However, Geoffrey Martel had taken advantage of Guy of Talou's desertion in order to slip out and hide elsewhere, so hostilities could not be assumed concluded.) But William *was* temporarily cleared of the threat, and now merely had to focus on subduing his latest unruly relative. To judge from his increasingly impressive record, the odds were on that he would do exactly that.

Nonetheless, the sheer cruelty of what William had done to Alençon sat uneasily in Edward's stomach. In regards to the coldness, his father Robert had been the same, but at least a spell of mirth, however dark, would lighten the skies. Despite everything, Edward felt his late cousin had been a good man, if a misguided one. There was hope, however, that the next duke of Normandy might distinguish the name. Matilda had given birth to a son a few weeks ago, whom she had christened Robert. Edward considered it both a touching gesture – the marriage seemed genuinely happy – and a shrewd one. Although he was not personally acquainted with William's duchess, his experience of her mother was more than enough to conclude that she was not a woman to be trifled with.

But he could not sit about waiting for young Robert to grow up. And while Edward had no desire to be the next in line to betray William (especially knowing who was likely to win that encounter) he was deeply troubled. It was at these times when he felt guilty for racing off with Alfred when William was still fragile from his father's death, abandoning him to be shaped into the brilliant but brutal man that he was. Edward told himself dryly that if he *had* stayed with William, he would likely have been murdered anyway. Nonetheless, something really ought to be done about his heir. He was in Winchester for Easter, as Godwin's guest, in a further attempt to prove that their reconciliation was sincere. Surely he could ask the witan; they would be delighted to hear his misgivings about a Norman. So, on first opportunity, he did exactly that.

'Your Grace,' said Archbishop Stigand. Despite an onslaught of papal venom – Rome did not consider the see of Canterbury to be empty, on grounds that Champart was still alive – he continued to operate in the position. Additionally, he refused to cede his original see of Winchester, meaning that he held two dioceses conjunctly. This ecclesiastical outrage had resulted in his prompt excommunication, but Edward was much too weary to fight another war over Canterbury. Stigand *had* secured the peace with Godwin, and said the Mass without mumbling, so there was that.

'Aye?' said Edward.

'There may be another choice for your heir than the most fierce and frightening Frenchman.' Stigand bobbed his head; he was a rotund, balding man under the unfortunate delusion that he was funny. He looked around, ensuring that he had the attention of the assembled witan. 'There are whispers from the Continent, oh yes.'

'And?' Edward prompted.

Stigand placed a finger to his lips. 'I have heard – albeit with *much* rumour and uncertainty – *most* shocking news. I cannot know if it is true, but surely we hope that it – '

'Point, Stigand,' Leofric ordered brusquely.

'Indeed, my lord.' Stigand gave the Earl of Mercia his best oily smile. 'Well, here it is. I have heard that the two young sons of Edmund Ironside did not die in Sweden after all. That they not only survived, but that they do so to this day.'

There was a brief, thunderstruck silence. Then the council chamber collapsed into a chaos of talk, disbelief, and shouting.

Edward himself was blindsided by the announcement, and he wished that Stigand had shared the news with him first, privately. The idea that his nephews could be alive was one he had never considered. His elder half-brother Edmund Ironside had been crowned in April 1016 and buried that November, the only legacy of his brief reign the crushing defeat at the Battle of Assandun, where the Viking chief Canute had taken control of half the country and then all of it upon Edmund's death. Apart from Edward and Alfred themselves, already judiciously fled to their mother's homeland of Normandy, Edmund's two little boys were the only remaining heirs of Æthelred the Unræd's eight sons. Therefore they had been cast into exile, so as not to challenge the Danish usurper's claim to their throne, and it had long been rumoured that Canute had also ordered their murder. Nonetheless if they *were* alive. . .

Edward looked at Godwin, fully expecting him to object. After all, the bulwark of the Earl's manipulations had been put toward getting a son of *his* own blood onto the throne instead, and no matter how carefully Godwin was treading these days, surely he would not miss a chance to advance Harold's cause. It was, after all, indubitably Harold's now. (Sweyn, seized by guilt for his sins, had attempted a barefoot pilgrimage to Jerusalem and died on the way. Edward had not yet met a man mourning him.)

Sensing the room's collective gaze, Godwin gave a bitter smile. 'My lords, I suppose I cannot expect you to believe that I will support this decision, *if* the sons of Edmund Ironside are still alive. But I have never been driven solely by the desire to oppose the king or to see my own sons shoved into favourable positions, though that has happened along the way. If any man says he would have turned down the same opportunities, I will call him a liar. But if Edward and Edmund Aetheling are alive, I motion at once for a man to be sent to find them, and for Edward – he is the elder, I believe – to be welcomed to the throne that is his right.'

There was another rumble, this one indicating general consent. Stigand turned to Edward with an appealing smile. 'There, my lord, and how could that be tidier?'

'Not at all,' Edward conceded. A rush of sick relief filled him, even as he considered that it would take a few years at least to locate the itinerant aethelings, convince them to come back to England, and secure a promise to be king of what was essentially a foreign country. But blood did count so damnably much for some, and not for the first time, he felt a traitorous disappointment. Christ, if there was an Englishman, strong, kind, and just, a grown man, a soldier yet one who would never commit an Alençon, who knew the people, whom the people would trust. . . Someone, yet again, like Harold Godwinson. But that was impossible.

The Easter feast served at Godwin's board was always extravagant, but this year it was particularly so, with a king, a witan, and an archbishop as guests. They kept the Paschal Vigil in Winchester Cathedral, Stigand intoning the prayers and lighting the candles, then all repaired in much merriment to the hall. Yet Edward had never abandoned his monkish restraint in matters of food and drink, and so as always, he ate sparingly. On his left, Edith was lost in thought. On his right, Godwin was regarding his food with a rather pinched expression. He toyed unenthusiastically with his lamprey pie, then nibbled at a crumb of bread.

'Father?' said Harold. 'Are you well?'

'Fine,' Godwin said gruffly. 'Nay mind me.'

Harold gave his father a concerned look, but went back to flirting with Edith Swannesha, his common-law wife, who was pregnant with their fourth child. There was much confusion among the Church as to whether these offspring should be regarded as legitimate, as Harold and Swannesha had never bothered to be formally married, but among the laity, the matter was largely ignored. Harold already had three young boys – who, if precedent held, would cause no end of trouble in the reign of Edward Aetheling. So the elder Edward suspected, at least, but he was jerked from his meditations by Godwin's voice. 'Might I offer you anything, Your Grace?'

'Nay. Your hospitality has been scrupulous, my lord.'

Godwin smiled, taking a bite of bread. 'Surely Your Grace knows that I will – '

He stopped. His hand curled into a claw. It remained there, frozen, as blood surged into his face, the vein pulsing madly in his neck. He said, sounding confused, 'My lord – ?'

Edward wheeled back. Godwin's face continued to purple, and then he fell forward onto the table, sending a salver of soup flying. It landed on the floor with a crash that startled the suddenly silent hall. Everyone was staring at the stricken earl.

'Father!' Harold bellowed, vaulted off the bench, and seized Godwin by the collar, frantically pounding him on the back. But the bread flew out onto the table and Godwin showed no respite. He was making gurgling noises, eyes rolling back in his head, and Harold was holding him upright with both arms. 'Gyrth! Leofwine! Help me, for God's sake! Help me!'

Gyrth and Leofwine, who had been staring stupidly, came back to life at their brother's shout. They bounded across the dais and shook Godwin, whose mouth had gone slack, frothing. Then Stigand, babbling about the need for an archbishop, came blasting through, clutching his crucifix, but Harold batted him away. He and Leofwine lifted their father and carried him down the length of the hall, with Edward and Stigand in pursuit, into the king's own chamber and laid him down on the bed, the light catching in the green, wolfish eyes gone empty and mute.

Somehow, Godwin lingered for four days. The witan huddled and muttered, Leofric and Siward regarded their rival's downfall with no great relish but no sadness either, and a firestorm of lurid stories had already begun to circulate. The most fantastical of these was the one in which Edward had, on the spot, accused Godwin of murdering Alfred. To which, Godwin had dramatically retorted that if he was guilty, then let this piece of bread choke him. To which, God happily obliged with the truth.

Edward spent most of the time either pacing in an antechamber, or shut up in the chapel, praying. For what, he was not sure. Godwin's recovery seemed impossible, but his death was no savour. He disliked seeing Edith grieving so much. Whatever his flaws, she loved her father.

That was where Edward was at dusk on Thursday. The sound of bells was what drew him from his reverie – first one, then another, and another, until they were all tolling in deep and sorrowful concert. By the time the manservant came for him, Edward already knew his tidings.

'My lord,' he said softly. 'Godwin of Wessex is dead. May God rest his soul.'

Arques, Normandy
October 1053

Arques: the latest rebel pisspot he had to put under siege, continuing a pattern so familiar he could do it in his sleep. His men had been thronging outside the walls for weeks, waiting for hunger to rot within. As if he had nothing bloody better to do. Christ knew, maybe he didn't.

To William's delight, his swift attention to Arques had succeeded in pinning Guy inside the city. Henry and Geoffrey had vanished like rabbits after he'd retaken Alençon and Domfront, but he'd be damned if they weren't still out there somewhere. And while he hadn't yet turned them up, he *had* learned that he had yet another enemy. Unsurprisingly, this one also qualified as family. Enguerrand, count of Ponthieu, had never forgiven William for getting him excommunicated at the same Church council which barred William and Matilda's marriage, taking it as a cheap insult (which it was, but on the part of the Pope, not him). William himself maintained that the fault was entirely Enguerrand's, and he promised his sister Adelaide that he would find her a new husband more to her liking. Presented with this callous disregard on the part of his brother-in-law, Enguerrand had raced off to back up his other one. And that was where the trouble came in. His sister was married to none other than Guy of Talou.

William considered wryly how bloody often wars were fought over who was sticking his cock into whose daughter. As rebellions went, this one was really quite clumsy – he'd been expecting more from his uncle and less from his brother-in-law. *And folk have the nerve to call* me *a bastard.* In any case, Enguerrand was mustering a force, intending to march to Arques, break the siege, and liberate Guy. William found this an amusingly optimistic notion, especially considering that he heard every scrap of strategy Enguerrand made almost the instant he made it – Adelaide had proven highly adept at conveying her husband's intrigues to her brother. *So it is lucky for me that he vexes her so much.*

William stood up, stretching his arms. Shadows fell weirdly through the darkening trees. Things croaked and cried in the bushes, and somewhere nearby, some animal called in such unnerving imitation of a human infant that it made the hackles stand on his neck. On that topic, no matter its perils, being in the field was better than being at home, listening to the baby cry. He had been immensely proud of himself for begetting a son, and since the infant's name was, after all, Robert, William had grandiose plans for him. Yet he did not feel any of the paternal affection which his own father had lavished so profligately on him; in fifteen years or so, then he'd be of some use, the only thing William cared about. Nonetheless, children were power in a man's hand, and he hoped that his opportunity to avail himself of Matilda's bed had left her pregnant with another. She suspected, when he left again in September, but he would not hear for some months.

William refilled his waterskin. Then he slung it over his shoulder and set back toward the camp, irritated to find his heart in his throat when that horrible half-human scream came again.

Enguerrand did not arrive that night, contrary to William's expectations. There *were* all manner of delays that could befall an army on the road – though it was surely too much to hope that one of his barons had ambushed Enguerrand en route and done the job for him. He felt naked without Will fitz Osbern at his back, but Will was off investigating what Geoffrey and Henry were doing, so William knew where to go the instant he was finished with Arques. Some reports held that they'd withdrawn from Normandy entirely, but William would believe himself the Pope before he believed that.

Enguerrand did not arrive that night, no. But just past sunrise, he did.

Later, the details of that battle would numb and fade in William's mind, as if it could not pick itself clear. Perhaps it was because Enguerrand was only a secondary nuisance, or because he had known it such a foregone conclusion that there was no need to savour it. It was just another of the endless struggles that made up his life. But whatever the lack of memory owed to, it was not a lack of competence. William and his men charged out of the woods with the rising sun behind them, and slammed into the Ponthieu contingent at full roar, overpowering them before they had even had so much time to put away their cocks from their morning pisses and grab their swords instead. William dodged, turned, and amidst the clamour, caught sight of Enguerrand himself. 'My lord – you misunderstand – the men, I brought them for you – !'

Further feeble explanations on Enguerrand's part were cut short as William's blade whistled above his head. Abandoning any hope of subterfuge, Enguerrand ducked away, bawling for his men to go, catch the siege while it was still only the night watch. William had a moment to think that in the hands of a more competent man, this might have been halfway effective. Then he blasted free of the skirmish, raced down the hill, and ruined Enguerrand's strategy by the simple expedient of snatching a warhorn from the sentry and venting his lungs into a blast that shook the dawn. He tossed the horn back, snarled, *'Go!'* and tore away.

Chaos roiled against the walls of Arques like angry waves. There were shouts, soldiers arming in frantic haste, horsemen barging through the lines, riding down tents and firing at the escapees. William himself went straight for the heart of the matter, driving the Ponthieu men – the ones trying to protect Enguerrand, who was not a noteworthy fighter – down into the long dale before the city. He dodged as arrows chattered over his head, then shot a glance over his shoulder. Citizens, drawn by the sounds of the mayhem, were appearing atop the walls, tiny black specks in the bloody dawn. Good. He hoped his treacherous uncle was watching.

William forced Enguerrand and his guards almost to the gates. Some of his own men came pelting up to join him, the hooves of their horses gouging the boggy ground. They only skidded. They were the lucky ones. Enguerrand's horse took its footing wrong in the mud, slid, screamed, and threw him.

William reined up hard and plunged a hand down, catching his brother-in-law by the tunic and hauling him across the back of his own great grey destrier. Enguerrand began to gibber thanks, before he caught sight of the eyes beneath the helmet. His face turned a patchy, frostbitten white at immensely gratifying speed.

'Ho there, Enguerrand,' said William calmly, touching a dagger to his neck. 'I can't have you going anywhere.'

For a moment, Enguerrand appeared to be contemplating the merits of pitching himself back into the melee, but bravery was not one of his particular virtues either. Come to think of it, William was not quite sure what his particular virtues *were*. He wrenched Enguerrand's head back to look at the dim figures lining the walls of Arques. 'Which one is your sister?'

No answer, save for Enguerrand's teeth chattering.

William twisted the dagger. 'I *said*, which one is your sister?'

'My lord – please don't – my ransom – Adelaide – '

'Who do you think told me about your treachery?'

Something seemed to break inside Enguerrand when he said that, and William wondered in surprise if the wretch actually loved Adelaide. *Too bloody bad. Love will destroy you, don't you know that?*

'There,' Enguerrand whispered, pointing. 'That's my sister.'

William glanced up. 'Ah, I see. The ugly one.'

In fact Enguerrand's sister was small and rather pretty, certainly finer stuff than his toad of an uncle deserved, but remarking on this would not have the desired effect. Sure enough, Guy of Talou was standing beside her, and they were staring down with expressions nicely caught between shock and horror. William waved pleasantly at them. 'Recognise this miscreant?'

'My lord!' Guy's wife screamed. 'Please, let me ransom my brother – I beg you – '

'Surely,' William called back. 'Would you like this traitor to be drawn and quartered, or merely make a clean end of him now?'

Enguerrand made a choking noise and redoubled his efforts at escape. William restrained him lazily, gazing at his uncle. Seven months of being caged up like a rat in a trap had not done Guy any favours, and he looked more gaunt and wraithlike than ever. His mouth hung open, for once utterly at a loss for a glib rebuttal.

'Fancy seeing you here, I do believe I left you at Domfront,' William added. 'Your lady's choice, my lord?'

Guy's wife began to scream again, begging, pleading. All William could see in Enguerrand's eyes was blank, consuming terror. If he had been vulnerable to such things, he might have felt pity. Enguerrand was the sort who got eaten alive in clashes like this. Not that he didn't deserve it, but he had never stood a chance.

'My lord!' Tears were pouring down Guy's wife's cheeks. 'Please, be merciful, please – '

William looked up at her and smiled. 'For you, sweet lady, of course.'

He waited just long enough to see her face begin to relax. Waited until she stretched out her hands toward her brother. Then he seized Enguerrand's hair, yanked his head back, and cut his throat from ear to ear.

Arques surrendered unconditionally a quarter-hour later.

While his men were ransacking the city for the vanishingly scant provisions that half a year of besiegement had spared it, William went to pay a call on his uncle. He found the comital couple easily enough, by following the sound of weeping. He strode down a hallway, climbed a stair, and flung wide a door. Sure enough, Guy and his wife – William couldn't remember her name, he thought it might be Bertha – were inside, sitting on the bed. Guy wore a look of dull incomprehension, while Bertha was sobbing inconsolably. 'Murderer!' she shrieked, catching sight of him. She sprang up and rushed at him, small fists hammering; he caught them with one hand and easily held her away. Still she went on screaming. 'Murderer! Murderer!'

'Spare me.' William tightened his grip on her wrists, until she moaned and tried vainly to wrench herself loose. She thrashed against him, making noises of unspeakable pain.

'Are you going to kill her too?' Guy's voice came, rusty, from the bed. He got to his feet in the slow, stilted fashion of an old man, and turned to face his nephew.

'I'm tempted,' said William. 'If only so she'd leave off her wriggling.'

Bertha, who clearly had no intention of leaving off, twisted and struggled, making a commendable effort to knee him in the balls. William wrenched her hard, and there was a sudden, sickening crack. Her wrist contorted horribly in his hand.

Bertha's legs gave out, and she sank down, mouth opening and closing in soundless gulps. William eyed her in dismay; he really hadn't meant to damage her that badly. She was so small, her bones so fragile – *she* was not his enemy, and it made him think of how easily someone could do the same thing to Matilda –

That thought terrified him, which made him furious, which gave him power and dropped him back on his feet from what had threatened to be a catastrophic misstep. Leaving Bertha huddled on the floor, he advanced on his uncle. 'Who is Aubrey de Hauteville?'

That, happily, took the whoreson completely on the hop. Panic seared in Guy's eyes. 'I – my lord, you can't think – '

'When he carried the news to me that you'd deserted the siege of Domfront,' William went on, 'young Warenne also mentioned that you were heard to say you'd been waiting for this chance ever since Aubrey de Hauteville. Who is he, and why have you been waiting since him?'

'William – Mauger knew, it was Mauger who did it, not – '

'What did Mauger have to do with Aubrey de Hauteville?' William repeated.

'Aubrey – he was nobody – no account – '

'That scarce meshes with your fervent desire to finish his noble work. All these years, you've been biding your time, building up wealth and connections. Your equally repellent brother even got himself into the fucking Archbishopric of Rouen.' Icy truth was falling over William like sleet. 'How many deaths were you two responsible for? How many? My great-uncle? Gilbert? Alan? Osbern? Convincing others so they did the dirty work, and you remained distant, pure as the driven snow? Or was it more?'

A horrible idea pierced him, coiled cold into his heart. *'Or was it more?'* He couldn't even speak it. Could see in his head the boy he had been, waiting in vain for his father to come home from the Holy Land, and the persistent whispers that Robert had not died a natural death, that he been poisoned by some foul unseen work, a hidden agent of some nefarious rival. *My uncles. Of course it was my uncles.* 'Is that who Aubrey de Hauteville was? Is that what he did?'

Guy stared at him. A queer, savage smile curled up his thin lips. He said nothing.

'Men called my father a kinslayer,' said William at length. 'Whether or not it was true, it weighed him down like a millstone. I will not have it said of me. So, Guy of Talou, I am sending you into exile for the remainder of your days. You will be free to end it at any time by leaping off a tower, finding a sharp knife. Or poison. That was, I understand, your favoured weapon.'

The dragon was burning unbearably hot, but his voice was calm. 'Be less than nothing. Be anathema. May everything you love wither and die, and when it comes to you, may you have no rest. May crows eat your eyes and maggots rot your heart. May demons hound you in hellfire for all eternity. That is my sentence. My lord.'

Guy looked back at him without expression. Bertha was sobbing hopelessly, helplessly. Morning sunlight crested through the window. It could have been just another day.

William waited until he heard his soldiers coming, then turned over the reprobates to them, to cast them out of Normandy forever. When they were gone, he sat down on the bed. He would drown in his tears sooner than shed one – he had promised himself that, after Joscelin. Yet sometimes, he felt he would crack apart like a badly made dam.

Oh God, he prayed. *My father has been gone eighteen years. I have avenged him at last. Now, let me put it aside. I still must be strong enough. Amen.*

The world looked almost at peace. William could hear the shouts of his men, the sounds of sobbing, the call of bells and the clatter of hooves. He waited a moment longer, to be sure he had not missed anything, then got to his feet and went outside to join them.

CHAPTER FIVE

Mortemer, Normandy
February 1054

THE STAND OF ALDERS cut the sunlight into pale shadows, ice dripping from the branches and the crunch of bracken underfoot sounding abnormally loud. The wood had just a hint of a green springy smell, though winter was still its master. But the trees were sparsest by the river, and that was where the road had been cut, a narrow track that sheared in and out along the riverbank. Although it was a nuisance in the extreme to move heavy cavalry along said road, it paid tithe for its trouble – it kept no secrets. The mud was already chopped and churned from an earlier passage. Aye, someone else had come this way.

William studied the mayhem of tracks, trying to decide if they had been left by Angevins or Capets. By now, he no longer knew whether it was Geoffrey or Henry egging the other on, which it was more crucial to stop. No time to waste, in any event. William's mouth tightened and he turned away, hauling himself back into the saddle. They were close. For now, he would take that.

They rode until nightfall and made camp by the bluffs. William sent out scouts, gnawed on half a stringy capon for his supper, then rolled himself in his blanket and lay down by the fire. He must have dozed off, for he dreamt that Will fitz Osbern had arrived. But when he woke in the grey, cold dawn, the fires had all gone out, and he was still alone.

'Your Grace,' said one of the returned scouts, dipping a bow and perching on the log beside William. 'There is both good and bad news. Which would you start with?'

'The good,' said William.

'Henry Capet had an apoplexy?' Walter Giffard said hopefully.

'Not quite, my lord. But the gracious allies *have* had a spot of disagreement. Geoffrey has amassed the Angevins nearby, on the east bank of the Seine, and is champing at the bit to fight you. But it seems that Henry has had an attack of second thoughts. The Capetian force is on the west bank of the Seine, while Henry dithers about whether or not to go for it.'

'Henry always was a ditherer,' William commented, stoking the fire. In truth, the news heartened him immeasurably. Somewhere in a dark part of him, he had been seriously concerned that having to face both the buggering whoresons at once would spell an end to his preternatural fortitude in battle. 'I take it you were not nearly so clumsy as to let Geoffrey see you?'

'Of course not, m'lord,' the scout retorted, looking miffed.

'Very good indeed.' William took a bite of the capon, chewed experimentally, and spat it out. 'Well, now I suppose I am sufficiently fettled for the bad news.'

'Er, well, it is quite bad. The king's brother Eudes Capet, Rainald de Cleremont, and Guy de Ponthieu have banded together to invade the east of Normandy. Guy took quite poor to your treatment of his brother and sister at Arques, so now that he's count, he's decided to pay it back.'

William raised an eyebrow. 'Another small-time traitor. How, pray, is this collection of luminaries occupying themselves?'

'Rape. Pillage. Burning. The lot.' The scout seemed to realise halfway through that he was not treating this recital of injuries with the proper gravitas, and hastily papered on a look of dire disapproval. 'Their devastation is really most awful, m'lord.'

William opened his mouth, then stopped. Something had just occurred to him. As much havoc as Henry's henchmen were undoubtedly wreaking, the scout dismissed it because he was sure that William would speedily handle the matter, mete out justice, and smack the oafs straight back into oblivion. William himself had known that long ago, but was wholly unused to anyone besides Will and Matilda sharing the opinion. He (mostly) trusted Warenne, Walter Giffard, Richard fitz Gilbert, and the rest, but only since they did what they were told. To meet with such uncomplicated faith was as gratifying as it was unexpected.

William cleared his throat. 'Fetch my captains. We must have a council of war.'

Most of the barons he had sent summons to had actually answered them. This miracle was followed up with a second one when they convened at his command. Once this was achieved, they went for a record by agreeing that his plans were sensible. If he was prone to such things, William would have fainted dead away.

'Warenne, Walter Giffard, Robert de Eu, Hugh de Gournay, Roger de Mortemer,' he ordered. 'I'm sending you ahead. Robert, you lead the attack on Henry's brother. Will, you lead it on Geoffrey Martel. As for me, I will be attending to Henry myself. Try not to kill Eudes Capet, but anyone else who wanders into range is perfectly acceptable. I'll even offer a bounty to whichever of you nicks the latest bloody Count of Ponthieu. Christ, I hate that house.'

They forded the Seine at night, well upstream of Henry's camp. It was a harrowing experience; though the ford was shallower than the rest of the river, it was still deep enough to come almost to a stallion's withers. At places the bottom fell stomach-lurchingly away, and contrary currents seethed and foamed. The moon was at a wane, and the night was very dark.

They arrived safely, though not without a few close calls, and pitched camp in the trees. William stripped off his wet clothes and rolled up in his blanket. But as he was lying down to sleep, he thought suddenly of his twelve-year-old self, on the run to Brittany with his uncle Walter. Asking about his mother, and the thought of Herleva set off a small, indefinable pain. He tried to hold onto it; he would be fighting Henry tomorrow, for his dukedom, his wife, his life. The stakes never got any lower. But just as before, he could not make this pain into anger, or power. It merely hurt, a dull throb like a diseased tooth, and went on hurting until he fell asleep.

He was woken before sunrise by one of his men shaking him urgently. 'M'lord? M'lord!'

William was by long practise and necessity a very light sleeper, but he had been in the middle of some muddled dream and it took him several heartbeats to recover his whereabouts. 'Wha?' He sat upright, kicking off the blanket. 'Whazit? Henry attacking?'

'No, m'lord. Across the river. Come.'

William stumbled after the soldier to the edge of the camp. Dawn was just beginning to limn the horizon with furious crimson, scorching the underside of the stone-smoke clouds. While it was hard to see much, he didn't need to. Just across the river, there were dark figures swarming, the distant clatter of spears, screams of wounded men, and he grasped it at once. 'That's Mortemer. So Robert de Eu and the rest of the barons must have made it. Given Henry's minions a surprise they shan't soon forget.'

The man nodded. The two of them stood marking the progress, trying to judge who might be gaining the victory, though it was impossible to say. But William at last turned away, gave the order to mount up and move out. Before the day was done, he intended to cross swords with a king, and if it so pleased God that one of them must die, by Christ His Son it would not be him.

The Normans rode like a thunderstorm, hoping to catch the Capetians off guard while they were either celebrating a victory or reeling from a defeat. Henry had installed himself at the mouth of a narrow valley, bottling it up, and while it was a defensible ground, it was easily possible to turn it into a trap – it was bordered by steep bluffs on one side, the Seine on the other. William wondered if Henry remembered how they had driven the rebels into the Orne to drown like dogs, seven years ago at Val-ès-Dunes. To judge from the evidence, perhaps not.

The French camp was visible just ahead of them, gone riot with activity. Horns called, horses stamped, and men ran about like startled chickens; they'd seen the Normans. William decided that this was a fine time to begin the enterprise. He raised his fist, and two flanks broke off and stampeded forward, the sun catching brilliant on helmets, hauberks, lances. Then William put two fingers in his mouth and whistled, and the stanchion tilted upwards until the breeze caught it. His banner flared out, stark as blood.

'Normandy!' the men were screaming. *'Diex aie!* William! William and Normandy!'

William felt a visceral, surging thrill. He glanced back into the camp, tracking the small figure that must be Henry. His men kept up their howls like a pack of hungry wolves, drawing the noose tight. The first volleys of arrows were beginning to fly –

And then –

William turned just in time to see a lone rider in Capetian colours, plunging down the embankment. At once he closed one eye against the sun, lining up the shot – it was a long one, and with cross-breezes, but if anyone could make it, it was him; very few men could even bend his great bow. He thought again of the day, very long ago, when he had struggled to draw his father's. *Before you loose, you had best be prepared to kill the beast – or the man – on the other end.* Back when the idea of killing even one man was unthinkable.

Flustered, he let the shot go too soon, and it fell into the grass well shy of its target. The rider ducked, looked around madly for the direction it had come from. Then his horse leapt a thicket, and he vanished into the madness of the camp.

William cursed. *Will you bloody forget about your father? Look what it made you do!* He reorganised a flank that had gotten out of order, scanned the scrum to assess how the battle might develop – then saw something extremely odd. The fleur-de-lis banner prancing on the wind had suddenly tipped, swayed, and toppled.

William blinked. He reminded himself to congratulate whichever of his men had penetrated to the centre of the enemy camp so quickly, when he realised that none of them had. Which meant that one of Henry's own men had struck it. Which meant –

Confused shouts tumbled down the valley. Henry could be seen riding this way and that, the crown of France gleaming golden over his battle-helmet. But the French army itself was abandoning its position, turning, fleeing, thundering out of the riverlands. Far from trying to stop them, Henry was foremost among them, and the Normans watched this spectacle in amazement. A few raised their bows, but were stood down; shooting a fleeing foe in the back transgressed the unspoken codes of warfare. William, equally bewildered, kicked the grey over to join them. 'What in the name of Mary God's Mother?' he bellowed at the nearest captain.

'Not entirely sure, m'lord. Far as I can tell, that rider was coming to deliver news, and – '

'Evidently not good news. For them. Good for me.' William grinned. Perhaps it was a blessing after all that he'd missed shooting the man.

'Aye, m'lord.' The captain's face split in an answering smile. 'Robert de Eu and his lads kicked Frenchie arses black and blue. Henry's underlings were busy pillaging like the swine they are, had no idea it was coming, and Robert and the others made 'em wish they'd never been born. When Henry got the news just now, he decided to cut his losses, stick his tail between his legs, and run.'

William nodded, thinking of the battle he had witnessed from across the river that morning. So the five barons had done their job, wonder of wonders, and he had won. At Val-ès-Dunes, it had been thanks to Henry. But he owed this victory to no one.

'Was Guy de Ponthieu killed?' he asked abruptly.

'Sadly no, m'lord.' The captain was still jubilant. 'He was, however, taken prisoner, and we'll clap him in irons until he learns his lesson. He may even be of use in the future.'

William made a noise that suggested he thought this possibility remote in the extreme.

'Doesn't matter at the moment, though,' the captain went on. 'A victory with barely a shot fired, how about that? And now they're out of Normandy for good.'

William shook his head, eyes fixed on the fleeing army now only distant figures on the horizon, their dust choking the sunlight. 'No,' he said at last. 'They'll be back.'

Be that as it may, the triumph was considerable. While beating his hasty retreat, Henry had considerately collected Geoffrey as well, and they had tripped over each other's feet trying to get out. Consequently, William returned to Caen in April with his reputation higher than ever. Not just France but the whole of Europe was realising that the young lion of Normandy had become one of the most fearsome warriors on the Continent.

William stayed a few weeks with Matilda, who was seven months pregnant with their second child, before he was off again, this time to Rouen, to order his uncle Mauger deposed from the archbishopric on grounds of grievous treachery. Mauger protested and pleaded and put up very unconvincing pretensions of innocence, but it did him no good. Just past Easter, at the synod of Lisieux, he was declared traitor and anathema, false servant to lord and Lord. As Mauger *had* been a churchman, it was not proper to kill him, but there was no way he would be permitted to remain in the duchy. He was given the same sentence as his brother: life exile.

Once Mauger had been thrown out on his ear and a new, ideally less treasonous prelate bestowed with mitre and crozier,

William still had work to do. He terrified petty officials who had been remiss in their duties, went through the cartularies and tax-records and hanged a few embezzlers, and in recognition of years of faithful service, raised his loyal Will fitz Osbern to the rank of lord, granting him the castle of Breteuil. Then he wed his sister Adelaide to Lambert de Lens, Eustace de Boulogne's brother. With all this industry achieved, he managed to return home soon after the birth of his second son, a few days past the Feast of St Boniface. 'We'll call him Richard, for my great-grandsire who was known as the Fearless,' William decided. Privately, he thought it a shame they could not name this one Robert instead. The holder of the name was a fat, whiny toddler who, in William's opinion, sulked to excess.

When he complained about this to Matilda, however, she gave him a strange look. 'Robert's a *baby*, husband. Of course he does. Your sons will be men in time, but pray God they do not have to be grown at the age of seven like you. Let them be children first.'

William supposed a mother would see it like that, and did his best to hold his tongue. Mayhaps it was just a reflection of other problems. Both Robert and Richard were of uncertain legitimacy; they'd been born into wedlock, but one the Pope still did not recognise. William himself did not regard them as anything besides his trueborn sons, but he needed men, sturdy heirs, fellow warriors, and was vaguely dissatisfied with the two he had thus far been equipped with. Perchance a different one would suit better.

By Michaelmas, Matilda was pregnant again. William welcomed it, rather more than she did. As small as Matilda was, the birthing bed was a considerable chore, and this was her third in three years. But she understood as well the need for children, and she adored her two small sons. They kept her company when William was gone, as he was three-quarters of the time.

As if to prove this, William went tearing back off to Maine, as he considered himself the winner of the wager he'd made with Geoffrey at Vitry-aux-Loges, and he spent Christmas in the castle at Le Mans. The rightful heir, Herbert, was only seven years old, and something about him reminded William of himself. Not that it stopped him from asserting himself as the true ruler of the county, but it did occasionally strike him as too ironic to be permitted.

The year turned. His sister was almost immediately widowed again – he would have said before she was bedded, if not for the fact that Lambert had managed to get her with child before rushing out and dramatically perishing in some inconsequent venture. 'William,' Adelaide said dryly, 'if it's all the same to you, I'd rather wait a while before marrying again.'

'Indeed. You devour mates like a spider.' William had brought his sister back to Caen for now, and he made a note not to wed her to any man he cherished too much. 'Guy de Ponthieu?'

Adelaide smacked him.

'Only jesting. But it might ensure that I got rid of him.'

'I have no interest in being a serial widow.'

'Before long the rumours will be about that you poison them,' William said jauntily.

Adelaide turned a chilly blue gaze on him. 'You dispensed of any chance of that by dramatically cutting Enguerrand's throat before a hundred witnesses.'

'I thought you didn't care for Enguerrand.'

'No, I didn't. That, however, is not the point.' Adelaide shifted uncomfortably; she was six months pregnant, and she and Matilda were pleased to have the other to commiserate with. They were alike in another respect, as they were among the few, man or woman, who were not afraid of William in the slightest, and spoke their minds to him as they pleased. William supposed he could permit it in them. As long as they did not give anyone *else* ideas.

Spring came. Geoffrey recovered his feet, and he and William went on scuffling over Maine. However, William scored the most lasting coup by whisking young Herbert and his sister Marguerite off to Caen, where he betrothed Marguerite to his son Robert. Geoffrey groused and fulminated and set various villages on fire, so William marched out to smack him on the wrist.

That summer, Adelaide and Matilda both gave birth to daughters, much to William's consternation. A daughter was very well and good, but he needed sons. Cecilia – that was the girl's name – was a sweet enough babe, and she had the decency not to cry much. Nonetheless, if the Pope wouldn't recognise the children, he'd bloody shove it down his throat. This sentiment, however, was not necessarily shared.

'Another?' said Matilda wearily. 'Must we?'

'Aye.'

'You don't even like them that much.'

'I still need them.'

'I understand we must have children, William. I understand also that we must have more. But must we have them all at once?'

'Why not?'

Matilda smiled with extreme dryness. 'If our positions were reversed, perhaps you'd understand better.'

'I am out fighting nearly all the bloody time. This is the least you can give me back.'

'Do not,' Matilda said evenly, 'accuse me of not making sacrifices.'

'I – no. That is not what I meant. I'm sorry.'

'Too many sons is as much a bane as too few.'

'Are you unwilling?' He felt a sudden stab of fear.

'No.' He heard her cross the floor, felt her small hand between his shoulders. 'Just tired.'

He turned wordlessly and took her in his arms. That was the last they spoke of it. When in October their fourth child was conceived, Matilda told him with a smile. The next morning he was off to skirmish with Geoffrey again. As he rode away in the mist, he was left to reflect that Matilda had done it because – despite all the excellent reasons to the contrary – she loved him.

He wondered if he could afford to let her. He wondered if he could bear to make her stop.

London, England
November 1055

If Edward had been informed a scant four years ago that his chief occupying issue over the feast of Martinmas would be a rebellion by a son of Leofric, and that his chief assistant in quashing said rebellion would be a son of Godwin, he certainly would not have hesitated to call the informant a liar. That, he supposed, was the beauty of the fact that only God knew all the days of a man's life. Still, he could have done without it.

'Your Grace,' said Harold, bowing. 'If you have a goblet of mulled wine, that would be most welcome. This weather is attempting to kill us all.'

'Indeed.' Edward could hear it lashing the windows, had been forced to suspend work on his great church while the storms crouched over London like a thief. 'Sit down, my lord, you look soaked to the skin.'

'To the bone, I fear.' Harold took a fistful of his cloak and wrung it out into the rushes. 'Ah, thank you,' he added to the servant, clutching the goblet in both hands.

Edward let the bedraggled Earl of Wessex recollect himself. Then he said, 'So tell me of Ælfgar. I've heard all sorts of rumours.'

'Where do I start?' Harold tipped half the goblet down his throat, still shivering. 'It is true that Ælfgar seems – er – to have taken a lesson from my father's defiance, but I can't quite fathom why he had to bother in the first place.'

'Nor can I.' *Though Leofric did warn me.* Ælfgar, Leofric's only son, had decided earlier that year that he was not receiving due honour as Earl of East Anglia – he'd briefly been dispossessed of the position when Harold was restored to it, but when Godwin died and Harold became Earl of Wessex, Ælfgar had gotten it back. Evidently this was insufficient for his purposes, as he launched a rebellion, got himself exiled, and fled to Ireland. Successful in acquiring ships, he had next enlisted the aid of England's other chief antagonist: Gruffydd ap Llywelyn, the self-styled King of Wales, who had been thrilled to do a bit of plundering, robbery, and rapine. They had then proceeded to cause so much pandemonium that Edward ordered an army raised and put Harold in charge of it. Harold had finally cornered the miscreants in Herefordshire, where Edward's nephew Ralph was earl. (Ralph had done his best to muster a defence, but utterly botched it, ensuring that he would be known unflatteringly as 'Ralph the Timid' from this day forth.) Harold had ambushed them as they were trying to make a victorious exeunt, chased Gruffydd back into Wales, and hauled Ælfgar down to London to face his reckoning. Edward too might need several goblets of wine before he was up for that.

'You have my gratitude,' he said. 'If it is money you desire, name your price.'

Harold shook his head. 'Nay, thank you, my lord. I have wealth enough.'

'Surely there is some gift I can make?'

Harold paused. 'Well, now that you mention it, there is one possibility. Is it true that Earl Siward is dead? In Scotland?'

'Aye.' That still saddened Edward. Last autumn, Siward had gone north with young Malcolm, the rightful heir to the Scottish throne, and launched an assault on the usurper Macbeth, who had killed Malcolm's father King Duncan and installed himself in his place. Malcolm had spent the last decade in exile at Edward's court, but now that he was twenty-three years old, he felt it time to reclaim his birthright. Although he and Siward had defeated Macbeth in battle, it had not settled matters conclusively. Macbeth had escaped, Malcolm pursued him, and it was left entirely in his own hands after the old Earl of Northumbria succumbed to a bloody flux. Siward's elder son had died as well, leaving Northumbria without an heir apparent. (Waltheof, Siward's younger son, was the product of a second marriage, his brother's junior by near thirty years. Edward, having seen the ruinous effects of a minor attempting to rule in Normandy, was in no hurry whatsoever to repeat the experiment in his own domains.)

It occurred to Edward that perhaps Harold was going to ask for Northumbria in addition to Wessex. He was not at all sure how he felt about this. Harold had proven himself loyal, competent, valorous, and kind, far more agreeable to work with than his late father, and if there was any Godwinson whom Edward trusted to hold half the kingdom, it was him. Nonetheless, the idea had to be considered with caution.

'I do not ask for myself,' Harold added, reading the look on Edward's face. 'I am content with Wessex. But if Your Grace would allow. . . perhaps my brother Tostig?'

Edward blinked. If there was any Godwinson he did *not* trust to have jurisdiction over more than a furlong, it was Tostig. Although he had mellowed from his truly unbridled youth, he was still erratic and volatile. In addition, he had little talent for administration and even less for hanging onto his money, two factors which made him about as unsuited a candidate for public office as one could imagine. However he *was*, like all his brothers, a skilled and fearless warrior. That might be more important, when it came to bashing the unruly northerners into compliance.

'I understand it comes as a surprise,' Harold went on. 'But since Sweyn's death, Tostig is the second eldest son after me. It is time he had a domain of his own.'

73

'That could be settled with a nice manor,' Edward countered. 'Northumbria is quite a large part of the kingdom, with a marked independent streak. Tostig is a southerner, and – '

'He's half-Dane, at least,' said Harold, 'and the north is still more Danish than English. I understand you may still have misgivings about him, but I ask that you grant him a chance to prove himself. He is different now, I swear it.'

Edward considered. 'Why Tostig?'

Harold's eyes met his steadily. 'He is my brother.'

You mean that if he holds it, that's another chunk of the kingdom I'm not in danger of giving to a Frenchman. Edward sighed. News of Robert Champart's death in Jumièges had come last Christmas, and despite the manner in which their association had ended, he could not help but grieve; the man had been his friend. 'And why else?'

'I believe in my country,' said Harold. 'I believe in my kin. Your Grace, grant us this boon, and both myself and Tostig shall repay you in kind.'

I scarce have a choice. I need to keep you bloody Godwinsons on my side – God Above help me if I have not learnt that. 'Aye,' said Edward. 'Well. Mayhaps it can be arranged.'

Three days later, in gratitude for Harold's service, Tostig was appointed Earl of Northumbria – a paradox that did not escape those present, least of all the king. Siward's memory hung long over them, as if his shade was whispering, asking *why*, pray, his earldom was being granted to a Godwinson. *A southerner.*

If Tostig himself was conscious of any improprieties, he did not show it. He was dressed for the occasion in a long green tunic with gilt embroidery, his cloak was marten fur, clasped with a silver chain, and he was fully cognisant and appreciative of the fact that every eye was on him. Harold was handsome, manly, virile, but Tostig was almost eerily beautiful, with thick golden hair, high cheekbones, and wide green eyes holding the glint of a private jest. He resembled a faerie in more ways than one – you were dazed by the splendour, but retained a dark, uneasy sense that at any moment it could all melt away and leave you trapped under the hill, the prisoner of a thing at once mirthful and merciless.

Edward hoped very much that whatever filial affection Tostig felt for Harold would restrain the younger Godwinson's venom from undue manifestation. He administered the oath of fealty and Tostig repeated it, with apparent sincerity. His timid little Flemish wife stood behind him, and Edward smiled at her. Judith was his cousin, as close kin to him as William, and as that occurred to him, he realised that doubtless Harold knew it too. It made him wonder if he'd just played into their hands more than he thought.

The pact made and sealed, Tostig rose to his feet. He smiled at the Northumbrians in the back of the hall – Siward's old subjects, passing through London on their way back north to fight with Malcolm in Scotland. It was a smile in which Tostig did not trouble to conceal any of his strong, white, remarkably sharp-looking teeth.

'Your Grace,' said Leofric, later. 'You will soon sit in judgment of my son. I make no excuses for his conduct. But. . . perhaps you might find some cause for leniency?'

Edward studied his friend thoughtfully. Leofric was the last of the three great earls, and had weathered decades of storms like the sturdy old oak he was. Yet with both Godwin and Siward dead, Leofric saw the writing on the wall. If he perished with Ælfgar still out of favour, what would stop Mercia from being peddled off to the next Godwinson in line, uniting England in the hands of one family? There were a number of things Edward would do to forestall it, even if it was a family he trusted more. No one should have that much wealth and power, and the Godwins were hardly known as an incorruptible lot. Please God Ælfgar would be humble and contrite, to preclude it from even being thought of.

'It depends,' he said, in answer to Leofric's question. 'Your son has caused me a deal of trouble I could have done without, left my nephew Ralph a laughingstock and Herefordshire in tatters. At least your grandsons did not join their father in his villainy?'

'No, m'lord,' the old Earl of Mercia said at once. His grandsons, seventeen-year-old Edwin and fifteen-year-old Morcar, were his pride and joy, a pair of strapping lads who swaggered around with the pissant braggadocio endemic to young noblemen. But even they had had better sense than to gallivant off with Ælfgar.

'That is fortunate.' Edward gingerly stretched his back. He himself was not at all young any more – past fifty, with the creaking limbs and fading eyesight and weary bones. At least having his castle precluded the need to tramp about in the mud.

Leofric nodded. 'Forgive me, Your Grace. But with Siward's death and Tostig's appointment, your heir must be thought of again. The rumours of your nephews – '

'They will be attended to.' Aye, they bloody well would be, now. 'You have my word.'

Leofric nodded again. 'What have you been doing in the nonce, my lord?'

'Trying to decide whether it was worth the risk.' Edward accepted two goblets of hippocras and offered one to Leofric. He nodded the page out before he continued. 'I have had men asking, yet it is time we mounted a full-fledged effort to find them. But it is not even certain that they *are* alive. For all I know, some cunning sort found two tall fair-haired men he can pass off as English.'

'But at the same time,' said Leofric, 'there are already enough factions at another's throats that the sudden appearance of a pair of well-nigh foreigners would be badly tolerated.'

'Precisely, my lord. But if Edward Aetheling lives, the throne of England must pass to him. Then to his son if he has one, and so forth. Then we can be quit of this succession fiasco.'

Leofric was too tactful to mention that Edward himself had been responsible for a great deal of it; Edward could tell, however, that he was thinking it. Then the old earl said, 'It is my experience that there is little a man will not do, with a crown at stake.'

'Mine as well. Don't you dare die and leave me alone with the Godwinsons, my lord.'

Leofric laughed, which turned into a cough. 'As Your Grace commands,' he wheezed. 'Don't worry. I'll manage until you find the aethelings, at least. I'll see England's fate settled before I go to my grave, so perhaps. . .'

'Perhaps?'

Leofric's gaze turned serious. 'Perhaps, my lord, you should make sure of it.'

Edward's Christmas court began, and the witan convened. Aside from the usual matters of taxes, laws, and marriages, they had to discuss Ælfgar's sentence. Leofric appealed passionately for clemency, arguing that if even the Godwins could be kissed and forgiven, surely the same could be spared for his son. 'Humour an old man's attachment, if nothing else. Ælfgar acted foolishly, we agree, but in the end he will serve his king.'

'Ælfgar is nine-and-thirty, my lord,' said Harold, son of the man who had perfected the art of double-crossing kings. 'That is well beyond the age at which fits of pique are expected or tolerated. It does not serve England for the king to be disrespected at yearly intervals.'

There was not another Godwinson who could have gotten away with that, but Harold had never incurred any censure for his personal conduct. Even during Godwin and Edward's standoff, he had done his best to maintain loyalty to both kin and king. The witan knew that, as did Leofric, and Harold continued courteously. 'I do not, however, suggest Ælfgar receive any punishment that my own father and brothers were spared. If the king will consent, then may Ælfgar be welcomed back into his peace.'

A murmur spread across the room. Then a Wessex ealdorman stood up. 'That's true and good, but how many times must the king thank a rebellious whoreson and ask for another? If he keeps forgiving the bastards, he'll keep having the problem. Mayhaps we should whack one. For a message.'

Harold gave his man a distasteful look. 'I fought Ælfgar, by my king's command, to bring an end to his pillaging. That was done. I do not endorse cold-blooded murder now.'

The witan deliberated. Leofric stole glances at Ælfgar, who sat quietly, chained to a chair. By contrast Tostig, attending his first witan, appeared bored and restless. The Northumbrian ealdormen were giving him suspicious looks, which grew increasingly aggravated as the debate wore on. When asked pointedly if he had anything to contribute, Tostig gave a negligent shrug. 'Are we off Leofric's tedious son and onto taxes yet?' he drawled. 'If so, aye.'

Harold shot him a reproving look. 'Not yet. We merely wish to ensure that every man has spoken on the matter of Ælfgar, before we ask the king for his judgment.'

Tostig shrugged again. 'You know what I think of the bugger. Have his head off, I won't weep.'

Harold's lips tightened. His gaze lingered on his brother, as if to say, *I did this for you. Don't embarrass me.* Then to smooth the moment, he turned to Edward. 'My lord?'

Edward drew himself up. 'Ælfgar Leofricsson has confessed his misdeeds and applies to me with a penitent heart. Thus may all men know that I welcome him back as my Earl of East Anglia, and into the sight of God.'

The witan stirred. Harold nodded. Tostig sighed. Ælfgar sat slightly straighter, despite the chains. Leofric let go a breath that he seemed to have been holding all council.

That was one promise. The next wouldn't be near as easy.

'Where,' said Edward, 'are my nephews?'

'Exactly, Your Grace. Exactly.' The Archbishop of Canterbury bit off a loose thread and patted his cassock back into place. 'When I first heard the rumour, they *were* in one somewhere, but certainly they could now be somewhere else. Somehow.'

Edward restrained the urge to roll his eyes. Stigand's propensity for dreadful humour could grate very thin, now especially. 'I'm having a *scop* in the hall tonight, you can practise your riddles then. Let us try again. Where are my nephews?'

'In the Kievan Rus', my lord. One of them married a daughter of the Grand Prince Yaroslav. The lady is a most – '

'Very well, very well.' Edward reached for his goblet. 'How certain are you that it *is* them? How recent was your information? From a firsthand source or a second?'

'I am certain, my lord. It was the Metropolitan of Kiev – a good and learned man, Ilarion by name – who shared the news. His predecessor officiated at the wedding of Edward Aetheling and the Princess Agatha. Sadly, Yaroslav died last year, and his son is rul – '

'The Kievan Rus' is a large place. Might you know *where* we should begin our search?'

Stigand blinked again. 'Oh. . . in Hungary, I believe. One of Agatha's sisters married the Hungarian king, and the aethelings, Ilarion said, established themselves at his court.'

Edward took a deep breath. 'Thank you, Stigand. You have performed a great service, I shan't forget it.' Surely the man would want money, though he seemed to possess it in plenty. Far more than an ecclesiastic required, truth be told, and Edward doubted that Stigand's unlawful double dioceses ever saw a penny of it.

'Your Grace, if you would permit me to travel there myself, it would be the greatest of – '

'Thank you, Stigand,' Edward interrupted again. 'You are excused.'

Stigand bowed himself out, and Edward watched him go, considering. Aside from the honour that would accrue to him by such a mission, Stigand surely intended to take a side excursion to Rome, in an attempt to reverse the tidal wave of pontifical disapproval crashing down on his head; the newest edition, Victor, had barely gotten his arse onto the Chair of Peter before he promptly reinforced Stigand's excommunication. And the prohibition against William of Normandy's marriage, for that matter. Edward sighed. *I could force Stigand to relinquish Winchester, but though he may be a glutton, an excommunicate, and a terrible jester, he is on my side at least. He fawns instead of plots, and all he truly cares for is trimming his cloak in gold and sitting before a warm fire. But sending him as an emissary for the delights of England, its godliness and appeal, to my nephews who have been exiles their entire lives? They'd be racing the other way before he finished his greeting.*

The Christmas season passed, the year turned. On the feast of the Epiphany, God's Year 1056, Aldred, Archbishop of York, was officially commissioned to travel to Hungary and convince the exiled aethelings to come home, restore them to their rightful inheritance at last. It was, in theory, a nobly intentioned plan. And now all he could do, Edward thought wryly, was wait to see not if it went wrong, but how badly it did so.

Yet nonetheless, he could not stop himself from hoping.

CHAPTER SIX

Caen, Normandy
March 1056

'H E *WHAT?*' William repeated. 'Are you sure?'
'Aye, m'lord.' His informant, a sparse, weedy man in a
tattered tunic, kept a prudent distance from the duke. 'He
sent the archbishop of York, swear on my son's life. To Hungary.'

'And these nephews are indeed alive? How convenient.'

'It came quite a surprise to them all, I do think.' The
informant perched cautiously on the settle, looking as if he would
leap up again at once if his employer got too close. 'Surely you can
understand that the good king Edward wishes his heir to be of his
own blood. His nephew – '

'Is even more foreign than me, and likely a heretic to boot, if
he stayed with the Patriarchs of Constantinople when they broke
from Rome two years ago.' William himself was no votary of the
Papacy, especially considering the continued nuptial roadblocks it
was presenting for him, but he was excellent at using righteous
wrath to trip up his enemies. 'And as for you, Abelard, you seem to
be forgetting who's paying you.'

'Not in the slightest, m'lord.' A thin film of sweat showed on
Abelard's lip. 'I was merely – it's understandable why Edward – '

'Perhaps. But he made me a vow.'

'He didn't – know his nephews were alive then, surely – '

'Are you arguing with me?' William enquired.

'C-course not, m'lord.'

William sighed. 'Here,' he said, tossing the spy a sack of
silver. 'You've done well. Come back once you've found out more.'

Abelard, still sweating, bowed himself out post-haste.

'My lord!' Maud Peverel looked up with a flashing smile, sweeping her curtain of red-gold hair out of her eyes. She alone among the fashionable ladies of Caen did not wear it braided and veiled, letting it tumble like an unwed lass. Various disapproving clergymen had complained about this to Ranulf, but he, as besotted with his wife as the day he'd run off to marry her, continued to let her do precisely as she pleased and to bugger with St Paul. 'What an unexpected surprise!'

'The pleasure is mine. If you might do me a favour?'

'Of course.' The smile was pure Maud coquetry, that tilt of her head and flash of the cornflower eyes. 'Anything for you, m'lord.' She stepped closer, put her hand warm over his.

William shrugged it off. He had enjoyed her charms before, of course, but that was *before;* there was no woman for him now but Matilda. Besides, the task he had in mind had nothing to do with the carnal. 'I want you to teach me Saxon.'

She blinked. 'My lord?'

'You're the only person I know who speaks it,' William elaborated. While Maud's French was now nearly perfect, she still retained a slight flattening of the consonants, an arching of the vowels, that recalled her London origins.

'Indeed, my lord, I'd be glad. I'm teaching my lads, would you like to sit with them at their lessons?' Again the teasing in her eyes. 'But then, it may take something different for you.'

'It doesn't matter. I need to learn it.'

'Any reason, m'lord?'

'Excellent ones.' William cracked his knuckles. 'When can we begin?'

Maud blinked again. 'I can fetch a quill and ink if you like. Ranulf was kind enough to let me learn reading and writing.'

Of course he did, William thought, but didn't complain. So he nodded, then sat down to wait while she went upstairs.

Maud had just gone when a door banged at the back of the house, and two young boys came dashing in. Their clothes were bedecked in mud, and one was shouting, 'Will! Mine! Will! Mine!' but failing to retrieve whatever the other had thieved from him. They were just to the point of coming to blows in earnest when they caught sight of the unfamiliar man in their kitchen, and froze.

'Ho there,' said William. 'You must be Maud's rascals, aye?'

'Aye.' The elder of the two drew himself up. He was about five, a small, sturdy lad with tangled golden hair, his mother's blue eyes, and the face of an angel. 'My name is William Peverel,' he said formally. 'I am your servant, messire.'

William, abruptly, felt a bolt of lightning go down his spine. He'd not thought of the possibility in several years, had all but put it from his mind in the tempest of invasions, scuffles, and skirmishes. 'Is that so. My name's also William.'

'I'm called Will, though,' the child added. 'This is my little brother Ranulf. He's smelly.'

'Am not!' The impugned party, a year or two younger, glowered heatedly up at his sibling. He was more closely his father, Ranulf senior, with a narrow face and brown hair – in fact, the boys did not look at all alike. It bit at William's mind, pulling at him.

'He is, don't mind him,' said the boy archly. He had a way of standing – and something about the shape of his head, perhaps. William's heart started to pick up speed. Aye, this was what –

'Will! Ranulf!' Maud reappeared at that moment. 'My heavens, don't stare like gawks! Make your courtesies to the Duke!'

'We did!' Will protested. Then the rest of his mother's words hit, and he wheeled around to stare at William. 'You're the *Duke?*'

'I am.'

'You can't be. The Duke's a big scary man on a horse.'

'The horse's outside.' William stood up to his full height. 'And I *can* be big and scary if I wish, no matter.'

Will Peverel almost put his neck out of joint craning up at this unbelievable apparition. Then a grin spread across his face from ear to ear. 'You're *great!*'

William could not fathom what in the world he was feeling. The heat had escaped its containment inside him, made him dazed. He desperately desired to go and pick the boy up, play with him, roll about with him. It was not a feeling he had much, if at all, with his own sons. But he wanted it to be true. God almighty, he wanted it. He should not have, had sworn that he'd never father a bastard. But in all technicality, Will Peverel was not. He had been born into respectable wedlock, this confident, precocious, prepossessing little boy. As if preserving a happy childhood for him could make up for the chaos and agony of William's own.

William swallowed the ache in his throat. He reminded himself why he had come in the first place, told himself to forget about it. But no matter what, it remained, the strange, tender, tentative adoration frightening him almost as much as its presence.

The days grew warmer, which normally portended a return to warfare, but all was currently quiet on the Angevin front. William heartily distrusted this; it meant Geoffrey was plotting something. He would hear of no let-up in his own arrangements, keeping men prowling the marches and bringing him constant news from Anjou, from Maine, from Brittany, from Paris. He spent his time riding up and down his duchy; he could appear without any warning, and at such speed, that it kept his magistrates, barons, clerks, and clerics terrified into doing their jobs properly, lest he turn up and hang one of them to make a point. But whenever he could, he returned to Caen and continued his lessons with Maud.

That he often found more challenging. He learned extremely quickly, but had never been fond of books, and Saxon was such a bloody crabbed, complicated language that it made his head spin. Nonetheless, sheer stubbornness kept him at it. That, and the chance to see young Will. The boy clearly thought he hung the moon, and would always shout with joy when he arrived to commence his latest round of scholastic indignity. William could play with him, to a point, and Maud was thrilled that they got on so well. Yet one day he'd seen her eyes flick from her son to him, back, and back again, and knew that she was beginning to wonder the same thing.

He has to be mine. He can't possibly be Ranulf's. Each time William saw the boy, he was more certain of it. *My son.* It seemed the words had been made to fit nobody but Will. Whether he was giving law, paying an unwelcome visit to another baron, attending the consecration of the new cathedral in Coutances, the thought was always there.

It was June, and William had just returned from a spate of trouble in the Cotentin. He'd pissed this ember out, as usual, and was greatly anticipating the thought of seeing Will again; what with one thing and another, it had been over a month. He hoped Will had missed him too, and decided, as a token of his regard, to bring the lad a gift. After much thought, he settled on a toy sword. Will would be six in January, soon old enough to begin training.

William stealthily attempted to carve one, but his artistry was in battle, not craftwork; it was crooked and splintery. He abandoned it in disgust and went off to engage the services of one of his men, Pierre fitz Bertrand, who had more skill in this arena. 'A nice wooden sword, aye? Is it for your son, m'lord?'

William was furiously tempted to answer in the affirmative, but that left the possibility for far too many complications. 'Nay. But that's no excuse, so do your best work.'

'Aye, m'lord! Some little lad is going to love this.'

'So I hope.' William treated Pierre to one of his incomprehensibly rare smiles. And then, even consenting to whistle, he turned away and strode back up to the castle.

Two days later the project was finished, exactly to specifications. Pierre had even made a small leather scabbard with the lions of Normandy worked in gilt, and a belt of braided leather with a garnet in the buckle. The sword itself was perfectly sized and weighted for a child, tapered and fullered, a thing of utter beauty. 'Will this do, m'lord?' Pierre asked, grinning.

William turned it over, trying not to show how pleased he was. 'Aye, it's satisfactory. How much do I owe you?'

'Oh, never mind that. Just one thing. Might I know which lucky lad will use it?'

William did his best to sound casual. 'Oh, just Ranulf Peverel's boy. Will.'

'Will Peverel, is it?' Pierre's grin turned sly. 'Not that I'm one to gossip,' he added, lowering his voice to a conspiratorial whisper, 'but there's a good chance he's mine.'

For a heartbeat, five, ten, William could not breathe. It felt as if he'd been hit in the stomach. His voice didn't sound a thing like his. 'What the devil are you talking about?'

Pierre blinked. 'Well, let's just say sweet Maud was very. . . free with her charms, aye? It was Jean Longsword and me with her when you turned up that one night and cleared us out. But nay worry, we got it back from her later. Oh, and so did Roger de Rouen, and I think there may have been one else. But that was that, then she ran off and married Ranulf Peverel, of all the bleeding idiots.' He sighed nostalgically.

William still couldn't breathe. Rather belatedly, it occurred to him that he had been tremendously foolish to assume that he was the only man Maud had slept with on her visit. He hadn't thought of it, hadn't cared, and would have continued not to care if only it wasn't for Will. All the fantasies he had cherished, all the moments he had ever imagined, were going up in smoke before his eyes. What was worse, all three of them – Pierre, Jean, and Roger – were men of decent height, if not matching William, *and* they had light hair. He might never know.

'M'lord?' said Pierre worriedly, when William's dumbstruck state persisted.

He tried to say something. Everything inside him had been slammed into a wall, swept onto the floor. He scrambled for the only thing left, the only way he could gain control: his anger. 'Get,' he croaked. 'Get out.'

Pierre frowned. 'My lord?'

'*Get out!*' William lashed out with the wooden sword, and Pierre yelped and ducked. He missed, but not by much, and swung about to try again.

'My lord!' Pierre pleaded. 'Did I say – I didn't mean – '

'Go, I bloody said. Pack your things. Tell Jean and Roger. If any of you are still here when I come back, I'll kill you.'

And with that, leaving the terrified Pierre to twist in the wind, he departed.

'Ohh!' Will Peverel's eyes went as big as trenchers when he unearthed his present from its wrappings. Tremulous and speechless, he drew out the sword and stared at it – then broke out in a grin that could have melted Lucifer. 'It's so pretty, my lord!'

'You like it?' William knelt beside him. 'Pick it up, let me see how you grip it.'

Shaking with excitement, Will ripped the scabbard off and grabbed the sword. 'Did you make it all yourself?'

'I did,' William told him, rearranging the small, deft fingers on the hilt. 'Aye, there you go, that's not bad at all. We must find you someone to spar with, aside from your brother.'

'He'll be so *jealous!*' Will's wide blue eyes sparkled with glee. He was so full of life and energy, strong and solid. 'Can I learn to fight, my lord? Can I? Can I please?'

William swallowed, with an effort. He had never wanted anything so much as to scoop the little boy up, bury his nose in the sunny hair, hold him to his heart and never let him go. But there were only certain gestures a duke could make to a minor nobleman's son, and this went beyond the pale of all of them. 'You shall,' he promised. 'When you're a bit older.'

Will went off into ecstasy, and raced inside to acquaint his mother and brother with his improbable good fortune. William sat back on his heels in the garden, feeling the late-afternoon sun warm on his shoulders. His chest still felt peculiarly tight, his eyes stinging. For the third or fourth time in his life, he was in grave danger of needing someone. *Get hold of yourself. The last thing you need is to give rise to rumours, put the boy in danger, undermine your own position. Stop it. Stop it now.*

He tried. God in Heaven, he tried. But despite everything, for that moment alone, he was at peace. And no matter what he did, he couldn't make himself break it.

That night after they had retired, Matilda said, 'Well, that was an intriguing afternoon.'

William had his back to her, yanking his tunic off, but something about her voice made him think he should reorient himself, and swiftly. He did so. 'What are you talking about?'

Matilda regarded him from where she was propped against a stack of pillows. The child was expected in a scant month, and she tired easily. 'You know what I'm talking about.'

'Very well then. What are you accusing me of?'

Her eyes glittered. Since she was so small, advanced pregnancy had a way of strangely distorting her; her face and hands and limbs were still slender and graceful, but the swollen core made her look as if she'd been reflected wrongly in water, a creature not quite herself and not quite another. William's hackles, already piqued, rose still further. 'Well?' he pressed.

Matilda purposefully let the silence reach the uncomfortable. Then she said, 'Pierre fitz Bertrand, Roger de Rouen, and Jean Longsword surely left in a great hurry.'

'Aye, they did.'

'Ah. To spare themselves your jealousy, perchance? Indeed, you've been spending time aplenty with the Peverels. And if you think I haven't heard the stories about that slattern, then – '

'Jesus bloody Christ!' Her suspicion infuriated William. 'I'm not sleeping with Maud! I told you, she's teaching me Saxon!'

'I believe that,' said Matilda, 'solely because I am married to you, and know exactly why you are doing it. Yet be that as it may, I consider Maud Peverel only a secondary temptation. I know why you're down there every moment, why you're in such good cheer when you get back.'

'Do you?' William growled. 'Then why did you ask?'

Matilda's eyes flashed. 'Why do you bloody think?'

'You know nothing about this. Nothing!'

'Oh, don't I?' Matilda screeched, finally losing her temper in earnest. 'It's very well and good for you, you can keep on using me as your broodmare, then ignore the children after they're born! You've wasted no time in betrothing Robert, who is all of three, to get a leg up in your demented little game with Geoffrey Martel! And all the while, you steal off and show more love to your bastard in one day than you've shown your trueborn children their entire lives! That, William, *that* is what I know!'

She subsided, gasping for breath, and a thunderous silence fell. For the first time in a very great while, William was honestly stunned. 'Matilda,' he said at last. 'Don't shout so much.'

There was no conciliation in her dark eyes. 'Listen to me. This is the only time I will say this. I will work to support your ambitions, I make no objection to you gaining as much wealth, prestige, and power as you can. But God as my witness, if you continue to treat me and our children like this, you can do it alone.'

That thoroughly rattled him. 'Matilda – '

'It would be unconscionably easy to obtain an annulment, you know. Seeing as the Pope still doesn't even recognise that we're married. It would solve a great problem for you – and, for that matter, Henry Capet. Don't make me do it.'

'Matilda,' he said again. 'Don't. Don't leave me.'

The tension crackled for another horrible moment. Then she shifted, offering an opening, and he took it, swung up beside her, pulled her against him. The curve of her belly pressed into his side, her small cold feet on the long bone of his shin, the weight of her head on his shoulder and the fragrance of her long black hair, unbound and sifting through his fingers. All at once, he felt the anger run out of her as if from a punctured waterskin.

'No,' she said indistinctly into his chest. 'No. I couldn't.'

William said nothing, watching the night sky through the window. A breeze tousled the sheets, the moon paved the floor. All he could hear was their breathing. For the first time, he wondered if she too could not bear to need him as much as she did.

She shifted again, her hip opening under his hand, and he steered them down onto the bed, rucked her shift up and took her quickly, from the side. It was effected in silence, save the sharp gasp she gave at the end, the way she bucked back into him as if daring him to answer. Then they rearranged themselves, pulled the quilts up, and she drifted off almost at once.

William lay awake for some time, absently stroking his wife's head. He had been feeling terribly vulnerable in one form or another all day long, and he did not like it. Matilda's threat had unsettled him badly, even if he was fairly sure there was no chance she'd ever carry it out, and he sincerely intended to give her no reason to change her mind. But all he could think about, all he could imagine, was how badly he wanted to go back tomorrow and see Will Peverel with his wooden sword, flying across the grass with his eyes alight and his hair as bright as summer.

Their fourth child was born three weeks later. Matilda's pains started at breakfast, and William himself carried her up into the birthing chamber. Neither of them wanted him to stay, as he would be altogether more a hindrance than a help; besides, births were women's work, no place for men. So he retreated to the hall to drink and wait. He tried not to listen to the screaming; this was the first of Matilda's childbeds he'd actually been present for, and the first time he truly understood that this was as hazardous for her as battle was for him. And Matilda had no control over her enemy, could not train her life long and trust in skill to see her through – could only rely on luck, and prayers. Thus he prayed, hard.

Past noon, the midwife came down. 'Your Grace. All is well. They are resting.'

William did his best to disguise his shuddering breath of relief. He got to his feet, realising as he did so that he had drunk enough to become genuinely tipsy – he didn't think that had happened since the day he became a knight. 'Name him after me.'

'Your Grace.' The midwife paused.

'Aye?'

'The child is a girl.'

Another one. Very well, no matter, daughters had their uses.

'We'll call her Adeliza,' said William, eyeing the small white bundle critically. Asleep in his arms, she almost looked peaceful – at least she wasn't crying. 'For Will fitz Osbern's wife.'

'As it suits you.' Matilda's voice was hoarse, but she looked pleased. 'Well, two girls and two boys. That will suffice for now.'

William shrugged. 'Aye.' It hadn't bothered him as much as he thought. He knew where to find a satisfactory son – but eventually he would need one that was officially sanctioned, as little Robert, Richard, Cecilia, and Adeliza were still regarded as no better than bastards in the eyes of Rome. There were threats of another interdict, the same old tired tune. *Aye, they will try very hard to make me pay them a mint, or do what they say. And they will fail.*

The thought, obscurely, comforted him. He gave Adeliza back to Matilda, kissed his wife, and showed himself out. He went down to the hall, then to the stables to retrieve his new horse – a grey like his last, but a colt, and badly in need of breaking. Then he mounted up, successfully withstood the beast's attempts to throw him, and rode down the hill into Caen.

December

'Your Grace.' The monk of Jumièges was a pinch-faced specimen with a close, clipped way of speaking, as if the words would run out and escape if he opened his mouth too far. 'I imagine this visit came as a surprise, but I pray you accept it nonetheless.'

'Of course, Brother.' William eyed the monk's charges appraisingly. Both fifteen or sixteen, tall and fair-complexioned, and if they weren't Saxons, he was a horse's arse. 'Have you brought these fine lads to burden upon my hospitality?'

'Indeed I have, Your Grace. They have been at Jumièges for the last several years, but after my lord Robert Champart's death, it eventually came time to find them a better location. It was scandalous how the English treated Champart, simply scandalous.'

'Aye, I've heard.' William revised his impression of the young men's potential use – and potential danger – significantly. 'And their kin have been content to let them rot in Normandy?'

'Their kin have not had a great deal of choice.' The monk emitted an annoying little titter. 'There has been all sorts of turmoil back in England, and the Godwinsons must be very careful indeed not to set a foot wrong. Hieing off to start a war across the Channel is *certainly* not in their best interests. That is why – in strictest confidence, Your Grace, you understand – we give you the means to ensure the Godwinsons do not stretch their leash too far. Wulfnoth Godwinson, and Hakon Sweynsson. My lord Champart, may he rest in peace, justly removed them from London as he fled in 1051.' To the lads he added sternly, 'Make your reverences to the Duke.'

The boys made rather sullen bows. Whatever they thought about the changed terms of their captivity, they were careful not to show it. There was more diffidence in them than defiance, William decided, but he would be wise to employ a deft touch.

'Welcome to Caen,' he said, trying out his new Saxon. 'I hope you shall like it.'

The words were stiff and uncomfortable on his tongue, but both the boys' eyes flared in shock at hearing their native language. *Now they know they must go carefully.* William had spent a good deal of the fall chasing Geoffrey Martel around Maine, and he was in no mood to have to go back to looking for knives in his own castle.

'My lord,' Wulfnoth said. 'Your hospitality is. . . appreciated.'

William nodded graciously. 'No doubt you had a long and wet ride from Jumièges. I will have mead fetch – fetching from the kitchens.'

'Thank you, my lord,' said Wulfnoth. 'That would be kind.'

I will have to watch that one. William wondered if the monks had saddled him with the hostages on the idea that if there *was* going to be trouble, he was best equipped to deal with it. A flattering conviction. He hoped there'd be no cause to prove it.

When it came to his and William's continual disagreements over Maine, Geoffrey Martel got quite tired of coming up on the short end of the stick. Thus, just past the New Year, he decided that a change of battlefield was in order, an ambition in which he was supported wholeheartedly by Henry Capet. The king, who had been brooding over his humiliation at Mortemer for the past three years and burned with the desire to avenge it, sent once more for his Angevin ally. By Candlemas, they had mustered an army even larger than the last one and were marching on Normandy in force.

William reacted as he always did. He raised his levies, fortified his cities, laid in supplies at any castle likely to come under siege, and strapped on his well-used sword and longbow. And then, with his usual coalition – his half-brother Robert de Mortain, Will fitz Osbern, Walter Giffard, Robert de Eu, and Richard fitz Gilbert – he rode out to meet them. He was oddly relieved. He had been anticipating Henry's retaliation for some while, and now that it had finally come, they would finish the business left undone. War, again. After so much vulnerability and uncertainty, it was a blessing to go back to the one place where he always knew who he was. And whenever that should be done, it was one less obstacle in his way. After that, the only thing he need fear, and wait for, was time.

CHAPTER SEVEN

London, England
August 1057

'I HAVE NEWS from Rome, Your Grace,' said the messenger. 'Pope Stephen has announced that he will uphold the ruling of his esteemed predecessors. Thus, the excommunication holds. The Holy Father says as well that a man of your religious insight must certainly understand that a simonist cannot be confirmed as Archbishop of Canterbury, especially considering the unlawful circumstances in which the last occupant departed the post.'

Sometimes I do wonder whose pocket the Pope is in. This marked the third straight pontiff who had excommunicated Stigand, doubtless a fact Edward should pay attention to, but he still couldn't bring himself to initiate another fight over Canterbury. And besides, Popes were dropping like flies these days – he might come to an accord with one, only to have it undone by the next. Victor had barely lasted two years before it was on to this version.

'I see,' Edward said. 'What else?'

'There's news as well from Scotland. Lord Malcolm avenged his father Duncan, and killed Macbeth the usurper at the battle of Lumphanan. He married the daughter of Finn Arnesson, a Norse jarl, but though he may have a queen, he cannot call himself king just yet. A son or stepson of Macbeth was crowned in his father's place, so there's another battle ahead.'

'Malcolm has my blessings and dearest wishes for his success.' Edward sat back. 'Very well. You are excused. And – ?'

The messenger turned back. 'Aye?'

'Bring me news of the Archbishop of York. That is what I need.'

The man bowed. 'Aye, my lord. Of course.'

The requested information came a few days later. Edmund Aetheling's whereabouts were unknown, and he was widely rumoured to be dead. Edward Aetheling, however, was still alive, and after much bother, misadventure, harassment, and haggling, Aldred of York had finally found his way to Hungary. The Aetheling had not accepted the chance to be king as punctually as might be expected, however, and had debated for a considerable while before at last agreeing. The travelling party had departed a month ago, and God and the roads willing, would arrive in England near the Feast of St Bartholomew.

The news that the next king was on his way home spread like wildfire. Feasts and revels were planned, and any number of wealthy lords volunteered to welcome the Aetheling and his family into their households, thus to inculcate him in the customs (and language) of the country he hadn't seen since babyhood. While Edward found such eager accommodation gratifying, he also found it irritating as well. *See, you've the capacity to bend over backwards for a foreigner if it suits you. But would you do it when I asked earlier? No.*

Edward did his best to temper such pettiness, reminding himself that he had tried so long to not have to fight a war over his successor, and now he was spared the need. The Aetheling was a choice ironclad in legitimacy and acceptability, and he, as Edward understood, had a son, so that would be that. The line of Cerdic would continue, and so, all was settled. Or rather, almost. On the vigil of St Bartholomew's day, as Edward lay awake late, it occurred to him to wonder how good his nephew's diplomacy was, if he was going to convince William to cede gracefully. Or if it came down to it, his diplomacy with a sword.

'Your Grace,' Stigand announced. 'See you the purple sail of that longship? And the wyvern prancing on the wind? That will be Archbishop Aldred, and our sweet royal family.'

'*Future* royal family, Stigand,' Edward said tersely. 'And my eyes are not so aged as to be sightless, nor my wits run out into my porridge. I am perfectly capable of marking it.'

Stigand, chastened, clapped his mouth shut and kept it that way, which Edward used to examine the fleet proceeding up the Thames. The entire court waited to welcome them in their finest attire, gold and gemwork flashing at throats and wrists and fingers.

Edward stood at the front, hoping he wouldn't broil any further. He already felt like an overcooked goose.

Below, the longships were just bobbing into pier, making fast and tying sails. Edward squinted at the small figures as the party advanced up the road toward the castle, and as they came closer, he thought he could tell which was his nephew: the tall man on the chestnut horse, pale hair burning in the sunlight. He looked the part, at least. Pray God he would play it as well.

At last the trumpets sounded, the gates opened, and the procession issued into the bailey. After they had dismounted and rearranged, the moment was finally nigh. A herald announced, 'Your Grace! Your nephew, Edward Aetheling. His wife, the lady Agatha. Their children: the lady Margaret, the lord Edgar, and the lady Cristina.'

Edward Aetheling approached cautiously. He was a handsome but melancholic and gaunt-looking man, blue eyes deep-set in the fine, angular bones of his face. He reached his uncle and knelt, taking the king's hands in his own. 'My lord,' he said, in halting, heavily accented Saxon.

'Nephew.' Edward wished he could better remember what his half-brother had looked like. 'Welcome home. Did you have a good journey?'

The Aetheling gave him a polite, timorous smile, and Edward wondered how much he had understood. A servant was summoned to translate, and the Aetheling gave a longer and more mellifluous response in Hungarian. 'He says he is weary from the long journey, but glad to see his native land again, and humbly wishes to present his family to Your Grace. The children in particular have found it a trial.'

Edward imagined they had, torn away from their home and whisked off to a far-foreign realm, to satisfy the whim of some distant king. 'It would be my pleasure.'

Permission granted, the Aetheling's family was brought forward. His wife, Agatha, was a striking woman – not beautiful, not exactly, but striking, like a blow to the chest. She had thick olive-black hair, a hawk nose, and quick dark eyes that saw everything, sensual lips and white teeth. She held the hands of her daughters, twelve-year-old Margaret and four-year-old Cristina.

Margaret was a tall, skinny, intensely solemn heron of a girl, with two long braids just the colour of her father's. She had his blue eyes as well; there seemed to be nothing of her mother in her. She wore a plain, high-necked brown dress, and a small gilt missal hung from her girdle, a wooden crucifix round her neck. *A nun in waiting?* That made Edward feel a distinct sympathy, ex-monk that he was, and he smiled kindly at her. 'Welcome, great-niece.'

Margaret sank precisely to her knees to kiss his hand, then moved off. By contrast, her little sister Cristina was a jumping, energetic, eager bundle of black curls, as much her mother as Margaret was not. She surveyed Edward with lively interest, and tripped over her skirt making her curtsy. Then lastly came the Aetheling's son, Edgar. He was a thin and rather frail child of six years, his hair the same white-gold as his father's and sister Margaret's, with his mother's dark eyes that took up much of his face. He kept them fixed on his feet as he approached his great-uncle, bowed, then took the first opportunity to sprint away behind his mother. She put a hand on his head, keeping him close.

Aye, that is wise. One day, God willing, that small boy shall be King of England, and you are in the midst of those who will try to use him for their own ends. The danger is greater than you have ever known before.

The feast that night, as most feasts did, took forever. It was hot, close, and smoky, and the Aetheling appeared profoundly uncomfortable with the noise, the scrutiny, the questions that had to go through the servant first. Edward also noticed that the future king developed a slight stammer when flustered, which made his heart go out to him. *Aye, you could have been me.*

At last, to the Aetheling's transparent relief, the ceremonials came to an end. Lady Agatha, who had been a whirl of gaiety all night, charming the masses even without recourse to Saxon, leaned close to her husband and said something in a low voice. He nodded, squeezed her hand, then addressed his uncle. 'My lord? I can? Go?'

Edward nodded, giving his nephew a kindly smile. Once the new branch of the royal family had repaired to their boudoir, he offered a hand to his own wife. 'My dear?'

Edith took it, and as she got to her feet, he was surprised to see that she was crying. 'My dear?' he said again. 'What's wrong?'

Edith collected herself almost at once. 'I am sorry to cause you so much woe by bearing you no son. As well, I am glad that the Aetheling has been found.'

Even if it comes at the cost of disinheriting your own family? That was a question Edward would not ask – best to let some dogs lie sleeping. But there was no call to complain of the Godwinsons' treatment these days. Harold, Earl of Wessex, his close advisor and military right arm. Tostig, Earl of Northumbria. And Edith the queen, holding the King of England with not just duty, but love.

Sometimes I fancy it a blessing that I was spared being a monk. Otherwise I might have to sit about all day and actually riddle this out. Edward sighed. 'As I have told you, my dear,' he said gently, 'you are faultless in this. And the matter *is* settled. So come.'

He tucked her hand under his arm, and they departed the hall. Behind them, the great fire in the hearth burnt low, first to embers and then to ashes, leaving darkness in its wake.

Edward must have eaten too much potted veal at supper, for he was wandering in a demented dream when he first became aware of the shouting. It failed to rouse him, however; he merely rolled over and put the pillow over his head. Thus, he got in several more moments of sprinting feverishly through the castle, Godwin hotly in pursuit and attempting to lambaste him with a large dead carp, before he ran into something that looked like a door but wasn't. This resulted in his waking up with a jerk, an event coincidental with a servant ripping the pillow off.

'Whuff?' Edward shielded his eyes against the torchlight. 'What's this? It can't be time for Matins already?'

'No, my Grace. Your Grace. Your Grace, please – '

'What?'

'The aetheling, my lord, Edward – '

'What?!'

'He. . . my lord. . .' The servant took a breath, and visibly commended his soul to God. 'My lord, he's dead.'

Murdered. The word was on everyone's lips. The frenzy over the Aetheling's death exceeded even the frenzy over his arrival, and it took a truly stunning naïveté to believe that it had come about by accident. Apparently healthy forty-year-old men did not drop dead in the night absent any other contributing factor, and divining how was just one of the problems that the Aetheling's abrupt departure from the mortal coil had engendered. The poor man was not cool beneath his shroud when the quarrelling began.

Edward was possessed with a desire to laugh almost as great as his desire to shut himself up in his room and scream for an hour, neither of which he actually did. He insisted that his nephew be given a proper funeral, and promised to act as grandfather to the children. And then, since he knew exactly what everyone was going to ask, he took steps to keep it firmly tamped down. In a hasty ceremony at St Paul's Cathedral, Edward formally recognised young Edgar as his heir; Edgar sneezed for the duration. *This is what it has come to? He has no idea, none at all.*

Aloud Edward said, 'Arise. My grandfather was the first King Edgar. One day, my child, you will be the second. May Christ guard you until that time comes.'

For the first time since his arrival, Edgar smiled. He still spoke no word of Saxon aside from 'good morrow,' and if the Aetheling *had* been murdered, those responsible would find his son an even easier target. Edward felt a qualm of remorse; who was he, to do this to them? And yet nonetheless, it *was* done. Of all the eyes, he could feel Harold Godwinson's the most. Could imagine the question in them. *With the wolf across the water, this is the guardian you choose? A frail foreign child with a foreign mother?*

He did not answer. The possible repercussions haunted him just as well.

The autumn did not offer respite from the summer's cruelty. If anything, it was worse. Edward's nephew Ralph, who had never recovered from the humiliation visited on him by Ælfgar and Gruffydd, expired of a chill, and Leofric of Mercia followed suit on the Feast of St Jerome. At least the redoubtable old Earl had died in peace at his manor in Staffordshire, not on the battlefield or at the banquet-table, and Jerome was a suitable saint to chaperon him heavenward. But his death deprived Edward of both councillor and friend, and contributed to a further power imbalance.

There were, after all, two younger Godwinsons – Gyrth and Leofwine – poised to fill his vacancy, and this was nearly what happened. Leofric's son Ælfgar was confirmed as Earl of Mercia, but Gyrth collected his former seat as Earl of East Anglia. Thus the lines were drawn. Godwin's progeny held three-quarters of the country, Leofric's the one. The man that could unite them would stand well-nigh the king's equal, or better.

In the interim, all England could do was pray – for time, to let the young Aetheling grow up. For Edward's continued good health. And while the smallfolk knew nothing of such intrigues, some of the well-connected nobles with awareness of the wider world spared a thought for Henry Capet.

To be sure, he needed all the help he could get.

Dives-sur-Mer, Normandy
October 1057

Henry Capet, King of France, was really getting too old for this. He was just a year shy of fifty, a fact his bones punctually reminded him of every morning, and a man of his age and station would be perfectly justified in sitting at home, dandling his heir on his knee – five-year-old Philip, born almost exactly twelve months after Henry had married the princess Anne of Kiev. At least there *was* an heir now, so if he perished, it wouldn't be a catastrophe.

Then again, it well might be, considering the procedure for succession in his tatty realms. And Philip was why Henry was out here – so there'd be half a chance of giving him a kingdom when he came of age. Henry knew exactly what sort of mischief William of Normandy would get up to if left unchecked, and the fact that the bastard had had the gall to wed Henry's own niece did not help. Aside from *that*, William's henchmen had trounced the flower of France at Mortemer, culminating in Henry's embarrassing retreat.

Henry had muttered and stewed and brooded on it for the past three years, and if his age should have meant he knew better than to go picking fights with vigorous and unscrupulous vassals, it also made for more than a hint of desperation. Faced with the ever-dwindling boundaries of his royal demesne, his son a child and his own shadow stretching longer, it was Henry's last chance to make a statement, defeat a foe who had had his way with him ever since Val-ès-Dunes, protect his patrimony, avenge his defeat, secure his House's legacy, and win a God-be-damned battle. He had to.

And so, in one final attempt to accomplish this ambitious itinerary, he had, yet again, invaded Normandy. And so, here he was with Geoffrey Martel, the man whose help he hated to need, encamped on the estuary of the river Dives. Having learnt from the debacles of Alençon, Domfront, and Arques, they had not attempted any sieges; besides, they'd been harried off from any town they came near. That alone was proof that William was aware of their undertakings, but there hadn't been any sightings of the man himself. That was odd, to say the least, when dealing with a foe like this, but as this unburdened them from the need to wage warfare in secret, the French-Angevin army had adopted a straightforward policy of burning everything they came across. This had won them through the Bessin, and now they needed to ford the river before they could continue their march on Caen.

Henry licked a finger and tasted the wind. It had been contrary all day, ruffling the slaty surface of the Dives. Of course they couldn't have any bloody good weather, and he didn't much like the look of those –

'Your Grace?'

Henry jumped, then chided himself for being taken, seemingly as always, off guard. The honorific, though spoken most respectfully, was accompanied with a mocking flash of cat-eyes; he knew their owner well enough to judge. He turned. 'Aye?'

Geoffrey Martel didn't look a day older than when Henry had first met him sixteen years ago, one of the many things that made him seriously wonder if his ally did in fact have Lucifer in the family tree. 'My scouts have returned,' the Count of Anjou said. 'The far shore is deserted.'

'Are they sure?'

'Unless they are blind, aye.' Geoffrey's disconcerting smile was the same as ever, that little flicker of his lip like a flame catching in wood. 'We ought make ready to go.'

'Aye, of course. Give the order to your men, I'll do likewise.' At last, action. Sitting on the estuary for the past two days, awaiting fresh supplies, had made him incontestably fretful.

Geoffrey inclined his head. 'At once.'

Henry nodded and strode away, bellowing for his captains. But even as he tried to absorb himself in his plans, focus on how sweet victory would taste when it came, he couldn't stop himself from one last uneasy look across the empty grey river, to the empty grey plains beyond.

It was past dusk by the time all was arranged. The Angevins, cantankerous gargoyles, had delayed their departure with some inconsequent quarrel, and Geoffrey was obliged to step in firmly to restore order (not a role he could customarily be found playing). Then there were packs to load and saddles to fit, and several horses slipped a shoe. In all, the evening star was beginning to rise as the first vanguards finally splashed into the dark water.

Henry rode in the front, eyes peeled for any movement. Geoffrey kept sharp on his left, unruffled as ever, but to the nervous king, the glint of gold from the count's cloak seemed as bright as a torch. That wasn't the only factor contributing to Henry's unease. Fog was creeping in, obscuring the water, and the incoming tide was already well past the knees of his destrier. 'My lord,' he said. 'Perhaps we should. . . expedite the process?'

Geoffrey took a look at the steady flow of water. Whatever he saw affrighted him into actually sitting up. 'Aye, perhaps,' he agreed, giving his sorrel mare a dig in the side.

Henry's disquiet might have been assuaged when they reached the far shore and cantered up onto the stony beach unmolested, but it was not. For once, Geoffrey's half-smile was gone, and his eyes were narrowed. 'I mislike the smell, my lord.'

'You were the one who said there was nothing here.'

'My scouts said it.' Geoffrey curtly reined in the dancing sorrel. 'I pay them enough, I've no reason to doubt their loyalty.'

'If you say so.' Henry frowned at the army in the river, dim shapeless figures. For a moment, he had the queasy feeling that he was caught in a nightmare, mired down and unable to run, even though he knew that the legions were his own. 'We should go.'

'That's a bad idea, my lord,' said Geoffrey amiably.

'And staying here is a better one?'

Geoffrey began to make some answer. He was cut off by a terrible scream.

Henry's heart somersaulted into his mouth. He stared madly at the dark forest, expecting the worst, but the disturbance came from the river. One of the knights was in trouble, his panicked horse floundering and plunging as the dark water coursed beneath its nose. There were similar shouts from the others, and a captain called, 'My lords! The tide's too high!'

Henry cursed. 'Hurry, then!'

'Your Grace, we can't! It's coming in too fast – we won't make the far side!'

'Then go back!' Henry would be damned if he'd watch them drown. 'Quickly!'

The captain bellowed this order, and suddenly the morass of horses was straining back the other way, fighting the current, struggling for footing. And then –

Henry's hackles stood cold. He nearly fell out of the saddle twisting around to look at the dark trees again. They seemed deserted, he had received every assurance that they were, but he knew, suddenly and unshakeably, that they *weren't*.

Geoffrey, sensing the same, turned so sharply that the sorrel almost sat down. He fumbled for his sword, yet for a moment, nothing happened, they could almost believe that nothing would –

And then the woods exploded with men, charging from all sides at once –

Geoffrey screamed an obscenity and vanished. The half of the French army that hadn't yet made it into the river was trying to gallop upstream and cross there, but arrows were clattering, harrowing, constantly reducing the number of sprinting shadows. Some of the Normans had waded in with knives in their teeth, hacking and slashing. For Normans they were. Henry looked up to the hill – and there he was in the flesh, astride his grey stallion. His golden head caught the moonlight, his hauberk showed a deep steel sheen, and his teeth were bared in a wild, white, mocking smile.

'I'm sure you paid your spies handsomely, my lord,' said William the Bastard, his voice carrying on the wind, audible even over the slaughter. 'But I paid them more.'

Henry raced one way and then the other, trying to get something, anything, in between him and the attackers. He took brief refuge with a flank of Angevin spearmen, but then William's reserves turned up and drove them apart. Henry thought briefly of Val-ès-Dunes. *My God, I'm going to die. The whoreson is going to kill me.* And that was as far as he had time to get before another Val-ès-Dunes parallel announced itself in emphatic fashion. Henry felt a violent shock in his back, then his arse was parted from his horse, he was flying through midair, and his face was full of mud.

Bloody hell, I really am too old for this, but it doesn't seem I'll get much older! He flailed about for his mount, or even his bearings, but both eluded him, along with his sword. *Bloody, bloody buggering –*

Henry was not given a chance to complete this thought either, as a rider suddenly loomed up in front of him. He prayed it was an ally – at this point he was ready to give Geoffrey half the kingdom if he helped him get out of this –

It was not Geoffrey.

Henry had one final thought of Val-ès-Dunes, the nineteen-year-old he had ridden to war with, the young man who had pulled him up on his horse, saved his life. The young man he had saved as well. The two of them stared at each other, Henry muddy and breathless, and William towering above him. All Henry could hear was the wind. Then the Duke spoke.

'My lord. Have you learned your lesson yet? Each time you set foot on my lands, I'll smash you. Try this again and there will be nothing for your son to inherit but your bones, so hear me now. Go away and never return, and take the Angevin whoreson with you. Do that, and I'll call off my men so you have a chance of leaving with some of yours. Do not, and. . . you can retrieve a few pieces.'

Henry wanted to say something. He wanted to proclaim his defiance. He wanted to show somehow, anyhow, that his kingship had not been an unmitigated failure, that he too was capable of defending what was his. But he couldn't. He was frozen.

'Well?' said William.

'You. . . Devil take you!'

'I'm not the one allied with Martel. I imagine if you ask nicely, he will.'

Henry couldn't answer. Couldn't force the words between his teeth. And couldn't see that he had any choice, couldn't understand how this could have possibly gone so badly. But he fumbled at his waist with nerveless fingers, then unbuckled his swordbelt – the symbol of a warrior's courage, a knight's honour – and threw it at his enemy's feet. *'Damn you!'*

William's smile remained. 'Thank you, but that's not necessary. By all reckoning, I lost my soul a long time ago. But I do keep my word. Farewell, Henry Capet.'

With that, he wheeled the grey around and blew a sharp whistle. The attacking men pulled apart, leaving corpses bobbing in the river, and his Normans, who had suffered only light losses, regrouped at their leader's side at once. *Bloody hell,* Henry thought, not for the first time that night. *They really* are *following him. He's theirs now. Their icon. Their lord. And they'll do anything for him.*

He struggled over to a boulder, still spitting mud. He could hear someone calling for mercy. Could taste the bile in his throat.

Philip, he thought. *I'm sorry.*

William's resounding victory at Dives marked the end of one era, the confirmation of another. As ordered, Henry and Geoffrey left Normandy and did not return. The last resistance in the duchy collapsed, and while Geoffrey continued to maintain scattered opposition in Maine, his back was so broken that it was more nuisance than threat. William returned to Caen just past the new year and got Matilda with their fifth child, who was born near the autumn solstice. This one was a blond-haired boy with a spitfire that was visible from the first hours, and William was delighted. Therefore, the baby was named after his father, but thanks to his ruddy complexion, soon began to be called Rufus by the family.

There was only one thing he lacked now: official Church sanction. And with Henry in marked disfavour, William had a sneaking suspicion that the Pope would ultimately surrender. Besides, Rome itself had just had to dispense with an Antipope and had damn near fought a war over it (William doubted it was much of a war, what with the fact that they couldn't wield swords, but that always tended to be forgotten when questions of power were in the offing). Thus, he had shrewdly dispatched support to the lawful claimant, who was now almost in a position to make good on it.

It was a gamble that paid off. In late January 1059, Nicholas II became the fourth pope of the decade, largely thanks to Norman assistance. He convened an Easter synod at the Lateran, and with this the case, William expected to see the long-toiling Lanfranc soon. He had sent word that he would return home the instant the ink was dry on the papal decision.

There were other matters to attend to. He had Will Peverel brought to the castle, to start his training as a warrior. He treated the Saxon hostages, Wulfnoth and Hakon, substantially better, and would talk and jest with them in their native language; his command of it was improving daily. Now that he had his feet so solidly under him, one might expect him to rest a while, take pride in what he'd done. One would be wrong.

'In God's sight, it's good to be back, Your Grace.' Lanfranc of Pavia straightened from his bow. 'Lombardy is my birthplace, aye, but my duty is in France.'

'I was beginning to think the Pope would never loose you from his talons.' William was having a new castle built, and the din of stonecutters and masons reached them faintly through the windows of his solar. 'Well? What sentence has Nicholas seen fit to pronounce on me, for all my gracious help?'

'The Church's view of Your Grace's marriage has indeed been altered. It may be owed to my intervention, but doubtless your own. . . arguments assisted.'

William caught a dryness to the abbot's voice, which he noted with approval. *Here's a man worth keeping about.* 'Well?'

Lanfranc bowed again. 'Your Grace. The Holy Father says that the marriage may indeed be fully approved, the children regarded as trueborn and legitimate, in exchange for one thing. That you and your lady wife both build and endow an abbey for the education of men and women, respectively, in the ways of our Lord and Saviour Jesus Christ and so – good heavens!'

William's whoop of delight startled the abbot greatly, especially when he followed it up by leaping out of his chair. 'You're joking! You're bloody joking! This entire time the Popes have been thumbing their noses at me like a little boy who doesn't like his supper, but all I have to do to get this one to stop is to build an abbey? That's *it?*'

'Well, Your Grace. I would suggest you accept it, and not give the Holy Father ideas.'

William, still grinning, clapped him on the shoulder. 'I do think I like you, Lanfranc of Pavia, and it's a shame you've been wasted on the bloody curia all this time. Very well, we will start at once. I hope you will do me the honour of becoming the first abbot of mine. Do you have a convenient saint I could dedicate it to?'

'Saint Stephen is always a foolproof choice, Your Grace,' said Lanfranc. A corner of his severe Lombard mouth twitched.

'Indeed. I like the symbolism, I was damn near a martyr myself.' William smiled again. 'You have certainly pleased me, and your abbey of Bec, I think, is about to find itself considerably richer. Aye, I have money now. It's a miracle.'

Later that afternoon, while William was strolling through the cloisters, he heard the sound of children shouting, followed it, and came upon a scene that almost succeeded in warming his heart. He paused in the corner of the courtyard, watching the three small boys sparring industriously, wooden swords whirring and clacking.

He was enormously proud to note that the chief player in the fight, eight-year-old Will Peverel, appeared to have a genuine idea of what he was doing. He knew how to block and parry, something of how to feint and lunge, while six-year-old Robert and five-year-old Richard were more prone to hack indiscriminately. They circled the older boy, jabbing like a pair of hornets. Robert was presented almost at once with a large opening, but missed it, his blade whistling harmlessly past Will's ear. Off balance, he stumbled, sprawling in the dirt.

'Put your shoulder into it, Shortstockings,' William called. 'And keep your feet.'

Robert popped upright, looked around, and spotted his father. William had recently bestowed him with his unflattering nickname in reference to his stature; he shared his mother's small frame and short legs. In consequence his younger brother Richard, who did take after William, was already significantly taller than him. 'Papa?'

Will and Richard, who had been continuing the engagement, drew up as well, and a smile spread across Will's face. 'My lord! We were practising. Soon we'll be big and strong like you.'

'Some of you, at least.' William smiled back at the boy.

'Me too,' Robert butted in. 'That wasn't really what I can do, Papa, I'm much better. Want to see?'

'Later.' William had more important things to do than watch him flail like a drunken windmill. And doubtless if Robert somehow managed to hit Richard, Richard would cry again. It might do him some good. William's second son was a gentle, sweet lad without much martial fervour, which dismayed him considerably. He needed warriors, not weaklings.

Desperate to prevent William from going, Robert changed the subject. 'What was the news? I saw riders.'

'You're no longer a bastard, Shortstockings,' William informed him, tousling his eldest son's hair. 'The Pope grew weary of our little game. I won.'

Robert glowed with pride at his father's success. Then the rest of William's words percolated, and a frown replaced his smile. 'I was a bastard?' he asked uncertainly.

'In the Church's view, little better. And now you are not. In technicality.' William smiled again, with a cut to it. 'Best prove to me that's the case.'

'Of course, Papa, of course,' Robert said hastily. 'Will showed me how to – '

'You showed him what?' William asked – Will, not Robert.

Will looked startled. 'Not too much, my lord. He's pretty good. Just sometimes I hit him too hard and he doesn't try. I don't want to hurt him, I don't!'

'It's good for him,' William reassured the child, hugging Will's head with his hand. It was a chancy gesture, aye, but there was no one around to see. 'Teaches him to be less lazy.'

'I'm not lazy!' Robert jumped in again, looking stung. 'Richard, tell him I'm not!'

'He's not,' said Richard dutifully, if somewhat untruthfully. Robert was apt to approach sweetmeats more enthusiastically than swords, which accounted for his podginess.

'We'll see.' Aye, as if those two would ever be worth anything. 'But not now, I've other things to do. Try not to put your eyes out.'

And with that, whistling, William strode off.

If William found the year 1059 to his liking, then he found 1060 even better. His new castle was completed, his abbey on the way, and his barons were the ones tiptoeing and pleading for favour. William himself, just past thirty, was in the prime of life, a warrior and a statesman atop his universe. By far the year's crowning achievement, however, was that it killed off both Henry and Geoffrey – Henry in August, Geoffrey in November, on both of which occasions William threw a feast. Eight-year-old Philip Capet ascended the French throne with two regents: his mother, Queen Anne, and his uncle, Baldwin of Flanders. This ensured that France would not pursue any sort of belligerence against Normandy, not with Baldwin's daughter installed as its duchess. As if there was a man in the French army willing to plunge back into that hellhole, in support of an eight-year-old.

With the threat from the crown neutralised and Geoffrey's successor – his nineteen-year-old nephew, inauspiciously also named Geoffrey – swaggering around Anjou in pursuit of fetching young women, William emerged as the most powerful overlord in France. As soon as Marguerite of Maine and his own Robert came of age and were married, he stood poised to collect that feather for his cap as well. Without military opposition, William continued his incursions into the Vexin, always a territory hotly contested between duke and king. Now, he could take whatever he wanted. So long as he could win it. So long as he was strong enough.

He had been. He was. And by Christ, he would be once more.

PART TWO

The Gathering Storm

1062 – 1065

CHAPTER EIGHT

Rhuddlan, Wales
October 1062

LL HIS LIFE, Harold Godwinson had tried to riddle out what was meant by the word 'England.' He understood the boundaries of the land: the south, where it was green and gentle; the north, where it gave over to the barren fells and savage raiders of Scotland; the east, with its great forests, and the west, where his family made its seat, looking out to the beautiful mountains and equally savage raiders of Wales. So much of it remained a mystery, this island shrouded in mist and myth, settled by the hardy fair Saxons with steel and gold and fire, holding high the cross of Christ to chase away the pagan Britons. For six hundred years they had ruled England, ever since they had arrived in the warbands of Hengist and Horsa – then were forced to defend it against the attacks of the Danes, as they had once been the invaders.

Harold himself was half-Dane, on his mother's side. Therefore, it struck him sometimes as dishonest, to be prating on about what the 'English' people wanted. If that was the case, if Englishness was determined by blood, perhaps he had no right to it, or less. Yet then he would change his mind, forsake his apologies. He had been born here, served its king and people, made it his life and home. To be in this place, this moment, bound a man somehow, gave him a right to hold his head high and keep his pride.

Harold shifted position with a sigh, trying to coax the cramp out of his legs, and pulled the hood of his cloak over his wet hair – which did him no good, the hood being even wetter. In a way, it was for England that he was crouched in this dark wood, the trees stripped bare by autumn and the rain pelting the half-rotted leaves. Perhaps it was not so complicated as he thought. He was here because the King had asked him.

As always, it had been an eventful few years. Instead of maintaining the generous peace accord he had been given, Ælfgar had taken his elevation to Earl of Mercia to mean that he now had a larger stage to continue his disruptions. In 1058, he had married his daughter Edith to his partner in crime, Gruffydd ap Llywelyn. With the bride barely bedded, the newly minted in-laws had rattled straight back to causing mayhem, terrorising the marches and pocketing the spoils. This state of affairs would have continued for some time, giving the rest of England endless headaches, had it not been happily curtailed by Ælfgar's death just this past summer. In an attempt to write a permanent end to this sorry chapter, Harold had asked for and received Edward's permission to lead a force into Wales, pursuing Gruffydd back toward his capital of Rhuddlan. Put the bastard's head on a pike, and perhaps that at last would spell a respite. Peace. It seemed so ephemeral. *Another thing which it seems I have no right to claim. But Father did not rebel from pettiness. There are so many things I wish I had remembered to ask him, and that was one. How he knew. Or if he did not, when to take the chance.*

The rain was slacking off. Harold glanced up through the skeletal branches, trying to gauge how many hours before darkness. Gruffydd's keep, such as it was, was just visible on the hill below, screened by a curtain of shabby oaks. The Welsh had no castles, barely even a mead hall; small huts ringed a low sod building, and the whole was closed in a palisade of sharpened sticks. A feast was well underway, and smoke drifted skyward, the smell of roasting meat on the air. Harold himself had eaten little during the chase, and his empty belly rumbled dolefully, reminding him.

Darkness was drowning them instead of rain by the time the torches around the hall finally began to go out. Harold's men were edgy, but he kept them in check, waiting until even the last hound had ceased baying. Then they landed noiselessly in the grass, reached the hill and climbed it quickly, until the hall loomed before them, its black bulk veiling the dreary stars. It appeared to be quiet, sleeping, but Harold knew not to underestimate Welsh cunning.

Nonetheless, when nothing materialised, he looked from side to side at his men, then nodded. As one, they surged for the gates and scaled them as well. Harold was one of the first over, and he dropped lightly into the courtyard, drew his sword, and –

A torch blazed, and a voice howled something in Welsh. Harold ducked, then spun about, flinging himself against his opponent – a skinny, screaming sentry, dark eyes wide and furious. He tried to knife Harold, and failed resoundingly; Harold was wearing mail. Then Harold, who had half a foot of height, three stone of weight, and at least ten years on his foe, wrenched him off and sheathed a yard of English steel in him from belly to backbone.

The sentry's mouth opened in shock. He staggered backwards, and fell when Harold pulled the blade out. The torch, dropped, guttered in the mud, but the boy's ambush, clumsy as it was, had done its work. Voices shouted, more torches flared, and feet pounded madly as Harold blasted toward the main hall. There was a bar on the door, but that was of small account; he ripped the hand-axe from his belt and disposed of it. It yawed open, and he careered through – just in time to see Gruffydd's wild-haired silhouette vanishing out the far end.

Harold bellowed a challenge and leapt off the dais. Gruffydd was astonishingly fast for a man of his size, but Harold himself was no poor specimen, and he was confident he could recoup the distance. His long legs ate it up as he pelted across the dirt floor. Just a bit closer, just –

One moment Harold was running flat-out, and the next he had an opportunity to examine said floor in great detail, crashing face-first with no notion of who or what had grabbed him. His first, mad thought was that the sentry had rushed in to give it one last valiant shot, and he seized his assailant, rolled them over, and slammed his dagger against their throat. Now he'd see if this one was any more a man –

It wasn't. Considerably less, in fact. As Harold's instincts let go and his brain kicked back in, he registered in astonished disbelief that it was a woman, young and fair-haired, blue eyes frightened but defiant, her shift torn down the shoulder. As that came to him, it struck him as well who she must be: Ælfgar's daughter, Gruffydd's wife.

'Get off me,' she said. 'And you won't catch my husband, either.'

Harold was tempted to point out that if he did one, the odds were very good that he would do the other, but now was not the time for it. He hauled her brusquely to her feet, trying to think of a place to put her – he didn't want to turn his back on her – and recollect the time he was losing to pursue Gruffydd. There was a chance that one of his men had apprehended the fugitive king, but distant thumps, shouts, clangs and clashes attested to their involvement elsewhere.

Edith was breathing hard through her nose, but her face was calm. Sweat was moulding her shift to her body, revealing – *bloody hell, Harold, this is not the time* – a very remarkable bosom. Coupled with the smooth white skin and fine bones, it made for quite an appealing picture. *A pity she's a traitor's daughter, and wed to a barbarian. Now get on with it!*

He pushed her away. Then he vaulted over the benches, reached the far end of the hall, and wrenched the door open onto the night. He could just see Gruffydd, racing off aboard a pony almost as shaggy as he was. Harold prepared himself to sprint –

And then he was taken embarrassingly unawares for the third time that night, by a teeth-jarring *clang* in the back of the head. He staggered, seeing stars. Edith, running up behind him, had pitched a pewter tankard with commendable precision and force.

She's fearless at the least, though I should have expected that from Ælfgar's whelp. Harold, resisting the urge to employ some of his brother Gyrth's more colourful verbiage, instead bellowed at the nearest shadow that looked like an Englishman. 'GRUFFYDD! AFTER HIM!'

Startled, the man whirled, trying to locate the Welsh king, but Harold himself had lost track of him; the woods had already engulfed him. This was a problem, but it was at once superseded by another – a pack of Welshmen armed with spears came somersaulting into the torchlight. One particularly overexcited specimen threw his, and that was it. Harold reached behind him, fumbled, and caught hold of an arm. With a protesting squeal from its owner, he swung it around and restored the dagger to her throat. 'Stay back,' he warned the Welshmen. 'Or you'll lose a queen too.'

It didn't matter that his Welsh was highly rudimentary; it wasn't the sort of gesture that required translation. They exchanged angry looks, but didn't venture closer.

'My lord!' One of his own men hurtled round the corner. 'Gruffydd! He got away!'

'Really?' said Harold. 'I had no idea.'

The venture was, therefore, a failure. Harold was a fair hand at tracking, but Wales wasn't *normal;* it closed itself to outsiders like a nunnery, turned into a maze of death, mud, and befuddlement for any enemy army attempting to plumb its secrets. Moreover, Gruffydd had spent his entire life here, could vanish like a hare down a hole, and while Harold's men were equipped to go light and fast, they were not carrying many provisions, and winter was coming. The idea of trying to hunt Gruffydd in the mounting snow, with no food, in the fey landscape, was tantamount to suicide. No, however much it chafed, he had to make new plans.

Meanwhile, Harold and his men burned Rhuddlan. It did not cause much damage; the wood and sod were soaked. That didn't matter. That was not the purpose. And all the while, Edith stood in the middle of the muddy courtyard, barefoot, her hair coming undone from its plaits. She was clutching the hands of three small children, and for some reason that caught at him. He hadn't known she'd bred with Gruffydd, and the blank, consuming fear on their faces caught at him as well, even as he and his men departed. It was a mile back to where they'd left the horses, and then, on no sleep and little food, a seventy-league ride to London.

The memory of Edith's eyes troubled Harold for all of them.

London, England
December 1062
'Brother,' said Harold. 'I need your help.'

'That so?' Tostig took a gulp of wine. 'At what? Combing your hair? Extorting money? Bedding your woman?'

'None of those.' Harold waited for his brother to make his move. If he went for that rook, then he could hop his knight and. . .

'Then what?' Tostig flicked his bishop exactly where Harold hoped he wouldn't.

Harold cursed under his breath, scanning the terrain of the chessboard. It was a recent arrival in London, from the trade routes along the Silk Road, and thus their chief entertainment for the Christmas season had been in playing duel-to-the-death matches that they took only slightly less seriously than it appeared. Which reminded Harold – although he was enjoying his brother's company, there *was* the small matter as to why he was having it at all. 'I've been meaning to ask, why aren't you in Northumbria?'

'Northumbria's a miserable buggering place, that's why,' said Tostig, in between another gulp of wine. 'Besides, the king asked if I would spend Christmas here. He's getting old enough that I daresay he's beginning to like me.'

'Indeed. How fortunate for you.' Considering the rumours he'd heard, Harold wondered if this was a shrewd move on Edward's part, to measure the leash given to a potentially problematic underling. Come to think of it, it might not be a bad thing to keep Tostig out of Northumbria for a while.

'Don't sound so disappointed.' Tostig pressed his advantage with the bishop. 'You were always Father's favourite, and now you're Edward's. You can save a crumb for us little people.'

Harold blinked. 'Where did that come from? I've only ever supported you – Christ, I got you Northumbria, is that – '

'A venomous blessing, but a blessing all the same. One given in thanks for you besting Ælfgar, who then went on to trouble us for another seven years! A failure that might have been averted, had we a stronger king. And then the whispers, that poor Tostig would never have gotten an earldom if his big brother had not come along and put it in his paw. Don't you understand what it's like to live in your shadow? You can't set a foot wrong. Whatever any of us get, it will always be thanks to you! It will never be said that we earned it!'

Taken off guard, Harold answered more harshly than he'd meant to. 'Whatever the circumstances, you do have Northumbria. If you are weary of men saying that you do not merit it, then stop giving them cause to justify their suspicions.'

Tostig glared at him. 'Keep talking, brother, and you can see if the Earl of Mercia wants to help you with your little errand.'

'He will not.' But recently come into the position at Ælfgar's death, twenty-four-year-old Edwin would not be at all inclined to assist his father's enemy in hunting down his sister's husband. Besides, he was a grandson of Leofric. Harold was a son of Godwin.

'Why?' said Tostig. 'Why won't Edwin want to help?'

'First and foremost, because he is of Leofric's line. Secondly, because what I was going to ask, before we got so distracted, was your assistance in chasing down Gruffydd ap Llywelyn, this coming spring. If it's news of my failure you want, then there you are. He got away from me at Rhuddlan in October, and I was forced to retreat for the winter.'

'Indeed? What a shame. But it might give my Northumbrians something to do, apart from grousing about me.'

'You are supposed to be their leader, so lead. And put a halt to the Scots' raiding every once in a while.'

Tostig shrugged. 'I befriended Malcolm while he was at Edward's court. If his people want a few cows from time to time, who am I to stop them?'

This line of argument was profoundly flawed to Harold, but he tried to think how to explain so without setting his brother off. 'We all rejoiced when Malcolm came into his crown.' The Scottish prince had done so four years ago, by killing Macbeth's stepson Lulach – seeing as he was known as 'Lulach the Stupid,' it was accorded no loss to anyone. 'That does not mean either you or he should feel justified in thieving from the very people – Siward's old subjects – who supported him in reaching it.'

'Oh, because they're *English* cows? Do they moo with a different accent?' Tostig laughed. 'Is that how it goes, brother? How do you even define it?'

'Certainly not by letting Malcolm of Scotland filch your livestock. They are more than cows, they are sustenance for your people. And by letting this go on, you dig your own grave.'

'Listen to you sermonizing again. You missed your calling, you should have been a priest. Don't you ever wake up one fine morning, look at your face in your wash-water, and say, "Oh my, there's a pompous ass staring at me?" '

'Tosti, would you – '

'Don't call me that, *Harry*. Whatever we are, we're not children any more.'

'I've stuck my neck out for you time and time again, especially when everyone thought I was completely – '

'Oh, and now we come to it. You are worried about how I reflect poorly on you. You could say it, you know, instead of cloaking it in all this pretentious rubbish about what your country needs. Well, I'm not a bloody country. I'm a man. Forgive me.'

Harold was quiet. The accusations landed in some uncomfortable part of him – not true or at least he did not think so, but not able to be denied out of hand. 'So,' he said at length. 'You won't help me capture Gruffydd, then?'

Tostig smiled. 'A game of chess on it.'

Harold paused, then reached out to reset the board – it only seemed fair. But Tostig's hand caught his wrist. 'We've already been playing the game,' he said. 'We can't go back. We don't have the chance to start anew. We have to finish it.'

In more than chess, brother, Harold thought. *In much more.*

There was no more talk as the two of them hunched down, taking a drink or plotting strategy. A whirl of their remaining pawns chased about, trying to force each other into the custody of opposing knights or queens. *It is more than chess we are playing here. And yet it is. Is this what it comes down to? Is this how God sees it? Just a game? It almost seems simple.*

'Damn,' said Tostig, and tipped over his king. 'It seems you have your army.'

Harold looked up with a start. He had become so engrossed that he'd barely realised what was going on – as if the game, somehow, had been playing him. But he met his brother's eyes and smiled. 'I'm glad. Now let's show them all how to finish the job.'

'Hail,' said Tostig. 'What a pity it's winter. I could run out and kill something right now.'

The Christmas season progressed peaceably enough, albeit with a certain foreboding pall. Edward was unwell, and the constant sound of his dry, muffled coughing was the pulse to which beat the court's communal heart. In his infirmity, the real power was directed more and more to Edith, who sat on her husband's throne or in his seat with the witan, hearing cases and dispensing counsel and judgment. In theory she was supposed to confirm everything with Edward, but his trust in her was such that he rarely insisted on it. In return, Edith's protection of his interests was comprehensive and thorough. For a marriage that had started out looking almost comically doomed, it had grown and matured into one of deep respect and love.

Harold was happy to see his sister busy, the way the smallfolk would pull off their hoods and hail their good Queen, but he was also unshakeably aware that her increase in importance was coincident with her husband's increasing frailty. Edward was by no means incapacitated, but it was impossible to ignore that not only was he an ill man, he was an old one. And the one great question of his reign lay on them like dark clouds.

Edgar the Aetheling was still only eleven, a slender and fragile child whose grasp of Saxon remained uneven and whose cloistered upbringing was a source of consternation among the partisans who had hoped to get their claws into him early. The boy, his mother Agatha, and his two sisters continued to live at court, and while Edward was fond of them and treated them as his grandchildren, they kept to themselves. Consequently they had no particular allies among the witan, aside from those who supported the lad for his bloodline. Soon, sooner than anyone wanted to think about, he would be the last living male heir of the line of Cerdic. Such a distinguished pedigree could not be easily cast aside, but the fact remained that as currently constituted, Edgar – through no fault of his own – would make a singularly unsuitable sovereign. Naming a regent would be a disaster, as it would give preferment to one family and encourage their enemies to be even more ruthless, if access to a vulnerable boy-king was at stake.

There was no chance of naming Edgar's mother, who after all was foreign, and included in the equation solely by the fact that she had shared Edward Aetheling's bed. All in all, there was still no obvious solution to the succession quandary, and there were those – quiet at first but then more openly – who had begun to furnish possible alternates. It came into the open on the meeting of the witan on St Stephen's Day, 1062.

'My lord,' said Wulfstan, now Bishop of Worcester – he had been appointed to that position just this year, aided considerably by Harold. 'I have had an epiphany.'

'Have you?'

'Indeed. I trust you will find it likewise.' Wulfstan looked around, at the queen sitting in place of the king, the dripping sunlight prying at the windows. 'I propose, my lord, that you wed the Aetheling's elder sister Margaret. She is a lovely girl, almost eighteen years of age, known for her steadfastness of character and devotion to Christ.'

Harold frowned. 'From what I hear, she'd sooner marry Christ Himself, go and become a nun somewhere. And there is one other roach in the rushes. I *am* married.'

'My lord,' said Archbishop Stigand. 'Is it to Edith Swannesha you refer?'

'It is.'

'Well, unless aught has changed since last I looked, you and the lady Swannesha are not precisely married. You have kept her in the Danish fashion of your forefathers and mine, but you have never wed her in the Church.'

'The lady Swannesha has lived with me almost twenty years and borne me six children,' Harold objected. 'What else is needed?'

Stigand tittered nervously. 'My lord, your love for your sweet lady is admirable and true, but not particularly. . . *useful*. She is of common blood. She brings no swords or lands.' He hesitated, then went for the jugular. 'She could never be consecrated queen.'

An alarmed rumble went around the room. Harold himself experienced a most extraordinary feeling: one of desperate longing and aghast horror both, as of something he wanted terribly but had never dared to name, never dared to think of going that far.

'If you were lawfully married,' Stigand pressed, 'and to a daughter of the old line, surely that would settle any questions of your. . . propriety?'

How dare you talk about propriety to me, you bilious quack? Isn't it five Popes now that have excommunicated you? 'Be that as it may,' Harold said, 'the lady Margaret, though lovely and devoted *and* of impeccable birth, brings nothing in terms of property, sworn swords, or allies. It would be a symbolic marriage at best. And will any of you tell me that *symbols* will hold the Norman threat at bay?'

'Duke William is a godly man,' Stigand insisted. 'He would never disobey the wishes of his own kin, our good king Edward, nor take away the rights to which another man was born.'

'Firstly, that would be Edgar, not me, and it seems we ourselves already have. Secondly, your sacramental wine must be strong stuff, my lord, if you think William will give up anything he has a chance to gain. Every tale of the man says he's a fiercer fighter than Samson, and more covetous than the sons of Jacob.'

'If he *is* Samson,' said Stigand, 'someone must cut off his hair. Not so?'

Harold gritted his teeth. 'My lord, it is not that simple.'

'Why are we speaking of this at all?' demanded Edwin of Mercia, a tall, auburn-haired young man. His brother Morcar stood behind him, a silent dark shadow. 'Does it not stink of some treachery to be openly plotting to replace the king, when he is not yet in his grave?'

'It's plain you have little experience, Ælfgar's son,' Harold said coolly. 'That's the sole thing the witan has been doing ever since our gracious Edward was crowned.'

Edwin scowled. 'Even so, why is it you who would wed the lady Margaret?'

'Who else?' It was Archbishop Aldred of York who spoke. 'I ask not in antagonism, my lords, but genuine curiosity. Harold is Godwin's eldest living son, respected by all, skilled in battle, moderate in temperament, wealthy in means and spirit, and brother to the queen. He is a grown man, demonstrably capable of siring children, has consistently defended us against our enemies, and can call on three quarters of England's resources. I repeat, who else?'

Harold had never been quite as aware as he was that moment, how much so many eyes weighed. They were all looking at him – even Edwin and Morcar could tender no good reply. And if so, then he must do this. Do it with whole heart and never look back. Did it matter what he must give up, if the results were good? If he succeeded, surely he must be justified? For England? For him? Tostig's accusations still beat in his skull. *Who are you doing this for? Can you not even acknowledge it to yourself? Will you?*

Again, he shoved it aside. 'My lords. While marrying the Aetheling's sister is an intriguing idea, I feel that it would not achieve our aims. But I may, however, have another idea.'

The old year passed away, died quietly in the night, and the new one was born. Epiphany was celebrated and Yuletide came to an end, and Harold and Tostig accelerated preparations for their campaign into Wales. The time was almost on top of them, and Tostig departed for York, to whip the lukewarm northerners into battle-fervour. Harold himself had almost finished assembling the fleet he was to sail around Cornwall and into Welsh waters. Gruffydd was rumoured to have taken to the seas, living as a vagabond, in his attempt to stay one step ahead of his pursuers.

The night before he was due to leave, Harold took supper with Swannesha alone. The pie was hot and the stew savoury, but he barely tasted it. He had never realised how comfortable the silence was with her – how they had learnt when to speak and when to not, what the other was thinking. Almost.

'Harold?' She was still very beautiful, his Swannesha. The elegant neck that had given her the name, the braided hair, the kind eyes. Her body was somewhat worn and thickened after six children, but he loved her no less for it. 'What's wrong?'

At that moment, a terrible spear of doubt took him through the heart: that everything and everyone was wrong, that he had made an agonizing choice unknowing. He sat there, mute.

'My love?' She touched his arm. 'Have you had a dream? Some ill?'

'No.' Harold surfaced. 'I – Edith.' He barely called her that, even though it too was her name. To him, *Edith* was his sister.

She blinked. 'Aye?'

Harold took a breath. 'I am sorry to tell you,' he said, 'that I have to let you go.'

Her face did not change. She continued to sit there, as if waiting for a catch. 'Why?'

'Because I cannot be king if I do not.' There, dear God, he'd said it.

'Is that what troubles you?' She began to laugh. 'What else?'

'Stop!' he said fiercely. 'I am deadly serious, Edith. It was not my idea, I swear. But it has become clear that there is no choice.'

'Not your choice?' She tasted the words deliberately. 'But being king is?'

'Listen – '

'I am. I hear as well what you are not saying. Perhaps I ought not be surprised. So it is. But there is always a choice, Harold. This is the one you've made. So it will be the one you live with.' She rose to her feet. 'God's blessings and protection on you always.' Her lips touched his, fleetingly. 'I will pray for you, my king.'

And with that, leaving her scent in the room like a dream he had lost on waking, she went.

CHAPTER NINE

Snowdonia, Wales
August 1063

HEAT FRACTURED off the horizon, lighting the lakes aflame and making the shadows shimmer. Sunlight lay thick as honey on the steep-sided mountains, clouds drifted in the blue sky, insects hummed and birds chattered. The grass on the valley floor was long and lush, and a stream tumbled through a birch grove. Harold Godwinson had never seen such a beautiful place. Nor had he been more convinced that it wanted to kill him.

Every sense on edge, he proceeded through the underbrush, one hand shading his eyes and the other grasping his sword-hilt. Behind him, he could hear his men following, each in the prints of the next, afforded some cover by the jagged contours of the vale, the high piles of rocks, and the mud they'd liberally applied. He could still taste it in his mouth, but did not complain. He might be, at last, on the verge of catching the miscreant and ending this whole affair.

The Godwinson brothers had hounded Gruffydd relentlessly over the spring and summer, and the conflict was only intensifying. The Welsh king had spent by far the lion's share of it on the defensive, after Harold's naval ambush had resulted in the destruction of much of his fleet. Once the fight was relocated to land, Gruffydd's options for escape had been severely restricted by the arrival of Tostig's Northumbrians, who saw to it that he had no time to choose a new hideout at his leisure. Since then, Gruffydd had been scuttling to and fro like a mouse chased with a broom, but had not succeeded in getting free. They had been slowly drawing the noose around him, forcing him into a smaller and smaller pocket of Snowdonia.

There was one thing that surprised Harold, however: the utter lack of feeling with which he was carrying this out. He had no love for Gruffydd, was anticipating the moment his defeat was final, and hoped he himself would play a significant part. But at the same time, it was becoming increasingly detached from him. It was only a stepping stone, something to contribute to an overall whole, as slowly and carefully as the great church Edward was building in Westminster, and he took a running leap over a stream, waterskin sloshing against his back. Sweat pricked his temples, and he felt the grind of effort, the grittiness of sleepless nights. In a way, it was comforting – a reminder that he *could* still feel something.

A storm is coming. Harold pushed aside another screen of branches. He did not mean the weather. It – for now – remained as deceptively brilliant as ever, annealed to gold on God's anvil, so one's eyes were dazed by the light and saw not the clouds amassing dark on the edges.

It began to rain that night, as they were pitching camp a mile upwind of the Welsh. Harold's scouts informed him that the cornered king was running low on supplies and morale, and so far as they could tell, considerable infighting was breaking out. This was good news for the English, of course, and they built a fire, poured the last of their wine, and toasted to Gruffydd's continued discord. Nonetheless, Harold was in a very strange mood. He sat on a log, sheltered by a mossy overhang, watching the fire hiss when the drops struck it. In these long summer evenings, it did not grow fully dark until very late, and blood-red clouds scarred the western sky. This lent itself too easily to the portents he was seeing everywhere. Gruffydd knew that if he could hold out until the first snows, boost the likelihood of Harold having to retreat for another winter, the odds would tip in his favour. *I have to end this now.*

'Beor,' he said to one of his captains.

'Aye, m'lord?'

'Wake me at midnight. We'll assault Gruffydd at dawn. Prepare the men.'

Beor bowed crisply and strode off. Harold, still troubled, pulled his cloak off and rolled himself up in it. He'd been sure he wouldn't sleep, but he was wearier than he thought. The world softened to a haze, and he slipped under.

Waves. One after another, crashing into the bulwarks. The eerie scream of the wind, the darkness of the bruised sky, the torn sail flapping. Cracking timbers and the roar of water. He tried to grasp a rope, but it lashed out of his hands. Then out of nowhere, a wave smashed the mast full on, cracking it in half. Yards and yards of wet canvas slapped the deck as the ropes unravelled, the sail collapsed. Barrels pitched and rolled, and Harold stumbled and fell, just in time to see the wall of water.

He had only a moment before it rendered his world a screaming chaos of froth and darkness. He had no breath, and he hung in a formless void, almost at peace. Then he became aware that he was drowning, and began to panic. His cloak and boots were weighing him down, so he ripped them off. Kicked harder, lungs burning, this was the end –

Then his head broke the surface. His gasp was explosive, searing his chest, as he pitched up and down on the heavy seas. But in the near distance, he could see the dark line of land, and knew that his only hope was to swim for it.

The storm was clearing. The land took more shape – a jutting sweep of empty beach, rocks turning the water white. Harold felt his feet touch bottom, and let the next wave wash him ashore. Too beaten to rise, he lay clutching the ground and retching.

After a moment that seemed to last forever, he sat up. He could see nothing but mist, hear nothing but the continual hiss and crash of the waves. There was not even a seagull. He was alone. The coast spread bare and desolate, vanishing into the fog.

'Anyone there?' he called. 'Anyone?'

His voice did not echo, flat and dull. He took a step. Still no sign, no sound.

There was something in the sand at his feet. Shining gold. He tripped over it, then knelt down, picked it up, and brushed it off. He was only moderately surprised to see that it was the crown of England.

He wondered if he dared put it on. He wanted it. He had earned it.

A quork from behind him. He turned.

He was not alone after all. There were crows, circling down like sooty ghosts. One landed, and then several. They hopped closer, paying no mind to his attempts to chase them off.

The mist was receding. And Harold saw what surrounded him.

Bodies. So many bodies, more men than he'd even known were on the ship, drowned and bloated and blue, hung with weed and their eyes still open, staring. The crows were descending on them, plucking at hair, faces.

'Shoo!' Harold cried, or tried to. The crown – he didn't remember putting it on, but there it was – weighed heavy as lead on his brow, and when he tried to pull it off, it tightened. He stumbled. And when he lifted his own hands to his face, they were white and cold, and his wrists were garlanded with weed. It grew thicker as he watched.

A weight on his shoulder. A crow had landed.

'No,' Harold tried to say. 'No, I'm alive, I'm alive!' But the words were gone, stolen from his throat. Then the crow lunged for his eye, and everything went black.

'My lord! Wake up, it's not but a dream! My lord!'

Harold's eyes flashed open. He could still taste saltwater, see the corpses and the crows and himself, wandering like a crowned fool in a sordid mystery-play. Nonetheless, words blurted out by old habit. 'I'm all right.'

'You were thrashing something awful, m'lord.' Beor peered at him worriedly.

'It's nothing.' Harold sat up. 'Is it midnight?'

'Not yet. I was concerned for you.'

Harold wiped his forehead. 'No matter, I should prepare. I – what is it, Leif?'

Another of his men had just come running. 'M'lord,' he said in Danish, one of the three languages Harold had at his command (four, charitably counting his Welsh). 'There are visitors.'

'Visitors?' Harold was still addled enough to fear he meant the crows. 'Who?'

There was a look on Leif's face almost as peculiar as his. 'Welshmen, my lord.'

That shocked the grogginess out of him. 'Welshmen?' Perhaps Gruffydd had caught wind of how dire his situation was, and decided that his best chance lay in negotiating. That, however, seemed most out of character for the stubborn patriot they'd chased all over kingdom come. Harold immediately suspected a trap.

'Stay with me,' he told Leif and Beor, belting on his sword. 'Feather them at the first sign of treachery.'

Leif and Beor, faces grim, nodded and strung their bows. They were both housecarls, highly trained in the arts of war, sworn to die sooner than surrender to any foe, and proficient with every sort of weapon. The employment of housecarls was commonly exclusive to the royal family, and the fact that they had been sent with him was one Harold had not missed. Up ahead, from the fire in the main camp, he could hear a buzz of nervous chatter, and quickened his pace. What in the name of –

'My lord!' His men rose to their feet as he entered the firelight. 'Welshmen.'

'I see.' Harold regarded them narrowly. A pair of slight, dark Cymry, dressed in tattered leathers and – surprisingly – the green cloak that marked them as Gruffydd's own personal guard. His men had already taken the liberty of divesting them of their weapons, but there was one thing, curiously, they'd been permitted to keep. A good-sized basket, covered with a cloth.

'Greetings,' Harold said to the envoys, switching to their language. 'What business do the king's men have? Who are they?'

He saw the surprise in their eyes, then they bowed. 'I am Cynan ap Iago,' said the taller of the two. 'This is Bleddyn ap Cynfyn, the rightful prince of Gwynedd and Powys.'

Bleddyn, thin and debonair, smoothly inserted himself into the conversation. 'We come to bring you a gift, Harold ap Godwin.'

'A gift?' Harold repeated. Somehow he thought they meant a snake.

'Aye.' Cynan picked up the basket and thrust it at Harold.

Seeing nothing for it, hoping Leif and Beor had their bows at the ready, Harold pulled the cloth away. A whiff of decay reached his nose, and suddenly, with a revulsion that turned his stomach, he knew what it was. He reached in, grasped a fistful of hair, and drew out the severed head of Gruffydd ap Llywelyn, the stump still moist with blood and the eyes staring fixedly.

There was a rumble of disgusted curses as Harold held it up. It must have taken several blows to hack through Gruffydd's beefy neck, and he tried not to notice how inexpertly this appeared to have been carried out. 'What makes this so, Cynan ap Iago?'

Cynan smiled. 'Gruffydd ap Llywelyn had many enemies, my lord. My own father was ruler of Gwynedd before Gruffydd killed him. Justice has been served. The Welsh are not governed by one man alone, but many princes and lords, who rise and fall.'

'And who did this thing?'

'I did. My father's shade is at rest.' Cynan held up his hands – crimson stains still showed on them, his sleeves spattered with it. 'Are you pleased, Harold ap Godwin?'

Pleased? At the moment he felt sickened. But Gruffydd *was* dead. One part of the labyrinth had been completed, another stone laid. He was even less able to turn back.

'Aye,' said Harold. 'Indeed I am, Cynan ap Iago.'

'Well done, brother.' Tostig tied back his shaggy golden hair and gave Harold a sly half-smile. 'Well done indeed. And you come out smelling of roses again. No one can accuse you of having a king's blood on your hands, a dangerous foe of England is cut down, and his replacements are kissing Edward's arse.'

'The treaty was sufficient to both of us, and fair. Bleddyn ap Cynfyn is Gruffydd's half-brother on his mother's side – which for the Welsh counts full as much as the father's side.' Harold uncorked his wineskin and poured Tostig a goblet. 'Sit down and stop pacing, you're making me tired merely to look at you.'

'I'd hope you'd *be* tired after so much industry,' Tostig said, but did so. 'So you pulled another miracle out of your arse?'

'I gave the rule back to the lawful heirs – Wales is generally ruled by provincial princes, not one king. In return, Bleddyn swore to recognise Edward as his liege lord.'

'Clever of you, to give back what was his in the first place and make him pay for it.' Tostig smiled again. Their work done, the Godwinson brothers had been reunited on the far side of the Snowdon mountains, which were turning golden in the advance of autumn. 'And what was more, you made Bleddyn swear to the *King* of England, not Edward specifically.'

'I saw no harm in having him indebted to the office, no,' Harold said coolly. 'That might preclude the need for another war.'

'Keep telling yourself that, brother.' Tostig's voice was amiable, but something in his eyes was not. 'Oh, and by the way. I passed through Rhuddlan, just as requested, and brought you a present. Look.'

Harold followed his brother's pointing finger, and saw, sitting beneath a tree, the erstwhile Queen of Wales, back rigidly straight and eyes staring ahead. Her fair skin was dewed with sweat, and her hands were looped thrice about with rope.

Harold swallowed. 'You bound her?'

Tostig gave him a queer look. 'You killed her husband – or would have – and now you're scrupling about her comfort? Don't be fooled by her martyred expression – she can be sweet enough, if you persuade her. But she's still a damned dangerous little bitch.'

Harold did not answer, watching Edith. Then he got up from his brother's side, crossed the grass, and knelt beside her. 'My lady. Is there anything I might do for you?'

Her head turned slowly. 'No, my lord. I am quite well.'

'Surely you mislike these?' He began to reach for the ropes.

'Your brother thinks I might be a liability unbound.'

'Would you?'

'Surely nothing you could not manage, my lord. As skilled a warrior as you are.'

'I'm sorry about your husband. He was a brave man.'

'Perhaps too much for his own good.'

'Did you love him?' It was unexpected, startling them both, yet somehow he cared to hear the answer. Why, he had no notion.

Edith considered. 'No,' she said after a moment. 'He was old enough to be my grandsire, and hardly a maiden's fancy. My father's choice, an enemy of my country. Nonetheless, Gruffydd is – was – kind. Loyal. More than I expected. He defended me. So I defended him.'

Harold resisted the urge to rub his head. 'You certainly did.'

The ghost of a smile touched her lips. 'What mean you with me, my lord?'

'I mean to take you home to Chester. To your brothers Edwin and Morcar.'

A flash of genuine surprise showed in her sea-blue eyes. 'Thank you.'

Harold nodded in acknowledgement. Then he drew his dagger, sawed through the ropes, and helped her to her feet. This accomplished, he strode off to where his army was encamped, feeling her gaze as surely as it had haunted him on the long ride from Rhuddlan. It was not until much later, as he was taking supper with Tostig, Bleddyn, and Bleddyn's brother, that it occurred to him to wonder what had happened to her children.

Chester, England
December 1063

'I thank you for my sister, my lord,' said the young Earl of Mercia. He was seated across the warm solar, sharpening a dagger in a not-so-subtle statement. 'The time has come, therefore, for me to ask what you are expecting in return.'

Harold took a cautious sip of hippocras, swilling it around before he swallowed. He hadn't yet expired ignominiously, and he doubted that he would – if only because Edwin would find it far more satisfactory to run him through with a sword. Still, one could not be too careful. 'My lord,' he said instead. 'Our families have a history of rivalry, to say the least. Yet we must bring it to an end. A storm is coming, and England must stand united, or be destroyed.'

Edwin eyed him thoughtfully. 'What do you mean?'

'I mean that the King is old and infirm, and the Aetheling is a sickly child. We must not delude ourselves into thinking that *that* has a prayer of holding back the wolf in Normandy.'

Edwin's voice was wry. 'A lion on his banners, I thought it was. Are you sure?'

'Increasingly over the past few years, he has made small secret of it. All of Edward's informants sing the same tune. He is convinced the throne was promised to him, and he intends to claim it when the time comes. By force, if necessary.'

'So what? He thinks he can beat an entire country?' Edwin laughed. 'I'd like to see him try. One Frenchman against the whole of England?'

'Precisely, my lord. It must be the whole of England. Against that, he has no chance. But Wessex and Northumbria and East Anglia and Mercia must be united.'

'Yourself, two of your brothers, and me. Three of Godwin's line, one of Leofric's?'

'That is how the coin has fallen, my lord. Must we squabble about which of us is loyal to which dead man? Tostig and Gyrth will listen to me. But we need you, Edwin.'

'And then would we? Hold against the storm?'

Harold kept his gaze. 'I swear it.'

'Interesting. How would this be accomplished? Is it glory you offer? Gold?'

'Gold will hold a man for a time, but another could always pay him more.' The path was evolving before Harold's eyes, so vividly that he had no choice but to believe in its rightness. 'I will bind us with a stronger thread, my lord. I will make us kin.'

Muted surprise registered in Edwin's face. 'How?'

Harold drew a breath. 'If you so consent, Edwin son of Ælfgar,' he said formally, 'I will take your sister Edith to wife.'

Silence persisted. Edwin blinked. 'Forgive me, my lord, but I was operating under the assumption that you already had one.'

'Not legally. The Church does not recognise her. I cannot afford the distraction.'

Edwin's face changed to frank incredulity. 'Swannesha?'

'Aye.'

'You put her aside and she's been your woman for how long?' Edwin shook his head. 'I almost believe you mean it.'

'I am in deadly earnest.' Harold could see his faint reflection on the fogged window. 'If it so pleases God, I will make your sister Queen of England.'

'She was,' said Edwin, with some irony, 'Queen of Wales.'

'This will suit better. Do we have an accord?'

'We may,' Edwin said neutrally, but a sudden, avaricious gleam had leapt up in his eyes. 'It is assuredly an interesting offer, my lord, but a. . . tenuous one. You still hold too much power. If you can cast one wife aside, what's another?'

'What can I offer you as my surety?'

Edwin considered again. Then he smiled. 'Forgive me. Some habits are not easily broken. I'll send to inform Edith at once, and we shall make plans for a wedding.'

'Would you have it here?' Harold asked. 'Now?'

'Nay, just past the New Year – there's a better omen, and marriage is not permitted in Advent besides. And one other thing. Let's have it at York, your brother Tostig's seat, to show that this is more than an alliance between you and I. This is to safeguard our country's very future.' Edwin's gaze resolved cold. 'You promised.'

Harold had yet another of those sickening presentiments: himself staggering around the beach, with only corpses for company. That, he had absolutely no doubt, was a warning of what would come to pass if he failed. 'I did.'

Edwin smiled. 'I believe you.'

York, England
January 1064

York Minster was a squatting, sinister, draughty, scabby hulk of a church, a monolith of dark stone and unfriendly statues, glowering at supplicants from the shadow of their unlit grottoes. The bell-tower slouched like a sullen stripling, the columns were sooty, the floor-stones cracked, and while the iron crucifix behind the high altar certainly inspired fear, there was no corresponding sense of mercy. The canopy covering Aldred's cathedra was the finest stuff in the place – Byzantine silk, picked up during his expedition to acquire Edward Aetheling. A great illuminated Gospel lay chained to a mahogany rostrum. Racks of candles guttered and spat, overflowing with waxen gremlins. The lonely wind howled, the assembly coughed, water dripped, and the Archbishop's droning failed to muffle either. With all that taken into account, Harold thought, it made sense that they were currently attempting to hold a wedding.

He stood before the altar, hand in hand with Edith of Mercia. She did not look at him, repeating her vows in a clear, calm voice; as it had been at the wedding of his sister and Edward, it was too cold to take them at the door. There was still the nuptial mass to be endured, and he did his best, but he appeared to be standing directly beneath a leak in the roof. The deplorable condition of the minster was startling. It *was* over three hundred years old, and had survived burning, pillaging, storms, Scots, and Vikings alike, but that was no excuse. Tostig should mount an effort to restore it.

Harold stole a glance at his brother. Tostig stood near the front, magnificently handsome in gilt and vair. The looks he was garnering from his vassals, however, could by no means be described as admiring; the Northumbrians made no secret of the fact that they could not stand him. Tostig's open belligerence and unwillingness to compromise only made things worse. The campaigns in Wales, far from reassuring them of his leadership, had been kindling on flame.

But the criticisms were unjust. We succeeded. Harold said the words, gave his pledge. He meant it. Harold Godwinson did not make frivolous vows, and was far past the stage where he could make excuses. As cold and cynical as this marriage was, he walked into it clear-eyed.

Aldred pronounced them wed. Harold bent to kiss his bride. Her cool lips touched his, with no attraction or abhorrence. Above, the minster bells began to sound, in deep, doleful booms more fit for a funeral. But a smattering of applause broke out, and he turned to face them, standing on high, hearing the slap of rain on the vaults. *I will* be King, he thought. *And that is well.*

The rest was sombre and understated. They passed out of the walled cathedral precincts and into Tostig's manor, and, rather than applying themselves to a celebration of the gaiety which such a momentous event would seem to require, settled instead to a quiet supper. The mutton was undercooked and the ale weak, but nobody seemed to care. The most jocular of the lot was Edwin, and the most mordant was Tostig; Harold occasionally caught his brother throwing him blackly bitter looks. No matter the public proclamations of faith he'd made, no matter how much he did love him, it was impossible to ignore the fact that Tostig was now, by far, the most unreliable quarter of the newly formed coalition.

Harold stole another glance at Tostig, who was well along in the process of drowning his sorrows in wine. The Earl of Northumbria's face was flushed, but his cheekbones stood out stark and white. And briefly, in the uncertain light of the torches, Harold fancied that Tostig's green eyes had gone a murky, unreadable black, some demon drawn in the margins of a Gospel-book.

After that, he did not need to blame the mutton for his lack of appetite.

The bedding ritual was carried out as prescribed. Harold and Edith were undressed and taken to the bridal chamber, and Harold dismissed the unworthy thought that Tostig had stationed a man behind the door with a knife. The maidservants were the only ones to linger, trying to coax a smile out of Edith, but she submitted with the same calm, uncomplaining mask.

Harold was installed in the bed first. Soon his bride came to join him, naked as her name-day, making no attempt at false modesty. He moved closer, combed her long flaxen hair with his fingers, hoping to accustom her to his touch. She made no protest.

At last he pulled her down, and rolled on top of her. There in a tender and bewildered silence, both of them wondering how it had gone from her ambushing him in Rhuddlan to this moment now beneath the long eaves of eternity and death, he took her with thoroughness and care. She clutched at his shoulders, made a small noise in her throat when he lost himself in her. For a moment she was luminous, worthy of love and ripe to be kissed, and he did so, hoping that perhaps this would not be what he had feared.

She said a name under her breath, too soft to be made out. Harold's own breath caught, and he hitched himself up on her. 'Edith,' he said. 'Edith, you are beautiful.'

Aye, the shade of Swannesha whispered, somewhere in the searching dark. *Aye, so I was.*

'Brother,' said Tostig the next day, doubtless purposefully echoing their last conversation of substance over a chess-board. 'Was that not indeed guilefully done.'

Harold considered. Tostig had unwisely imperilled his rook on his last move, and Harold's queen stood poised to capitalise. Yet he felt strangely reluctant, as if the game was spilling into the world. As if this would make real something he had been avoiding.

'Go,' said Tostig, with no patience for his existential dilemmas.

Harold made a move, a safe and evasive one. 'What are you talking about?'

'Don't insult me.' Tostig relocated the rook as if it was a personal insult. 'If you don't know, it's because you don't want to.'

'Tosti. Talk to me.' Harold reached a hand for his brother.

Tostig didn't slap it away, but looked as if he was thinking about it. 'White always moves first,' he said with a bleak smile. 'You are, of course you are, and now you have.'

'What?'

'Admit it plain, brother. Save some of my respect for you.'

Harold tried to change the subject. 'York Minster could use some attention.'

'I'll get on that once I have the money.'

'But I've heard you doubled the earldom's taxes?' Harold prayed that that particular piece of gossip was a falsehood. The Northumbrians would riot on the instant.

'You didn't think your war in Wales was going to pay for itself, did you?'

'*My* war?'

'Spare me.'

'All right, my war. I am grateful for your help.'

'Seeing as what a tender bit of skirt it's got you, all under the guise of what is best for your country.' Tostig kept up the attack with his knight. 'What did Swannesha think?'

'She understood.'

'Aye, I'm sure she did. And with dampened eye, quivering lip, and fortitudinous bosom, told you that she knew your heart's nobility and that hers would ere be true, no matter the square-jawed housecarls that flitted across her path.'

'Believe it or not, but Swannesha let me do what I had to.'

'There's never what you had to. There's only what you want to. And what's your next betrayal?' Tostig looked up at him. 'Who follows her, Harold? Who else will you sacrifice for your ambition? And how will you justify it then?'

I will never, he wanted to say. *I'm alive*, he had wanted to say. And in neither case could he, but only choked, and watched the words go down into the green darkness and drown.

And suddenly, it came to him what he had to do next.

London, England
March 1064

'So you are wed, I heard?' Edward smiled. 'You ought have brought her to court, I much desire to make her acquaintance.'

'I left her at my court in Winchester, my lord,' said Harold. He was heartened to note that Edward, though sixty-one and still plagued with poor health, looked somewhat more healthful. Perhaps he would not have to make the last choice just yet.

'A pity. Though I welcome your return. Most of the court has been insistent that I sit and do nothing, as if I was merely a senile old man. Let them have the running of it.'

'My lord. . .'

'No matter.' Edward brushed it aside. 'I know you are doing your best to stitch together the cracks which split this country apart. I fear you will find it complicated.'

'To what does my king refer?'

Edward turned to look at him. 'There is one more obstacle you must overcome.'

Is he giving it to me? Harold caught his breath. 'Aye?'

'Is it true that you mean to travel to Normandy?'

So he has heard. 'Aye. I must have measure of the duke as a man. And I must rescue my brother Wulfnoth and my nephew Hakon from his clutches. They've been there over a decade now, so I do not know that they find the prospect so terrible. But they are my own blood.' *I will not betray my kin. I must show Tostig that.*

'Well then,' said Edward. 'Go to Normandy, with my blessing. But one thing.'

'Aye?'

'William is a lion,' the king said quietly. 'I knew his father, I knew him in his youth, I saw it when he came. Go, Harold Godwinson, and learn what you can. But in the name of Christ our Lord, you had best pray that you are Daniel, and that an angel will keep his jaws closed.'

Harold paused. Then he dropped to his knees, pressed Edward's hand with its sapphire ring to his mouth, and kissed it. 'Then I set sail for Normandy. Pray for me.'

'Each day,' Edward promised him, 'and twice on Sundays. Believe me, my lord. You will need it.'

CHAPTER TEN

Bosham, England
April 1064

ALL WAS SET, the men packed up, and only the last prayers remained to be said. Harold knelt before the altar in the stuffy little church, wishing the man beside him would stop drumming his fingers on the rail; it was distracting him. Organising an expedition to Normandy was a bloody daunting task, and he could use the time to plead for its success.

The air was warm, the smoke from the censer somnolent, and Harold allowed his mind to drift. Unbidden, it returned to his leave-taking in London just a few days past, as he'd bowed over Edward's hand in the misty dawn courtyard. Edward told Harold to convey his regards to his cousin, and Harold promised to do so. Then he happened to glance over and see a pair of dark eyes watching him from the cloisters. So he took his leave of the king and subsided inconspicuously into the busy courtyard, until he reached them. 'Greetings, Agatha's son.'

'G-Greetings.' No longer a baby at least, Edgar the Aetheling had matured into a tall, thin, intensely gawky fledgling of thirteen. But he was built more like a dancer than a warrior; there was no brawn in the slender shoulders, barely a touch of colour in the skin.

Harold studied the boy appraisingly. *No,* he decided, *still not enough.* 'You ought to be out more often, my lord. For your health.'

'My mother does not think it safe.' Edgar spoke both Saxon and French quite passably by now, though still with a lilting accent. 'After what became of my father.'

Harold decided not to remark on the fact that poor Edward the Aetheling had been struck down in his own bedchamber, or doubtless the family would take to living underground. But then it occurred to him why Edgar had risked incurring his mother's wrath by his unauthorised emancipation. With only her and two sisters for company, one of whom had a foot in the nunnery already, the boy must be intolerably lonely and bored out of his wits, and Harold had a sudden impulse to grasp him by the hand, smile at him. Speak him sweetly, take him under his wing. Starved for a father's affection, half a ghost before he was even grown, caught in the uneasy hinterlands of this place that was not quite home, Edgar would lap it up. Listen unquestioningly. Do what he was told. *And if I had the life of the rightful heir in my hands. . .*

Harold shook that thought away. He gave the Aetheling's bony shoulder a quick, bracing pat. 'I'm for Normandy now, but we will speak more on my return. Farewell.'

'Farewell.' Edgar inclined his shining white-gold head. Then, as easily and quietly as if he had never been, he turned away and vanished down the cloisters.

'My lord! We're to go now, are you awake?'

'Aye.' Harold blinked, the outlines of Bosham church resolving back into focus. He crossed himself, got to his feet, and gave the priest alms. But with all spiritual matters in God's hands, the rest was in his own. He followed the sunlight on the floor-stones, like a finger pointing, out of the church grounds and down the hill to where the horses waited.

They pushed into the Channel by the end of the afternoon, a stiff wind bellying the striped sails of the longship and the salty air clean but sharp. The captain had been dubious of starting a voyage so late in the day, but an extra sack of silver changed his mind, and England was soon receding in the grey swells. Harold stood in the prow, telling himself that he was an idiot to expect imminent catastrophe every time the ship so much as rocked. It was that damned dream again. At least if he ended up at the bottom of the ocean, fish nibbling the gold from his fittings and Ægir's daughters dicing with his bones, he couldn't say he hadn't been warned.

He very much hoped that it would all promptly be dismissed as a silly and groundless fear, but to his apprehension, this was not the case. The sun sank low, the wind picked up, and the blowing spume turned white. The moon vanished in the clouds.

Harold swore and spun away – just as a rush of salt engulfed the deck, putting out half the torches. The helmsman swore even louder, and the ship rose to meet the next wave, but skidded and began to wallow. The sail went slack, then snapped.

Bloody hell, Harold thought. *I'm not bloody drowning.* And as a matter of fact he wasn't; he had no fear of it, if only because he was supposed to turn up on the beach later, with a load of corpses. But the fear that the rest of it might then prove true as well made him throw himself forward and bawl at the captain, 'Get us out of this!'

The captain gave him a deeply affronted look, as if to ask who was to blame for them setting out against his better judgment. It was one of those freak spring gales that blew up in the Channel, arriving like a scorned wife, kicking and screaming. And while Harold was a good sea-traveller, he was not much use as a sailor, though his strength and size did enable him to handle the ropes that the wind had torn away from smaller men. He wrestled one of these back to what he thought was its rightful place, which he was relieved to have confirmed by the hands shouting at him to tie it down. He did so.

The madness continued, up and down and down and up, again, at last. For the longest time, the ship perched at the crest of the wave. It was a moment of eerie weightlessness, so quiet that Harold had time to hear his men praying. Then reality came thundering back, and they pitched headlong into the trough.

It went on forever. They did not sink, rising battered but unconquered from each fresh assault, and Harold began to wonder instead if this was the last test. If he'd misinterpreted the fear, been wrong to live so consumed by it, that all they had to do was pass through this. The thought gave him strength. He kept hanging on and waiting for the dawn, knowing it had to come, the night couldn't last forever. And was just congratulating himself on overcoming his foolish superstitions when there was an ear-splitting crack, a blinding light, and a darkness that swallowed it all.

A small eternity later, Harold Godwinson remembered who he was, and opened his eyes.

Sunlight above him. Sand below. A gentle breeze. Blue sky. The crashing of the ocean, the sound of gulls. *Oh,* he thought. *I'm dead.*

He did not have time to dwell upon this revelation. 'MY LORD!' A loud voice, uncomfortably close at hand. 'Wake up!'

Harold blinked, discovered that everything hurt, and had an urge to slip back into the darkness, where this was not the case. This was followed, however, with a much stronger one to lurch to his knees and vomit an appalling quantity of seawater, which was exactly what he did.

'Oh, thank Christ. You're alive. Easy there, m'lord. Easy.'

Harold wiped his dry mouth with his sleeve. Sitting up, he was in better position to take stock of his surroundings, and could see that it really did appear to be a fine spring morning on the coast somewhere. Far from being surrounded by corpses, he was instead accompanied by the vast majority of his men. *It was just a dream.*

Harold squinted against the sunlight, which was either causing or encouraging his head to ache terrifically. 'What happened?' he croaked.

'Ship broke up on the rocks, just offshore. Look.' The man pointed.

Harold squinted some more, and thought he could discern a faint, cockeyed line near the horizon, which may or may not be the mast of a foundered ship. 'When?'

'Almost dawn. Part of the jib fell and knocked you cold, though. It gave us quite a terrible fright. We dragged you ashore, but you've been gone a good bit.'

That accounted for the headache, then. 'Where are we?'

'Normandy, I think. Although how far off course, I daren't wonder. Once we reconstitute, we'll find somewhere and ask our bearings.'

Just what he needed, Harold thought. The word to spread that an Englishman had come to Normandy. But there was nothing for it, so he struggled to his feet. 'Sensible.'

His man hovered at his elbow as he strode toward the camp. It *would* be helpful if he knew where they were – on the coast, clearly, but Normandy was plentifully equipped with coastline. Yet God must have taken notice of this question, and decided to provide it with an expeditious answer. Harold heard a shout of alarm from a nearby bluff, and then another of his men came crashing down it in a cloud of haste and sand. 'My lord! Riders!'

Harold's heart leapt into his throat, but he did his best to disguise it. 'Well then, we'll find out whose company we're keeping, aye? Then we can get on with it.'

His man goggled at him, thinking this unlikely in the extreme, but did not argue. There followed a considerable ruffle as the English did their best to look less beggarly, wringing out cloaks and improvising splints, until the reverberation of hooves in the ground announced the fact that they were out of time. The castaways huddled together, still trailing weed and dripping saltwater, as a band of mounted knights thundered around the bluffs. They reined to a halt with no sound, save the stamping of their horses and the continued rumble of the waves.

Harold stepped forward, preparing to negotiate; his long years in Edward's court had given him a competent, if unspectacular, command of French. 'My lords. I have come from – '

'Silence,' said one of the knights, none too warmly.

Harold, supposing it a sufficient boon that he could understand him, decided against pressing matters at this delicate juncture. He glanced at his men, doing his best to communicate this, but the preponderance of weapons on the Frenchmen and their own lack ensured that they had already arrived at the same conclusion. The two parties eyed each other suspiciously, and after a moment, Harold tried again. 'Your Graces. I would be much obliged if you could tell me where I have landed. I was – '

'I'll tell you.' The voice came from the back, and by the deferential way the knights drew apart, the speaker must be a figure of some authority. However, the short, weasel-faced man who came riding through, decked in marmoset and satin, did not nearly match up to what Harold had been led to believe. *Lion? He's barely a stoat.*

'You,' said this resplendent personage peevishly, 'are on my land, foreigner.'

Harold inclined his head, wondering how on earth Edward could have gotten his cousin's estimation so badly wrong. 'Duke William, my deepest apologies. I was hoping you might – '

'William? *William?*' His captor looked mortally wounded. 'I thank God I am not that kinslayer. I am Guy de Ponthieu, the count of these lands, and you and all your men are under arrest.'

Harold blinked. 'Guy de Ponthieu?' he said, attempting to match the name with his patchy recollection of the Norman fiefdoms. If he was correct, they were considerably far north, nearly to Flanders. He wondered just how astray the storm had blown them. 'But we did not – '

'I demand,' said the count of Ponthieu, 'your weapons.'

'Your Grace, we have none. We are – '

'You are wearing a swordbelt.' Guy's beady eyes fixed on it – Harold's was of good leather, clasped with gold, and the empty scabbard was chased in gilt. 'I will take that.'

Harold hesitated, and not only because both the belt and the now-lost sword had been a gift from his father. To yield it to an enemy was the most shameful thing an Englishman could do, forsaking his honour, courage, and prowess all at once. He did not know if it was likewise in France, but then again, death was the same no matter the language. And if the dozen longbows trained on him were any indication, Guy's men were most eager to prove it.

Slowly, feeling the eyes of his men on his back, Harold undid the belt and handed it over. 'Perhaps we might – '

Guy de Ponthieu had not let Harold finish a sentence yet, and he did not appear inclined to break such a sterling record. To his men he said, 'Take them.'

'My lord! We were shipwrecked, it was an accident – '

Guy raised an aristocratic hand, and the Frenchmen rode forward. The English looked to their lord for directions, but when Harold offered no resistance to the enormously smug Ponthieuan who hopped off his horse and tied his wrists, they unwillingly submitted as well. No, now was not the time. Any impertinence, real or imagined, would result in being promptly shot and left for the crows. And not until they were well away from the beach, and not even for some time after, would Harold consent to believe that he had escaped that fate.

Guy de Ponthieu had the English captives immured in his castle at Beaurain by the time the bells began to call Vespers. They were given a bowl of broth and a chunk of bread apiece, and shut into a tower. There were no luxuries, but there were hay and blankets, and Harold's exhausted men subsided into sleep soon after sunset. He himself sat by the tower window, watching the stars embroider the velvety spring night. He wondered what Guy wanted, if he had escaped the trap only to fall into another one, yet at least he had survived the dream. He was his own man again, the future blessedly murky. And for that, he was grateful.

It was some time before he slept. He lay down, but was so beaten and sore that he could not get comfortable. At last, however, sheer exhaustion won out.

The last thought Harold remembered having was that it was a pity that Guy de Ponthieu was not, in fact, William of Normandy. But at least he would have time to prepare. He would find a way out. And then he would look the lion in the eye, and not be afraid.

Dol-de-Bretagne, Brittany
April 1064

'Your Grace,' said Turold. 'We've some considerable news to share. The English earl Harold Godwinson has washed ashore on your lands.'

William started to attention. 'Mine?'

'Well, not your own demesne, my lord. Guy de Ponthieu's.'

William groaned. 'Why is it always a bloody de Ponthieu?'

'Because they have a capacity for trouble nearly as great as your own, my lord.' Turold had an uncompromisingly brusque, straightforward manner, which was one of the things William liked about him. He was an excellent spy with an eye for detail, no whisper of divided loyalties, and a lack of scruple almost as pronounced as his master's. There was one other pertinent fact about him: he was a dwarf. A giant in mind, to be sure, but the body had failed to keep pace, being born short and misshapen.

That, however, was where his effectiveness came from. Turold and his companion, a half-daft jongleur named Ivo Taillefer, had escaped from a travelling fair after years of being exhibited for the public's amusement. However, rather than collecting a few fistfuls of silver and buxom milkmaids and calling it a day, they had decided to reach somewhat higher, and presented themselves at William's doorstep, suing for a job. His guards had laughed them off three times before Turold succeeded in cadging an audience.

William himself, however, had taken one look at them and decided that he had the perfect spies on his hands. Their sheer improbability meant that no one else would ever take them seriously either. So, he told them, he was willing to see what they had to offer, and it had proven a remarkably astute decision. Turold could tumble and tell stories and stand on his head, and Taillefer could juggle anything, sing in a honey-sweet tenor voice, at least when he wasn't going crazy and claiming to predict the future. Thus, the two earned their keep at every inn, tavern, and brothel across Normandy – and at each, collected a healthy dose of gossip and rumour along with the silver. It was thanks to one of Turold and Taillefer's intelligences, in fact, that William was here in Brittany. But of course this would happen the instant he left.

'Go on,' he said, returning his attention to Turold. 'What is a Godwinson doing here?'

'I do not believe Guy has been able to wrest that out of him just yet. So far as I make it, Harold was shipwrecked and washed ashore in Ponthieu, where Guy – no doubt acting only as your loyal vassal – promptly clapped him into irons.'

William snorted. 'I'd hoped the two years Guy spent in my dungeon after Mortemer would knock some sense into him, but it seems I underestimated the density of his idiocy. Then again, Guy's not forgiven me for killing his brother, which I fail to understand. Enguerrand being the paragon of manly virtues he was.'

'I know a song about a man with virtues,' Taillefer piped up. 'He loses them when he meets a red-haired whore.'

William shot a disdainful look at the jongleur. Taillefer was a bizarre, gangling individual with pale lantern-eyes, long black hair, and a bristling moustache, the latter two of which made him unique among the Normans. It could not be denied, however, that he did seem able to predict the future – albeit only at sporadic intervals, and in mumbling so cryptic that it was more trouble than it was worth to riddle it out. William wondered how many times Taillefer's mother had dropped him on his head when he was a baby, which might account for both of these gifts.

'So,' said Turold, commandeering the conversation before Taillefer could wander off with it any further. 'What would you have me do, my lord?'

William had to think about that. He was in Brittany for very good reason, and advantage could be lost if he pulled up stakes and returned to Normandy – but then again, an opportunity like this might never come again. Harold Godwinson. . . aye, he knew the man, at least by repute. And knew as well how Harold had been entertaining himself for the past few years. His man Abelard, and Will's little brother Osbern, kept him punctiliously updated.

'Crowns and corpses and golden dragons in the sky,' Taillefer sang. 'One ran red and one was dead and one with an arrow in his eye. . .'

'Shut your beak, fool.' William turned back to Turold. 'I'll send you and Cassandra with my messengers. Force that arrogant whoreson Guy to release Harold into your custody, or I'll rip his head off and stuff it up his dead brother's arse. I'll conclude my business with Rivallon and ride up to join you.'

'Very good, my lord. Should I say it in so many words?'

'No. It's not your job to start wars, Turold.'

'Indeed, I try to avoid it, seeing as most longswords are taller than I am and even more frightening when attached to a righteously outraged man.' Turold sprang to the ground with his acrobat's dexterity. 'One other thing. If you do support Rivallon in his rebellion, there will certainly be war with Brittany.'

'Shockingly perspicacious of you, dwarf.' William smiled.

'Therefore, this is your way of arranging a welcome for our honoured guest?'

'Something like that. My grandmother was Breton, did you know?'

'I did not, Your Grace, though I suspect I grasp your meaning. Well, I'll gather the men, and we'll ride for Ponthieu within the hour. No reason to make poor Harold suffer Guy's company any longer than he must.'

Later, after the dwarf and the fool had gone, William ducked out of the tent and stood looking at the walls of Dol-de-Bretagne. It was good to be back in the field. He lived for it. As it happened, though, he was not burning or besieging this particular city; in fact, if all went to plan, he would be assisting it. Rivallon of Dol, a powerful Breton vassal, had tried the time-worn act of rebelling against his lord – who in this case was William's rival, Duke Conan of Brittany. Therefore, when Turold and Taillefer had informed him of this, William had raced off to talk alliance with Rivallon. Ever since Henry and Geoffrey died, he needed someone to loathe.

This animosity, however, was far more than military posturing. It ran far back and bone deep: Conan was the son of Alan of Brittany, William's old warden. Alan had been poisoned in 1040, ending William's brief and star-crossed sojourn in Rennes, and leaving Conan to also come into his inheritance at the age of eight. He blamed William bitterly for his father's death, not without good reason. But his regent, that old bugger Eudes de Penthièvre, had not been killed; in fact he'd made such a zealous job of it that Conan had to forcibly depose him. William, for his part, had never forgotten the contempt with which the young Conan had treated him, when he lived at the Breton court as Gervase the tanner's lad. *Get that smelly boy out of the way. . . Throw him off the tower!* And his own voice, answering. *Only if you'll do it yourself, Your Grace.*

William shook his head. Christ, that had been a long time ago. But some causes grew more just, instead of less. Mayhaps he'd finally throw Conan off, as he so richly deserved. And then. . . what could he dare to dream of, with Brittany leaderless, that imbecile strutting around in Anjou, and Maine already his? (Marguerite of Maine, a sickly child, had died a few years ago, cancelling the betrothal between her and his son Robert, but William had marched his men into the county and won a few more battles to ensure that it stayed his.) And further afield. . . that pious dolt in Aquitaine, a loathed and blasphemous tyrant in Burgundy, and a boy on the French throne. . . Well, that might be more difficult, as Baldwin was serving as his regent and William didn't want to kill his father-in-law. Matilda would certainly never forgive him.

But for the rest – it could be done. *Impossible* was not a word William gave much credence. By all rights, it was impossible that he had survived his childhood, won so many victories, risen to where he was, but he had. Time and again he had proven that he could take what he wanted. Now it was time to test that on the grandest scale of all. He'd burnt and buried that frightened child he used to be, he had no weaknesses now. And so that imagining he had shared with no one, not even his wife, lest it perish in the speaking –
William the Bastard, King of England and of France.

'You will remember me,' William said aloud. 'I don't know who you are, but you will.'

He paused a moment to be sure they had sunk in, held the weight of oath. Then he turned away, and went to take his supper.

Beaurain

Harold was awoken that morning by a matter-of-fact kick in the ribs. 'Get up.'

The impact jarred through him, rattling every bone that had, improbably, succeeded in hurting even more than yesterday. Sleep had stiffened and disoriented him; he felt thick and sick and altogether reprehensible. As Harold struggled to his knees, the thought came to him that he felt the weight of his forty-two years a little more every day, but the man who had resurrected him did not have time to spare for philosophical observations. 'Up,' he repeated. 'The lord Guy requires your presence, prisoner.'

With an incredible effort, Harold got to his feet. He gave the minion an exceedingly cold look, which did deflate him slightly. 'Of course. One moment.'

The minion sullenly retreated. Harold pulled the hay out of his hair, did his best for his wrinkled clothes, then made sure no one was watching and was quietly sick in a corner. Then he staggered to the door and was met by a pair of glowering guards.

The halls seemed inordinately long. One sprang out of another, doors blurred past, and finally he was brought to a forceful halt, turned about, and inserted through one of them, which slammed shut behind him. He leaned against it, closing his eyes to wick away the bright colours assailing them.

'Ah,' said a voice. 'My lord.'

Harold pried his reluctant eyeballs open and perused the room, which only grudgingly consented to take shape. He did, however, manage to locate the source: Guy de Ponthieu, reclining in a great carved chair, clearly fancying himself a lord of much more than one piddling countship. 'Forgive me,' he said familiarly. 'I fear I was too hasty with you yesterday. Wine?'

'Nay, my lord.' As if he'd drink anything made sight unseen.

'You look pale. Have you eaten?'

'Nay, my lord. I hit my head in the wreck and have not felt quite right since.'

'I'll have my physician look at you, if you wish.'

'Nay, my lord,' Harold said a third time, mistrusting Guy's benevolence even more than his belligerence. 'What do you require of me?'

Guy's smile still held, but fixed. 'Why have you come here?'

Harold racked his dented skull for a decent alibi. 'My lord, it is all an error. I was merely out sailing with my men, when the storm came up and wrecked us.'

The look in Guy's eye said that Harold really must take him for a truly stupendous idiot. 'How fascinating,' he said pleasantly.

All Harold wanted was to crawl into a dark hole and lie down. He couldn't take the questioning much longer, and hence his gratitude knew no bounds when there was a brisk rap on the door, and one of Guy's men entered. 'My lord, I'm sorry to interrupt, but we have visitors.'

Guy's face flashed annoyance. 'Who?'

The messenger drew a finger significantly across his throat.

'Not the bloody Bastard, surely? How did *he* hear of it?'

'Not him in person. His envoys. And he hears everything, you know that.'

Guy looked deeply displeased. 'Well, show them in, then.'

The messenger bowed and went out. Presently he returned with a remarkable company – three men wearing the lions of Normandy, a fool in motley, and a dwarf. Eschewing all but the essential preliminaries, they began to haggle at a speed which far exhausted Harold's finite French. He contented himself with watching the shadows change on the wall, until he was at last brought back to earth by a sharp voice. 'My lord?'

Harold jumped.

'Come then,' said the dwarf with a smile. 'It's been arranged. You're free of that.'

'That,' better known as Guy, wore a look as if he'd been forced to drink vinegar. Not at all sorry to escape his clutches, even if he still had only the vaguest idea of what was going on, Harold ambled over to join the Normans.

'Taillefer will see to you,' said the dwarf, nodding at the fool; he moved forward, humming gently. 'When you're better, then we'll go to meet him.'

'Him?' Harold asked, confused.

'Why, my lord William, of course.' The dwarf's smile widened. 'Duke of Normandy.'

Harold indeed began to heal under Taillefer's unorthodox care, in one of the tents the Normans had pitched outside the walls of Beaurain. The fool proved equally mercurial, sometimes showing himself to be a quiet, kind, and lonely soul, other times a capricious, hard-eyed trickster who found nothing more amusing than his rhymes about death – still, it was a relief to be shot of Guy. In addition, Harold's men returned to the shipwreck and managed to salvage some of their weapons and food, thus rendering themselves marginally less destitute.

'How do you fare, Lord Fairhair?' Taillefer asked him, several evenings hence. 'Are your troubles at an end? Do you feel on the mend?'

'Better than I was.' The fool's habit of speaking in verse had ceased to annoy him, too much, and he had walked around the entire day without once having a headache and the strong desire to vomit. 'I – will we go to meet your lord soon?'

'Soon, soon, at the turning of the moon.' Taillefer steeped some sort of evil-smelling tea and foisted it on Harold. 'Or yet on the morrow, so come, no more sorrow!'

Harold, lacking an adequate response, drank his tea and held his tongue.

Taillefer's latter prediction, as it happened, was accurate. The next morning dawned warm and clear, and the hour was deemed right that the newly repaired Earl of Wessex should make the acquaintance of the Duke of Normandy at last. As Harold mounted up on his borrowed horse, he even felt confident. Now that he was compos mentis once more, he was quite anticipating the upcoming chess-game with William. He hoped his practise with Tostig had prepared him, and the Normans had even supplied Harold with a goshawk, which made the ride more enjoyable; he hadn't had a chance to hunt for pleasure in a long time. This he could knew. This he could manage. And no matter how audacious it seemed, he was beginning to think that he could retrieve both Wulfnoth and Hakon and be on his way home (ideally with no shipwrecks this time) by the feast of St Egbert.

The designated meeting-place was a grassy meadow rimmed in trees, and Turold, Taillefer, and the Englishmen arrived first. Harold was tempted to dismount and walk a bit, but he restrained. He had no intention of being taken off-guard again.

'My lord,' he said to Turold, as they waited. 'What does the Duke look like?'

Turold gave him a strange look. 'First, I'm no one's lord. Second, you'll know Duke William when you see him.'

Harold found this answer both ominous and unsatisfying, but said nothing. Soon enough the ground began to tremble, and the vivid crimson banners of Normandy unfurled on the horizon. Beneath them was a host of considerable size, moving closer at speed, and Harold inspected it carefully. *Lion,* Edward had said, and sounded very convinced. Aye, well, but –

Oh.

He rode at the front of the queue, with the easy, unconscious effortlessness of a man who'd spent his life astride. His mount was a barrel-chested grey stallion, a beast wholly suited to its master. William of Normandy was bloody *big,* not an observation Harold – himself a tall and strong man – made lightly, and his close-cropped head flashed golden in the sun. A longbow was slung on his back, a longsword at his side. He was an impressive figure even from a distance, but it was when he reined in and cantered close enough for conversation that Harold finally understood. Years of war and hardscrabble living had tarnished some of William's lustre, but furnished the assurance of an experienced commander who feared nothing under the sun. Yet it was the eyes Harold watched. You could tell much about a man from his eyes, and the Duke was no different. It was just *what* he could tell that was disquieting. The icy grey gaze held cunning, ruthlessness, ambition and arrogance at once, though the lips were offering a smile that could nominally be termed friendly. 'Welcome, Harold Godwinson,' they said.

'My lord.' Harold gave a courteous nod.

No. Edward hadn't exaggerated a thing.

'I am sorry your visit has been so tumultuous,' William went on. 'Guy de Ponthieu's no friend to me either, and rest assured that if you'd come to land where you were supposed to, my lady wife would have made you a much better welcome. Have my servants done well by you in the meanwhile?'

'Very well, I thank you.'

'Good.' William smiled. It still didn't touch his eyes. 'So. Why are you come?'

'To offer you the regards of King Edward,' said Harold, deciding on the spot that he did not want to be caught out in a lie by this man. 'And see if there is some term we can arrange that would allow the return of my brother and my nephew.'

'Mayhaps there is. We will have to discuss it. But certainly not in the middle of the sward like a pair of pagans. We will ride to Caen together, my lord, and then see what can be done.'

White always moves first. The opening gambit was struck, the knights in motion. Harold offered a smile in return. 'Lead the way,' he said. 'It would be my pleasure.'

CHAPTER ELEVEN

Caen, Normandy
April 1064

I T WAS A CONSIDERABLE distance from Beaurain to Caen, not a ride that could be made in a day, and Harold spent most of the three that it took attempting to work out what William was going to try to extort from him. Their combat was subtle, mental, delicate, feeling each other out, advancing and retreating, parrying and prodding. Harold found that his lack of complete fluency in French worked to his advantage, as he could say one thing and later claim that he had meant another. They both jested and jousted, never elsewise than courteous and lordly.

They reached Caen on the morning of the fourth day, as the bells were calling Terce, and the gates flung wide to welcome them as they rode up the hill to William's great castle. Pennons fluttered, chains creaked, and they proceeded into an eager crowd. Harold's boots were touched by small inquisitive hands, as the children in the courtyard tried to guess what to make of him. He smiled at them, missing his own. God only knew when he'd see them again.

'My lord!' A thin, handsome, golden-haired stripling, who must be William's own son, came running. 'You're back!'

'Indeed.' William dismounted and clapped the stripling on the back. His stern, harsh face had changed, wreathed in the first true smile Harold had glimpsed. 'By God, lad, it's good to see you.'

The boy glowed with excitement, and Harold dismounted as well. 'You must be Robert,' he said, smiling at the lad in turn. 'You look just like your father.'

There was a horribly awkward moment, and then the boy's expression changed, shut off. 'No, no, I'm not. I'm the trueborn son of Ranulf Peverel. His Grace has been kind enough to take a hand in my upbringing, nay more.'

That surprised Harold immensely, and he felt a twinge of pity. *The idea of being a bastard must be more frightening than anything else, if the tales of William's childhood are true. How many men want to kill you for something entirely out of your hands.* He looked at them again, studying the profiles, the golden hair. *There must be talk. No doubt that's why he's so sensitive. But God almighty, Harold, when will you stop leaping to conclusions? You'll put your back out.*

'Forgive me,' he said, to cover the gaffe. 'Your name, lad?'

'Will Peverel, my lord.' The stripling bowed, cheeks still flushed. 'Your servant.'

'And yours.' Best to get him inside – and then he'd mistake the Duchess Matilda for a serving-maid, if his record held up. But as Harold trailed toward the castle behind his host, it did not escape his attention that William himself had not denied it.

This thought receded, however, as Harold entered the high hall. He couldn't help looking around; it wasn't a style he'd seen much of in England, though he recognised elements from Edward's castle and almost-completed great church. He cast a particular eye at the lion banners hung from the rafters. *Aye, I am in his den now.*

'My lord?' a servant called.

Harold, ashamed to be caught dawdling, quickened his pace. He reached the sun-drenched dais at the far end, on which was set a magnificent chair of mahogany, also carved in the shape of a lion. At least so far as Harold could tell, since William had already taken the liberty of occupying it. 'My family, my lord.'

Harold turned to see a small woman, black-haired and beautiful, with three solemn-faced children to each side of her; a nursemaid held the baby. He bowed deeply and kissed her offered hand. 'Duchess Matilda? I am honoured, my lady.'

'Aye,' she said graciously. Good, at least he'd got that one.

'My eldest son, Sh – Robert.' William indicated a short, chubby boy with black curls, who looked about eleven. 'The second eldest, Richard.' This one was a tall, graceful, golden lad, perhaps a year younger. 'My eldest daughter Cecilia, nine.' She looked enough like Richard that they could be twins, and they stood close together, holding hands. 'And my second daughter Adeliza, eight.'

This child was also golden, and Harold surreptitiously glanced between her and her siblings, then back at Will Peverel. But then, it would be impossible to say. . .

'And this,' said William, with distinct approval, 'is my small William. We call him Rufus, though.'

Little Rufus was a stocky, glowering child of six or so, with spiky yellow hair, smudges on both cheeks, and fists pugnaciously clenched. 'Who are y-you?'

'That's an important visitor, lad,' William told him. 'And I've told you not to stammer, it makes you sound a fool.'

Harold gave Rufus a kindly smile. 'He sounds quite well.'

'Aye?' William paid no attention. 'Well, that's my sweet Constance. She's two.'

Constance was her mother to the life: tiny, dark-haired and dark-eyed, with a quick, darting energy like a robin on a branch. She was also clearly quite the coquette already, and gave Harold a big smile and curtsy. Enchanted, he grinned back at her, thinking that he would be most content if William would merely let him roll around in the rushes and play with the children. Not, of course, that this was remotely likely.

'And that's the baby, Agatha,' William finished up, pointing to the bundle in the nursemaid's arms. 'Born just past Candlemas. So, my lord, what do you think?'

'They are beautiful. You must be very proud.'

William grunted. 'They serve their purpose. Now, my lord, say I was to ask you which of the girls you'd like to marry. What would your answer be?'

Harold blinked, revolted. The eldest of them was not yet ten! Did William truly think he would stand here and look at his young daughters as potential brides? Wherever this was leading, Harold had lost his taste to play along. 'I beg your pardon?'

'It's merely a rhetorical question. Answer it.' William smiled.

'Adeliza,' said Harold, improvising.

The child – charming, lovely, innocent – was far too young to understand the implications. In fact, she looked downright hopeful; she was at the age when little girls dreamed of weddings. 'Really, Papa?' she asked tremulously. 'May I?'

'We'll discuss it later.' William rose to his feet. To Harold he said, 'I've ordered a great feast for your welcome, this evening. In the meantime, there's someone waiting to see you.'

For a moment, Harold could not fathom who he could be talking about. Then a door opened at the side of the hall, and a tall, reed-thin young man, pale hair cut close in the Norman fashion, stumbled through, looking confused. He looked around, spotted William, and made a hasty bow. 'My lord? Are they. . .?'

'You've a visitor, lad,' William said lazily.

Harold stared at the newcomer, teetering on the brink of recognition – and then it happened. The memory of the boy he'd last seen twelve years ago shifted and stretched, settling into the lines of this familiar stranger. He stepped forward, a lump in his throat. 'Wulfnoth?'

His little brother spun around so fast he almost fell over, provoking giggles from the children. Neither Godwinson cared. Wulfnoth raced across the floor and hit Harold like a boulder, and Harold caught him and held him close for all he was worth, Wulfnoth's stubble rasping against his cheek. They rocked on the spot, Wulfnoth weeping silently, Harold none too steady himself, as he patted Wulfnoth's back.

'Is it really you?' Wulfnoth pulled away at last to grasp Harold's shoulders, staring into his face. 'Christ! You look so old!'

'I thought you wouldn't remember me. You've been captive half your life now.'

'It's not so bad,' Wulfnoth said bravely. 'But I want to go home. Oh God, I do.'

'I'll do anything I must to get you there,' Harold promised. 'Even fighting a war.'

Wulfnoth stiffened, looking over his shoulder, and Harold followed his gaze in puzzlement. It was William, attending to some bauble Rufus was showing him, but he didn't appear to have heard them. Besides, they were speaking in Saxon.

'What?' Harold asked.

'Nothing.' Wulfnoth bit his lip, then smiled. 'My lord was so kind as to promise that I might spend the afternoon with you, and I don't want to waste any of it. Come on!'

The rest of the day was like something from a dream. Harold and Wulfnoth were allowed to take horses from the ducal stables and venture out around Caen. Wulfnoth's French, unsurprisingly, was much better than Harold's, and there were a number of people – young women, mostly – who greeted him warmly. He and Harold were talking as fast as possible, trying desperately to cram twelve missed years into one afternoon. It wasn't enough time, couldn't be enough, and as they finally had to turn back to the castle, they finally fell silent.

'Are you treated well?' Harold asked at last.

'Well enough. I certainly don't get to do this every day.' Wulfnoth grinned wanly. 'I don't know. I'm half-French but still English forced to be French. I'm not quite here or there.'

Harold reached out to clasp his brother's hand. 'Courage,' he said. 'I'll settle it.'

Wulfnoth looked at him with trusting eyes, and Harold remembered the tousle-haired scamp he had been, always following him around. *He wanted to be me. And now I must let him have the chance to be himself.*

The feast that night was as splendid as advertised. Harold was very hungry after his misadventures, and this was the first time he'd had the chance, or desire, to eat a good meal since arriving in Normandy. So he did so, careful to be served only from dishes that William was. As with Edwin, he didn't *think* it likely, but still. . .

'How do you find our hospitality, my lord?' Matilda asked, after the swan had arrived.

Harold swallowed his mouthful. 'Scrupulous,' he assured her. Then, lowering his voice and leaning closer, he added, 'I am sorry about that. . . scene earlier. I had no idea William meant that. Truly, my lady, I have no designs on your daughters.'

Something that might have been relief showed in her dark eyes, but was gone too fast to be sure. Besides at that moment, William's powerful voice cut through the din, and the hall went quiet. He stood at the centre of the high table, tall and striking, the candlelight shimmering in his hair. 'The moment has come,' he said, 'to welcome Harold Godwinson, Earl of Wessex, to my board and to my family. For he has done me the great honour of agreeing to marry – when she comes of age – my daughter Adeliza.'

Harold's jaw dropped. His first impulse was to surge to his feet, explain that this was a terrible mistake, that he was already married, that it was quite impossible for a dozen different reasons. But then those freezing eyes caught his, then performed the briefest sideways flick toward Wulfnoth and Hakon – making their meaning abundantly clear without a word spoken.

Harold experienced that horrible feeling he'd had all too often: staring down a long dark tunnel, the ground falling away. *Say it. Say whatever you must to get the lads and get out of here.* And so he managed to rise to his feet, bumble through a speech in French, of how the Duke honoured him and the girl would make a fine wife. Adeliza, sitting with her siblings, clapped and giggled in starry-eyed delight. *Lies, child. It is a court and thrall of lies.*

'Very good,' said William, when he had finished. 'And to celebrate our new alliance, you will help me fight a war.'

Harold should have been on his guard for anything, but that still caught him badly off it. 'What?' he demanded of his prospective good-father. *Bloody Christ, he's younger than me.*

'Conan of Brittany and I are in a state of rather deteriorated relations,' William said pleasantly. 'I shall have to launch a campaign against him this summer, and it will serve as a mark of your pledge if you came and fought beside me.'

Harold was doing his best to keep up with the revelations, each of which he liked less, but this one might actually be a blessing in disguise. Get to know William. Find out how he fought, how he thought. His skills, his methods, his plans. At the least, it would give Harold a chance to take something from this damnable trip, potentially even what he'd come for.

'Your Grace,' he said, after a moment. 'Of course.'

William smiled. 'You honour me. My lord.'

Avranches, Normandy
June 1064

The sun was spilling down the horizon, tumbling through the clouds and dyeing the ocean rose and red and gold. High on this promontory, Harold imagined he could see forever. The river Couesnon meandered through the lowlands and the green country rolled, and the beautiful, remote island monastery of Mont-Saint-Michel lay in the distance. It occupied a spit of land just a few hundred yards offshore; for most of the day, it was surrounded by bare sand, but in the morning the tide went all the way out and in the evening it came racing back in.

The other salient feature of Mont-Saint-Michel, aside from the fact that its influence far exceeded its size, was that it was located almost exactly between Normandy and Brittany – which meant it was hotly contested as to who had the right to exercise said influence. With William and Conan at loggerheads again, the point had become more pressing than ever, and William was intending to pay a call on the abbot to remind him of the correct answer. They would then begin the offensive into Brittany, in particular Dol-de-Bretagne, where Conan (having hastily dispossessed his rebel vassal Rivallon of the city) was mustering an army.

Harold returned his attention to the sky. It was almost midsummer, and the light lingered far into the evening; it was past the usual time for Compline, and the sun was only setting now. It cast brilliant over the glassy sea, silhouetting the monastery on the horizon.

'I always think it will hiss when it touches the ocean,' said a voice behind him. 'Like a great candle snuffed out. But it never does. It merely falls away. As if it could breathe water, as if it could transform who it was, before it rises again. Kill itself and make itself stronger, until perhaps it could not stop now even if it wanted.'

Harold recognised the voice, yet was astonished that its owner should be expressing such poetic sentiments. A faint unease went down his back at the fact that he hadn't heard him approach, but he offered a friendly smile. 'My lord. It is a lovely sight.'

'Isn't it.' William was wearing a leather cuirass over his tunic, but his sleeves were rolled up and he had set aside his heavy mail. Indeed, he looked almost relaxed. 'I thought I'd best see what was occupying you so intently out here.'

Harold let him be. Despite all the excellent reasons which advocated the contrary, the two of them had formed a – well, *friendship* was too optimistic a word, but an understanding. They respected each other's formidable gifts, skill at warfare and shared ambition, and both of them had a habit of slipping in sly wit – no doubt to trip each other up, Harold thought, but it surprised him how much they had in common. To a point.

William said nothing until well after the last light had faded, and the sky was a deepening blue. Then he turned to Harold and asked, 'Do you love your brother?'

Harold decided to tread cautiously. He was already wondering just what price he was going to have to pay for Wulfnoth, and if he *could* afford it. But surely William knew that –

Hold on. Something caught at him, twisted him back around. It had managed not to occur to him until just that moment that William had put the question in *Saxon*.

'My lord,' said Harold, extremely flustered. 'I did not – '

William shrugged. 'Do you?'

Harold didn't respond at once; he was mentally reeling through all his previous conversations with his men, trying to work out if he'd said anything particularly illuminating or incriminating. He was, yet again, badly thrown, and disliked the feeling immensely. If he wasn't careful, he would put himself out of this game – and much more – at humiliating speed.

Answering in Saxon, he said, 'My lord, I care for my brother and my nephew very much, and would do them all the duty owed to kin. Within limits.' *I'll do anything I must to get you there. Even fighting a war.* Another promise it seemed he would not be able to keep. But God almighty, what would it cost him if he did?

William was still looking at the horizon. 'Commendable.'

Harold shrugged. 'You speak Saxon well, I am surprised. It's not a language I think you'd need in Normandy.'

'Well,' said William. The rising moon caught on his teeth as he smiled. 'Perhaps it's not Normandy I think to need it in. Come, supper's still hot.'

And on that thoroughly disconcerting note, he went.

Morning came with depressing promptitude, and Harold struggled out from beneath his blanket and assisted in the preparations for departure. With these completed, the company rode across the flatlands to the estuary, to where Mont-Saint-Michel rose great and stark before them, still clothed in shreds of morning mist. Part of William's haste was due to the fact that he wanted to reach the island before the morning tides went out – while it was possible to walk across the sands, it was ill-advised. He hoped they could conclude their mission in a few hours, get back just ahead of the tide, and be on their way to Brittany that day.

It was quickly decided that William, Harold, and a few of the men would try to accomplish this, and they pushed a longboat into the bay. It was such a short distance that they didn't bother running up the sail, and all eight pulled an oar. With seven strong Norman backs and one strong English one, they bumped against the pier in no time flat.

There were a few stone huts on the lower flanks of the island, built for pilgrims, but the expeditionary party took the narrow, precipitously steep dirt path up to the abbey. At the top, William banged on the door and terrified the novice on night-watch into fetching the abbot straightaway. While he went to haggle, the rest of the men were invited to hear Prime.

Harold stood in the back of the cool sanctuary, head bowed. It was obscurely comforting; church was church anywhere. The monks sang the same Latin, moved through the same motions, offered the same devotions. Mayhaps God was even here as well. *I will not break my troth. Let me find favour in your sight, Lord. Let me do what is right. Let me get home.*

A great silence pressed in. Something Edward had once said floated into his head. *Prayers are always answered, aye,* the king had remarked. *But almost never in the way we expect.*

When the service was through, Harold went out onto the abbey promenade. It boasted a stupendous view in all directions – the rivers, the green lowlands, the broad pane of the ocean and the rocky outcrops. However, with the sun well up, he saw that the receding of the tide was similarly advanced. *William had best hurry.*

Noticing the same thing, the Normans began to confer, and one of them was dispatched to inform William, who was certainly taking his time. Whatever the delay, he was in a foul temper indeed by the time he emerged, trailed by several monks carrying sacks. 'Get that down to the quay, and be quick about it. You all! Let's go!'

Harold and the men snapped to attention and followed him off at once. By the time the party arrived at the longboat, however, there was no water on which to float it. The sediments of sand stretched before them, carved with deep runnels and shallow puddles. The tide, for its part, had guiltily retreated all the way to the horizon, and Harold learned quite a number of French obscenities as William took stock of the situation.

'Bugger it,' William announced at last. 'It can't be more than a hundred yards or so, we'll take our chances. Spread out, test your weight. Now come.'

With that, he hoisted a sack over his shoulder, almost lifting the slight monk attached to it off his feet. The Normans appropriated the rest, and then, following their fearless leader, jumped off the quay and onto the sand. Once or twice Harold had the stomach-lurching sensation that his footing was going to vanish entirely, but he was a good hunter and knew how to go quick and light. He and William leaped almost in unison, skirting pools and looking for solid ledges. Slowly, it was becoming a race to see who proved worthier, who reached the far side first –

'My lord! Hel – *aughh!*'

Both William and Harold swung about madly, just in time to clap eyes on a horrifying sight. Two of the men had stepped directly on a vein of quicksand, and were already submerged up to their waists, groping furiously. Another moment, and –

Harold and William moved at once, but Harold was faster. He sprang down, landed knee-deep in a tidepool but didn't care, racing over the treacherous sands toward the flailing Normans. Skidding to a halt, he untied his belt and flung it at them; one of them managed to catch it, and seized his friend's collar with the other hand. Harold set his feet and hauled with all his strength until he got the men close enough to grab their wrists. Almost there, almost –

At that moment the sands shifted again, and Harold nearly lost his balance. The two men started to slide back, an inexorable counterweight – and then, another set of incredibly strong arms seized Harold from behind and gave them a hard jerk onto firmer ground. Gasping, grimy, and badly shaken, the two men sat down, wheezing .'Many thanks, m'lord. I'm indebted.'

'It was nothing.'

'Quite some nothing,' said William, composed as ever. 'Now, I suggest we get moving.'

Harold gave the men another hand up, and they set off once more. Soon they scrambled up the rocks, were given a hero's welcome by those who'd witnessed the whole thing from shore, and gratefully accepted William's commandment of a restorative ration of wine apiece. With the sacks slung on the pack-horses and the wind at their backs, they put Mont-Saint-Michel behind them, forded the Couesnon, and were on their way into Brittany by early afternoon.

Prior alliances with Rivallon proved soluble. William burned Dol-de-Bretagne anyway.

To be sure, he rather regretted it, as he was galloping around in the dust and smoke and bawling orders at his men. But it was only a flicker, then gone on the wind, as he wheeled his horse about and got a few more shots off. He was down to scavenged arrows, and as he turned to look for more, he caught a glimpse of Harold. The Saxon was riding hard and fighting well, but it was plain that he was unused to doing both at the same time; the English would ride to the field, but dismount for the battle. But Harold had not allowed the unfamiliar circumstances to daunt his courage, or used it as an excuse to hold back from a clash that he had no stake in. The same way he'd unhesitatingly gone after those men. *My men. Maybe he really is as noble as everyone bloody says.* For the briefest moment, William felt remorse for trapping him into this.

But not much. Not for long. And then it was gone even faster than his feelings for Dol itself, and there was nothing left to do but fight.

By evenfall smoke was drifting skyward from the bruised city, and isolated fires still smouldered in broken beams. The gate and half the wall was staved in, and dead men sprawled where they'd fallen. The groan of the wounded not yet fortunate enough to join them echoed the evening call of the birds. Otherwise, it was silent. But to William, it sounded like victory.

At that moment, a roan courser plodded up beside him and its rider pulled off his helmet, letting his sweaty hair spill down over his shoulders. 'The reports aren't promising,' Harold said. 'You've won the city, but it appears Conan has escaped – indeed, was gone even before we arrived. He left Dol dangling as bait, while he concentrated his efforts elsewhere.'

William's mouth tightened. 'That explains why they all broke so badly at the end. Though they gave us a fair fight for a decoy force,' he added, grudgingly.

'Aye.' Harold unhooked a waterskin and took a long slug, then tossed it to William, who applied himself in turn. As they drank, a crow swooped overhead, then another and another. They landed, and congregated on the nearest dead man.

Harold tensed. Then he dismounted, picked up a rock, and flung it at the scavengers. It exploded into their midst, setting off a storm of croaking and feathers. The target of their depredations was in no state to be grateful for the intervention, but Harold went to retrieve the stone. He knelt by the dead man, whispering a prayer that William's Saxon wasn't quite adroit enough to capture. Then he reached out and closed the staring eyes.

William, observing curiously, said, 'He was a Breton.'

Harold drew the dead man's cloak over his face. 'Then he died in defence of his homeland. He must have been honoured.'

'That's a queer sentiment.' William shrugged. 'Dying for your country is a good bit less useful than living for it.'

'If you say so.' Harold rose to his feet. 'It'll be dark soon. Come.'

William, wondering how the man thought to give him orders – and, even more perplexingly, why he was obeying – nonetheless put his heels in the grey, and followed.

From Dol they struck south to Rennes, hot on Conan's heels. Until then, the campaign had had almost an air of light-heartedness, but the narrow shave at Mont-Saint-Michel and the assault of Dol had hardened it somehow, made it in deadly earnest. They rode for hours at a time, periodically skirmishing with the Bretons, and it never failed to amaze Harold how quickly William could have his men at arms and closing ranks. Despite the frequency of the Breton ambushes, the Normans had only lost two of their number.

They fight for him. He is the lodestone that guides them all. William possessed an almost supernatural ability to steer a battle, sensing when a flank was on the verge of breaking or if the archers hadn't sufficiently seasoned it, if someone was going to charge him, and if they were going to employ a lance, sword, hatchet, morningstar, or poniard while doing so. Harold had never seen a more toweringly competent commander – or a more single-minded one. Everything was immaterial to William but the victory.

Break him, and you will break the Norman threat. That cold, analytical voice was always in the back of Harold's head, accumulating individual moments – the way William always rode in the thick of battle, never taking a safer position, or the way he would dip up his stew at supper, the firelight stark on his face. Yet at the same time, he did not care for the thought of their being enemies. Partly for having seen his prowess, and partly not. He admired the man, deeply in fact, but could not say that he liked him; William's callous and oftentimes indiscriminate brutality tasted sour to a nature that tended to hope the best of people. Yet occasionally he would let slip some remark that made Harold curious as to how deeply suffering and loss had left their mark on him. Who had he been, in those long dark years before he was the highest and the strongest?

Personal considerations did not and would not constrain Harold; he did not feel as if William's defeat would be undeserved. But there was nothing to be done for it now.

And so the engagement dragged on. A brief and messy affair at Rennes led to further decimation of the embattled Bretons, but this time they managed to pay back their own in kind, and William lost half a hundred men. He never dwelt on losses, as long as the larger victory was secured, but he was strangely melancholic that night. It was the first time he'd been back to Rennes in twenty-four years, and it felt too soon. This was where, after being soundly thrashed every time it lifted its head, his childhood had gracefully taken the hint and expired.

'Are you well?' Harold asked, startling him.

William shook himself. 'Fine.'

Harold nodded an acquiescence and moved off. Pausing at the far side of the fire, he said something to one of the men, who laughed and nodded.

William watched him narrowly. It was hard to pin down just what he thought of his ally (at least, so he was for the time being). Almost to his embarrassment, he found himself liking him – Harold was kind, brave, and funny. But for all that, William could not say that he admired him. *He chooses to do things that he himself does not want, until by now he's convinced of his own delusions. He's not his own man, he's a bloody mouthpiece.* But then he wondered if Harold was not in fact far more dangerous than he thought. He *believed* it. That was the problem.

Displaying an art for extricating himself from tight corners that a weasel would have envied, Conan managed to fortify Rennes and escape. So William and Harold duly chased him back up the way they'd just come, except this time Conan was making for the village of Dinan. But despite a good run, he was now out of options, trickery, and hideouts, and everyone concerned knew it was there he'd have to make his final stand.

'I don't think even bloody Gruffydd was this much trouble,' Harold said as they were crossing the river Rance, stripped to their braies in the trenchant heat.

'There's the Bretons for you, my lord.' William wiped his face. 'But they are descended from the Celts, so it's no wonder they're a passel of pagan bastards.'

Harold laughed. 'Well then. They and the Welsh will be sure to keep each other rousing company in hell.'

With the rest of us bastards? William thought, but did not ask.

Dinan, Brittany
August 1064

Great towers of cloud roiled in the sky, crackling prongs of lightning. Thunder rumbled sullenly, and a dark stain of rain swept in over the river. Even a downpour, however, could make it no worse; the air was so hot and thick that to breathe it felt like drowning, and made the wearing of heavy armour an unmitigated misery. William would have taken off his own, dared the Bretons to find a mark from this far, but they'd recently gotten lucky. Damp fingers of salt slithered down his back. He kicked his grey around, looked for the weak spot in their line – and found it, where the roan's rider had just seen the same thing.

The two of them, galloping full tilt, fell into perfect synchrony, the world whirring away behind them. The same shout burst from their throats. There was a moment when William fancied he could see the whites of the Bretons' eyes – in that final instant before impact, when they knew the candle of consciousness might snuff out forever. And then he and Harold, doing their best to make this prediction come true, slammed into them like an avalanche.

Chaos reigned. Men and horses screamed. Lances shattered and arrows zinged. William could smell smoke, hear the shouts. But there was none of that, nothing else important but that he was alive and they were not, they were too slow and he was strong, strong enough, the strongest. His sword melted to his hand, steel and bone together. And so he detached from everything, until time itself was gone, and all there was, was peace.

Conan surrendered in late afternoon, just as the thunderstorm was passing. He put the keys to the gates of Dinan on a lance and shoved it through the window of the tower, so William helped himself, unlocked them, and marched in to demand an accord. In the meantime, he left the Normans free to terrorise, just to be sure the lesson had been piquantly learned.

Harold kept well clear, remaining outside the walls to supervise the aftermath. The crows were gathering again, but he couldn't stand to sit by and watch. So he went and chased them off again, watched them scatter into the dusk. Now they'd just –

By his feet, a hoarse voice whispered, 'Water.'

Harold started. He looked down.

It was another young Breton, speaking French. He could not have been more than eighteen, and his eyes showed shocked and huge in his bloody face. He was missing his ear, most of his right arm, and the sweet stink of death was already rising from him. He fumbled at Harold's boot. 'Messire. Water. Please.'

Harold could feel the weight of the waterskin on his back. Could see as well the ruin of the young man's stomach, and knew it would make it worse. Away toward the west the thunderheads had faded, revealing a deep, beautiful crimson.

'Water,' the young man rasped. 'Please. Please, messire.'

Harold knelt next to him. 'Enough,' he said in Breton, one of the half-dozen words of the language he had picked up. 'Quiet.'

The young man's eyes widened. 'Water?' He reached up with his mangled right arm, gave a gasp of pain, and fell back.

'Aye.' Harold gently put his hand over the young man's face. 'Rest. Quiet.'

'Water?' the thin voice whispered.

'Aye.' Harold drew his misericordia from its sheath in his boot, and found the faint, skipping pulse with his fingers, brushing the stubble of the beard the young man would never grow. It was just beneath it, in the hollow of the throat, where he socketed the blade hard and fast, with all his weight behind it. The young man made a brief, choked sound, and went limp.

Harold drew the blade out. 'I know you wanted water,' he said quietly. 'I'm sorry.'

For his valorous conduct in the campaign, Harold was deemed fit to receive a knighthood, and of course, nothing should do but that William bestow it himself. So the ceremony was solemnly held on the shattered bones of Dinan. With the sunshine in Harold's hair and his shoulders held proud, there was not a man who did not own that he cut a marvellous figure. He knelt before William, and was vastly surprised when the duke conferred on him the treasured sword-belt that he had thought was lost forever down Guy of Ponthieu's rat-hole.

'My lord. . .' said Harold, blinking hard. 'I cannot – '

'I reward those who do me good service.' William's hand cupped Harold's chin, tilting his face back. It was the gesture a man might make to a lowborn knight or an unblooded stripling, and Harold found himself instinctively resisting it. But William held fast, one thumb stroking Harold's cheek. 'I have given your honour back, Earl of Wessex,' he said. 'Remember that.'

There is no chance I will forget, Duke of Normandy. Mark me on that. 'Of course.'

William smiled, and raised Harold to his feet. They exchanged the kiss of peace, and the Normans let loose a proper shout. Though Harold understood only half of what they were calling him, he knew it was felicitous, and was glad of it. He had been trying hard to win them; making men love him was something he could do with little effort. Who knew if one might later check his blow, or hesitate half an instant. Harold was well acquainted with the small threads of fate that might swing a battle one way – or the other. *And what does it say, that I am already thinking of a battle?*

He cast a look at William's back. *Well. I've come. We've taken measure of each other. We respect and even rather like each other, and understand each other perhaps far too well. And now we must prepare to rip each other apart.*

'My lord,' said Harold on the ride back to Normandy. 'May we conclude our bargain?'

'Indeed.' William's face looked almost guileless – clear, warm, generous, dazzling. He could get like that when he was in a high mood, and he was in a particularly high one at the moment. The campaign had now assumed its rightful place as a summer amusement, nay more, but Harold thought of the dead man, whispering in the twilight. *Water. Please, messire. Please.*

'I beg your pardon?' he said, having missed William's last remark.

'But of course we must.' William smiled. 'I have sent a letter informing the great men of the duchy to assemble at Bonneville, near Rouen – that is where we are making. There you will publicly acknowledge your intention to marry my daughter, and we will finalise the matter with your brother and nephew. After that, you will be free to return to England with my blessing. I will give you a ship, treasures, provisions, to replace everything lost in the wreck.'

He's as hard as stone, but he does have a ruthlessly fair streak. Ruthless being the operative word. If that was all, Harold could cross his fingers and do it. Adeliza wouldn't be of marriageable age for half a decade at least, and a great deal could happen in that time. Getting custody of Wulfnoth and Hakon and buggering out of here was all that mattered, and it was in reach. For the first time since setting foot in the lion's den, Harold felt downright hopeful.

'Well,' he said, with an answering smile. 'It's a deal. I'll race you to that tree.'

'Done,' William replied promptly, crouched low to the grey's neck, and proceeded to leave Harold in a cloud of dust.

It didn't matter. It wasn't this race he meant to win.

CHAPTER TWELVE

Bonneville, Normandy
September 1064

EXCLUDING TWO OR THREE sulking barons, almost all the flower of Normandy had indeed assembled in Bonneville, there on that sunny Feast of the Exaltation. The ceremony was held outdoors, on a great dais, and William held pride of place. His long tunic was blue and gilt, his belt done in bronze knotwork, and the gold of his hair set off the silver of the ducal circlet. He appeared to be unarmed, but Harold knew there was a dagger up his sleeve.

Something I would be wise to keep in mind. Harold ascended the steps and knelt. He could see Wulfnoth and Hakon in the crowd, and it gave him heart. *Almost there.*

He held out his hands, but William did not take them, as a lord customarily would when accepting a vassal's oath. Instead he gave a nod, and a dwarf and a jongleur – the same improbable pair who had rescued Harold – moved forward, each carrying a box covered with an ornate cloth. It was testament to the solemnity of the occasion that nobody snickered. Turold and Taillefer put the boxes down, bowed, and retreated.

What's this about? Harold regarded the setup with both interest and caution, wondering if William wanted him to handle a serpent or something else dramatic. He half-expected the boxes to start hissing, and was relieved when they did not.

'My lord of Wessex,' William said. 'Place your hands on those, if you please.'

Harold did so. The crowd's murmuring went quiet.

'Now. Do you swear to marry my daughter Adeliza at her maturity?'

'I do, my lord,' Harold answered, priding himself on how natural the lie sounded.

'Do you swear to maintain our alliance and continue as my liegeman?'

For a time. 'I do, my lord.'

'And so do you, Harold fitz Godwin, swear to stand by the promise my cousin Edward made to me, and do all in your power to secure my accession to the throne of England upon his death? And in so doing, deliver to me as your pledge Dover Castle and all its strength and men?'

What? Bloody what?! Harold felt as if he'd been hit in the stomach. *What am I supposed to do?* Say no? With a pack of Normans breathing down his neck?

Vying for time, Harold looked up, and caught sight of young Will Peverel. The boy's face was shining with devotion; there was something damnably familiar about him, but Harold couldn't work out what. He looked to the other side, to the tall, black-haired clergyman William had introduced as his half-brother: Odo, Bishop of Bayeux, who had been lobbying vigorously to have the oath taken at his cathedral. Robert, Count of Mortain, William's other half-brother. His leading barons – William fitz Osbern, William de Warenne, Walter Giffard, Roger Bigod, Richard fitz Gilbert, Robert de Eu, Roger de Montgomery, all the rest. No help. *If this is the serpent's bite, I can manage it. Later, I can. Once I'm gone.*

'I do, my lord.'

William smiled. 'Everyone has heard you swear, and we all know you for a man of faith and character, so we retain every confidence that it will be kept. Yet even the greatest of us can be tempted into transgression. So I will require two conditions.'

'Name them, my lord,' said Harold tightly.

'First, I will keep your brother Wulfnoth in my care until such time as I am on the throne. Then both he and your nephew Hakon will be released to you, but not before.'

To hell with being *hit*; he felt as if he had been *stabbed*. The one thing he needed to do, the one thing he'd risked everything for, gone on that bloody wild goose chase –

'And the other,' William concluded, 'has already been accomplished. Turold. Taillefer.'

The odd pair moved forward again. Harold wanted to shout, leap up and run them through – find some, any way to forestall the terrible scene that was suddenly unfolding – but he was paralysed.

The dwarf and the fool whisked aside the cloths covering the boxes. And so it transpired that in fact they were not boxes – or Gospel-books, as had been Harold's other guess. Nor psalters nor jewels nor charters nor chests. They were reliquaries.

Turold opened one of them, revealing a few browned bones and a scrap of cloth. 'My lord. You have sworn your oath on the holy relics of one of Christ's own beloved saints. It has been made therefore doubly binding, in the sight of God and man. Breaking it condemns you to the deepest levels of blasphemy and anathema. Do you understand?'

Aye. A knife up his sleeve. I knew that. I bloody knew *that.* It was his imagination that a cloud had come over the sun, that the world had gone silent, that he could barely breathe and all he could see was that triumphant smile on William's face. But it did not matter.

Oh, Harold thought, sick to his stomach. *That was the serpent's bite.*

The rest was a blur. Harold barely remembered being packed off in ostensible honour, forced to part from the brother he'd just begun to know again, escorted to the coast and set aboard a new ship. About the only thing he *did* remember was fearing to speak, lest he reveal the storm of betrayal raging in his heart.

William had executed the entire thing in a masterpiece of subtlety. The closest he'd ever come was that cryptic allusion in Avranches, about it not being Normandy that he needed Saxon for. It was all congruent with Harold's admiration for the man's incredible gifts, but it poisoned his mild dislike to something teetering on the brink of hatred. How could he have been so *stupid?* He had been so focused on two things – retrieving his relations and surviving the process – that he walked obligingly into every snare it pleased William's devious mind to set. And another reason, just as bitter, was that somewhere, subconsciously, he had assumed that Edward fundamentally overestimated William's danger. To a man like Edward himself – sensitive and intelligent, but withdrawn, cautious, and pacifist – yes, the duke was a threat. But not, Harold had thought, to a man like him. One who was better, stronger, more courageous, more skilled. And in a few moments on a sunny autumn day, that delusion had shattered into a thousand pieces.

As they rode to London, Harold began to rationalise. Surely God would understand that the oath had been extracted by trickery and false pretences, under coercion and with no possibility of refusal – if he was fond of his limbs, that was. Surely, then, it was not him but William who was damned, for using the sacred relics of a saint to such lying and loathsome purpose. Aye, and likely they weren't relics at all, but some mangy bones he'd dug up somewhere and successfully used to give Harold the scare of his life.

With these and other arguments, Harold (mostly) succeeded in salting away the sickening end to the venture, and decided to focus on the positive – he had, after all, gotten out alive. And next time, he would not be so unprepared. Next time, he swore, as he strode to the throne room and vowed William would never get within sniffing distance, he would be ready. *Mark me on that.*

'It is good to see you, my lord.' Edward smiled. 'Pardon me if I do not rise, I have been informed that I may be taken faint if I walk too far – which I most sincerely doubt, but it gives my physicians something to do. I trust your trip was fruitful?'

'Quite,' said Harold. *In trickery and lies, aye, and it taught me an important lesson. Better now than later.* 'I am glad to be home.'

'Well, the Norman sun seems to have agreed with you.' Edward's tone was slightly nostalgic. 'Here it rained without cease, all summer. But you look well.'

Harold wished he could say the same, but in fact his first sight of the king had shocked him. Edward's hair and beard were pure white, his tall, thin frame had become stooped, and while his eyes were blue as ever, the face that contained them was deeply lined and worn. 'Aye,' Harold said instead. 'I suppose.'

'Good. You've come back just in time.' Edward's smile vanished. 'I apologise for letting you have no leisure with your wife, but I need to send you to Northumbria at once.'

'Northumbria?' Harold hadn't thought it was possible to feel any queasier, but as ever, he was farcically mistaken. 'Surely – '

'Your brother Tostig,' said Edward, 'has acquired the remarkable notion that the laws of the kingdom do not apply to him. I do not know if he made mention of it to you, but he took it upon himself to double the earldom's taxes. Which, as you can imagine, was *very* well received.'

'He. . . did mention it. To pay for my wars in Wales?'

'Indeed.' Edward took a sip of some foul-looking potion. 'But it gets worse. While you were away, representatives from several prominent Northumbrian families decided to pay a call on your brother, to enquire about these measures. Well, Tostig must not have felt in an explanatory mood, or a sane one, for he had them killed. Under his roof. When they were his guests. While they were bearing a charter of safe conduct.'

Harold had been picking up a goblet of wine. At this, he set it back down. 'God's wounds,' he managed. 'Why?'

'I suspect indeed that God's the only one who knows.' Edward's lips were thin. 'Needless to say, this fantastically stupid action has frayed your brother's tether to its last thread. Northumbria has been arming, and is on the brink of civil war.'

Happy homecoming, Harold. 'Your Grace – I – '

'You told me to appoint Tostig. That's a mistake that can't be undone, but we mayhaps – mayhaps – can avert a catastrophe. Take a full force of housecarls and ride north at once. Do whatever you must to stop it. I'm trusting you, Harold. Don't fail me.'

Once he had seen a dead man torn apart by wolves. Limbs and head and heart ripped asunder, guts spilled steaming on the snow. It must have felt like this.

'Your Grace,' said Harold. 'As you command.'

Caen, Normandy
February 1065

'I've been thinking,' said William, 'that Cecilia has a calling to the religious life.'

'Really? And where might you have come across this fascinating idea? Is it too much to hope that the girl herself said something to you?'

'Nay, she didn't. But she's the solemnest in temperament. And she always does her devotions before the nursemaid asks. But most of all – ' William rolled over to look at his wife. 'The nunnery for your Abbey of Saint-Trinity is nearly complete. What better way to honour it than by placing your eldest daughter in its care?'

'I – what?' He reached out for her, but she held back. 'Cecilia's not quite ten! And as *your* eldest daughter, might justifiably expect a more glamorous lot.'

'I don't give a rat's arse about glamour. How could I make a better marriage for her than with Jesus Christ? If it pleases you, I'll ask her. Now come here.'

He pulled her into his lap. She let him, but her disapproval coloured the air between them so patently that he looked up from what he was doing and said, 'What?'

'Are you afraid that too few people pray for you, and you had best remedy that if you would cast yourself as God's avenger?' Matilda knew her voice was sharp, and knew as well that by law, William could do whatever he wanted with his daughter. But this, she had not anticipated.

William frowned. 'If I say Cecilia will enter the abbey, she will enter the abbey. It's here in Caen, after all. I'm not sending her away. You'll see her often enough.'

Matilda said nothing. Unbound, her long black hair fell over both her shoulders and William's, thick and luxuriant. *He has always loved my hair.* Now was one of those times, however, when she wondered if he loved anything else.

'I'm not trying to make you wroth,' William went on. 'But who else would it be? Adeliza's betrothed, and Constance and Agatha are far too young.'

'Or perhaps you ought make Richard a monk,' said Matilda coolly. 'You complain often enough that he has no taste for war.'

William looked at her strangely. 'No. I need my sons.'

A pang of helpless anger went through her – not at him, per se, but at everything, a conveniently vague target. There was so much of him that had been damaged before she ever had a chance, and so much was nothing she could have changed anyway. She didn't blame him, and yet she did. It was troubling and confusing.

To eclipse her own thoughts, and because she knew that he did not want to hear any more debate, Matilda leaned forward and kissed her husband. He responded at once, his hands coming up to cup her face, and for a long moment there was no sound but the soft, deep ones of their passion. Then he took hold of her and pulled her down, and – for a little while, at least – they slipped away into that place where they never misunderstood each other.

There was no more debate. Cecilia was installed in the abbey a few weeks later, in the early days of March – right before the start of Lent, which Matilda considered a distinctive cruelty. Not only would the girl have to abruptly acculturate herself to life within the cloisters, but to do it at a time of particular austerity, in the fasting and deprivation that marked the Lenten season. Matilda took some solace in the fact that at least Cecilia had been accepting of her fate – or rather, well aware of what pleading and resistance would accomplish (which was to say, nothing). She knelt before the abbess, her graceful golden head looking peculiarly fragile as it bowed, and repeated her vows in a small, clear voice. Matilda wondered how on earth a child could understand their weight.

The rest of the ducal family, watching from the choir, evinced several different reactions. Adeliza had announced archly that at least *she'd* never be a nun, on account of marrying a great English lord, and little Constance and Agatha hadn't grasped that Cecilia was leaving. Thus, they were quite untroubled, with their chief irritation being how long the ceremony was taking. The boys felt likewise, and were causing more of a difficulty. Robert sulked, Rufus trod on his toes, and Richard wept voluminously; Cecilia was his favourite sibling. Matilda squeezed his shoulder and whispered that he could visit her, but William glanced down in irritation. 'Stop blubbing. You're eleven, not one.'

Richard turned up a supremely downcast countenance, but at that moment, there was a piercing yelp from Robert. 'Stop it!'

Heads turned throughout the sanctuary, and the abbess looked startled. Matilda hastily nodded to her to continue, and addressed her firstborn quietly. 'What's amiss, Robbie?'

'Rufus won't stop stepping on my foot.' Robert shot an accusatory glance at his brother. 'He's *mean.*'

Matilda sighed. She loved Robert – she loved all her children, but him in particular – with a singular intensity, possibly because he came in for far more than his share of his father's disdain, and she felt she had to compensate. It was not to be denied, however, that he was a very young twelve, and petulant with it. To add more spice to the pot, Rufus at seven was an almost unmatched hell-raiser capable of driving a saint to blasphemy.

'Rufus,' Matilda said. 'Apologise to your brother.'

'Shan't,' Rufus said virtuously.

'He started it!' Robert insisted.

Matilda did not doubt that in the slightest, but she had no intention of marring Cecilia's ceremony with a full-blown fiasco. So she took hold of their shoulders, and managed, by sheer maternal will, to keep them quiet through the rest of it. But that was all. No sooner had the slight, veiled figure of her daughter vanished into the cloisters than Rufus kicked Robert again.

Robert let out a squeal of indignation, and William swung around. 'For God's sake, Shortstockings, you sound like a pig being butchered.' To Rufus, he added, 'Come, lad.'

Rufus, grinning, scrambled after his father. He had secured William's affection – even for Rufus, *love* was a reach – by being as much an angel within his presence as he was a terror without. Aside from that, he was a fierce, strong child who did not sob or simper and had no qualms about proving it. His sisters tried to avoid him.

William himself made no secret of the fact that in his opinion, Rufus was the only child of his who would ever amount to anything. On more than one occasion, Matilda had overheard her husband jesting that he had one son and six daughters, which never failed to elicit gales of laughter. It always made something clench in her stomach, as it did now. She loved Rufus too, difficult as he was, but sometimes, against all sense, she resented him for being the only one to have any currency with William – a fact he mercilessly exploited. William was also halfway fond of Constance and Agatha, but they were girls, and therefore not worth as much.

The family emerged from the abbey and into the chilly spring sun. Richard, still sniffling, cast a bereaved look back and asked Matilda if he could be a monk when he grew up. Adeliza flung her arms out, twirled in a circle, and asked her father if it would be this beautiful when she went to England, to which he replied with a grunt. Constance, a neat and delicate little lady, lifted her skirts out of the mud, and Robert let out another scalded-cat shriek as Rufus scooped up a handful and pelted him in the face.

William snapped. 'Bloody *enough,* you mongrels,' he said, seizing the miscreants by an ear apiece and banging their heads together. 'Do that again, and I'll geld the pair of you, put you in dresses, and marry you off to the next rich idiots I can find.' With one more knock to undergird this threat, he let go and strode away.

Rufus beat a sullen retreat, but Robert fled to Matilda, knowing he would find comfort there. Tired of having to play conciliator whenever her husband and her eldest son were feuding, which was to say always, she looked up angrily for the former. William, who stood head and shoulders taller than most men, was easily visible even at a distance, and she picked him out from the crowd by the stables. She could see as well, standing nearby, the tall, thin silhouette of the fourteen-year-old Peverel boy.

Again, Matilda felt that clench in her gut. She had no cause to fear for William's fidelity; he didn't even look at all the nubile maiden daughters his barons pushed under his nose, hoping one would take his interest and thus their influence. She knew as well that she was indispensable to him, as he rarely did anything without consulting her, and she always had complete command of the duchy whenever he was in the field. They were rivals, best friends, lovers, and soul mates, and neither could imagine life with any other partner. That much could not be doubted.

Yet for all that, Matilda thought, there was something she had failed to give him. She'd borne him seven children, and was willing to bear him more. But part of him was always looking outwards, attracted by something, somehow, that Will Peverel offered. Matilda did not know if the boy was William's or not, though certainly they looked enough alike, and William had long shown such interest, that there were a swarm of rumours speculating on connections of all sorts. Yet that was secondary.

England. That was what troubled her. William had made his intentions explicit at Bonneville, but the reality was something she dreaded to contemplate. Surely he knew that Harold Godwinson would not merely step aside, no matter the oaths he'd sworn. And while Matilda had not said so, she took serious leave to doubt that the Saxon had any more intention to marry Adeliza. And so, armed with broken promises on two fronts – but even her brilliant, extraordinarily capable, nerveless husband, surely he couldn't –

And if the price for losing this wager was death, and William had rolled the dice –

That was when Matilda finally realised the truth. Cecilia was her daughter, and she loved her, but it was too late. That move had been made, and this was not a game that could be undertaken half-heartedly. And if William did not win, he would die.

Matilda felt almost afraid as this new revelation settled over her, cold as snow. So that was how it must be, and she was ashamed that she had not seen it before. Everything, or nothing, and she gave Robert a quick embrace, then let him go. 'You mustn't take it so hard,' she said softly. 'It brings out the hunter's instinct in them.'

Robert gave her a miffed look, as if he thought he was still entitled to more sympathy, but nodded. Apparently deciding to take his medicine like a man, he squared his shoulders and subsided in the direction of some of his friends.

Matilda watched him, unable to put a finger on her half-articulated fear. Then she turned away, lifted her own skirts out of the mud, and went to join her husband.

'Your Grace,' said Lanfranc, rising from his desk. 'You should have told me that I was to be honoured with a visit. I had no time to prepare.'

'Well, we wouldn't want you at a disadvantage. Should I go out and come back in again?'

'Happily, my lord, that will not be necessary. I have already managed the shock.'

William laughed. 'I should give you a promotion,' he said, stepping inside the study and relocating a stack of parchments off the only available stool. 'Or no, I already did. Once a bit more of St Stephen's is built, you can actually get round to abbotting it.'

'I await that day in breathless eagerness, Your Grace,' Lanfranc assured him. 'What may I assist you with?'

'Law. As concerns my claim to the kingdom of England.'

Lanfranc raised an eyebrow, but commenced rummaging in one of his innumerable piles – a delicate proceeding, in order not to avalanche it all at once. His study had one high window, and a beam of early-April sunlight showed a golden flurry of dust motes. William waited impatiently, tapping his foot and trying not to sneeze, until Lanfranc unearthed the pertinent diagram. 'Ah. Yes. Have we another charge to add?'

'Let's review what we have first.'

'Indeed.' Lanfranc cleared his throat. 'To begin, there is the fact of blood kinship. King Edward and your late father were cousins in the first degree, as the king's mother Emma was sister to your grandfather Richard. Thus it *is* on the female side, which can't be helped, but – '

'That doesn't matter. It's there. Next?'

'Secondly is the centrepiece of the case – when you visited the King in London, in God's Year 1052, did he make you a clear and unambiguous promise of the throne?'

'He did.'

'A pity he gave you no charter nor mark to prove it, but that can be finessed.'

'It was a promise,' said William, close to a growl. 'Next?'

'Certainly, Your Grace. Thirdly – ' Lanfranc squinted at his own handwriting – 'we have a pair of contributing factors concerning outrages done against your countrymen. One of these occurred when the king gave the town and incomes of Steyning to Fécamp Abbey, in thanks for serving as his home during his long years in exile. Steyning is a wealthy burgh in England with a royal minster and mint, and surely the abbey merited it. But Earl Godwin and his sons, on their return from exile, unlawfully dispossessed the Normans and took it for their own.'

'Scandalous. What was the other? Robert Champart?'

'Indeed. The English treated this consecrated man of God with appalling sacrilege. First they would not let him serve as Bishop of London, against the king's express wishes – it took two years to sort that out. Then they vigorously opposed him as Archbishop of Canterbury, again against the king's express wishes, then blamed him for their own strife and forced him to flee.'

'Rome got that one back,' William pointed out. 'They've excommunicated Champart's successor something on the order of half a dozen times.'

'Five, since Alexander of Lucca took the Chair. And with good cause. After the English destroyed Champart, they thought a wretched usurer would prove a better fit. In addition, Stigand continues to commit the sin of pluralism by holding the dioceses of Winchester and Canterbury concomitantly. Highly representative of the English Church as a whole, Your Grace. A thoroughly rotten and backwards institution.'

'How tragic,' said William. 'I suppose it's a mercy they worship Christ at all, instead of Woden or Weyland or what else.'

'Practising Christianity as badly as they do is worse than not practising it at all. And may I add that during my time in Rome, I developed a certain rapport with the Bishop of Lucca, as the Holy Father was known then.'

'I never thought there'd be an upside to you squabbling so long with the curia. Though you did achieve what I sent you for; I've been married for fourteen years, and the world's not ended yet.' William tapped his knee. 'We'll discuss it further. And the last?'

Lanfranc consulted the chart. 'Another damning one. At Bonneville, before every man of worth, and by his own free will, Harold Godwinson swore that he would support your claim. What was more, I am given to understand that he did so on holy relics – an astute bit of theatre, my lord. Taken together – ' Lanfranc rolled up the parchment and fixed his dark gaze on William – 'it forms a formidable body of justification. Some might say self-evident.'

'There are a multitude who won't. So tell me, my lord, the odds that the English will decide they're in the wrong and defer to our superior wisdom? Slim to none might be a kind estimate. And so, this takes on another dimension, beyond dried-up academics scribbling on parchments. No offence to present company.'

'None taken. If it does, Your Grace, I am not the right man to confer with on that subject. I can fight with letters all you wish, but when it comes to lances, you must look elsewhere.'

'I will.' William sat back on the stool; he couldn't find enough room among Lanfranc's rubbish to properly stretch his legs. 'So tell me. Do you think I could do it?'

'It is my experience that it is at best unwise and at worst suicidal to oppose you, Your Grace. But let us abandon the hypothetical. Do you truly mean a full-scale invasion of England?'

'If it comes to that. But it may not. My cousin Edward made me a promise, and he may yet formalise it. Then all the English have to do is send for me.'

'All things are possible,' Lanfranc agreed. 'Including that we may drop dead on the morrow. But, I think, less than probable.'

William shrugged. 'I had opportunity to acquaint myself with Harold Godwinson last summer. He seemed to be a man of honour. He might keep the oath. Might.'

'Were it you, Your Grace, would you stand aside?'

'I'd die first.'

A long pause. Sunlight fell across the floor.

'Well then,' said Lanfranc at length. 'I fear you may have your answer.'

This conversation was a spur in the side of a horse already galloping flat out. William sent a letter to London, demanding to be apprised of the king's health, and received assurances from Osbern fitz Osbern, Will's younger brother and Edward's chaplain, that it was feeble. In fact, Edward had not been seen in public for some weeks, fanning rumours that he was dying. When informed of this, William sent another letter formally requesting that the King name him heir. To this, however, he received no response.

The summer passed in something almost approximating peace. He had beaten Brittany so thoroughly into submission that there was not a whisper from the marches, and anyone else with rebellious sentiments had the sense to keep them very deeply submerged. Thus, William was at liberty to spend most of it in Caen with Matilda, a rarity they almost never enjoyed. The other person whom he saw more of than he had in years was his old friend – in fact his oldest friend, Will fitz Osbern himself, who had come up from Breteuil. He rode in one day near Midsummer, and after he and William had exchanged embraces and cuffs on the back, said, 'So what's this I've heard? You're going to be king of England?'

'Oh, aye.'

'You've been invited?'

'Nay, but I *will* invade it, if necessary.'

Will laughed heartily. Then he choked when he noticed that William was not. 'What?' he spluttered. 'You were serious?'

'Would you expect anything different?' William asked dryly. 'Besides, I'd best give you something to do before you rust away.'

'I resent that,' Will said, as they strode into the bailey. He was a very fit forty-five, strong and bluff and vigorous, but it gave William a start to see the streaks of frost in his hair. 'Speaking of which, why didn't you invite me to Brittany? I missed the fun.'

'Because I would take no chance of you dying on a less important mission.' They evaded a vociferous disagreement between the cobbler and the blacksmith and scattered a flock of chickens, ducking through a door and gaining the ladder to the north tower. Over his shoulder as he climbed, William added, 'For all I know, you've lost a step.'

Will scoffed. 'You're lucky I'm such a feeble old man, otherwise I'd beat your arse. Are you really going to do this?'

'Aye.' William shoved aside the trapdoor and stepped out onto the wallwalk. 'But even I can't take on an entire country by myself. That's why I need your help.'

Will joined him at the overlook, which took in the cottages of Caen, the green hills beyond, the gleaming coil of the Orne. 'What do you want me to do?'

'I don't want to make any plans just yet. There might be no need. But if there is, I will need all my barons behind me. And I'll need them to fight.'

'Christ.' Will shook his head. 'Get them to care about England? What do they know about it, or want to fight for it?'

'That's part of your job. It's a wealthy country. And my barons *are,* as both of us know, a bloody rapacious lot. Therefore – '

'I don't know. I'll go with you to hell, but invading and conquering an entire *country*? Especially one as strong as England?'

'I can do it. England belongs to me. God Himself knows it. One way or another, I *will* have the throne.'

Will hesitated. 'I do believe you mean it.'

'Bloody well I do.' William turned to look at him. 'So do this for me. Be my man. Stand forth and say it.'

'Aye.' Softly at first, then louder. 'Aye, I'll convince them,' Will said. 'Though they *will* think I'm insane.'

'They've thought that from the beginning.' William loosened his grip, but didn't relinquish it. 'This is it. What it's for. When, in all the time you've known me, have I ever intended to lose?'

'Never,' said Will. 'Not since the days you were fighting Pimple in the bailey.'

William gave him a dirty look. 'When you woo my barons, feel free to miss that part out.'

'What should I say, then?'

'Gold,' said William. 'Lands. Glory. And one other thing.'

'Aye?'

William smiled. 'Victory.'

CHAPTER THIRTEEN

Northampton, England
October 1065

THE WORLD was a sea of grey, from hills to horizon. The remnants of a snow flurry were settling over the dead grass, and the air was damp and frosty, but even that couldn't make him feel any colder at heart than he already was. He could see them, camped on the far side of the river. By his best estimate, there were at least a thousand, and that was the Northumbrians alone.

Harold sat for a moment, the wind biting his face. He could feel ice crusting in his beard, and his horse kept spooking at the shouts from the camp. She was a blood mare, bred for speed and not trained for battle, and the most unstable damned beast imaginable, but she had brought him north in record time. He wished very much, however, that there was no call for it.

Upon his first arrival in November of last year, Harold had managed to prevent the Northumbrians from coming to out-and-out blows, but they were even angrier that another southerner, brother to their loathed leader, had turned up and tried to stop them from taking their fully merited vengeance. For his own safety, Harold had been forced to retire to Winchester for a time, but had gone back just past Easter. The housecarls he'd left behind had been the only thing that kept a civil war from breaking out, and he received no warmer a welcome than before. The Northumbrians announced flat-out that they would not accept the king's judgment if it meant forcing them to keep Tostig, and Harold was left in the position of having to bow to their demands and undermine royal authority, or insist on it and lose the North. At last, seeing nothing for it, he agreed to let them decide their own fate. This made them downright conciliatory, and they promised that if he departed, they would cause no further trouble. He had believed them.

Harold had been in London when the news came, just a fortnight ago. The Northumbrians had revolted en masse, descending on the city of York and putting all of Tostig's henchmen to the sword. Only Tostig's absence had spared him the same fate, and the Northumbrians were through with even a shabby charade of loyalty. They declared Tostig an outlaw, traitor, and apostate, and announced that Morcar, Edwin's younger brother, would henceforward be recognised as earl in his place. Edwin had arrived with his own forces to back up his sibling's appointment, and now the lot of them, Northumbrians and Mercians alike, were on the march, pressing south to coerce Edward into their point of view.

Sitting there (just out of arrow range) Harold felt a hollow desolation. This was the choice he had hoped all along he wouldn't have to make. But every rope Tostig had ever been given, he had used to hang himself. Like their brother Sweyn, and look what had happened to him. What was worse, it was all on Harold himself. Fearful that it appeared a Godwinson was leading an army against Leofric's grandsons, he had elected to go alone. They were his own brothers-in-law, after all, and it was true that the situation might not be irreparable. But the thought of what he might have to do was making him even colder. *I cannot turn back.*

Harold lifted his reins, and rode into the camp.

'Brother.' Having been summoned to greet him, Edwin of Mercia smiled, more or less warmly. 'What an unexpected surprise.'

'You must have known I was coming.' Harold swung down. 'Otherwise you'd have feathered me long before.'

'There were rumours.' Edwin shrugged. 'And you *are* family. My sister Edith has surely had enough of her husband being cut down by men supposed to be his allies.'

It was an oblique barb, but it caught in Harold nonetheless. 'Aye. Well. Half the kingdom for myself and my brother Gyrth, and half for you and Morcar. Surely that's more than fair.'

'Aye.' Edwin shrugged again. 'Only if you choose to keep to that state of affairs, of course. It would be entirely understandable if you argued that we have terminally overreached ourselves by declaring Tostig an outlaw.' *But not very wise, I think.*

Harold glanced uneasily at the grim-faced Northumbrians. 'I bring King Edward's regards from London. He understands your discontent, and wishes me to negotiate – '

'There will be na negotiation.' One of the thegns stepped forward. 'We'll never take that whoreson Tostig back. If the king says we must, we stuff it up his arse. Aye?'

'AYE!' the Northumbrians bellowed. Birds startled off the trees into the twilight.

'We'll keep m'lord Morcar,' said the spokesman, nodding at Edwin's brother. He was clearly the brawn of the two, whereas Edwin was the brain, and didn't look like the sort of man that one would want to meet on a moonless night in the Southwark stews. 'Least he's na a Scot-loving southerner like yon last useless shite.'

Harold looked around at them. Until that moment, he'd still had some faint fraternal impulse to argue for Tostig, to hope that the situation could be resolved. But then, he felt the last of that fallacy evaporate. And when it was gone, it was gone, shattered beyond a ghost of recall. *I have,* he thought. *I have done it. I have betrayed Wulfnoth, and I have betrayed Tostig.*

'My lords,' he said. 'From here, I ride to the royal council that the king has called at Oxford, and shall send word to my brother to join me. He knows that I have been doing my best to help him – I think he will obey.'

An angry rumble circulated through the mob at the reminder, and Harold went on quickly. 'Then I will sanction what judgment you have made in your own interests, and the king likewise. Tostig will be named an outlaw, but. . . spare his life.'

'His life's worth less than a brass groat if he falls into our hands,' the spokesman growled, another sentiment enthusiastically seconded.

'Do *not* kill him,' said Harold. 'If you do, there will be retribution from the crown, and I speak with the king's voice. That is not a threat, only a promise.'

There was another discontented murmur, but nobody was quite so carried away as to openly oppose king and country. There was still a reluctance, a sense that this would be a point of no return, and Harold prayed it held. The alternative didn't bear thinking of.

'Swear,' said Morcar, the first time Harold had heard him speak. His voice was deep, rasping, like grinding stone. 'Swear that you will stand for us at the king's council.'

'I will,' said Harold, 'but you needn't take my word for it. Come yourself.'

'Without being tied up and imprisoned?'

'Why? Do you feel you have done something wrong?'

A pause. 'No,' said Morcar. 'Brother.'

'Good,' said Harold. 'I'll see you there, then.'

The northerners offered for him to pass the night in their camp, but Harold, mindful of what had happened the last time he'd taken their word that they'd cause no more trouble, refused. He mounted up and trotted away, crossing the lonely fells alone. It was just about twelve leagues due south from Northampton to Oxford, and he could make it if he rode all night.

It was dawn by the time he finally had to stop, tying the mare's reins to a branch and striking a fire. He felt an emotion in defiance of all logic: relief. The path before his feet had never looked so clear. There was no question that he must walk it.

Harold scoffed an unappetising breakfast of leathery jerky and soggy bread. It was starting to snow again, softening the barren downs. His tracks would be covered by nightfall.

He swung into the saddle, and rode toward his future.

Oxford

The tower of St Michael's-at-the-Northgate was built of stone and wood, the sigil of its patron saint fluttering dismally from the top. Inside, it was furrowed with tight staircases, a few smoky rooms, and narrow window-slits that looked over the city wall. The current structure was only a few decades old, but there had been a castle there (in an optimistic sense) for several centuries, first built in those uneasy days when four kings ruled England. Before the great Alfred and his son and grandson had knitted the disparate pieces together, seamed over the cracks. Harold wished that they were about today. England could have used them.

The tower itself was too cramped and filthy to lodge a proceeding as august as a royal council, so it had been moved to the longhall below. Harold had never seen the witan more angry and anxious, emotions fuelled by the pale spectre of Edward. The king was gaunt and wasted, and when he pressed a cloth to his mouth to cough, it came away stained with blood. It was a miracle that the journey to Oxford hadn't done him in.

'No,' said one of the East Anglian thegns. 'Christ, no. Northumbria's long been labouring under the delusion that it can do whatever it wants. Recognising this gaggle of rebels and upstarts will only encourage them.'

'I trust you did not mean to call my people traitors,' Morcar rasped.

'Your people? They'll be someone else's tomorrow. You can't trust northerners.'

There were shouts of hostility to this blazing brand of a statement, and Harold saw Edward close his eyes. So he sprang to his feet and bellowed, 'ORDER!'

His voice rang out over the turmoil, and the combatants turned grudgingly to look. Harold had already noticed that they were drawing their cues from him, rather than the king, and that for better or worse, he was at the centre of the room's energy. He now took advantage of it, striding into the fractured silence. 'The current situation may lack something in how it came about, but it is better for the entire country. Four great earls, two of Godwin's line and two of Leofric's. It should be plain to the blindest among us that my brother Tostig simply cannot rule the Northumbrians. Making them take him back is simply madness.'

Gyrth and Leofwine watched him sharply. 'Brother – '

Harold could not stop, not now. 'Therefore, I endorse the recommendation I made before. That the king and witan officially condemn Tostig Godwinson as outlaw and exile, and recognise Morcar Ælfgarsson as Earl of Northumbria in his place.'

'But what would we do about – '

'You could,' said an ugly voice, 'ask me.'

Heads spun. A shocked murmur roiled the uneasy witan. The outlaw himself, teeth bared and eyes madder than ever, pushed off the doorpost where he had been leaning, and sauntered in. His golden hair fell in tangled knots past his shoulders, and he looked as if he hadn't washed for weeks. He stank of hard riding and rough living, having to stay a step ahead of the amateur assassins who would have gladly ended the matter for free.

'What a surprise,' said Tostig conversationally. 'You must not have thought I'd turn up. I didn't think I would either. But I supposed that I couldn't let you kill me without hearing why.'

'Brother,' said Harold. 'We do not mean to kill you.'

'Pull the other one.' Tostig came to a halt. 'Even now you cling to your hypocrisies. As if it wasn't you who started this rebellion! All along, you wanted to take Northumbria away from me, once it was plain I would not be your toady. You saw I was a danger to your ambitions, and so you had to destroy me. And now you have, in the most cowardly way imaginable.'

More shocked whispering. 'My lord,' said Archbishop Stigand, 'you cannot be accusing your own brother of – '

'Shut up.' Tostig wheeled around. *'Shut up!* Why is it that whatever I say is never believed, so long as it is measured against him? My perfect brother! He is a worse traitor than I ever will be. I've only betrayed a pack of northerners. He's betrayed his soul.'

'Tostig – ' Gyrth began. 'Listen – '

'No!' Tostig screamed. 'I'm sick to death of it! Harold giveth and Harold taketh away! Harold the good, the benevolent, the kind! He is offering me up as a sacrificial lamb, and you will sit here and let him do it! I warned you! I warned you all!'

Gyrth frowned, sat back down. Tostig's shouts were still ringing in the air when Harold moved. He descended from his place beside Edward into the cauldron of the benches, until he was directly across from his brother, and looked Tostig in the eye. 'I warned you too,' he said. 'A hundred times I warned you. That if you continued to run amok, you would pay the ultimate price. England faces the greatest threat since Svein Forkbeard at the least, and you alone will destroy us if you continue on your feckless course. I'm done with you, Tostig. You are *niðing.*'

A stunned gasp as Harold named the worst thing an Englishman could be – a villain, an outcast, and a traitor, honourless, exiled, and damned. Tostig might have flinched, but it was hard to tell. He did not flush, but remained pale, burning white, then took a step. Then another, cold and inexorable as death.

'Very well.' Tostig tore the wyvern brooch from his cloak, flung it into the rushes. 'You have denied me, Judas, so hear me in turn. I deny your blood. I deny your father. I deny your name. You are not my brother. And – ' Tostig took another step, close enough to kiss, snarling into Harold's face. *'You will never be my king.'*

'Get away from me, traitor. Or must I have you dragged?'

'Nay need.' Tostig stepped back. Raising his voice, he added to the witan, 'Enjoy him while you can. It won't be long. I'll be back, and next time I'll have a sword in my hand.'

'You won't be the only one.'

'Aye, but you won't dare to kill me. How horribly might it reflect on you! I always said – '

'You've said enough.' Harold raised a hand, and the housecarls began to advance. 'Men. Take this traitor and see to it that he's off English soil by the feast of All Souls. That's five days. If he's not, cast him into prison and keep him there.'

Tostig sketched a brutally mocking bow. 'Your Grace. My pleasure.'

The housecarls marched him out, none too gently. The reverberations of the fatal confrontation still poisoned the silence. Then, very softly, Edward's voice broke it.

'God have mercy,' he said. 'Now there will be war.'

Shattered and shaken and riven with suspicion and dread, England staggered into Advent like Lazarus into the tomb, rather than out of it. Harold rode south to keep the Christmas feasts at court, but there was no savour in it. The Oxford council and its catastrophic denouement took something vital out of Edward, and near Martinmas he had had a seizure. He was now declining so swiftly that there were fears he might not live to see his great abbey completed; the workmen were toiling day and night. The first ceremony it would host would all too likely be its patron's funeral.

Everything became worse on Christmas Eve. Edward briefly appeared to be on the mend, and had made plans for a celebration in a well-meaning attempt to lift the court's spirits, but as he was hearing Mass that morning, he suffered a seizure so violent that it took three brawny housecarls to hold him up. Unconscious and bleeding from the nose, the king was carried to bed at once. Aldred of York and Stigand of Canterbury were on constant standby, and the chamber hummed with nervous dismay.

Harold came to see him. Edward looked like a pale statue, no colour to him at all, heaped with a pile of blankets. It seemed unlikely that the king would ever speak again.

'My lord?' Harold whispered. He took Edward's fragile hand in his. 'My lord?'

Edward's eyelids fluttered – yet if he knew who Harold was, he gave no sign. Then his head fell back on the pillow. He slept.

Christmas Day arrived in unadulterated grimness. Rain pelted the keep and the cold snuck in like a thief, no matter how many times the fires were stoked. The full witan was gathered in London, and there was supposed to be a feast, but what looked certain to be Edward's final illness put paid to that. The royal family ended up taking a private, sparse supper in their rooms, under the shadow of the king lying mute and stricken.

Edith ate nothing, pale and strained. Gyrth and Leofwine attempted to introduce a note of levity by telling French jokes, which only served to remind everyone of the threat hanging even more palpably than the rainclouds. Edgar the Aetheling sat in a corner and said little. He was not quite fifteen, a graceful and handsome youth, but still delicate, inexperienced, and painfully naïve. Harold thought that if he hadn't been told it was a holiday, he never would have known.

The Feast of the Holy Innocents, three days after Christmas, brought remarkable tidings: St Peter's Abbey had been finished the night before, the last stone laid. They fetched Aldred straightaway, and a ceremony was hastily thrown together. It was another miserable day, and the distant bulwark of the new church, built on the outskirts of London near the misty, brambly marshes, was barely visible through the rain. The consecration took place in appropriate glumness. The workmen had managed to provision in everything except candles, and the sanctuary was so grey and dark that it was almost impossible to see Aldred at the high altar. Harold stood at the front, one hand under his sister's elbow. Gyrth stood on their other side, while Leofwine tapped one foot nervously. The place was so quiet that it already sounded like a tomb.

There were no Twelve Days of Christmas, no Lord of Misrule (aside from Gyrth and Leofwine's unofficial efforts, which were generally disapproved of). The year dwindled down, wearing to a stump, and the new one arrived in heavy gloom: God's Year ten hundred and sixty-six. Its inaugural act was to oversee a storm even more violent than its predecessors, ripping out thatch, downing trees, and killing livestock.

No one would have been outside even if the weather wasn't so anguished. They haunted the royal bedchamber, and at least two of the Godwinsons were in earshot at any given moment. Edward had been drifting in the wastelands of delirium for the past week, sometimes waking enough to make scattershot bits of sense but more often not. So all they did was wait.

It was the afternoon of the fourth of January, and Harold had been dozing intermittently at his good-brother's bedside when he noticed a slit of blue beneath Edward's cracked eyelids. As he struggled stupidly to absorb this, Edward said in a faint but clear voice, 'Fetch my wife. Archbishop Aldred. And my lords.'

Harold was loathe to wake his sister, who had just been persuaded to get some rest, but dared not disobey. He went stumbling out, shouting; everyone arrived with such alacrity that they all thought Edward was rattling his last breath on the moment. But when they had gathered in the dim room, he looked peaceful enough. Edith sat at the foot of the bed, weeping, wiping her face with her mantle, as the men muffled clandestine tears of their own. How brief life was, how fragile – like a sparrow flying through the mead-hall, briefly sheltered in the warmth before being cast back out into the tempest. How unstoppable was the power of *wyrd*.

Edward smiled drowsily. 'My lords. Do not grieve. I am casting off this old and used body, and going to meet my Christ.'

Edith paid no heed. She bent in half, shoulders shaking with agony.

Edward's eyes turned to his queen. 'Dear heart.' It sounded as if words took a considerable effort. But then, in a greater one, his wasted arm rose into the air. One bony finger pointed at Harold.

'I commend my wife and my kingdom into your hands.' Edward's voice was barely a whisper, lips blue. 'See them safe.'

And there it was.

Harold stepped forward and put his arms around his sister, pulling her to her feet. She melted against him, burying her face in his chest and sobbing, and he held her, stroking her hair. Aldred administered the final sacraments, which Edward took with difficulty. He avowed renunciation of all his sins, and was proclaimed assoiled. By then he was beginning to lose coherence, and they knew that this time, he would not surface again. So they stood and waited, watching the shallow breaths that stirred the blanket less and less, until cold draughts began to extinguish the candles and leave them in darkness.

All Edward could see was light.

It was pleasantly bright, never grew dimmer, held steady like a flame burning without a breath of wind. He was aware, somewhere very far away, of a gathering of shadows, but their edges were softening, receding, like waves rolling out to sea. Yet he was walking, drawing nearer to the strange and sourceless brilliance. It might have hurt his eyes, but he had none.

It grew brighter and transformed, became green and gold. And in that moment, he was *enough*. Everything he had done and hadn't, known and loved and lost and ruined and saved, all was taken and understood and known. For he was not made of darkness, but of life itself. And there was a voice, a warm one, speaking to him, and in him, and through him, to his very soul.

Do not be afraid.

And Edward – who had spent so much of his life being afraid, called coward, by others or in his own self – was not.

They barely noticed that there was not another breath.

'My lords,' said the archbishop. 'Edward son of Æthelred and Emma, King of England these twenty-three years, is gone to Christ. May God rest his soul.'

Hands moved to cross themselves in the darkness. Edith continued to weep, a dry, catching, heartbroken sound. Harold held her. Every gaze was on them – him, there, with the queen of England in his arms, and the promise made and kept. Aldred's eyes in particular lingered on him. 'We must convene the witan at once, and formally bestow the crown on the King's heir. England must not be leaderless. My lord – ' this to Harold – 'comfort the queen as best you can. And then come to the longhall.'

Harold nodded, turned to go, carried his sister to her quarters and put her to bed. He kissed her and left, the moment of this change and transformation fixed forever in his head. It was the wee hours of the morning, January the fifth, 1066.

The deliberation of the witan – it happened just past Prime, but all the city bells had been sounding since the moment of Edward's death, so it was hard to be sure – took almost no time at all. 'There is no question,' Wulfstan of Worcester declared. 'Edgar the Aetheling may have the best claim by blood, but he is yet a green stripling. Do we want a boy to defend us, or a man?'

'My lord forgets that there *is* another option,' said the Bishop of London, who was a Norman. 'If we honour our king's wishes – '

' – Then we respect the man he commended his queen and country to.'

'He might have meant only for safekeeping, to deliver to Duke William – '

This was resoundingly voiced down by the rest of the witanagemot. Harold thought of Edward, being prepared for burial, not even cold yet – and rose to his feet. 'MY LORDS!'

Silence came just as reluctantly as it had in Oxford.

'Edward bequeathed the kingdom to me. I intend to abide by it. I *will* be king. I *will* defend you, as I have done my life long, and no man among you can say differently. We waste time. Name me by acclamation, and let us turn to the true enemies.'

Silence still, a moment. And then, the first shout –

'Harold King!'

And another –

'Harold King!'

And another, and another, and another, until the rafters shook with it –

'HAROLD KING! HAROLD KING! HAROLD KING!'

And thus, that simply, it was done.

Edward's funeral took place that afternoon, under a dour, brooding sky that nonetheless withheld the rain long enough for the procession to arrive at St Peter's. It was a solemn and subdued event, but the whole of London tried to cram into the church; Edward had been a well-loved ruler. He'd always done deftly at stopping the earls' infighting from spilling over into all-consuming bloodshed, kept the treasury full and the harvests good, and never stinted at helping those in need. His legacy was a rich one, and surely, as the Archbishop promised, his reward would be still greater in heaven. But on earth, the ordeal was only beginning.

The next morning in the same church, the *Te Deums* shaking the vaults and the bells of the entire city booming in great and terrible concord, Harold Godwinson was crowned King of England. He walked up the aisle in a tunic of white and green, a cloak of darker green and his torque and cuffs of gold. It seemed the bells had not stopped all night. They were sounding in his bones and in his very soul, punctuating each word like a sacrament.

Do you swear to guard, to protect, to rule? Archbishop Aldred asked. As Archbishop of Canterbury, Stigand should have had the right, but Harold would take no chance of the coronation being declared void due to Stigand's ecclesiastical foibles. He knelt as Aldred anointed him. He took the vows, accepted the sword and ring. And then, at last, it was time.

Harold looked up at the circlet of gold descending toward him. And then it was set on his head, and the church thundered as if to shatter the firmament. He rose, and looked out at all the faces. There were so many of them.

A movement near the back caught his eye. He looked, felt a shock. In that moment he might have abandoned his dignity, run down the aisle after her, but it was too late. It had been too late for years. For Edith Swannesha pulled her hood over her hair, and vanished softly into the crowd.

The feast tasted ashen in his throat. He couldn't get used to being called *Your Grace.* He couldn't countenance the idea of sleeping in Edward's bedchamber. Every moment, he was calculating how long it would take to reach Normandy. But if it was a war, he would fight. This was it. The last. For everything.

The king did not sleep that night. He spent it practising with his housecarls.

Caen, Normandy
January 1066

William was hunting when he received the news. He had been, as always, the first to spot the approaching rider, and was very galled at the idea that he might be obliged to let his five-point buck escape in order to attend it. Nor was he pleased by the fact that when the dust cloud came closer, it proved to consist of a horse dead on its feet and a seriously quailing Abelard. 'M-my lord,' he stammered. 'You won't – I didn't, the tale from England, I – '

'Now,' William ordered. 'Tell me.'

'Harold Godwinson. . .'

'What?'

'He. . . no, my lord, please don't shoot me – King Edward died the fifth of January. Harold got the queen and then the witan said that Edward bequeathed them. . . and he. . . he. . .'

'WHAT?' William snarled. 'Make bloody sense!'

'He took the kingdom.' Abelard covered his head with his hands, spoke between his fingers. 'He seized it. He was crowned on the Feast of the Epiphany.'

There followed the most terrible silence that anyone in the hunting party had ever heard. Several of them began to back away. William stood motionless, as the colour surged out of his face and an icy, remote whiteness replaced it. Those who had known him any length of time backed away still further. He was twice as dangerous in this calm than when he was raging.

'What,' said William. The word fell like thunder.

Abelard cowered. 'And he – he is. . . it transpired that he was already married, Your Grace. When he agreed to wed your daughter Adeliza. He could not have done so. He is faithless twice over, making vows he never had any intention of keeping.'

William thrust out a hand for the crumpled parchment that Abelard was clutching, read it, then tore it up. Only the flare of his nostrils and the frozenness of his eyes betrayed the depths of his rage. 'He took it,' he said, half to himself. *'He took what belongs to me.* He swore an oath, and then he broke it. *He took it from me.'*

And what he had done all his life was now, forever, for everything or nothing –

'He seems to want a war.' William's head came up. A slow smile curled across his lips, shivering with frost. 'He damn *fucking* well can have one.'

PART THREE

The Battle

1066

CHAPTER FOURTEEN

Lillebonne, Normandy
January 1066

MEN HAD BEEN riding in since before dawn, dismounting and milling about, pitching tents and starting fires, a great dark throng against the hills. It was the first time in considerable memory that writs had gone out through the entire duchy, summoning the full levies of men, and the number-one topic of gossip was who they were supposed to be fighting. Some of the lords who'd been at Bonneville had more than an idea, but they themselves were not going to do anything about furthering this ludicrous proposition, without significant incentive.

They're about to bloody well get it. William was standing incognito at the edge of the camp, taking note of everyone who arrived. What he'd heard thus far had not been promising. By the second day, the rumour had made the rounds that England was in fact the object of his attention, and the reaction vacillated between laughing disbelief and utter horror. William had expected this, which was why he had convened a council of war in the first place. He didn't think they'd refuse outright; after all, they had lived under his rule long enough to know what became of rebels. But for once, he was put in the awkward position of needing them. He couldn't smash them if they did refuse. He'd have to compromise.

That may be the hard *part. When it comes to the actual fighting –* *that, I can manage.*

The council of Lillebonne opened as it meant to continue: with an argument. Emboldened by the fact that it was their own necks they'd have to risk, the barons argued passionately against the idea, that they had enough to manage with their Norman estates, that it was ludicrous to attack a country as strong as England, that this would end in their destruction and even that of the dukedom itself. William let them have their say. Then he got up and went to town.

He demanded that they cleave together and stand behind him. He told them that it was right that they fight – and die, if needed – in whatever service he required of them. He demanded to know if they were cowards, if they still doubted his abilities. He slandered their manhood and questioned their motives, praised their abilities and slammed their reticence, until he had worked them up into a froth with visions of blood and gold and glory, English lands and English wealth, under a lord that no one would dare to challenge again. Soon the hall was rocking with cheers, so carried away that he thought they might start killing each other on the spot. Then one Doubting Thomas put his hand up and chirped, 'And how in God's name are we supposed to *do* this, Your Grace?'

The barons stopped cheering, remembered their objections, and began to mutter worriedly.

William could have launched into a detailed plan of strategy, but he didn't bother. Standing before the high seat, he waited until the balance tipped. Then he said, with utter and absolute conviction, 'Because I am going to win. That's how.'

No matter how rousing this ultimatum was, the debate dragged on. The council broke to take supper that evening with nothing resolved, and William and Will had both gone hoarse from all the shouting they had been doing. They recouped privately with a goblet of wine, sitting in silence to give themselves a rest.

They convened again after supper and argued for a further four hours. The barons tried every trick in the book: cajoling, wheedling, and flattering, to reasoning, to rationalising, to pleading, to threatening. But no matter how heated their exertions got, there was one incontestable fact at the end: there was not a man of them brave enough to stand up and tell William flat that he was wrong and they would not obey him. Hence, they only disbanded for the night when they'd argued to a standstill, and William crawled into bed in grim determination. His resolve had, if anything, strengthened. *I'm coming, you bastard. Just you try to stop me.*

The next morning William said, 'I've had an epiphany.'

'Out with it, then,' said Will, shovelling fried fish into his mouth. 'Save us another day of quarrelling.'

'Oh, I doubt it will.' William began to smile. 'I'm going to send an ambassador to Pope Alexander. We've ample evidence that if Stigand is anything to go by, the English Church is a stinking viper's den of perverts and malfeasants, and if I argue that my kingship is the only way to restore the truth. . . Rome has spent enough bloody time making itself a pain in my arse. Well, the hour has come for repayment. Ah, I feel rather benevolent! Nearly enough to thank Henry Capet for opposing my marriage in the first place, so Lanfranc had to go to Rome and get to know Alexander!'

'That's quite benevolent indeed.' Will washed down the fish with a gulp of yeasty brown ale. 'Sounds dangerous.'

'Mayhaps not that much, then.'

'Mayhaps not.'

Armed with this new dimension, William and Will went back to work scything down the barons' last crop of arguments. The session only lasted the morning, instead of the day, and by the hour of Sext, they had succeeded in forcing them to the brink of agreement. The first of the opposition to break was also the one who had heretofore stood the stoutest: Peter de Valognes. He stepped forward, knelt and pledged to do whatsoever his lord asked of him.

'Do you swear to serve me as duke and king, of Normandy and of England?'

'I do, my lord!'

'Do you swear to fight and help me win?'

'I do, my lord!'

'And will your sons serve my sons, once they rule after me?'

'They shall, my lord!'

'Good.' William clapped a hand on Peter's shoulder and pulled him to his feet. 'Then you'll have the honour of riding alongside me, and a greater share in the spoils. There is much at stake. Riches, titles, lands. Normandy and England alike, so long as my line endures. Follow me, and what is mine is yours. My opponent is a perjured blasphemer and I have the might of the True Church behind me. How could we go except to victory? *Diex aie!*'

'*Diex aie!*'

The shout came readily enough, though sparser than he'd like. Then Will fitz Osbern bellowed, 'What's wrong with you palsied buzzards? Are you Bretons? Angevins? Toadies for the stripling king? Or are you Normans? You bloody don't look it! You look a gaggle of old women! Fretting and farting and whimpering! Now *scream it,* or I'll wring your necks myself! *Diex aie,* you miserable cocksuckers! *DIEX AIE!'*

'DIEX AIE!' they thundered, a hearty full-throated roar. They surged to their feet. It caught at some vague memory in the recesses of William's head – something he wasn't sure he even *did* remember. But he did remember blood. His own, sealing it.

He drew his knife. He held out his other hand, raised it, then slashed it, quick and fast. And then Will stepped up beside him, unsheathed his own knife, and cut his palm as well.

The two of them clasped their bloody hands. He soaked in the feeling, the snarl of power. Yet the moment itself meant nothing. All it showed was that the real work had now begun.

This was proved quite true the very next day. To start with, William had to work out how many men and supplies each vassal owed him, a process that he wished he had a better method for aside from grabbing each vassal by the collar and demanding how many men and supplies he owed him. There were also innumerable egos to balance, provisions to stockpile, and tasks to delegate. Will fitz Osbern was, as always, his right hand and second in command. His half-brother Robert de Mortain was an honest, stolid man of few words but a good head for figures, so William appointed him clerk-in-chief. Richard fitz Gilbert, Roger de Montgomery, William de Warenne, and Robert de Eu were loyal men who had served faithfully, so they would have the honour of captaincy in battle. Geoffrey de Montbray, bishop of Coutances, was more warrior than a priest, so he was included as well. Besides, if they were claiming Godly right, it followed that there should be a bishop along.

And then, of course, there was the other bishop he had to reckon with: Odo, as different from Robert as vinegar from wine. Spending the last seventeen years in Bayeux after being ambushed into the episcopate had done nothing to dull Odo's brash nature, and once he got over his resentment at William's battle-axe tactics, he discovered that he liked his new position quite well. It served as a useful way to deflect any charge of ill-doing, gave him an influence he never would have otherwise enjoyed as the son of a minor vicomte, and was his so long as he lived, provided that he said aye to his half-brother at the appropriate intervals.

Odo was doing that at the moment, in spades. In fact, the chief difficulty lay in shutting him up. William had ordered vast quantities of timber felled and transported, and a makeshift shipyard was beginning to take shape at Dives-sur-Mer. But whenever he visited, Odo went with him, and persisted in trying to instruct the carpenters and builders in the plans he thought they should be following. He took an even more grandiose vision of the enterprise than William, and liked nothing better than to fete its supposedly inevitable success. 'What a marvellous fleet it shall be! The Saxon dogs will run for the hills at the very sight!'

William cast him a cool look; he thought quite little of boasting. In his experience, the more a man did it, the less of it he could back up. 'We'll send you ashore first, then. Getting a good look at your face ought to speed the process.'

Odo shrugged, unrepentant. 'Once your messengers return from Rome with the Holy Father's blessing, it will be even more so. Those English curs are cowards. They won't fight.'

William pictured Harold Godwinson's face in his head. 'No,' he said. 'They will.'

The weather began to get warmer, and the preparations even more industrious. William thought his mood could get no higher when his emissaries returned bearing not only a papal seal of approval, but a consecrated banner to be flown above his army. As well, Matilda discovered that she was pregnant with their eighth child, which pleased him more; he felt it was time for another boy. It served as a useful reminder of his vitality and potency, a man who could make both himself and his sons a king.

Battalions were marching in daily, and not only Normans. Thanks to his lovely wife, there were a goodly proportion of Flemings, but as well some intrepid Frenchmen with no battles to fight for the wet-behind-the-ears Philip, rebel Bretons who appreciated the schooling he'd inflicted on Conan, and Boulonnais, led by the ageing pepperpot Eustace himself – still nursing his decades-old grievances against the Godwinsons. Some were mercenaries, some wanted the adventure, or had heard whispers of generous remuneration. Most knew approximately what to do with a sword in their hand, but others had never fought in a proper army before. So William promptly sicced Will fitz Osbern on them, to reassemble them into a seaworthy unit. And in the meantime, surprising him, he received appeals from two diverse personages.

The first was simple, at least on the surface. He had been in his hall, listening to a report on the status of the shipbuilding, when he became aware that there was someone watching him from the corner. When he had concluded the audience and dismissed the head builder with a dire threat to find more canvas or else, he turned and said, 'Come out, lad.'

A pause, then a guilty-looking Will Peverel sidled out from behind one of the tapestries. Another flash of memory caught at William, but he pushed it aside and smiled at the young man. 'It's all right, I'm not wroth.'

Will looked relieved. 'My lord. I – this is an errand of God, truly, and I do not wish to be an imposition. But of all the boys my age, I'm the best at fighting, and the master-at-arms said I might even be good enough to ride on campaign, and – '

'And you want to come along.'

Will flushed. 'Aye, m'lord. I – I do.'

William studied him. A youth of fifteen, tall and remarkably striking. It briefly occurred to him that there might be something else he could not bear to lose, but he pushed that aside as well. He smiled at Will Peverel again. 'Kneel.'

The lad looked astonished. 'My lor – '

'Go on, kneel.'

Still flabbergasted, Will did so, and William drew his sword, tapping it on the youth's shoulder. 'In the sight of our Lord and Saviour Jesus Christ, and by my authority as Duke, I dub you William Peverel, knight of Normandy. May you guard the unguarded, help the helpless, stand as a shield for all that is good and true, and keep to your calling as long as you live. Amen.'

With that, William sheathed his sword and offered his ring, but Will seized his hands and kissed them with fervent devotion. 'In life or death, I am your man, my lord.'

'Let's hope it's life.' William gave the new knight a hand to his feet. 'And Will?'

The young man, already poised to bound off, stopped.

'Next time,' said William, 'no spying.'

That one was straightforward enough, though it did give all the busybodies an excellent opportunity to renew their speculation as to just why William's notoriously hard-to-earn favour had been so freely dispensed on a handsome stripling. The second proved somewhat more complex.

It was nearly the Ides of March. The thought of every day Harold spent with his arse on the throne of England was infuriating to William, but if there was one thing all those sieges – Brionne, Domfront, Arques – had taught him, it was a merciless patience and meticulousness. He must hold the wildness in check, do precisely what was logical, one step at a time. It would wear down the Godwinsons as it had everyone else. They'd chosen their side, they were his enemies, that was that. That was why William could not have been more surprised when one of them turned up on his doorstep, offering allegiance.

'Kinsman,' said the spectre, making an elegant bow. He was tall, and had once been almost disturbingly beautiful, but the beauty had been wracked and ruined away, leaving only the disturbing behind. 'I offer you my greetings.'

'Kinsman? I was unaware of such a situation.'

'Aye.' The man glided forward. 'I am wed to your wife's aunt Judith, who I believe is also your first cousin. How damned incestuous a web we weave. But I am – '

William held up a hand. 'Tostig Godwinson? It can't be.'

'In the flesh.' Tostig showed his teeth in a smile. 'If you fear that I'm here to spy for my brother, you needn't. I've sworn to kill him the next time I see him.'

'Oh?' This unexpected news brightened William's mood considerably. 'Did he betray you too?'

'Indeed he did. And I'm his kin by blood, more's the pity. So we could debate whether he did the worse wrong to you or me, or we could merely join forces and kill him.'

William laughed. 'I do like your thinking. Where have you been all this time?'

'In Flanders with Baldwin – your father-in-law, my brother-in-law. He gave me a home and even a fleet, but he won't help me fight a war. You seemed more likely. Here I am.'

William surveyed the itinerant Godwinson thoughtfully. 'What do you want?'

'To kill my brother.'

'Yes, I gathered that. Anything else?'

'I want to show them all what I can do.'

'You want to be king?'

'Why bloody not?' Tostig laughed like breaking glass.

'What a difficulty,' said William. 'I'm going to be king.'

'Be my guest. Just give me Northumbria and Wessex.'

Let half the country be held by you? A Godwinson and a lunatic? I don't bloody think so. 'I don't see what you have that I need.'

'Information.' Tostig smiled mirthlessly. 'I can tell you all about Harold. What he's like. What he'll do.'

'I observed him at length two summers past,' William countered. 'I know.'

'If you think so,' Tostig said, in a tone implying he did not. 'I'm offering you help.'

'No. You're trying to use me for your revenge.'

'Mayhaps I am. You're a wise one.' Tostig let loose that ghoulish laugh again. 'But if you won't help me, someone will. The king of Scotland or of Norway, the princes of Ireland or of Wales. You may wager on it. And I will take whatever I win.'

I almost rather like him. 'Go ahead and try,' said William pleasantly. 'I'm quite serious. We'll see who comes out on top.'

'My lord. You're too kind.'

'That's something I've never heard before.' William rose to his feet. 'So get you going to whichever of these bold men you think will serve your purpose. If you wanted to cause trouble for Harold on the way, however, I am sure we'd both appreciate it.'

'Now that,' said Tostig, 'was something you needn't tell me.'

Winchester, England
April 1066

He was having that dream again. Twisting, thrashing, struggling to escape, as the crows scratched at the window and flapped through the air. The bedchamber was flooded and there was water in his lungs, the bed broke apart to sink. He was watched by the dwarf and the fool, sitting atop the curtains as the water continued to rise, as he struggled to keep his head above it. It was the crown, the bloody crown, it was weighing him down –

One of the figures threw something at him. He clutched at it – a reliquary with his own face, staring at him – except it wasn't a painting, it *was* him, he was bound to it –

And he lost his grip and fell into the water and drowned.

Harold awoke with a strangled scream, sitting nearly upright. His heart was racing, and he could not quite make himself believe that there were no crows infesting the bedchamber, that it was not flooded, that his bed was not in pieces, and that Turold and Taillefer were not crouched atop it. But in fact the worst damage lay in the quilts, which were knotted furiously. It was very early, and grey predawn suffused the air with a silvery fineness. He reached out for the presence that should be beside him, but his fingers found only a fading warmth. He panicked, whipped around, and saw his wife kneeling in the corner, being quietly sick into a pot.

'Edith?' Concern cut through his terror. 'Are you well?'

Edith glanced up, began to nod, then clapped a hand to her mouth and retched one more time. She remained bent over, panting, then got to her feet.

'What's wrong?' Harold asked. 'How long has it been so?'

Edith took a goblet of water from the salver, rinsed her mouth and spat it out. 'I've been sick the past three mornings.'

'Should I call a physician?'

'You don't know? What, and Swannesha bore you six?' Edith smiled, without warmth. 'I think I'm with child, my lord.'

Harold flinched at the mention of Swannesha, but did his best not to let her see. 'That – that is very well, my lady. Mayhaps you will give me a son, aye?'

'There could be no greater honour.' Edith crossed the floor and climbed back into bed. 'After all, you have several already, but they're not "trueborn." And it would be indeed a pity if we had to go through all this again.'

Harold felt another pang of foreboding. He lay down and wordlessly offered his arms, and Edith let him hold her. She was not stiff or cold to him, but she never treated him anything other than politely. He knew he could not blame her, and knew as well, with a creeping shame, that it was not always her he meant, when he said her name. He was the sort of man who needed a woman in his bed, and she uncomplainingly paid her marital tithe. Yet ghosts always hung between them, tangible as the grey air.

In the distance, the morning bells began to sound. 'That will be for Prime,' said Harold, trying to break the silence.

'Oh? Aye,' Edith agreed.

The silence stayed.

'I was thinking,' said Harold instead, 'that I might crown you as queen. It *is* your right.'

'If it please my lord. To take it away from your own sister?'

'I love my sister dearly, but her husband is dead. I am king now. And you are my wife.'

'Indeed,' said Edith. He thought he heard a trace of scorn, but couldn't be sure.

It began to grow lighter. Harold supposed he ought to be getting up; there were endless things to do each day. But no sooner had this thought crossed his mind when there was a rap on the bedchamber door. 'Your Grace?'

Harold took the necessary moment to remember that they were addressing him. 'Enter.'

The door opened, and a servant edged in. 'Your Grace, I'm sorry to disturb you, but the Bishop – well, the Archbishop there, but the Bishop here – that is Stigand, said I should come fetch you.'

Harold wondered how long one had to be a king before one was sufficiently prepared to quarrel with an archbishop. Possibly never, to judge from Edward's example. 'What?'

'He said. . . there's something you need to see.'

Apocalyptic visions of night attacks, slaughtered sentries and poisoned wells, immediately crowded Harold's already morbid thoughts. He shot out of bed and seized a tunic, before stuffing his feet into his boots and shrugging on his mantle. Thus haphazardly clad, he faced the manservant grimly. 'Well? Show me.'

Since Harold had expected the worst when he emerged into the courtyard, his first thought was to be relieved that nothing was on fire. Indeed all looked almost peaceful, servants and stablehands hurrying on their morning errands, but a crowd was starting to gather. Heads were craned up, staring at something in the sky.

'What's going on?' Harold demanded, shouldering his way through the scrum. He was grateful that nothing was dead or about to be, but he had been left highly unsettled by that damned dream. Then again, the last one hadn't come true, so perhaps he was just –

'Make way for the king!' men cried, and he took the steps cut into the wall two at a time. At the top, he said again, 'What?'

'M'lord – Your Grace – look.'

Harold looked. He could see, low on the horizon, a strange celestial body – a fist-sized lump, enshrouded in a hazy aureole. It had a long dusty tail, as if it had been smeared across the heavens with a milky finger, and its light was beginning to be outstripped by the advancing dawn, but remained steady.

'It's a portent, Your Grace,' said one of the men nervously. 'But for what?'

'Don't be ridiculous. It's just an unusual star. Doubtless something a learned man could explain to us. I'll hear no more of that talk, do you understand?'

There was a murmur of assent, but their eyes didn't move from it. And as he turned to go back inside and get properly dressed, he knew that even if in itself it meant nothing, he would have to move very quickly to retain any hope of it staying that way.

Whatever it was, it didn't leave their minds. It did not set, but remained visible throughout the next several days and nights, burning palely. But Harold had real threats to trouble about, not this nonsense transforming otherwise sane men into two-bit raving prophets. The news trickling in from across the Channel was what stopped him from having even more of those disturbing dreams, mainly because he never got to sleep in the first place. Trying to avoid alarming the country before absolutely necessary, Harold had resisted calling up his levies – the housecarls were training harder than ever, but the fyrdmen had received only a quiet notification that the king might have need of them in the near future. He had ordered the royal fleet to be repaired and expanded, and set every smithy in England to churning out new swords and spear-heads. But once the levies were mustered, it would be real. Irreversible.

'Your Grace,' said Stigand. 'I have done my best to divine of the leading minds of the country what this phenomenon may – '

'Get on with it,' Harold ordered.

'Very well.' Stigand oiled closer. 'I've enquired as to what the celestial object is. They say it is likely a fixed star that has fallen into this sphere. As to why it has come *now,* most believe it a. . . a sign to bless your kingship, Your Grace.'

'Do they?'

Stigand hesitated. 'Well. . . except for one Eilmer, Your Grace. A most old and venerable man, a monk at the great abbey of Malmesbury. He – er – '

Harold could see that the archbishop was fumbling for a palliation, and said coolly, 'The truth, my lord. Now. And Eilmer. . . the name sounds familiar, why?'

'Oh, Eilmer was a bit of an adventurer in his day. He – '

'Don't change the subject. What did he say?'

'He said that it will bring tears from many mothers. That he has seen it before, but it becomes more terrible now.' Stigand paused, all his usual melodramatics quite gone. He sounded grim, almost frightened. 'That he sees in it the very fall of his country.'

'Eilmer of Malmesbury can fuck his mother!' Harold snarled, driven by frustration to uncharacteristic obscenity. 'I'm trying to keep England together, stop it from terrifying itself! I don't need this! Eilmer – aye, I remember him, our nursemaid used to tell us stories about him. Was he not the lunatic who broke both his legs thinking he could fly?' Indeed, by strapping wings to his back and leaping off the roof of his abbey, to soar magnificently and then crash in general and utter failure, which had been one of Harold and his brothers' favourite yarns as boys. The memory hurt now.

Stigand looked shocked. 'Your Grace, surely you do not mean to cast aspersions on a – '

'I'll cast aspersions on whoever I damned well want, and don't you start playing the sanctimonious angel, my lord. This will go no further.' Harold clenched a fist, took a deep breath through his nose. 'Thank you. Now go.'

Stigand bowed and absented himself. Harold sank into his chair, rubbing his temples. *It's nothing.* Eilmer of Malmesbury was just another voice. Saying something false over and over did not make it true. Yet nonetheless, he knew the time had come at last.

It was a fortnight later that they received the news. Tostig had arrived with a Flemish fleet and was harassing and ransacking the English coast, pulling it like a heretic with an altar-cloth, so the sacraments crashed to the floor. But Harold's response was quick and decisive. He sent the lithesmen to force Tostig into retreat, putting a halt to his depredations and throwing him back on his heels. This show of royal power convinced a number of Tostig's cohorts that continuing with him led to nowhere but an early grave, and they promptly abandoned him, but Tostig was undeterred. He sailed north and made a great nuisance of himself in Lincolnshire, but Harold ordered his brothers-in-law, Edwin and Morcar, to engage him there. They did so, defeated Tostig resoundingly, and returned to Winchester to report smugly that there wasn't much chance they'd be hearing from him again.

'Is that so.' Harold did not want to ask, but had to. 'Did you kill him?'

'Nay,' said Edwin. 'He got away. But the remainder of his men deserted him as well after we thumped him, they can see he's mad as a potted hare.'

'Where was he making?' Harold looked out at the darkening sky. It was a warm May evening, and the odd star was barely visible anymore. He wondered if anyone would connect its vanishing with the fact that he had just masterminded a pivotal victory over a dangerous enemy, but that was doubtless too much rationality to hope for.

Edwin shrugged. 'Scotland. He ran there, at any rate, and Malcolm took him in. I suppose he was hoping to reap the benefits of how damned friendly he was to the Scots when he ruled in Northumbria – Malcolm owes him *something,* for all those cows Tostig conveniently mislaid. But don't worry. If he comes back, we'll smash him again.'

Harold didn't answer. As twisted and charred and trodden-on as his love for Tostig was, it still remained, somewhere in a dark corner of his heart. Briefly, he remembered them when they were boys, running and playing. *Catch me. You can't catch me, Harry.*

'No, Tosti,' Harold murmured. 'I have to.'

'What was that, my lord?'

'Nothing.' Harold rose to his feet. 'I'll be riding for London on the morrow, to oversee the raising of the fyrd. I hope you will accompany me.'

'We will, brother.' Edwin likewise turned to go, but paused. 'Does this mean the war has started?'

Christ Almighty, I think I can stop it? As best tell the waves of the ocean to turn back, as Father said Canute did once. 'Aye,' said Harold quietly. 'It has.'

CHAPTER FIFTEEN

Dives-sur-Mer, Normandy
July 1066

A FOREST OF SAILS had sprouted in the harbour – square, striped, run up on masts that proudly punched the sky. The longships brimmed with activity, men loading provisions, weapons, armour, tools, tack, rope, barrels, and the pieces for the wooden castles that William intended to erect as soon as he got to England. All was ready save for one rather crucial factor: the wind. It seemed impossible that something usually so variant could remain so persistently contrary, but it had been blowing out of the north for a fortnight now and appeared to have no inclination to stop. They would have set sail long ago if only it would have been obliging enough to blow from the west, but it hadn't. So they stayed at anchor, the heavily-laden ships riding low. There were so many of them that they were all the eye could see in either direction.

William kept his army in brutal order, forbidding any looting or skirmishing, but he was well acquainted with the deleterious effect boredom had on soldiers, and hoped he didn't have to hold this commandment forever. He kept them drilling, shouting at them, sparring with them, cobbling the diverse contingents into one force. At that he had been highly successful, as usual. He was the core that held it all together, a burning star.

Speaking of burning stars, the one they'd seen that spring was universally held to be an omen; the changing of the guard, Taillefer said. 'The sky it flames bright, and well it spells doom. But which of the crowns will the battle consume?'

'Silence, fool,' William said shortly.

Taillefer dodged away. 'One king already is dead, *mon aime*, and Senlac Hill will run red as its name.' With that, he'd gone mumbling out.

William, however, remembered that particular day for a different reason; Taillefer was always jabbering nonsense. It had been when a party of riders arrived from Caen, and he'd ducked out of his tent to meet them. Only to find, to his immense surprise, Matilda at their head, sitting regally side-saddle.

'Good morrow, you,' William said, sweeping his wife off her chestnut palfrey. 'Should you be riding?'

Matilda shrugged. 'I've ridden until the seventh month with all our previous children, and it doesn't appear to have done them irreparable harm. I've missed you.'

William bent to kiss her. 'Aside from that, what are you doing here?'

'I've brought you a gift. I trust you'll enjoy it.'

'I'm sure I will.' He raised an eyebrow. 'Something apart from the radiance of your presence, I am to understand?'

'Indeed. Come.'

Curiosity piqued, William followed her on the path she was taking, away from the camp. They climbed down the bank of the estuary, then turned onto the sandy headland where it silted into the sea. He wondered what the gift could be to demand such an excursion, and hurried to catch up with Matilda, who despite being half his size had managed to outstrip him. 'Where are we going?'

'Almost there.' Matilda turned onto a narrow track that switched down the bluff, and he did as well, skidding on the stones. There was a screen of trees at the bottom, but she proceeded straight through, to the rocky inlet that they sheltered. William followed her, ducking under a branch – then stopped, blinking.

There, pulling at anchor as the waves rolled under it, was a magnificent longship, with sleek, sharp lines, a purple sail, and a forbidding bronze figurehead. It was so new that it still smelled of pitch and pine, and the lions of Normandy flew twin from its mast with brightly coloured gonfalons. Its ropes creaked, and water broke white around its prow.

William, genuinely dumbfounded – something which did not happen often – opened his mouth, then shut it. He even had to do it twice. 'It's – I – it's beautiful. What is it?'

'Yours.' Matilda was smiling, enjoying his astonishment. 'I had it made and fitted from my own money. Her name is *Mora.*'

It belatedly came to William what else it meant. It meant that she had forgiven him for Cecilia, that he had her blessing and her hope, and that in this, as always, they stood together. Without a word, he took her in his arms, and she nestled comfortably.

'She will be my flagship,' William said at last. 'And you my regent, of course. When will the babe be born?'

'December,' said Matilda. 'You expect to be back by then?'

'No idea. Who knows how much subduing the Saxons will need? Oh, and one other thing. If it's a boy, name him Henry. That way we can continue to claim amity with the French crown, prove that it needn't worry about what I'll try once I'm a king in my own right.' To judge from William's smile, this might be intended to lull them into a false sense of security, but it was hard to be certain.

'Indeed,' said Matilda. 'What for a girl?'

William shrugged. 'I don't care, you can choose.'

'I'll call her after my mother, then,' Matilda decided. 'Well, I should stop detaining you from your other duties, so let's get back. I trust you like your gift.'

'Very much. I'll send some of my men to fetch her round.' William led the way up the steep bluffs, and they returned to camp in equitable silence. Then he dispatched a task force to retrieve the *Mora,* and went to see Matilda on her way back to Caen.

'My dear?' she said, as he was lifting her onto the palfrey.

'Aye?'

'I understand this may be difficult, but please. Do win.'

'I understand this may come as a shock, but I have every intention of doing so.'

'You haven't a fear that Conan of Brittany or some other opportunistic weasel will decide to up and invade your lands while you're gone?'

William laughed. 'No,' he said. 'I haven't.'

He sounded so sure that Matilda thought better of asking the reason.

That had been almost four months ago, and he meant it, if possible, even more than he had then. But the furthest distance the *Mora* had sailed – indeed, the only distance she had sailed – was up from the inlet to the main anchorage in Dives harbour. The wind remained so stubbornly unfavourable that even William – who, unlike many of his men, put no stock in superstitions – wondered if the English had employed some pagan conjuror. They couldn't squat forever, using up provisions and patience, and every day gave Harold more of a chance to fortify his resistance. This was an intuition which William was especially displeased to have confirmed.

'Aye, m'lord, it's not going quite as well as we'd hope,' the spy reported. 'The King of England – the *false* King of England,' he amended hastily – 'has mustered his levies, called out his brothers Gyrth of East Anglia and Leofwine of Kent, and marched the whole affair down to the south of the country. Which is where he is sitting, waiting for you to invade.'

William cursed. 'How strong?'

'Some seven thousand. Some housecarls, most fyrdmen.'

'Cavalry? Archers?'

'None and few, m'lord. The English fight on foot, behind a shield-wall. It's tempting to say that there's no way they'll stand up to a mounted charge, but I've heard too many stories to be sure. The housecarls will fight to the last man, and die sooner than serve an impostor.'

'By that logic, they should all keel over right now. And no sign of Tostig?'

'None, m'lord. They seem quite sure that there won't be.'

William cursed again. He had been counting on the rebel Godwinson to cause headaches for his traitor brother – what fine stock that family was, indeed. Even though the wind showed signs of shifting, he was not at all keen to sail straight into the teeth of the waiting English army.

'So what do we do?' the spy asked.

'We delay. More.' William raised a hand. 'Taillefer!'

A pause. Then the fool trotted out of the darkness, and sat down in a clatter of ill-assorted limbs. 'My lord?'

'What do you see?' William asked briefly.

Instead of answering, Taillefer closed his eyes and began to hum. William found it so irritating that he was strongly tempted to curtail the divining session on the instant, but forced himself to keep his peace. The fool went on buzzing like a great bee, growing louder and then softer, until his eyes shot open and he gasped.

'What?' William ordered.

'Many ships. Many men. Many leave but few return. A king of hard rule. A golden worm and a faerie flag and blood upon the bridge. It is a harvest moon. The solstice gone. Brother grips brother and all the world shatters on the forge. From it only one can stand.'

William was so surprised by how Taillefer sounded – deep, rasping, quite unlike his usual singsong – that it took him a moment to realise that the fool was not speaking in verse. He had as well the most unsettling impression that something ancient, primevally sentient, was staring back at him from the wide lantern-eyes. A little smile quirked Taillefer's mouth. 'The tree,' he whispered. 'A rose upon it. Withered. A lion comes for it.'

'Tree? What tree?' William turned to the spy. 'Do any Englishmen use it for their sigil?'

'No, m'lord,' said the man, looking unnerved.

'*Blood*,' Taillefer boomed, startling them both. 'The only price. Kingsblood.'

'All right, that's enough,' said William. 'Come back now.'

Taillefer paid him no heed. Instead, the fool turned his head and met William's eyes directly, with a sharp and lucid intelligence. 'Soon,' he said, sounding pained. 'Soon the swords will drink their fill and the thorns will pierce the heart.'

'Aye, but who?' William demanded. '*Who?*'

Taillefer continued to ignore him, gazing at the sky. 'Aye, my lord,' he said, to something that was not William. 'Aye.'

His eyes closed. His head drooped. And with that, he fell asleep.

Sussex, England
August 1066

The encampment stretched up one side of the rise and down the other, a sprawling jumble of men, horses, tents, food, shields, lances, axes, hauberks and helmets, cookfires and latrines, earthen fortifications, barrels of rainwater. Banners snapped in the hot summer wind – the golden wyvern of Wessex, and Harold's personal standard, the Fighting Man – and men worked stripped to the waist, cutting down trees and laying in the beginnings of a palisade. The camp was like a great hive of bees jabbed with a stick, a nervous energy not at all helped by the continual false reports that the Normans had been sighted.

Harold was always to be found striding through the whirlwind, keeping an eye on the goings-on and doing his best to ensure that it resulted in quantifiable progress. It had, but that did little to assuage his misgivings. They had been sitting here for two months, and there was still no sign of William – but that, of course, didn't mean in the slightest that he wasn't coming. What was more, the harvest season was fast approaching, and since so much of his army consisted of fyrdmen, it meant they had duties back home to think of – duties that might make the difference as to whether or not their family ate that winter. Harold had the best tent, which he shared with Gyrth and Leofwine, but he was running ragged from all the sleepless nights. And not due to Gyrth's snoring, either.

'Sit down, Your Grace,' Leofwine said, that evening. 'Otherwise you'll perish before the battle, and that would be a great disappointment.'

Harold gave his brother a chafed look, but consented to sit and accept a bowl of murky stew. He was so hungry that he inhaled it without complaint, using a stale chunk of bread to sop up the remainder. The men were always heartened when he ate with them, and so he tried to do so, learn their names and stories. If he was going to ask them to die for him, he owed them that much at least.

There was Broca, a big fair-haired lad barely old enough to grow a beard, who was rapturously in love with a girl in his village named Gunhilda, and whose conversation consisted of little else. There was Edwulf, an old smith who'd lost an eye fighting for King Edmund Ironside at Assandun. (He was one of the lucky ones; most had lost their lives.) There was Hengist, a quiet young man worried that the war would cause him to miss the birth of his first child. There was Lucan, a salty character who swore like a sailor and had a fearsome temper, but would always pat his mare and give her an extra sugar-lump. There was Eoghan, a towering red-haired giant with a great bushy beard, who despite his formidable appearance proved to be one of the gentlest souls Harold had ever met. They were kind men and cruel men, passionate men and phlegmatic men, brave men, men who loved to fight and those who did it because they must. The men of England. *My men.*

It was Eoghan who turned a friendly smile on him. 'How goes it, m'lord? Do ye think we'll die on the morrow?'

'It doesn't seem so.' Harold could not say if that was good. At least if there was a chance, it would mean the battle was nigh, and that was preferable to this God-be-damned waiting. 'The report that the Normans had sailed turned out to be, yet again, false.'

'We'll smash the French bastards whenever they come, see if we don't,' said Edwulf. 'And then Hengist will go home and meet wee Hengist, Broca will vanish into a hay-rick with Gunhilda for what precious little time he has afore her father turns up, and the rest o' us will fall down drunk.'

There was general laughter. Young Broca looked mortified that anyone could take his intentions toward his beloved as something so scandalously carnal, and started into an indignant defence, which no one paid attention to. Hengist himself looked downtrodden. 'Aye, I hope. Elda would never forgive me if not.'

'Well, I daresay she won't hold *that* much of a grudge,' said a jaunty voice. It was the dark, wiry man named Corbin, one of the sort who seemed to love fighting for its own sake, and also one of the sort that Harold wouldn't want left alone with his wife or daughters. 'So the odds are good she'll let you back in her bed to make another one.'

There was another round of laughter at Hengist's expense, but he looked almost teary, and Harold could sense the strain. He laid a comforting arm over Hengist's shoulders. 'My wife is with child too. I'd like to be there to welcome the birth of a prince.'

'Ach, I've the six weans meself,' Eoghan added. 'I miss them so much sometimes I can't even ken, but that's why we're here, no?'

They all agreed, watching the last light fade beyond the dark hills. Then Harold put his bowl down and stood. 'Forgive me, but I'm fair exhausted tonight. I think I'll retire early.'

They all assured him that there was nothing to forgive, and he went to his tent and crawled onto his pallet. It took an eternity, but to his astonishment, he slept.

'My lord.' Edgar's voice had broken, and he sounded, at last, much less like a boy. There was even the first hint of strength in his shoulders. 'I heard that you are for the south with a great army. I beg the honour of accompanying you.'

'Nay, lad,' Harold said gently. 'I am afraid I cannot grant that.'

He could see by the flicker in those dark eyes that Edgar misliked being called 'lad.' He went on, 'I would take you if I could, but there almost certainly will be a battle, and while I do not doubt your heart, you have no experience. It would be much too dangerous. Besides, it is far easier for a man to be brave in the abstract, when he has no idea of the horrors of war.'

'I'm fifteen, I should be blooded!' Edgar insisted. 'I want to fight!'

Harold wondered if it was a great boon or a great tragedy that Edgar was still young and green enough to be disregarded – but not, he felt, for much longer. The apron-strings were clearly beginning to fray, as he could not imagine Lady Agatha approving this venture for her recklessly gallant-minded offspring. She knew the boy was her path to power, and she played the game with such careful skill that she would never let a fit of youthful petulance bring it crashing down now.

'My lord,' Harold said. 'You do me honour by asking. But no.'

'Why not?' Edgar pressed.

'Because I am the king.' Harold reached out to put a hand on the boy's shoulder, but he twisted away. 'I say so.'

Such a simple answer, on its face. Yet God alone knew the force behind those words.

Edgar went to sulk; Harold, to the final meeting of the witan. 'I'm leaving most of the fleet here. I'll keep the city safe, you have my oath. The word from Normandy is that William is almost ready to sail, so it should be only a matter of days until the war comes.'

Murmurings. More, when he told them of his decision on Edgar. Most of them, however, supported it – and for a reason he found profoundly disquieting. 'If you should. . .' Stigand licked his lips. 'Should fortune not be with you, Your Grace, it is indeed best that we keep young Edgar here in London. If you were, God forbid, not to come back, we would need a new king. . .'

You fool, *Harold wanted to scream.* You utter, blibbering fool! If I die, it does not make one bleeding bit of difference who you name king! Choose Edgar or choose the court jester! Do you think it matters to William? I am the only hope this kingdom has! But what *he said, through gritted teeth, was, 'My lord bishop makes a point. So it is decided. I trust that if there is any news of the former Earl of Northumbria, you will see that it reaches me at once.'*

They agreed. The meeting ended. He walked out into the courtyard. It had been such a lovely afternoon, so succulent with sunlight, that it seemed impossible to think of it catching to a halt, spilling out of its place and cut loose from its moorings, falling down and down and down.

St Bartholomew's day arrived in the last week of August, with no sign of William and no news from London. Accordingly, Harold's forces were ravaged with a plague of cabin-fever, and bouts of infighting were breaking out. He'd disciplined the perpetrators harshly – so harshly, in fact, that the body of the worst offender was still hanging from a sapling a few hundred yards upwind. That had promptly quashed the bickering, but it was still sitting badly with Harold.

August shimmered away. Still nothing. On the first of September, Leofwine asked the question they were all thinking. 'How much longer can we afford to wait, brother?'

'I know we cannot afford to leave!' That was Harold's worst fear – that the instant they decided to up stakes for good, the wily bastard across the Channel would catch wind of it, pack up army and self, and set sail quicker than one could say 'usurper.' But on the other hand, the matter of the harvest was becoming urgent.

'Give me one more week,' he said instead. 'Then, if there's no sign. . .'

William could have always fortuitously sunk halfway across, one never knew. But Harold was deeply loathe to make any move placing himself at a disadvantage. Considering the foe they were facing, even a minor one might be fatal.

'One week,' he repeated. 'Then. . . if that's still the case. . . we shall disband.'

This compromise was accepted. The week passed in exquisite tension. Harold couldn't fathom what was taking William so long. The Normans had been prepared to sail at least a month ago, and it beggared the most fertile imagination to think of the duke deciding to call the whole thing off and go home. But the seas and the shore remained empty. The promised day, the Nativity of the Blessed Virgin, arrived, and in some ways, Harold was almost sickeningly relieved. He was still sure that the battle would commence the instant he laid down his sword, but he had no choice.

He gave the command, and the English army disbanded.

Dives-sur-Mer, Normandy
September 1066

It was the night of September eleventh when the messenger came galloping into camp, gasping and shouting. It was the morning of the twelfth when the Norman fleet raised anchor, set sail to a strong westerly wind, and struck out for England.

For the first hour or so, all was going so well that William was sure he would set foot in his new kingdom by evenfall. But then the wind changed, chilled, and began to moan. The sky turned green, the waves turned black, and frothing salt thundered over the sides. The *Mora's* prow rose nearly vertical, then crashed down with a violent splash; she was so loaded that she could only lumber, rather than roll. It was difficult to tell what was happening with the others, for the storm had forced the ships to break formation. Lightning scalded the sky in adder's tongues, and thunder rolled like drumbeats.

The idea that the entire expedition might unravel thanks to the one thing he could not control was absolutely maddening to William. In fact, he caught himself thinking that he should just throw himself overboard, rather than limp back to Normandy in disgrace. But as fast as it came, his old survival instinct erased it. Aye, was this all they could muster? Was this their last gasp? Did they think a bloody gale could stop him? Indeed William, rather incongruously, found himself grinning, even as the ship continued to pitch and yaw. The storm went on – for how long, he didn't know. It was immaterial. There could only be one outcome.

The tumult passed at last, the dark anvil of clouds breaking apart to reveal the Norman fleet tattered but more or less intact. This was not, however, a universal fortune. William could see one ship on its side, another with a broken mast, and for others, nothing but an ominous patch of debris. He felt a pang of anger; the ocean had stolen something that belonged to him.

He climbed into the prow of the *Mora*, water sloshing around his boots, and began to take stock. Almost immediately, he spotted land off to his right, a hazy line, and wondered if it could be England after all, but he didn't think they'd gone nearly far enough. So he plucked the bow-lantern from its hook, emptied it, and quickly had it burning again. He summoned one of his men, had him sound a warhorn, and began to semaphore them into shore.

Their new anchorage turned out to be a small port named Saint-Valery-sur-Somme. It was well in the northeast of Normandy, near Flanders, and while its lord had had no idea that he was going to welcome his bedraggled duke and a host of dripping compatriots for supper, he compensated admirably for the surprise. As they sat in the smoky hall, appetites sharpened by their brush with death, he said timidly, 'So – so you still mean this venture, my lord?'

'Aye.' William ripped a wing off his capon.

'Even after – '

'Aye, I said.'

'As you will, Your Grace,' said the sire de Saint-Valery, limited courage running short.

William said nothing. Inwardly, however, he was furious. They'd never again have an opportunity as perfect as the one that had just been squandered. Now Harold would hear they'd tried to sail, and race to reconvene his army. That had been the moment, and a bloody storm had to bloody fucking blow up and ruin it.

Nonetheless, William's determination had become even grimmer. In a way, he'd always known it would come to this – army to army, man to man, hand to hand. Everything or nothing. And God in His wisdom knew the rightness of his claim. Knew that Harold was the worst thing a man could be: a traitor not only to earth but to heaven, and to his very soul.

London, England
September 1066

It was before dawn. It always was when he woke. Yet something was different this time, as Harold surfaced from what – he was astonished to note – was not a nightmare. He didn't have his usual sense of fear and futile protest. For the first time in a thousand mornings, he merely woke, and was. As easy as coming up for air.

The quilts rustled as the woman next to him turned over. He had a memory of falling asleep with his hand tracing a line from breasts to navel to the lingering slickness between her thighs. She was a maidservant in the castle. He thought her name was Serenna.

Harold hadn't meant to. But Edith was back in Winchester, and he simply could not bear the thought of being alone one more night – as he was even with her sleeping beside him. He desperately craved kindness, warmth, love, and Edith gave him her body, but never her heart. He knew as well that it was his fault. That he'd had it, and given it away, sacrificed it at the altar. He still didn't know if Edith had loved Gruffydd, but he knew that he loved Swannesha. But he'd judged it less against everything else at stake.

If it was a mistake, it was too late. It was done. But every day he walked deeper off the path, until by now he was lost in the wilderness. It was very simple. He couldn't go any further.

So he had waited until the court was scattered for the night, then went to find Serenna. He had noticed her before. He liked the way she seemed to glow, the way she was kind to everyone. He hoped she would be kind to him too, and she was, flattered by the king's attention. He hadn't needed to do much talking, and soon they were alone in the bedchamber.

At first he kissed her shyly, lips closed. Her hair smelled like sunlight. He was trying to be gentle, but she drew him into her, and he broke. He'd needed her so much, given himself to her so eagerly. If it was not love she touched him with, she did it well enough not to matter, and as he came back to her the second time, he realised he was crying. She didn't say anything, but brushed his cheek. Once more when they woke in the night, and clung onto each other in the darkness. Then the morning came, and that was no small thing.

Harold rolled over and sat up. Serenna stirred, but he pulled the quilt over her, and she subsided. He dressed quietly and went out, going through the breezy corridors to the chapel. He knelt, crossed himself, and began to ask forgiveness, but stopped. He wasn't sorry. If it was only him now, then there was no one to wound but himself, and he had committed his graver sins long ago. Perhaps Tostig had been right. But that was still irrelevant.

It was there that they came to find him. He heard the door scrape, the sound of footsteps on stone. Could hear as well the hesitance, judge the moment they would speak. 'Your Grace.'

He kept his eyes closed. 'Aye?'

'There is news. From the north. Fulford.'

The north? A sudden stab of foreboding went through him. 'What do you mean? There's no way the Normans could have gotten to Fulford – they'd have to sail past miles of English coastline. Someone would have seen them.'

'Your Grace.' There was a blanched, sick look on the man's face. 'It wasn't the Normans.'

The words hung in the air, not making sense. Then, horribly, they did. 'It's Tostig,' Harold said. 'Isn't it?'

'Aye. Not just him.' The man paused. 'He's made alliance with King Harald Hardråda of Norway. They came ashore with a great host – it's said there are three hundred dragonships. Edwin and Morcar gave battle to them at Fulford, but they were badly beaten, and. . . Tostig and Hardråda have taken York, my lord. Hardråda's proclaimed himself King of England. They sent word that they are waiting your. . . your surrender.'

'My surrender.' Harold spoke the words with toneless mockery. 'My brothers-in-law. Are they alive?'

'Aye, though they took heavy losses. My lord, I – '

Harold paid no attention. He was already off, bellowing at the top of his lungs, pounding on every door he passed. 'Awake! Awake! To arms! Rise! For England! Rise!'

Shouts and questions followed him. But men were already moving, snatching up weapons, kissing wives and throwing on coats of mail, ready to fight for king and country. The city turned upside down. Bells sounded, and citizens rushed out to watch as the army galloped through Aldgate. It was barely four hours since the news had come.

Harold rode at the front of the column, wearing a face like grim death. For a brief moment, he could not help but wonder if this was the last time he'd see London, but he put that thought aside. He wondered if he'd be forced to kill Tostig himself. Then he put that one aside as well. He had sworn an oath to England, an oath above all others, and by God, he would keep it.

To ask forgiveness for something meant that you regretted it. And he did not, could not, and all that was left was to ride as if the Devil Himself was on their heels.

Or, as the case may be, his son.

CHAPTER SIXTEEN

Stamford Bridge, England
September 1066

FOUR DAYS. That was how long it had been – four days and four nights, riding until they had to stop or kill the horses. The army had been largely made up of housecarls and the London levies when they set out, but they had collected more men along the way, arriving in York in the wee hours of September the twenty-fifth. Finding that the citizens' submission to Hardråda was merely conditional on him being out of their sight and hence not able to murder them, Harold was able to cozen intelligence from them; they told him that they had been ordered to furnish further hostages and provisions to the invaders at a place called Stamford Bridge, a league outside the city. Harold thanked them, promised to protect them, and promptly departed again. Now he and his army were gathering in the river-bottom, just a hilltop away.

It was an unseasonably scorching day, and Harold was broiling in his heavy mail and leather. He couldn't remember the last time he'd slept more than a quarter-hour, and he saw everything with a weird, eerie clarity. Nonetheless, he had never felt more resolved. This was the hour of the wolf, the moment he must be smelted in the forge.

He rode in and out of the lines of his army, chivvying them into order, supervising the formation of the housecarls into their shield-walls. They pulled on helmets and checked their weapons, until at last they became one body, breathing and thinking as one. Harold, an experienced soldier and commander, could hear this transformation as it happened, as audibly as a click, and galloped into position at the head. 'Now,' he said. 'For England.'

'*For England!*'

And forth, so, to destiny.

Tostig Godwinson was in – pardon the audacity – a downright fine mood. The day was clear, blue, gloriously hot, and the men were soaking it up. Most were wearing only their tunics or tabards; their armour was still on their ships, which had been dragged ashore at Riccall, four leagues off. But this was no concern. There was no way Harold could have heard of their victory at Fulford yet, let alone raised an army and left London. All they needed to worry about was when those thrice-damned Yorkmen would get off their arses and bring them more food.

It amused Tostig more than he could say, in an utterly pitch-black way, to force them to bow and scrape to him now. Relations between him and the city had always been tense at best, homicidal at worst, and he had secretly hoped that they would proclaim their defiance – Christ knew they'd done that to *him* enough – so he and Hardråda would have an excuse to storm it and kill them all. But the Yorkmen had taken one look at the fearsome Viking and his army, and capitulated at once, disappointing Tostig greatly. He didn't care about being king. He didn't want to rule. All he wanted was revenge. As long as Hardråda permitted him to kill his brother, then let the Norwegian king march south and add another crown to his collection. Tostig hoped that when they did win, Hardråda's first venue to make an example of was Northumbria. He'd never met a place more in need of *Hard-rule*.

Tostig pushed his hair out of his face and turned to locate his ally; they needed to talk strategy. Harald Sigurdsson was one of the few warriors as good at thinking as he was at fighting, and Tostig was happy to let him direct the enterprise. In his youth, Harald had served in the Varangian Guard of the Byzantine Empire, and had much experience at putting impostors out of business. (Including, if the tales were true, one of his own emperors.)

Tostig had taken exactly one step toward Hardråda's tent – his banner, Land-Waster, said to be a gift of the faeries, was fluttering from it – when there was a raucous shout from the men. It did not, however, sound triumphant. In fact, it was remarkably similar to one of startled alarm.

Tostig wheeled around. 'What?' he barked at the nearest underling. *'What?'*

'My lord – ' Eyes wide and frightened, the man jabbed a finger at the hill-crest.

Tostig looked. And blinked hard, hoping that it was the heat. That he was hallucinating.

He wasn't. A vast line of men had materialised atop it, sunlight catching on chain mail, swords, and axes. At the front was a tall figure on a horse, except the glint from his head was that of gold. Even without it, Tostig would have known him anywhere, but he could not process the immensity of the shock. They'd had no inkling that there was an army nearby – had been so sure that Harold would not have even received the –

'That chancred whore of the Virgin Mary,' Tostig breathed. 'It can't be.'

Even some of his own men flinched at the pungency of his blasphemy, but Tostig paid no attention. He whirled and raced towards Hardråda's tent, only to be intercepted by Hardråda himself coming out of it. 'What?' the Norwegian king demanded.

'We've been caught,' Tostig spat. 'Take a look.'

Hardråda did, then uttered an oath at top volume that almost matched Tostig's. Both of them knew that they were at an immense disadvantage – one half of their army was on the west side of the river with them, and the other half was on the east, twelve miles away, guarding the ships at Riccall. The Vikings were abandoning their basking and scuttling around for their weapons, cramming on whatever oddments of armour they could find.

The English, however, made no move to advance. The tall figure on the horse held them in their lines. Then he galloped down the hill, alone, into no-man's-land. He drew rein ten feet shy of Tostig and Hardråda, regarding them with icy blue eyes. 'Greetings,' he said, in Norse. 'I've come to make you an offer.'

Hardråda laughed. 'I am King of this country. I make no bargains. Surrender now, and mayhaps you will leave with some of your men. I fly Land-Waster. I cannot lose.'

The rider stared back with an utter lack of fear. His face was hard, but something in it almost cracked as he turned to Tostig, speaking in Saxon. 'Listen to me. If you and your men turn on this Viking usurper, I will restore you to your earldom of Northumbria.'

Tostig laughed. 'Fuck Northumbria. Fuck it bloody. And besides, what would Hardråda receive for his trouble?'

The rider looked straight at the towering Viking. In the king's own tongue, he said, 'Seven feet of English earth, seeing as he's taller than most men. Aye or nay?'

'Nay. Here's a counteroffer. You throw that crown at our feet and surrender.'

'When hell freezes.' The rider gathered up his reins. 'You've made your choice?'

'I made it a long time ago.'

A pause. 'Very well,' the rider said. 'I'll retreat. Just this once, provided you do the same. From. . . filial duty.'

Watching as the rider galloped back toward the English lines, Hardråda looked rather impressed. 'Who was that? What man's valorous son?'

Even you? Even bloody you? When does it end?

It ends now.

'That,' said Tostig, 'was the man I once called my brother. King Harold Godwinson.'

With that, he turned to his soldiers and waved to put down their weapons. 'It's all right. The king is too cowardly to fight.'

The Vikings looked dubious, but slowly began to relinquish the axes they were clutching. A dust cloud rose; the English vanished, but Hardråda watched with a look of deep suspicion. 'I do not know that we should trust the withdrawal. Your brother, though a short man, sat very proudly in his stirrups.'

Tostig shrugged, thinking that anybody looked short when you were seven bloody feet tall. 'He still thinks he can redeem me. Benevolently correct the error of my ways. Even now, after he named me a traitor and sent Ælfgar's sons – *Ælfgar's sons* – to attack me! I'm glad Father keeled over before he had to see his beloved Harold come to this.'

Hardråda grunted, but turned away. Tostig glanced to the ceorl beside him. 'There. I told you so, no?'

'Indeed. I'm glad he didn't, it would have been a problem.'

'Harold wouldn't dare.' Tostig laughed wildly. 'He'll even choose to retreat rather than besmirch his precious self. That's why we'll break him, we'll – '

The ceorl began to agree – then stopped. Grasped at the arrow in his neck. Frothy blood gushed from his mouth, and he stared in a mix of befuddlement and accusation. Then he toppled over, and as if to true-north, Tostig's eyes swung to the hilltop opposite, the one just behind where the dead man had been standing. He looked, and looked, staring just as blankly.

The Vikings were cursing, screaming, scrambling. The English army surged over the rise, a thunder of steel and shields, arrows peppering the sky with hissing streaks. And leading them on, bellowing, drawn sword molten in the sun –

'Oh, Harold,' Tostig murmured sadly. 'I should have known. All of it wasn't enough. You've betrayed me one last time.'

And then the charge hit, and that was the end of thinking.

Everything was madness. The English smashed through the off-balance and under-equipped Norwegians like a scythe through ripe wheat. Their first harrow left a ruin of crushed bodies on the riverbank, and then they wheeled around for another. The Vikings fled madly over the bridge, and the English plunged after them. But here the Vikings ran into an unexpected piece of good fortune: a giant axe-man, one of Hardråda's own bodyguard, planted himself in the middle of it, single-handedly staving off the English advance. The tenor of the battle briefly shifted. The Vikings got their hands on a few archers and sent volleys back across the water.

The English flung themselves ever more furiously against the giant, but could make no headway. At last, young Broca had a stroke of suicidal inspiration. He raced upstream, commandeered an empty barrel from the Viking camp, grabbed a lance, and bundled himself quite without fear into this makeshift apparatus. He rolled into the river and floated directly under the bridge. Then he slammed the spear up through the slats.

All the English – and the Vikings – saw was the giant bellowing in pain, then staggering as a spear erupted from his belly. Then he fell with a titanic splash into the river.

Broca's barrel hit a rock, cracked apart. A Viking archer spotted him. Aimed. Loosed. Blood flowered brilliant once more. Heavy armour pulled him under. Broca would never kiss his Gunhilda in the hay-rick.

With the bridge clear, the English swarmed into the breach. The delay, however, had given the Norwegians time to forge their own shield-wall, and they turned aside the first charge. So the English spun off, mustered up, and crashed into them again. Now it came to heavy, brutal hand-to-hand fighting, two lines squaring off like the hammer and the anvil: a tangle of flailing limbs, grunts, steel biting into flesh, blood slick, bones crunching, bodies crumpling. But the English were much better armed and armoured, and they began to chew inexorably into the tattered Viking front. Hardråda could be heard bellowing terrible imprecations at his men, promising that he would personally kill anyone who didn't get in there and back it up. They were briefly heartened. The sun crept down the sky, and still the fighting continued.

And then Hengist, with a perfect shot at the great Norwegian king, and an arrow, flying true in the madness –

Hardråda let out an even more horrible howl, and staggered, then clutched at his eye and fell as Goliath must have, Land-Waster torn from its stanchion and vanishing into the fray –

And after that, the disintegration began full-blown.

Late in the afternoon, a desperate battalion of Viking reinforcements arrived from Riccall, gone on such a mad march that some began to fall down and die of exhaustion before the English had even struck a blow at them. The fight was almost over, and their valiant counterattack crumbled into the devouring maw. The remainder routed, broke and fled. The English drove them into the river and drowned them, just to be sure.

Slowly, the battle ground to a halt. The English were utterly spent as well, and they began to sink to their knees and retch, many of them bleeding from wounds they hadn't noticed in the insanity. Shadows twisted. Crows gathered croaking in the trees.

Gyrth Godwinson took off his helmet and shook out his tangled hair. 'Harold?' he shouted. 'Leofwine?'

Another tall figure reeled out of the carnage. It was Leofwine, bleeding heavily from the shoulder, but likewise breathing. His eyes were staring, a smear of viscera striping his cheek like savage war-paint. He reached out for Gyrth, but fell backwards. 'God's fucking Mother.'

Gyrth tore a strip from his tunic and began to tend his brother's wound. 'You seen Harold?' he panted, unwilling to think about what it meant if not.

'No. I'd – ah! Christ on the cross, watch what you're doing!' Leofwine grimaced. 'I last saw him over there – ' He waved in an indiscriminate direction. 'A while ago – '

Gyrth pulled the bandage tight and tied it, then got to his feet and began to look around. At last he caught a glimpse of gold in the fading light, and felt relief seize his stomach. Could see the distant figure of his eldest brother, standing up. And then, falling as if mortally stricken.

Horrible thoughts crowded Gyrth's head. He left Leofwine and scrambled across the bloody grass, evading corpses and some who were not yet. A crop of housecarls were moving around the field, dispensing mercy to both the Vikings and their own.

'Harold!' Gyrth reached his brother. 'What are you – '

Harold did not answer. He was on his knees, holding someone in his arms.

Tostig's eyes were blank, beautiful. His head fell back, cradled in the crook of Harold's elbow. Impossibly, he still seemed to be smiling, though blood was oozing out of his mouth and congealing on his chin. The blow that had killed him had landed deep in his chest, leaving shreds of the leather gambeson brutally embedded in the torn, sucking wound.

Gyrth's own breath went out of him. He knelt beside Harold and put a hand on his shoulder. Leofwine came staggering out of the dusk to join them. The three of them said nothing.

'It had to end like this,' Leofwine said at last. 'Him, or you.'

Harold nodded, but still didn't speak. A faint, contained tremor of agony ran through him. Then he reached out, closed Tostig's eyes, and let his brother's broken body fall to the ground. With Gyrth's hand under one elbow and Leofwine's under the other, he rose to his feet. 'Two rebels dead now.' His voice was hoarse, catching. 'But that will not be all.'

The few remaining Norwegians surrendered absolutely. Harold accepted it, allowed them to limp away without further harm, in exchange for their solemn pledge never to attack England again. With a generation lying dead on the riverbanks, the water running red, it was easy. As well, there were a considerable number of dead among his own men – including not just Broca but Hengist, something which caught him in a peculiarly vulnerable spot. He'd lost soldiers before, but this was different. It was as if they were fragments of his country itself. He was trying so hard, but it was still being taken away, one piece at a time.

They returned to York well after nightfall, with Gyrth and Harold carrying Tostig's body in a makeshift litter. While the rest of the English army found quarters in the city, assured the inhabitants that they were relieved of their need to tender any more sustenance to the invaders, the Godwinsons slipped off to York Minster. *The church I told him he ought to rebuild, now where he'll lie for eternity. One of our chasms – but where did it start? Where?*

The minster looked older, scabbier, and more formidable than ever, statues looming out of the darkness and giving them a bad turn. There, by the light of a lone candle, they wrapped Tostig in a shroud and interred him in a side aisle, by Leofwine's suggestion. 'He wouldn't want people trodding on him all day,' the youngest brother said, trying to smile.

It was heavy, wretched work, prying up the stones and digging the dirt beneath. Gyrth and Harold were shaking with fatigue, but the task nonetheless fell largely to them; Leofwine was not much help on account of his wounded shoulder. He did the best he could, however, and they laid their brother to rest with mumbled, badly memorised bits from the Office of the Dead. Then it was another torturous task replacing the stones, but they did.

They stood there forever, but at last could barely remain upright. They made to go, footsteps eerily loud. Harold hesitated as if to blow out the candle, then turned away and followed his brothers, leaving it burning silent in the darkness.

Saint-Valery-sur-Somme, Normandy
September 1066

The wind must have realised it had caused problems the last time it materialised. Its solution was to vanish completely. For a fortnight now the Norman fleet had been riding at anchor, again forced to engage in the one activity its leader hated the most (apart from losing). A few days to mend after the storm had been welcome, but a week showed cracks, and two officially opened the breach. The extra time to think about the sheer improbability of what they were planning to do, in addition to the fact that the corpses of the men drowned in the storm kept washing up on shore, had helped to sow serious doubt in their hearts. It was almost October, they argued. Surely William did not mean to press forward with what could easily become a winter campaign, in a hostile and unfamiliar land? That was not to say the venture was unjustified, but they might find God's promised favour more freely dispensed should they retire for the time and set out again in spring.

William himself, of course, abhorred the idea. He announced that any man who wished to withdraw could do so, as he needed no cowards behind him, but when he returned with his crown, he would be certain to hang the lot of them as traitors. The knowledge that this was not at all an idle threat maintained order, if grudgingly, but the whole undertaking lay on an excruciatingly delicate fault line. It was him alone that kept it knitted together. With Flemings and Frenchmen and Bretons and Boulonnais and Normans all in the same army, and the old enmities entrenched with them, this was a masterly feat of legerdemain.

'You juggle more skilfully than I, my sweet lord,' Taillefer remarked that night, the twenty-sixth. 'Should you wear the motley and I wear the sword?'

William grunted. 'Heaven forfend.' He had even less patience than usual; in fact he was in a vindictively foul mood. He had spent the day exhausting every single one of his commodious ideas, resources, and gifts in an attempt to impress upon the men the urgency of the enterprise and how much they ought to *pray for good weather* – which entailed walking a very fine line between theatricality, sermons, blood-and-gall, and downright witchcraft. Upon finding out that the local saint after whom Saint-Valery was named was known to grant the requests of the needy, he had not merely gone to the shrine but ordered the bugger dug up, so intervention could be made more directly. This cavalier treatment of holy remnants had sent the delicate sire de Saint-Valery into conniptions, and he would have retired to his bed, but for the fact that William was in possession of it. To say tempers were at the brink was an understatement.

'If the wind shan't blow, we shan't go,' Taillefer went on. 'Yet the bridge bleeds and the fighting man flees and fear not, it must ever be so.'

William turned his head sharply. 'What did you say?'

Taillefer looked blank. 'Say?' he repeated nervously.

'Aye. Say. You do it enough.'

Taillefer continued to look confused. William groaned and stood up; why was he humouring a madman of a fool? (Although considering the rest of the day's activities, it was by far the least exotic.) 'You think on it, if you're even capable. As for me, I need some bloody air.'

Outside, the night was tinged with autumnal frost. He could see the dark ships, the flash of moonlight off the glassy water. No good. Wind, where was the bloody wind? William was just wondering if there was any incantation he had forgotten (whether to saints or otherwise) when he caught movement out of the corner of his eye. His hand went by habit to his sword, even as he recognised it. 'Bit chilly for a place to think. Though I can see that being about the rest of the men might drive you mad.'

Will Peverel, who by contrast appeared to have had no idea that he was being observed, jumped a mile.

'Sorry, lad,' said William. No, Will had never needed to scrutinise every shadow, listen to every step, mistrust every face, in case it veiled an assassin. 'Should I leave you to it?'

'It wasn't much.' Will summoned up a wan smile. 'I don't want to burden you.'

'You couldn't burden me with anything more, I promise.'

'I suppose.' Will paused, then burst out, 'My lord, is battle – is it very terrible?'

William blinked. 'What?'

'I'm sorry. I just thought. . . when the wind does come up, we'll be crossing, and then. . .'

Even William's terrible mood could not fail to nudge slightly upward at the lad's unquestioning loyalty and belief. 'And then we'll have to fight?'

'Aye. And I just thought. . . you might tell me what to expect. Sparring in the bailey, I know, it's. . . it's nothing like it.'

'Nay, it's not,' William agreed, with feeling. 'My first real battle was exactly half my life ago. Val-ès-Dunes. But I'd been fighting long before.'

'I don't want to embarrass myself. With cowardice.'

William regarded the young man appraisingly. He opened his mouth, intending to dispense some reassuring advice – and then, quite suddenly, found himself lost for words. Did he speak of the rise of the berserker, when the wildness overran him and drove out all sense? Of blood, of never knowing how much of it there is in a man until you run him through? How did he explain that? Of how skin is stronger than you expect, and you have to shove without hesitating to break it, and the horrible yielding sensation when your blade goes home? The way blood will bubble in someone's mouth if stabbed in the heart, the short punched gasp if stabbed in the back? Should he explain the way it felt, the wet, tearing rip of slicing heart and lung? Did he tell of how grown men could soil their smallclothes, and how some shrink and fail, and others turn into animals? Did he tell him not to be frightened? And yet that was the greatest falsehood of all, for no man in his right mind went to war unafraid. Sometimes, not even him.

It was only when Will frowned that William realised he had spoken aloud. 'Surely, my lord, you must never fear,' the lad insisted. 'Men call you a lion, the bravest, the best.'

'Do they?' said William. 'It matters not what a man says to your face, should he turn and say something different behind it. And there, I will never be called anything but the Bastard.'

'It seems to me that they can call you whatsoever they want, if it helps them find solace in losing to you. Though I do not see what, if you are supposedly so unworthy, it says of them.'

'Splendour of God, that's my lad!' said William, laughing for the first time in days. He moved to put an arm round Will, tousle his hair, as he had often done when the boy was younger.

But this time, Will tensed, gave him a queer look. 'My lord?'

William paused, then dropped his hand. Of course, Will was old enough now to hear all the various sensational fictions that circulated, but it was more than that. *He does not want to be my son. My dearest knight, my loyal man, my protégé – all that. But not my son. He knows – just as I did – that bastards are cursed. It is crucial to him that he never have any thought, any chance, that he might be one.*

'My lord?' said Will. 'I didn't – '

William swallowed. 'Nay, it was my offence. I thought of you as a child, when you are a man now in truth.'

This served its intended purpose of restoring Will's equilibrium, and his face brightened as he smiled. God, he was so *young.* Not quite sixteen. 'Well,' he began. 'I will surely – '

He stopped. Sprang to attention, like a hound getting a whiff. 'Did you feel that?'

'Feel what?' William put a hand to his sword again.

'No, my lord, no!' Will's eyes were alight. He began to skip in place, pointing. 'Look!'

William looked. He saw the dark trees, the ships – nothing – and then he did. The trees bending. The sea rippling, its fortnight-long doldrums cracking like a broken mirror. He could feel it in his face, feel it whisk his cloak, could hear Will Peverel's delighted laugh, as the vaults of heaven opened and the wind began to blow.

After a day of mad preparations, panicking every time the breeze lulled, they departed on the evening tide. It was the twenty-seventh of September.

The weather in the Channel was as placid this time as it had been ferocious the last. It was a clear and starry night, the wind steady from the southwest. The Norman fleet looked like a ghostly armada, and every man was occupied, minding the lines or the horses or the navigation. The *Mora* sailed at the forefront, its lighted lantern dangling from the prow, and William stood at the centre of the deck. He had prevailed again, and the coming of the wind had heartened quailing spirits, convinced them that the saints had rewarded them for their fervent prayer sessions. William did not care what it was, so long as they were behind him.

He glanced back. Normandy had faded to a shadow, falling off the edge of the world. The lines hummed, timbers creaked, and they surged through the dark sea. Feeling – knowing – that this was the reason he had survived, William nonetheless kept his homeland in sight as long as he could. He watched until at last a cloud passed softly over the horizon, and it was gone.

CHAPTER SEVENTEEN

Pevensey, England
September 1066

B Y DAWN THE AIR had changed. It smelled different, somehow, and a flock of screaming seabirds wheeled overhead. Fog had rolled in overnight, but it was thin enough to reveal the broad bay ahead. To William's great surprise, it was deserted, but that meant nothing. The Saxons could very easily be parked up in the abundant stretch of trees further inland, waiting for him to get his forces ashore before launching a screaming attack. That was likely going to be the case anyway, but he preferred to have it at a time when he could plan for it.

Thus, he undertook the landing very, very carefully. While the ships stayed a safe distance out, one longboat was sent in loaded with Bretons; they were armed to the eyeballs, and if something *did* go wrong, they were, after all, Bretons. William was excruciatingly on edge, waiting for the shouts, the arrows. But the Bretons splashed onto the beach and unloaded with as much commotion as possible. Still nothing. One of them wandered off alone, which should have done the trick. But they debarked all their weapons and supplies, without the slightest disruption.

'God's teeth,' Will fitz Osbern remarked. 'I do believe the Saxons simply are not here.'

Not warranting it, William studied the shore intently, but at length he was forced to conclude that Will appeared to be right. The *Mora* sent out the signal for advance, and the fleet surged into the breakers. It was a rough ride, but then they were through, and men jumped into the water, catching ropes thrown to them. Then there was a final bump and splash, and the *Mora* rode up onto shore.

William grinned, turned, and raced to clamber down onto his new land. But in his eagerness he slipped, falling with horrendous indignity off the rope ladder. He flailed in midair, then sprawled in the wet sand, and heard a sudden hush. He pulled his face out, spitting and swearing under his breath, and saw that his men were watching him with superstitious horror. After the ordeal it had taken to get out of Saint-Valery, they were even more attuned to portents of an apparently ominous nature. *Bugger.*

'Your Grace,' said one nervously. 'England rejects you.'

'What bloody nonsense.' William sprang to his feet. 'Ho, my lords! See what I have done! By the Splendour of God, I have taken possession of English soil with the whole of me, and what is mine is yours! Now *get* to it! Forth Normandy to the crown! *Diex aie!*'

'*Diex aie!*' The answering cry startled the seagulls off the rocks. Spirits were reassured. Industry resumed. William brushed himself off and strode away to help.

The Normans worked all day, still so nervous that they nearly killed a number of their own fellows by accident (and two or three deer on purpose). It was slow, gruelling business, and every man was starved by the time dusk was falling. After posting a double watch, they built a great fire on the beach and roasted the deer. There was also fine drink in the casks they'd appropriated from the sire de Saint-Valery, who was likely never going to recover from their visit. When William slept at last, it was rolled up in a blanket on the deck of the *Mora,* his sword tucked alongside him like a lover. For once, he was so tired that he did not dream.

The next few days saw them penetrate steadily inland. William had one of his wooden castles built as a base of operations, at a place a few leagues east of Pevensey called Hastings. It was a sporadically forested, green and rolling ground, cut with meandering streams and witchy thickets. Moreover, there genuinely did not appear to be an enemy soldier in the whole of it, and William wondered where in creation Harold was. But one did not look a gift horse in the mouth.

William set up several earthen fortifications to buttress his castle, and turned his men loose to raid the surrounding crofts for victuals. The appearance of these heavily armed and ruthless spectres was more than the poor rustics could comprehend. It took only one or two examples before they shrank away, offered up what little they had, in exchange for remaining unmolested. This was a covenant mostly but not always honoured; William left his men at leisure to inflict any sort of injury they felt was merited, whether to garner obedience, supplies, or simple fear. He knew more than anyone how effective a weapon it was.

'That's about the last of it, m'lord,' Will fitz Osbern said, riding in with a sack of grain slung across his saddle. It was dusk, the second of October. 'Bunch of bloody mutes in the village. I had the boy here question them – ' he jerked his head at Will Peverel – 'but they weren't singing a word about Harold's whereabouts.'

William grunted. 'Perhaps they truly did not know, they live at the arse-end of nowhere. If we have what we need, then we may leave off the foraging. For now.'

Fitz Osbern nodded and trotted off. William turned back to Will Peverel, who was looking dispirited. 'What's amiss, lad?'

'Nothing,' said Will unconvincingly.

William waited.

'I – I've no wish to gainsay you,' Will burst out. It was plain, however, that he did. 'Why must we take from them, my lord? We've provisions enough, yet it's their only succour for the winter. And they will soon be your own people.'

William looked at Will in surprise. He was reminded that the boy, no matter his contested paternity, was indisputably half-Saxon on his mother's side, and had grown up hearing her speak their language, tell their tales and sing their songs. Understandable, then, if the lad had a slightly erroneous view of current activities.

'They are still Harold's for the moment,' said William, 'and will not easily become mine, I think. Besides, it is a vassal's duty to give tithe to his lord.'

'And a lord's duty to maintain his vassals.'

'Lad, a lord can do as pleases him with his vassals. Including taking what he deems needful, or punishing them as he sees fit.'

'But should another lord do precisely the same thing to them, it is cause for war, and furious accusations of the other's barbarian nature.'

Caught off guard, William laughed. 'You've a good mind and a fair point, lad. Keep your sword as sharp as your wits, and I will be well-served.'

He moved to ruffle Will's hair, remembered this was now forbidden, and changed it to a manly clap on the shoulder. Then he set off toward the fires. The night was mild, but the wind was rising to an eldritch whine, and the waning moon had already been swallowed by the clouds.

York, England
October 1066

Harold had been in a sleep so dead and heavy that even as he was sinking into it, he felt as if he would never wake. This prediction might well have proved true if not for the valiant efforts of his brother, which succeeded in raising him to the level of mere stupor. 'Harold!' He had never heard Gyrth sound like that. 'Rood of Christ, wake *up!*'

Harold wondered why he could not have one morning without someone needing something, bringing bad news, waking him from a nightmare. This, however, did not appear to be the opportune moment to ponder the question. He opened his sticky eyes a crack. 'Whuh?'

'Get up.' Gyrth looked as if he'd dressed in a windstorm. 'God's bones, I thought someone had poisoned you!'

'What. Is. Going. On.' Harold shoved upright.

'It's them. They've come. Landed at Pevensey. Six days ago.'

There was no need to ask who *they* were. 'How many?'

'Seven thousand, or more. The messenger wasn't sure.'

'Where are they now? Still at Pevensey?'

'No. They've built a castle near Hastings.'

Another moment. Then Harold tossed the quilt aside and surged out of bed, throwing on clothes and armour and weapons. He blasted out the door, across the courtyard, and into the great hall, where the soldiers were sleeping. The men startled awake at his voice, startled even more at the look on his face, and raced to make their own preparations. There was an air of great alarm, but not panic. The red dawn grew brighter, lending the sullen clouds a glow like the heart of a forge. The army was ready to march in two hours, rumbling down the road in three.

Last time, Harold had been aware of four days, four nights. There was no such distinction this time. All of it was a blur. Nothing but the thought that he must keep moving. He drove the men

240

unmercifully, could always taste dust in his throat. They stopped only long enough to collect Edwin and Morcar and their own forces. The might of England united at last: Wessex and East Anglia and Mercia and Northumbria. Come what may, at least they would stand together.

Harold began to feel that he was existing permanently just outside his body, watching his own doings with a detached interest. He regarded the tall, fair-haired, grim-faced stranger with the golden circlet on his head, the cool emptiness of his eyes. It was brought upon him to wonder, then. *My God, who am I?*

They arrived in London at last, as sundown dyed the Thames a bloody red and the bells were calling Vespers. It was the seventh of October.

Harold spent the next several days in a fury of work. He had forges running constantly, and ensured that the harvest had been completed enough to lay in a tolerable amount of food. Then he ordered barricades built at each of the six city gates, and deployed a gang of masons to shore up any weak spots in the great Roman wall that guarded London. His attention to these details did not go unnoticed.

'Harold,' Gyrth said. 'I hate the thought of the Normans on our soil as much as you, but we absolutely must stay here longer.'

'Why?' Harold marked another twelve paces along the wall.

'What levies there were in London, you took north already. We need time to gather fresh men. The army is exhausted from the two long marches, and Stamford Bridge between them. Another march to Hastings, another battle. . .'

'That would be well indeed,' said Harold sharply, 'if we had the time to spare! Don't you think I would love to have the luxury of putting together a proper defence? By the time I finished, William would be advancing on London, wreaking God alone knows what havoc! What message would it send if we let ourselves be penned up in the city, unable to make a stand? God Almighty, Gyrth, I may die, but on my hope of heaven, it will be with a sword in my hand!'

Silence fell, ringing, and Harold belatedly seemed to realise he had been shouting. 'I'm sorry. But our enemy is already here, and giving him more time to do as he pleases will make it much worse. I know the man. He's like a wolf on the scent of blood.'

The brothers stood staring at each other. Harold's fists were clenched, and heat still burned in his face. For a moment Gyrth looked, really looked at this gaunt, careworn man, crushed beneath a burden far too great for anyone. *My God, who are you?*

Harold, finally, broke the silence. 'Come. We still need to reach Ludgate.'

Gyrth nodded, said nothing more, and followed.

The frenzy grew even more white-hot. Disturbing reports drifted in almost hourly. Raiding, pillaging, crofts burnt down. Harold went paler with fury at the news of every outrage. Nearly there. Nearly ready. Then they would settle this once and for all. *You may be a lion, William. But I am a dragon.*

It was very late afternoon, the eleventh of October. He was in the deserted throne room, leaning back in the great gilded-wood chair. Deep golden sunlight lay on the flagstones. He was almost too tired to breathe, yet somehow he had gone on living.

'My lord?'

Harold opened one eye. 'Aye?' he murmured.

Edwin stepped through the side door and closed it behind him. 'I am sorry to disturb you, brother. But there are a few matters I would have settled afore you go.'

'Speak.'

'Very well. Who will hold London?'

'You will.' Harold sat up. 'I do not doubt your bravery, and I could use you at my side, but I cannot place all four earls at the brink together. You and Morcar stay here. Guard the Aetheling – especially from himself. He may be all we have left.'

Edwin frowned. 'My lord, you sound as if – '

'I have no intention of dying. By God Almighty, Christ His son, and all the saints and angels, no man will take England from us while there is breath in my body. Yet I have already given it almost everything, and should it come to that, I must give it all.'

Edwin was quiet. 'If you do,' he said at last, 'should we – '

'Fight. All you can. One day, God grant, there will come a time when we are free again.'

'Should this come to pass, then what of my sister?'

'Tell her to flee. Get her out, take her to Chester, somewhere away. My own sister as well.' Harold closed his eyes again. 'And one more thing.'

'Aye?'

'Tell Edith to name my son for me.'

Edwin nodded. 'When do you leave, my lord?'

'Tomorrow morning. First light.'

'To Hastings, then?'

'Aye.'

'We will look to the south for your joyous return.'

'Do that.' Harold stood up. 'One of us will die there, Edwin. Him, or me.'

'I know,' his good-brother said. 'So did you. Long since.'

I did. I do. If it comes to that. At last. Everything.

The English army departed London the next morning. Thursday, the twelfth of October. Harold had never heard the raucous streets so quiet – the only sound was the clop of hooves, the clinking of mail, and the scouring of the wind. Distant came the bells of St Peter's and St Paul's. Men took off their hoods. Women covered their faces. Some stretched their hands toward him. He knew again the weight of so much love and fear – knew it afresh, asked to bear it just a little further. The one thing he could not let go of. Not this. Not ever.

They passed through Aldgate, as they had the last time. Gyrth and Leofwine rode beside him, Leofwine's shoulder still bandaged beneath his armour. The banners caught in the leaden breeze: the golden wyvern and the Fighting Man. Behind them the army kept coming and coming. The housecarls and the fyrdmen. Spearmen and axmen and swordsmen. Edwulf, Lucan, Corbin, Eoghan, and all the others. Breath and blood and bone and sinew.

Harold looked back only once. The towers and parapets were already receding. Still the bells called, but fainter and fainter. Then he gave the command, the army began to move in earnest, and London was gone into the mist.

CHAPTER EIGHTEEN

Hastings, England
October 1066

'THEY'RE COMING! Harold and his army! They're coming!' Will Peverel dodged a boulder, leaped a tussock, and slammed to a halt in front of William. 'The men saw them on the road. A great host. They've arrived just north of here, at a place called Santlache Hill.'

William's Saxon was sufficient to translate this as 'sandy stream,' which seemed a rather deceptively pastoral sobriquet. But oddities of name aside, he cared more for the rest of Will's news. 'At last. I was beginning to think I'd misjudged the man.'

'Of course you didn't, my lord,' the boy said loyally. He fell into step with William as they crossed the camp, supper-fires pricking the encroaching dusk. 'Some of the men said we should have begun to march on London, rather than waiting for him.'

William raised an eyebrow. 'I bloody hate sideline generals. None of them were bold enough to venture this puissant opinion to me, I notice.'

'Why – why didn't we?' Will was tall enough at fifteen that he could almost match William's strides, though he still had to walk fast to keep up entirely.

'Harold is the first of my enemies I've ever respected.' William shrugged. 'Admired, no. And he *is* a godforsaken traitor, he broke his oath, and what have you. But I'll still let him have the chance to fight for it. Trial by battle. He deserves that at least.'

To judge from Will's expression, he was both awed at William's faith in the matter, and praying it would prove to be justified. 'Odo is informing the men, my lord.'

'Good. We'll be marching as soon as it's dark. Help see to it that they're ready.'

Will nodded, then sprinted away, and William watched him go. So it had come at last, as he had known it would. The wind from the north smelled of foreboding. By this time tomorrow it would smell of blood. But the lingering reek of smoke made his thoughts wander back to a few days past. When everything was finished at Pevensey, and they had built the last fortifications at Hastings, he had given a peculiar order.

'Burn them,' he said, indicating the ships. 'I have kept a sufficient number for our later use, and my own *Mora*. The rest must be put alight. The English may drive us to the shore, but they shall drive us no further. If the ships are spared, some of you will think of fleeing. That must not be.'

'Burn them?' Odo repeated, goggling. 'But they – '

'They have served their purpose.' William met his half-brother's eyes coolly. 'Does anyone else question my decision?'

No one did. So it was done. The ships were drenched in pitch, had a torch thrown onto the deck, and were pushed out into the bay. At first the flames mumbled, flickering only in embers. Then they touched the tongues of oil, and fire raced up, caught, and screamed. Burning, the ships were eerily and starkly beautiful, masts showing skeletal, ropes crashing down in flaming coils. The orange light dyed the darkness for miles, smoke rising wraithlike against the moon. One by one, as each ship burnt to the waterline, it was transformed into a shapeless hulk, steaming and hissing and snarling, until at last even the most fearless demons plunged into the dark ocean and perished in its depths.

The Normans set out as ordered, under cover of darkness. It was only a short march, a little over a league, but the ground was uneven and marshy and seven thousand men could not be transported in any sort of secrecy. The tramping echoed through the woods, torches flared, and outriders raced on ahead. Far in the distance a wolf howled.

The moon was well in the sky by the time the Normans reached their final camp. It lay just a scant mile away from the English, who they could see as the glitter of a thousand fires. Harold had chosen his ground wisely; Santlache Hill was a formidable ridgeback of limestone, hemmed with scrubby trees, and the English had established themselves at the very top. Behind was the vast forest, and in front was a steep slope of loose, sliding rock and grass and mud. Any attack would start at a serious disadvantage, but William was unfazed. He strode through the camp, keeping spirits up, and ordered the men to get what sleep they could. 'You may have to die for me on the morrow, you know. You don't want to go yawning to Our Lord.'

They laughed nervously. Death was on all their minds that night, as tangible as if it prowled just outside the firelight. William paused, then spoke again. 'You very well might. You are in a foreign land. Winter is coming. You will have to fight, and you will win or you will die. I have shown you already that retreat is not an option. You face men who have nothing left to lose. You stand with everything to gain. We give them battle on the morrow. We arm at first light. It will be a day long remembered. *Diex aie.*'

With that, he retreated, leaving them to murmur. He walked among the tents, looking for nothing in particular, until he found it. He turned and said softly, 'What do you see?'

Taillefer did not answer for the longest moment. Then he lifted his head. 'Nothing.' His eyes were cold and empty as snow. 'The crows shall feast well by the evening bell. *Death*, you dread king. The only thing. Everything.'

Santlache Hill
Midnight

'Your Grace! Your Grace!' The lookouts pelted in, breathless and muddy. 'They're – the Normans – they're here!'

'We know, Alwin.' Harold rose to his feet, grim. 'Where?'

'Just beyond Telham Hill, my lord.' The lookout made a flustered bow and accepted the waterskin. 'You can't see their camp from here, but for certain you can smell it. A stink of murderers, usurpers and madmen,' he added savagely.

His fellow lookout, however, appeared to be confused. 'My lord said that the Normans are fierce warriors. But I do not understand why the duke has brought so many priests with him.'

Harold looked at him blankly. 'Priests? No, they're – oh.' He had to smile as he realised the source of the confusion. 'The Normans wear their hair short, and their faces shaven. I fear you will taste the wrath of those "priests" soon enough.'

'And they'll taste ours,' said Alwin stoutly.

'I pray God so. Take some rest, you deserve it. Morning will be here much too soon.'

Alwin bowed and retreated. The English camp was mostly dark – though not silent, thanks to the rumble of snoring coming from the men; they looked like scattered logs, shields and helms and axes heaped beside their owners. To show that they had no fear, and nothing to hide, they had spent a great deal of the night singing and drinking, until finally dropping off. Harold had a feeling, however, that a goodly number of those men were feigning sleep – lying half-dozing, wondering if this was the last night they would have on earth. Even a veteran of a hundred battles might not rest easy – perhaps even less so, knowing that eventually his luck would have to swing in the opposite direction.

Harold himself had been functioning so long without sleep that he was afraid that to do so might leave him bleary and muddled, in a time when he had never needed his wits more. He reached for his wineskin again, and prodded the fire back to life. Then he noticed Gyrth regarding him with his square jaw set, wearing a dogged expression that meant he was about to ask something unpleasant.

'Aye, brother?' Harold prompted.

Gyrth took a deep breath and shot a look at Leofwine. Finding no help, he turned back to Harold. In a voice which said he did not expect to be heeded in the slightest, he said, 'I ask leave to command Your Grace's forces in the battle tomorrow.'

'I – *what?* What in God's name makes you think I'll come this far and sit out?'

Gyrth flushed, but did not look away. 'Whatever the circumstances, you did swear an oath to William on holy relics. If you take the field against him, you may be in defiance of heaven. If that is the case, then. . .'

'We would undoubtedly lose,' Leofwine completed.

Harold gave the pair of them an aghast look. 'This is the – I – no. No. First, the oath was not binding, it was extracted from me by trickery and deceit. Secondly, I swore to help him take the crown for himself. Well, I bloody well didn't. It's been ten months, and I haven't been cut down. I've united England, defeated the Vikings. Hardly the victories expected of a perjurer.'

'Aye, but those weren't against William,' Gyrth persisted. 'I – I only meant – '

'I know.' Harold gazed into the darkness. 'But you must know what my answer is. It is for me that these men are here, and for me that they fight. I must command them myself. And then the night will be over, and we shall not be afraid.'

Gyrth said nothing. Then, eyes still downcast, he nodded.

'We go where you go.' It was Leofwine who spoke this time. The youngest of Godwin's sons save Wulfnoth, still captive in Normandy. Yet even he was past thirty, and his boyish handsomeness was beginning to grow worn and gaunt. 'To death, or to victory.'

Harold nodded. He held out his arms, and they grasped hard. Three brothers, a king and two earls. The last remnant of their powerful family, with one great task left.

The fire guttered. Harold thought of that candle in York Minster. 'Stay with me,' he said. 'I don't want to be alone tonight.'

Leofwine smiled. 'Never.'

The three of them lay down by the fire, sharing blankets, watching it fade. The night seemed expansive and dark when it did. Almost silent, almost peaceful. Harold hovered just beneath the surface, not asleep and not awake. The warmth of his brothers was comforting. Leofwine's breathing deepened, grew slow.

The moon set. The hours waned away like sand in a glass. Harold turned over carefully to look at the sky. It was brilliant, star-flecked and depthless as a woman's eyes.

He was under no illusions about what came in the morning. He knew that it would be a fight to the death, exactly what sort of foe he faced, and that William would impale himself on his own sword sooner than surrender. But Harold meant the same. He trusted his men. He believed in the rightness of his cause. He had faced the fire, and now he must walk through it. There was no way but forward. He was at peace. With God, and with himself.

Harold turned over again. Vaguely, on the edges of awareness, he realised that the lack of snoring meant he was not the only one who could not slip under.

But at last, only a few hours before sunrise, he did.

Telham Hill
Dawn

The beginning announced itself gradually, a deepening red flush in the east. It burned through the clouds, casting shadows over the pockmarked ground. It was time.

The horses were stirring restlessly. Men moved about like ghosts, or crammed bread down their throats, or said quiet prayers, or were sick in a bush when they thought their fellows wouldn't notice. They struggled into their armour, fingers stiff with sleep.

William didn't think he had ever had so much time in the calm before the storm. His battles usually presented themselves cock-a-hoop, and he was lucky to have a few moments of notice that he would be required to fight them. It was racing here or there, ambushing this or that, sitting at a siege, twisting an arm, doing all the things he did so well, and thus why he had survived. The only thing that felt even remotely comparable was Val-ès-Dunes. His first real battle, half his life ago. Since then, he had never faced another with such a real threat of being his last. Of course, they had all been a gruelling gauntlet – hard-fought, damaging, draining. There had been no certainty that he'd win. But those had been for other things: fealty, money, power, lands, Church, wife. Nothing less than his whole existence, in one great cosmic sum, had been wagered at Val-ès-Dunes. For what, he'd never known. Until now.

He was not frightened; he was imbued with stony, unassailable resolve. But even he, William the Bastard, was – at long last – slightly intimidated.

He stood looking in the direction of Santlache, could see the dark stain of the English camp. 'You can't win,' William said softly, his breath silver in the chill air. 'You should have kept your oath.'

Silence, almost. Then came the strident crack of Odo's voice, hailing him. William started, crossed himself, and went to prepare.

It was a cumbersome business getting one's armour on, especially in haste. There was, after all, a great bloody deal of it. Chainse, gambeson, hauberk, tabard, vambraces for the arms, greaves for the legs. Then over the hauberk came the studded-leather cuirass – it had a front piece and a back piece, and tied under the arms. William was trying to get it on, and his squire was trying to keep up in order to not be shouted at, and so it was the logical consequence that the boy put the cuirass on backwards. This, by the nervous Normans attending their duke, was immediately and very rationally interpreted as yet another ill-meaning omen.

'Oh for Christ's sake,' William said in exasperation. 'You, dolt – ' such as he customarily addressed his squire – 'put the blasted thing on right, or I'll leave you for the Saxons. The rest of you, stop your damnable simpering. Why, I daresay it bodes very well. For I too shall be changed about today, from duke to king.'

That shut them up nicely, and the rest of his armouring was accomplished without incident. But there was still one thing left. 'Turold,' he called. 'Taillefer.'

The dwarf and the fool stepped forward, carrying the reliquaries which had made their last, and highly effective, appearance in Bonneville. William hoped they'd retain the same potency today. He waited calmly as Turold removed the bones, which had been tied together with a bit of ribbon. Then because Turold was much too short, William was much too tall, and had no intention of kneeling to be bedecked by a dwarf, the honour of conferral was given to Odo. Praying loudly in Latin, he raised the relics high, then placed them around his half-brother's neck, as William consented to bow his head the barest bit. Then his squire brought forth his longsword, and William buckled it on. He cinched the straps tight; he would not bear his bow today. Just this, his old friend. Then he pulled on his gauntlets, leather sewn with steel discs. Last came his helmet, clasped under his chin.

'My lord,' Odo declared, in ringing tones. 'No man can stand before your face.'

'I see you've managed. And I would rather they fell beneath my sword.' William looked at them – Odo, Robert, Will fitz Osbern, Will Peverel, and the rest. 'Come,' he said. 'We have a battle to win.'

A thunderous shout greeted him when he stepped out of the tent. He raised a hand, acknowledging it, but said nothing; now was not the moment for speeches. His squire brought him his grey. He stroked its nose, then grasped the bridle and swung astride. From there he surveyed them – infantry, cavalry, archers. A forest of lances, gonfanons snapping at the top. The papal banner fluttering. And above them all, the lions of Normandy, crimson as the sunrise.

He knew the masses were watching him. He said nothing, let them keep doing so. Then, sudden as a bone breaking, he flung back his head and let loose an almighty roar.

It bounced crazily across the misty fens, was echoed back by seven thousand throats. Then and only then were they his, finally and forever his, with the demon in them, no more ghost of an idea of surrender or ill omens or anything save victory. He seized the lance handed up to him, then wheeled the grey around.

Behind him the landslide started. Their armoured feet beat and the ground rumbled and then they were pouring into the low plain before Santlache Hill, and atop it they caught their first glimpse of the seawall rising to counter their wave, and the sun, breaking from the clouds, glittered on countless swords and axes, the interlocking circular shields. Above this army flew the golden wyvern and the Fighting Man, and somewhere in the middle of them was the fighting man himself, the man with the stolen crown. And so it was a reminder that no matter the great columns massing beneath Santlache, no matter the shield wall that stood implacable at the top, it was much simpler, much smaller, than that.

Army to army. Man to man. Hand to hand.

Harold and William. England and Normandy. Now and forever. Just that. Always.

'Steady! Steady!' Harold had to bellow over the racket the Normans were making, and the answering commotion of his men, screaming and howling, axe against shield. 'STEADY!'

Behind the shield-wall of housecarls, the fyrdmen crowded in, spears jutting out: a merciless harvest of foot-long steel. Then more axmen, and the swords in reserve, defending the hill on all sides. Gyrth on his right, Leofwine on his left.

'*Men of England!*' Harold thundered. 'We have the high ground! As long as we stand as one, *we will outlast them!* Break ranks, and you will be sundered alike! Stand together! Stand for home, for hearth, for freedom! Stand for England! *STAND!*'

The noise was deafening. The very earth was rolling. Below them, the Normans had almost finished assembling. Archers in front, row on row, followed by infantry, and then the heavy cavalry. Lion and wyvern leapt above the opposing lines. The air resounded like drums.

Then, for a heartbeat that crashed in everyone's ears, it was quiet. Neither army moved. Harold felt he was about to snap with the strain, but kept holding, waiting, and then –

The Norman lines parted, and out came a –

A giant axe-man, an archer, a fire-breather, William himself? No. A fool.

Harold blinked, sure that he was seeing things. The fool who had saved him outside Guy's castle in Beaurain. Taillefer, his name was. What was William thinking, was this just some –

Taillefer prevented further quandary on the part of the English by taking hold of his tunic, flipping it up, and displaying his skinny bare buttocks. A rumble of fury ran through the housecarls, but they'd seen this sort of thing many times before. What they had not seen, however, was when Taillefer hopped up on a horse. With that, he began to sing.

The Saxons stared in communal stupefaction, but made no move to attack. At least, until a fyrdman on the lower reaches of the hill could bear the insult no further and – ignoring Harold's shouted command – went skidding down, hurtled across the field, and closed in on Taillefer like an enraged ox.

Taillefer whirled his horse around. He waited until the Englishman was almost on top of him. Then with amazing dexterity he snapped his hand up, dodged the man's blow, and socketed his dagger in the vulnerable hollow of shoulder and neck. The Englishman shouted, charge turning into a stumble. An explosion of blood showed on the grass. Taillefer stabbed again, and the Englishman crashed down. He writhed, then lay still.

Nobody on either side was laughing. Taillefer was no longer smiling. He dismounted and regarded his victim dispassionately. His teeth were bared, and he looked like something feral. He paced forward, singing deliberately, loudly.

Then turned away the Baivers and Germans
And Poitevins and Bretons and Normans.
Fore all the rest, 'twas voted by the Franks
That Guenes die with marvellous great pangs;
So to lead forth four stallions they bade;
After, they bound his feet and both his hands;
Those steeds were swift, and of a temper mad;
Which, by their heads, led forward four sejeants

Towards a stream that flowed amid that land.
Sones fell Gue into perdition black;
All his sinews were strained until they snapped,
And all the limbs were from his body dragged.
On the green grass his clear blood gushed and ran.
Guenes is dead, a felon recreant
Who betrays man, need make no boast of that.

The Saxons understood none of this performance, conducted as it was in French, but the body of their compatriot was all the understanding they needed. Another fyrdman, quicker and cannier than the first, came bellowing down Santlache. With one mighty heave he flung his lance, and Taillefer made no attempt to avoid it. He was thrown a good six feet back with the force of the blow, bony limbs flopping limp, landing just in front of the Norman lines.

'Blood,' he gurgled softly, and died.

'Steady!' Harold shouted again. He knew what was coming.

Provocation had been tendered. The Norman army gave a great shout and surged into motion. The archers nocked and drew. A breathless, unbearable moment, while the arrowheads went up. And then a thrumming snarl as they loosed.

'*Shields!*' Harold screamed. At once they locked together overhead, and the next instant the first volley began to fall, hissing and slamming, thundering against the wood like hailstones. Then the Norman archers nocked, drew, and loosed again. The sky was freshly split by all the screaming shafts, and again they fell. They cracked and thumped and zinged, pinging off, lodging in the ground like bristling grass. But still, the housecarls held.

'Fine weather we're having!' Leofwine shouted, grinning at Harold. 'All this rain? But I could do with a touch of sun!'

'I'm afraid we're under the storm yet!' Harold shouted back. He could hear a third volley, a notion confirmed an instant later by the shuddering impact. Through the line of housecarls, he could see that the archers had almost reached the base of Santlache.

There were half a dozen more volleys to endure. He was astounded that he was able to count; the world was a dream. He could hear the grunts of effort, taste the sweat, as the housecarls withstood the relentless pounding. But William must have thought they'd done their job, for then the terms of the battle changed.

'Infantry!' William roared. He'd never known an enemy to take that vigorous a peppering without at least some damage to show for it, and he didn't want all their arrows to be wasted at the outset. *'Charge!'*

Robert de Mortain relayed this command to one side, and Will fitz Osbern to the other. The first several ranks broke off and surged, and reached the foot of Santlache in truly remarkable time, clawing up the steep, rocky slope. But something had shifted. The battle, for once, was not unfolding the way he'd read it. And then the English boiled off the defensive. Shields rotated and raised. A hurl of stones, lances, anything they had to hand, came pelting down the hill. The barrage was furious, and from their throats came one, equally furious cry. 'OUT!' The trees bent, the air reverberated. 'OUT! OUT! *OUT!'*

They're not softened. It came to William in a flash. The shield-wall had done its work exceptionally well, rendering the English losses almost nonexistent, and now they were raining their wrath on the Normans below. For every man that gained a foot, two more fell. The English kept on screaming. *'OUT! OUT! OUT!'*

'DIEX AIE!' came the answering bellow from the Normans. They kept on climbing. A few archers were climbing with them, pausing to loose and fire, having more success at catching those who had exposed themselves to throw. The Norman infantry had been decimated, torn apart, but they still kept coming. Some of them were almost to the top, at close enough range that they could duck the missiles. Then they began to run flat-out.

'Stop them!' Harold seized another boulder and flung it into a cluster of climbing men; two of them lost their balance, one had his neck broken on the spot, and another was laid out clean, an easy target for the spear Leofwine threw. 'Steady – steady – *brace!'*

The housecarls braced. The next instant, the charge hit them like a snarling maelstrom. Steel screeched and sparked, and the ground was slippery with blood. Harold lost sight of Leofwine and Gyrth; he was hacking and hewing madly, back to back with some fyrdman. They were all still chanting, bellowing. 'OUT! OUT! OUT!'

He had no idea how long it had been going on. He thought they were doing well, all things considered; they had staved off the Normans from advancing any deeper than the first rank. A blow clanged off his mailed shoulder, and he spun and sheathed his sword in the attacker's gut. They were gaining the upper hand. He could sense it, in that way in which the army was his body, his bones and blood their own. Then he felt the ground beginning to shake in earnest, and when he spared a glance back down the hill, he saw that all hell had truly come unloosed.

'*Cavalry!*' William hadn't meant to resort to it just yet, but the losses the Normans had sustained just to get to the top of the hill were well-nigh ruinous. He shoved his heels into the grey and went careening off – his Normans behind him, the Bretons to his left and the Flemish to his right. Their infantry flung themselves out of the way, and the horses plunged up the slope, hooves striking sparks.

The English raced to reform their shield-wall. Lances snarled upright, axe linked with axe. William readied himself for the shock, but it was still titanic. Broken bodies snapped underfoot, and he threw his weight forward in the saddle, still clawing, dodging, arrows singing overhead. It happened so fast that there was no way a man could think consciously. But he had been trained for this, trained to the marrow of his bones.

The sun continued to move higher in the sky. It had to be going on noon. Almost all battles took three hours or so at most, but this one appeared to be just warming up. Still the sheer weight of the cavalry pushed it forward – but yet, for everything, despite the fact that they were mounted and the housecarls were not –

It came to William out of nowhere. *I am losing.* The English had given very little ground, and though their own dead were beginning to mount, it was nowhere near on the scale of the Normans. Confronted with the wall of swords and axes and spears, the horses were screaming, rearing, cut down, their riders falling into the morass and being trampled into the bloody mud. And then William had his eerie *sense,* a moment before it happened, and –

They were breaking. The bloody Bretons were breaking. The English had sensed it, were throwing themselves at the weakness, driving them back on their heels. Half a moment more and they would be in genuine rout. Dust choked the sunlight. It couldn't –

With no further preliminary, the Breton line collapsed completely. They turned tail and galloped down the hill in a panic, and with this precedent established, the Normans and the Flemish, who were also coming off the worse, immediately followed suit.

Suddenly there was only air behind William, and he was facing the whole mob of housecarls alone, and he was determined but he was not a lunatic. He turned and raced down the hill after them.

'No!' Harold screamed. 'Don't break ranks! Don't break ranks!'

His words fell on deaf ears. The English saw, at last, their unfathomable stroke of good fortune: the Normans tumbling away, heavily wounded and heavily damaged. They had withstood the worst the foe had to offer and lived, and euphoria and instinct won out. The shield-wall began to disintegrate, achieving in an instant what the Normans could not do in several hours, and the English poured hungrily down the hill after them.

'GOD ALMIGHTY, NO!' Harold could see the milling, panicked throng of Normans below. For a moment he hoped with a sick and desperate fury – if his men did get there in time, one great hammer-strike to end it, end it now –

And then he saw one lone figure riding like hellfire toward them, the grey stallion flying across the blood-drenched grass. He would have known it anywhere.

'STOP! STOP HIM!' Harold seized a lance from the nearest man and threw it, but it fell well short. All he was aware of thinking was that he could not, could *not*, let William get in among them. *No, no, get away from there, you bastard, get AWAY –*

And then, somehow, madly, he was certain that God had heard. The housecarls slammed into the rear of the scattered Normans – a moment where all the world held at bay, waiting –

And just like that, the grey horse and its rider were gone.

William never saw the man that struck the blow. He wasn't even aware that there was a man about to strike a blow. He had no idea why he reined up and dodged so hard. Then he heard a muffled whistling sound, followed by a bone-splitting crunch.

William wondered which unlucky son-of-a-bitch had taken *that* one. He turned the grey, except the grey wasn't turning. There was a horrible feeling of immobility and vertigo. Then the grey crashed to its knees, screaming, and threw him.

Somehow, impossibly, William had the sense to twist as he was going down, just enough to wrench clear of the horse. Its forehooves churned, its eyes rolled white. Its chest had been cleaved almost in half. Mercifully, it died a moment later.

William sprawled beside it, blood-soaked and dazed. He felt dreamlike, disconnected from the madness still going on just above him. He was sucking air fruitlessly, could barely see for the sweat in his eyes. But he could still hear. 'The Duke! Duke William! *The duke is dead! I saw him fall! He's dead! Flee! Save yourselves!'*

The madness overhead accelerated. And William, then, could see it. The balance tipping catastrophically awry. Everything gone. His life. His crown. Everything.

Well, he thought. *That simply will not do.*

He sprang to his feet, horses still swerving and plunging to every side. And, being William, he did what any sane man would have accounted a very stupid thing indeed.

'GET BACK THERE, YOU WHORESONS!' He found the buckle of his helmet, undid it, and ripped it off. He ran like a madman, locked onto the first riderless horse he saw, and leapt astride at full sprint, bareheaded. He wheeled around and belted off, getting between the retreat, galloping circles around them, still bellowing at the top of his lungs. He was dimly aware of his brother Odo rampaging by, waving a distaff and screaming far more blasphemous oaths at the deserters than was proper for a churchman. Not, at the moment, that he objected at all.

'GET BACK THERE AND FIGHT! OR I'LL KILL YOU MYSELF!' Slowly but surely, William pulled them back into order; with his helmet off, there could be no doubt that he was still alive. The Normans were turning, coming, returning, and Will fitz Osbern blasted out of nowhere to instil similar compliance in the Flemish. *Where* were the useless fucking Bretons – but it didn't matter –

William scalped off a band of Normans, turned back toward Santlache, and charged.

'God on the Cross!' Harold screamed. 'Get out of the way, Gyrth, GET OUT – '

He knew his brother couldn't hear him. Gyrth was wedged between William and the hill, a pack of housecarls backing him up. They were standing fast as – God *almighty,* how had William survived that, *how* –

'GYRTH! MOVE!' Harold flung himself forward. 'NOW – '

The rest of the words never made it to his lips. On flat ground, the Normans coming at a dead gallop, the outnumbered housecarls never stood a chance. William smashed into Gyrth, his sword erupting through the back of Gyrth's throat.

'NO!' Harold couldn't be seeing this, didn't register. No, this was not what was supposed to happen, why hadn't they listened to him, he'd told them not to –

Disorganised, out from behind the shield wall, the English were not nearly so invincible as they'd first appeared. The fyrdmen lacked the discipline of the housecarls. They tried to band together, but that only made them more convenient to cut down.

The two armies briefly drew apart, leaving a rubble of shattered bodies strewn across the field. In places they were two or three deep. Blood ran like a stream, and Harold flung a desperate glance at the sky. It was well into the afternoon. and no matter the fact that they'd been fighting for six or seven hours already, it gave him a sudden, lurching hope. If they could hold out until nightfall, they would win. Battles were not carried on past dark; both sides would have to retreat and wait for sunrise. And Harold knew there were fresh men marching to join him at this very moment, who would arrive before that sunrise. William would have no such succour, and a badly demolished and demoralised force.

The thought heartened him. He bellowed at the remaining housecarls to form up, and succeeded in getting the fyrdmen to hold the line, reclaim their entrenchments atop Santlache. They were standing, and would stand still. Not losing. Not now.

William lost his second horse on that attack. One moment it was running underneath him, the next it was gone, and he was crashing down. It winded him no less this time, and hooves flashed just as dangerously overhead. But by great good fortune, he hit a tree, dodged behind the trunk as a spear lodged in it, then raced back. This time, he did not even bother that the replacement mount be abandoned. He sprinted up to a good-sized chestnut, seized the rider, and threw him out of the saddle, before climbing up and kicking the beast back around, squinting – the shadows were growing tricky, and longer. The sun was sliding toward the horizon, and he felt a jolt of fear. If night came, he would lose.

He looked up at the tattered outfit still holding out on Santlache. There was still a shield-wall, but it was crooked and uneven, like a mouth of broken teeth. And that –

Something came to him. He wheeled around and galloped off toward the archers, pointing up, describing a long high arc with a hand. 'Over!' he shouted. 'Fire *over!*'

They saw at once what he meant. They raised their bows and began to fire long, well over the shields, into the tightly packed ranks beyond. This worked with stunning success. The English began to scream, topple, could not get replacements to the front line quickly enough. And William saw again what he had to do.

He raised a fist. Arrows screamed into the growing evening, clattering and thundering and falling. And then he brought the fist down, and one more time, they charged. Horses coming up Santlache like an avalanche in reverse, pushed on by their own inexorable, surging weight. And one more volley was loosed to show their way, and went up and up and up, singing and hissing, and up and up into the sun and vanished, devoured by the flame.

Nightfall. The thought was blasted into place by pain and fatigue, searing as if writ in fire. *Nightfall. Please God. Nightfall.*

The English army was driven together, gathered around the wyvern standard at the very crest of the hill, in danger of being forced into the trees below. Harold was surrounded by corpses, he was so tired, so tired –

And he heard a shout, somewhere –

'MY LORD! HAROLD! LOOK OUT – MY LORD – '

Leofwine, was that Leofwine? He had been searching for –

Harold, duly warned, looked up.

The next instant, there came the worst agony he'd ever known, animal and unbearable, boiling red-hot. Blood spilled on his cheek, he tasted it on his tongue, and half his world had gone black. He fumbled madly, grasped the arrow. Felt it break, cast the fletching aside. *No – please God – nightfall –*

And yet night was coming, they were at the shield-wall, they were breaking in –

Harold was, somehow, still upright. He could hear curses, screaming. 'Look to the king! The king! My God! No, God, mercy!'

But there was breath in his body, yet. Dimly, out of his right eye, he could still see, though the agony was making him hallucinate gory phantoms. He gripped his blood-slicked sword. *Come for me.*

They were coming. The English were shattered, Normans riding over them, housecarls still around him but being cut down where they stood. The horses reached him. He stared at them, knew them. William and five or six of his knights.

Harold bellowed a final defiance. The Normans charged. Just give him one good swing – the light turning blue and shadowy, the flickers of the trees, running –

Then they were on him from all sides at once. *Wolves.* He swung the sword, swung it, swung it still, for he was a warrior and would die as one. Gashes opened in him, long ribbons of silken soul blown on the breeze. The bright fire of steel was coming for his face, and in his leg and in his chest and in his heart. Then he was falling, never landing only falling, never hitting the ground, only in midair, shattered darkness, and all he heard was screaming.

EPILOGUE

Santlache Hill
Twilight

THE WYVERN STANDARD fell first. William cut it down. A crack of wood, a crack of mail, and a sword through the heart for its bearer. After that, the Fighting Man.

The English were taken with unholy terror. The fyrdmen were throwing down their weapons and fleeing, the housecarls fighting with a dull, dead look. The bodies were three and four deep at the top of the hill, and William had lost his third horse just as he reached it. He'd been able to leap off it and land on his feet, run toward Harold, where he knew Harold must be, and then –

Then he had seen him. Barely recognised him. There was an arrow in his left eye, and his face was a monstrous ruin. Blood everywhere, but he was still on his feet. Even as they broke him and overran him, Harold was standing tall, smashed into submission only by the rain of blows descending. Never defeated. Not truly. And then even so, he was dead and he was falling. William was aware that this was it, that it was done, but it made no sense and he kept on fighting anyway, fighting as long as the housecarls stood, until the last one went down and there was only a thunderous silence, that did not touch him and shook him to the remnants.

By twilight the battle was done. It was theirs. Lances and arrows broken, swords fallen from dead fingers, empty eyes staring. Santlache itself was an abattoir. The stream was red. The grass was red. It was such a shocking colour that William laughed.

'Your Grace.' A familiar figure staggered into view, pulled off its helmet. Then knelt, and grasped his hands. 'May I be the first to pay my homage to the King of England.'

That's me. Had this bloody mad idea worked? Or was it only bloody?

He looked down into Will fitz Osbern's battered, filthy face and smiled. 'Rise, my lord. This work is barely started.'

They walked the field as his men pitched his tent amongst the ruins, raised the lions of Normandy to fly in the gathering darkness. It was still ludicrous to William. The silence was oppressing him. He could not imagine it done. He began to laugh.

'My lord?' Another voice wavered out of the dusk, and he glanced up to see Will Peverel himself, looking sick and shocked. He was covered in a quantity of blood, but it did not seem to be his own, praise God. William offered him a hand, and Will grasped it hard. 'You won, my lord.' He gave an unsteady giggle. 'You won.'

'So I did.' William grasped harder, wondering – just for the briefest moment – who was holding who up. He undid his helmet and let the evening breeze run its cool fingers across his sweat-soaked face. He was shaking with exhaustion. He hadn't noticed.

'My lord,' said Fitz Osbern. 'Come sit.'

He did. He ducked into the tent. He sat down. Outside he could hear the looting going on. 'Put a stop to it,' he ordered his captains. 'And stop the hunting of the English. Any man who survived that battle has my respect. Bring them here. See if they've an interest in swearing their fealty. Any man who will be mine can live. Kill the rest as traitors.'

The captains bowed and departed. It was his half-brother Robert de Mortain who spoke next. 'Some of the English women have come to the field. They ask leave to recover their menfolk.'

William grunted. 'If they can find whatever's left of them, they're welcome to it. Deal harshly with anyone who tries to stop them. And one more thing.'

Robert glanced back. 'Aye?'

'Find me Harold. He died on Santlache somewhere.'

'Santlache? Is that what it's called?'

'Aye.' William blew out an unsteady breath. 'Of course, that name does not suit now, does it? *Sanglac* would better.' *Blood-lake.*

Robert raised an eyebrow. 'Indeed.' He left.

William sat with his eyes closed, listening to the distant sobs from the women hunting among the corpses. It was some time before his captains returned with the English they'd caught. They said there was some bloody treacherous and steep ground beyond the hill that had almost done for them, and a few of the Normans had indeed broken their necks at the bottom. 'All for this ragged-arse lot,' Walter Giffard growled. 'We've killed most of them already, we should just finish the job.'

'Peace, Walter.' William turned away and walked down the line of captives, sorting out which man was a coward and which man meant to stab him later and which man had merely been caught since he could not run fast enough. He ordered them killed, then turned to those remaining and demanded their oaths.

When this was done, it was full dark, and the stars were coming out. Robert de Mortain and Will fitz Osbern returned, and reported that they were having difficulty locating Harold; the butchered bodies heaped up on Sanglac made it impossible. The men *had* found what they thought were Gyrth and Leofwine Godwinson, and proudly carried in the mangled corpses for display, which William surveyed with a mildly revolted look. 'Aye, it is. Take them out to await their brother. And *find him*, I said.'

'We. . .' Will paused. 'We did find someone else you might be interested in.'

'Show him in, then.'

'Her, m'lord.' Fitz Osbern grinned. With that, he reached behind him and hauled in a cloaked and hooded woman.

'Gently, Will, gently, you needn't take her arms off,' Walter Giffard commented. 'She's a fair bit, if you know what I'm saying.'

William gave him a cool look, though he knew that with men's blood so up after a battle, they were apt to take it out in other ways. He addressed the woman directly. 'Who are you?'

For a moment she didn't move. Then her hands came up, and she pulled her hood off, revealing two long, thick plaits of pale hair. She had an equally pale, slender neck, an elegant carriage, and an unspeakable, crushing sadness in her eyes. 'My name is Edith,' she said, answering him in Saxon, 'though I am called Swannesha.'

He inclined his head, watching her warily.

'I came with the women to the battlefield,' she said. 'I would know where he lies.'

'Who?' he asked, knowing.

'My lord Harold.' Her lips pressed together, she bit them, but her voice did not break. 'He put me aside in life, but in death that makes no matter.'

'We searched for him, to no avail. If you can find him, we would be obliged.'

She nodded stiffly, then turned. He followed her, ducking into the chilly night. Will came after him with the torch, and Robert de Mortain and Walter Giffard and Roger Bigod and a few others. They climbed Sanglac Hill steadily in the dark, the light bobbing over the countless dead men. Swannesha looked neither left nor right, wading through the dreck of bodies, pulling them aside with her own hands. She folded down the tattered tunic and examined each bloody, ruined chest, then moved onto the next one.

William followed closely at her heels. She carried out her grisly work with a coolness he admired. She should have been queen – at least until now, as he had his own candidate in mind for the position. He wondered what in God's name had led Harold to cast her away.

He was brought back by a small, sharp sound from Swannesha. She was looking down at what indeed appeared to have been a tall man at one time, but was missing its head, one of its legs, and so many sundry bits of flesh that it could have been anything. It gaped from a thousand wounds. It was barely human.

'It's him,' said Swannesha. 'I know it.'

'Are you sure?'

Her lips went tighter. 'Aye,' she said, barely opening them, as if afraid she'd scream.

William made a brief signal. A pair of Normans moved forward and hoisted the slaughtered thing, rolled it in a blanket, and swung it over their shoulders. Recovery mission concluded, they made their way slowly back down Sanglac. Swannesha stumbled. William offered her a hand, but she ripped away.

He raised an eyebrow. 'Fine. Break your neck if it suits you.'

She didn't answer. He heard her breathing change, showing all the anguish she refused to speak aloud. They arrived back in the field. Harold was dumped with Gyrth and Leofwine.

'My lord,' said Swannesha. 'Their mother is with the others. She bids me tell you that she will pay her sons' weight in gold for their bodies. To give them proper Christian burial.'

'They died as traitors,' William answered coolly. 'Forsworn by God. I doubt Christian burial is a sacrament they merit.'

Her pale face floated in the dark like a spirit. 'So your answer is no, my lord?'

'Shockingly, yes.' William turned on his heel. 'You,' he said to Will Peverel. 'Escort this lady back to the other English women. See she's not harmed.'

Will nodded, moved forward, and took Swannesha by the arm. 'Come, my lady,' he said, very soft. 'Come now.'

They vanished into the dark. William stood watching them go, the carnage raw around him and the night that smelled of blood. He still did not quite believe it.

'My lord,' said Will fitz Osbern. 'What comes now?'

'We wait.' William paced a circle. 'Rest a few days. And see if the witanagemot in London has the good sense to submit at once. They can do this the simple way or the difficult way, but it *will* be done. England is mine now, and it will learn that.'

'And if the witan does not have such wisdom, what then?'

William turned. He stood with his face to the wind, breathing the scent of victory, but knew the hard work was only beginning. In a moment more he spoke.

'Then,' he said. 'Then we ride.'

To be continued in

THE OUTLANDER KING

DRAMATIS PERSONAE

The English Royal House

[Æthelred the Unræd], c.968 – 1016. King of England; called the 'Unlucky' or the 'Ill-advised'; father of eight sons and several daughters by two marriages; ruled thirty-eight years in the midst of unrelenting Viking attacks; driven into exile in 1014, briefly returned as king, but died soon after;

[Aelfgifu of York], c.970 – c.1002. First wife of King Æthelred; likely a daughter of northern stock; little known of her;

[Aethelstan Aetheling], ? – 1012. Eldest son of Æthelred and Aelfgifu;

[Egbert Aetheling], ?-? Second son of Æthelred and Aelfgifu;

[Edmund Ironside]; c.988 – 1016. Third son of Æthelred and Aelfgifu; succeeded his father to the English throne in 1016, earned his nickname due to success in battle against the Vikings; however, suffered a terrible defeat at the Battle of Assandun and was forced to give up much of his kingdom to the invader Canute the Great; died in November of that year, leaving two small sons;

Edward the Exile, 1016 – 1057. Eldest son of Edmund Ironside; was sent by Canute to Sweden while still an infant; escaped and ended up in Hungary; married Agatha, a princess of the Kievan Rus'; father of Margaret, Edgar the Aetheling, and Cristina; was recalled to England by his uncle to be his heir, but died within two days of his arrival;

Edgar the Aetheling, 1051 – 1126. Son of Edward the Exile and Agatha; rightful heir to the kingdom after his father's death, but was passed over by the witanagemot in favour of Harold Godwinson due to youth; had a long and eventful life;

[Edred Aetheling], ? – ? Fourth son of Æthelred and Aelfgifu;

[Eadwig Aetheling], ? – 1017. Fifth son of Æthelred and Aelfgifu; claimed the throne after the death of his elder brother Edmund Ironside, but was captured and executed by Canute;

[Edgar Aetheling the Elder], ? – ? Sixth son of Æthelred and Aelfgifu;

Emma of Normandy, c.985 – 1052. Second wife of Æthelred; daughter of Richard I of Normandy; sister to Richard II; mother of Edward the Confessor, Goda of England, and Alfred Aetheling; married Canute the Great after the death of Æthelred and was by him mother of a son, Harthacanute, and a daughter, Gunhilda; was deposed by her son Edward after his ascension to the English throne and kept imprisoned at Winchester, where she died;

Edward, 1003 – 1066. Known as *Edward the Confessor*, elder son of Æthelred and Emma of Normandy; spent his youth in exile in his mother's homeland; last of the House of Wessex to rule England; King from 1042 until his death without issue, sparking the war of succession between Earl Harold Godwinson, Harald Hardråda of Norway, and William of Normandy;

Goda, c. 1004 – c.1047. Daughter of Æthelred and Emma; sister of Edward and Alfred; married first to Drogo of Mantes, by whom she had a son Ralph (later called Ralph the Timid, earl of Herefordshire) and secondly to Eustace of Boulogne; life unknown;

Alfred, c.1005 – 1036. Younger son of Æthelred and Emma; younger brother of Edward and Goda; was captured and murdered by Earl Godwin's men during his attempt to take the throne.

The Great Houses of England

Wessex

Godwin, c.1000 – 1053. Earl of Wessex, a position he acquired under Canute after swearing loyalty to him following Edmund Ironside's death; was rewarded with marriage to a Danish noblewoman, Gytha Thorkelsdottir; implicated in the murder of Alfred Aetheling; swore loyalty to Harold Harefoot, Harthacanute, and Edward the Confessor in turn; rebelled against the latter in 1051 and was exiled; forced his return the following year, but died at Easter 1053;

Gytha, ? – ? Wife of Godwin, mother of their children;

Sweyn, 1020 – 1052. Eldest son of Godwin and Gytha; father of Hakon; misadventures included abducting the abbess of Leominster; was named *niðing* and exiled for life; died while attempting a barefoot pilgrimage to atone for his sins;

Hakon, c. 1040 – ? Son of Sweyn, taken as hostage to Normandy;

Harold, 1022 – 1066. Second eldest son of Godwin and Gytha; named Earl of East Anglia, but became Earl of Wessex after his father's death; led campaigns against Wales in 1062-63; travelled to Normandy in 1064 and forced to swear loyalty to William; named King of England after the death of Edward the Confessor; defeated the Vikings and his brother Tostig at the Battle of Stamford Bridge, defeated and killed at the Battle of Hastings;

Edith Swannesha, c. 1024 – ? Common-law wife of Harold Godwinson and mother of six of his children; he set her aside for marriage to Edith of Mercia; identified his body after Hastings;

Edith of Mercia, c.1040 – ? Second wife of Harold Godwinson; first marriage was to Gruffydd ap Llywelyn of Wales in 1058; married Harold in 1064 after Gruffydd's murder; had a son by him, also named Harold, born two months after his death;

Tostig, 1026 – 1066. Third son of Godwin and Gytha; married Judith of Flanders in 1051; was named Earl of Northumbria in 1055, but had a highly tumultuous tenure; deposed in 1065 and turned against his brother Harold; made alliance with Harald Hardråda of Norway and invaded England, but defeated and killed at the Battle of Stamford Bridge;

Edith, c.1029 – 1075. Eldest daughter of Godwin and Gytha; married Edward the Confessor in 1045 and became Queen of England; briefly banished to a nunnery due to her family's disobedience, but was reinstated; fled to Winchester after her husband and brothers died; died there in 1075 and was buried beside Edward in Westminster;

Gyrth, c.1030 – 1066. Fourth son of Godwin and Gytha; named Earl of East Anglia when his brother Harold became Earl of Wessex; fought beside him at Hastings, where he was killed;

Leofwine, c.1035 – 1066. Fifth son of Godwin and Gytha; Earl of Kent; fought with and was killed beside his brother Harold at Hastings;

Wulfnoth, c. 1040 – c.1094. Sixth son of Godwin and Gytha; taken by Robert Champart into captivity in Normandy, where he remained for most of his life;

Gunhilda, Aelfgifu, Marigard. Other daughters of Godwin and Gytha.

Mercia

Leofric, c.995 – 1057. Earl of Mercia, one of the three most powerful men in England after the king; married at least twice; stood with and supported Edward the Confessor during the crisis of 1051; died in 1057;

Godiva, ? – ? Best known of Leofric's wives; remembered in folklore as 'Lady Godiva of Coventry' for her supposed nude horseback ride; possibly the mother of Ælfgar;

Ælfgar, c.1015 – 1062. Only son of Leofric; became Earl of Mercia at his death; rebelled against Edward the Confessor in 1055 and was defeated by Harold Godwinson; allied with Gruffydd ap Llywelyn of Wales, but was again defeated; died in 1062;

Edwin, c. 1036 – 1071. Eldest son of Ælfgar; became Earl of Mercia in 1062 on his father's death; made alliance with Harold Godwinson; enemy of William the Conqueror; author of insurrections against the Normans; died in rebellion against them;

Morcar, c.1038 – 1087. Second eldest son of Ælfgar; became Earl of Northumbria in 1065 after the deposition of Tostig Godwinson; removed by William the Conqueror; rebelled with his brother Edwin and Edgar the Aetheling;

Edith, c.1040 – ? Daughter of Ælfgar; first marriage was to Gruffydd ap Llywelyn of Wales in 1058; married Harold Godwinson in 1064 after Gruffydd's murder.

Northumbria

Siward, c.990 – 1054. Earl of Northumbria; supported Edward the Confessor in the crisis of 1051; went north with Malcolm of Scotland in 1054 to depose Macbeth; defeated him in the Battle of the Seven Sleepers, but later died of a bloody flux;

Osbeorn, c. 1020 – 1054. Eldest son of Siward; died with his father;

Waltheof, 1050 – 1076. Second son of Siward; married Judith of Lens (daughter of Adelaide of Normandy); later appointed Earl of Northumbria in 1072, but rebelled against William the Conqueror and was executed.

Other English Nobles Great and Small

Eadsige, ? – 1050. Archbishop of Canterbury; succeeded to the post after Æthelnoth's death; crowned Edward the Confessor; death precipitated the crisis between Edward and Godwin;

Stigand, ? – 1072. Bishop of Winchester; named Archbishop of Canterbury in 1052 as a reward for negotiating the peace between Edward and Godwin; excommunicated five times; supported first Harold, then Edgar, then William as claimants to the English throne; deposed and imprisoned for simony;

Aldred, ? – 1069. Archbishop of York; led the expedition to find Edward Aetheling;

Wulfstan, 1008 – 1095. Clerk, prior, and eventually Bishop of Worcester; close ally of the Godwins; the only English bishop to retain his post after the Norman Conquest;

Ingelric, ? – ? Senior thegn of England, father of Maud;

Maud, c.1030 – ? Daughter of Ingelric; married Ranulf Peverel and settled in Normandy; mother of William and Ranulf Peverel the Younger;

The French Royal Line

{Robert Capet, 972– 1031]. King of France; father of Hugh, Henry, Adela, Robert, and Eudes; crowned his son Henry co-king in 1027; died in 1031;

[Constance of Arles, 986 – 1034]. Queen of France; third wife of Robert Capet; mother of Hugh, Henry, Adela, Robert, and Eudes; after the death of Hugh, plotted against her son Henry trying to get her younger son Robert on the throne instead, but failed;

Henry Capet, 1008 – 1060. Second eldest son of Robert and Constance; King of France after his father; made alliance with Robert of Normandy; became sole king in 1031, but had to deal with his mother and brother; made alliance with Geoffrey Martel of

Anjou; knighted the young William of Normandy; fought with him at the Battle of Val-ès-Dunes, but the alliance later turned sour; conducted campaigns with Geoffrey against William; twice tried to invade Normandy, in 1054 and 1057, but failed;

Anne of Kiev, c.1030 – 1075. Daughter of Yaroslav of Kiev; third wife of Henry Capet, who she wed in 1051; became regent for her son Philip in 1060;

Philip Capet, 1052 – 1108. Son of Henry and Anne; became King of France in 1060; later an enemy of William of Normandy;

Adela Capet, 1009 – 1079. Daughter of Robert and Constance; was betrothed to Richard III of Normandy, but he died before the marriage could take place; wife of Baldwin V of Flanders; mother of Baldwin VI, Matilda of Flanders, Robert the Frisian, Henry, and Richard;

Robert of Burgundy, c.1011 – 1076. Third son of Robert and Constance; schemed with his mother to become king at his father's death, but was defeated by his brother Henry; received the duchy of Burgundy as a placation; a ruthless and amoral robber baron;

Eudes Capet, c.1013 – 1056. Fourth son of Robert and Constance; led a French force into Mortemer in 1054, but was soundly defeated by the Norman barons; died soon after.

The Norman Ducal Line

[Richard II], c.963 – 1026. Fourth Duke of Normandy; son of Richard the Fearless and Gunnora; brother of Robert de Évreux, Emma, and Hawise; husband of Judith; father of Richard III, Adelaide, Robert, Eleanor, William, and Maud [the latter two entered the monastery at Fécamp and died young.] Father by his second wife, Papia de Envermeu, of Mauger and Guy de Envermeu;

Robert de Évreux, c.970 – 1037. Son of Richard the Fearless and Gunnora; brother of Richard II, Emma, and Hawise; became Archbishop of Rouen in 989; pronounced an interdict on his nephew Robert after the death of his nephew Richard III and was sent into exile; however the situation was resolved by diplomacy and he returned to Normandy; became the regent for his young great-nephew William in 1035, but died two years later;

Hawise of Normandy, c.978 – 1034. Daughter of Richard the Fearless and Gunnora; sister of Richard II, Robert de Évreux, and Emma; wife of Geoffrey of Brittany; mother of Alan;

[Judith], c.982 – 1017. Daughter of Conan I of Brittany; first wife of Richard II; mother of Richard III, Adelaide, Robert, Eleanor, William, and Maud;

[Papia], ? – ? Second wife of Richard II; mother of Mauger and Guy;

[Richard III, c.1002 – 1027]. Eldest son of Richard II and Judith; became the fifth Duke of Normandy after his father's death, but died mysteriously very soon thereafter, leading to accusations of fratricide against his younger brother Robert;

Nicolas, 1023 – 1092. Bastard son of Richard III by unknown mother; put into a monastery at the age of about three at his father's death; later Abbot of Saint-Ouen;

Adelaide, c.1003 – ? Eldest daughter of Richard II and Judith; married Reginald, Count of Burgundy, by whom she had a son, Gui;

Gui of Burgundy, c.1023 – ? Son of Reginald and Adelaide; nephew of Robert the Magnificent; tried vigorously to install himself as duke in place of his bastard cousin William; led the rebels at the Battle of Val-ès-Dunes; escaped and holed up in the castle of Brionne, enduring a lengthy siege before surrender and exile;

Robert, c.1005 – 1035. Second son of Richard II and Judith; called the 'Devil' and the 'Magnificent'; became the sixth Duke of Normandy on his elder brother's death, but was suspected of fratricide; father of William and Adelaide by his mistress, Herleva de Falaise; briefly married the Danish princess Estrid Sveinsdottir, but the union ended in annulment; went on pilgrimage to Jerusalem but died at Nicaea on the return;

Eleanor, c.1011 – c. 1071. Daughter of Richard II and Judith; married to Baldwin IV of Flanders; mother by him of a daughter, also named Judith, who later married Tostig Godwinson;

Mauger, c.1018 – c.1055. Elder son of Richard II and Papia; brother of Guy; became Archbishop of Rouen in 1037 following the death of his uncle Robert; deposed at the synod of Lisieux in 1054 and exiled for life by his nephew William;

Guy [William], c.1019 – c.1053. Younger son of Richard II and Papia; brother of Mauger; became count of Talou in about 1037; deserted the siege of Domfront in 1053 and declared his rebellion, but captured at Arques, defeated, and exiled by his nephew William.

Herleva, c.1007 – 1050. Daughter of Fulbert the tanner; sister of Walter; mistress of Robert the Magnificent, by whom she was the mother of William and Adelaide; later married Herluin de Conteville and by him had two sons, Odo and Robert, and two daughters, Muriel and Emma;

Walter, c.1003– ? Son of Fulbert; brother of Herleva; assisted his nephew William;

Herluin de Conteville, c.1000 – 1066. Knight of Normandy, created vicomte of Conteville; brother of Agnes, Martine, and Isabella; husband of Herleva; father of Odo, Robert, Muriel, and Emma; stepfather of William and Adelaide;

Agnes de Conteville, c.1004 – ? Sister of Herluin; wife of Ranulf Peverel, mother of a son, also named Ranulf;

Ranulf Peverel; ? – ? Son of Ranulf and Agnes; married Maud of England; named as father to two sons, William and Ranulf, but there is doubt about William's parentage;

William Peverel, 1051 – 1113. Known as Will, rumoured to be the Conqueror's bastard but this claim unclear; recorded as son of Maud and Ranulf Peverel; fought at the Battle of Hastings; afterwards, rewarded richly with the Honour of Peverel;

Adelaide, 1030 – c.1090. Daughter of Robert and Herleva; sister of William; married three times, firstly to Enguerrand de Ponthieu (killed at Arques 1053) secondly Lambert de Lens (died 1054) and lastly Odo of Troyes (in 1060); had three children by Enguerrand; by her second husband, a daughter Judith (married Waltheof of Northumbria) and by her third, a son, Stephen;

Odo, 1031-1097. Elder son of Herluin and Herleva; became Bishop of Bayeux in 1049; fought with his half-brother William at the Battle of Hastings;

Robert, 1033-c.1095. Younger son of Herluin and Herleva; Count of Mortain; fought with his half-brother William at the Battle of Hastings;

Muriel, c.1035 – ? Elder daughter of Herluin and Herleva; married William de Ferté-Macé;

Emma, c.1038 – ? Younger daughter of Herluin and Herleva; married Richard de Avranches.

William, 1028 – 1087. Son of Robert the Magnificent and Herleva de Falaise; known as *William the Conqueror* and *William the Bastard*; Duke of Normandy and King of England; took the throne in the Norman Conquest of 1066;

Matilda, 1031 – 1083. Daughter of Baldwin V of Flanders and Adela Capet; niece of Henry I of France; married William in 1051; Duchess of Normandy and Queen of England;

Robert, 1053 – 1134. Their eldest son, known as *Curthose* and *Shortstockings;*

Richard, 1054 – 1081. Their second son;

Cecilia, 1055 – 1126. Their eldest daughter; became a nun around the age of ten;

Adeliza, 1056 – ? Their second daughter; briefly betrothed to Harold Godwinson;

William Rufus, 1058 – 1100. Their third son; became King William II of England;

Constance, 1062 – 1090. Their third daughter;

Agatha, 1064 – 1080. Their fourth daughter;

Adela, 1066 – 1137. Their youngest daughter; wife to Stephen, Count of Blois, and mother of Stephen, King of England, and Henry, Bishop of Winchester;

Henry, 1068 – 1135. Their youngest son, called *Beauclerc* and *Lion of Justice,* later King Henry I of England and Duke of Normandy.

Other Norman Nobles Great and Small

Robert Champart, ? – 1052. Abbot of Jumièges; travelled to England with Edward the Confessor, where he became first Bishop of London and then Archbishop of Canterbury against the wishes of the Godwins; pushed for their exile; forced to flee the country;

Osbern de Crepon, ? – 1040. Nephew of Gunnora, Duchess of Normandy; seneschal to the Dukes; father of Rainald, William, Constance, and Osbern; warden of the young William of Normandy; killed in his bedchamber while defending him from an assassination attempt;

Emma de Ivry, ? – ? Wife of Osbern; mother of Rainald, William, Constance, and Osbern;

Rainald, 1012 – 1035. Eldest son of Osbern and Emma; went on pilgrimage with Robert the Magnificent, where he died;

William, 1020 – 1071. Second son of Osbern and Emma; Lord of Breteuil; close companion and captain of William of Normandy; rode with him in all his battles; fought at Hastings;

Constance, 1022 – 1038. Daughter of Osbern and Emma; died in defence of the young duke;

Osbern, c. 1025 – 1103. Youngest son of Osbern and Emma; travelled to England in the retinue of Edward the Confessor, where he became a chaplain; passed intelligence along to his brother William; became Bishop of Exeter after the Conquest;

Bertrand de Bernay. Captain of Normandy under Robert the Magnificent;

Alain de Bernay. His brother, went on pilgrimage with Robert;

Joscelin de Bernay, 1015 – 1047. Son of Bertrand; knight and warden of William, Duke of Normandy; died at Val-ès-Dunes;

Gilbert de Brionne, c.1000 – 1040. Warden of William, Duke of Normandy; murdered while riding near Échauffour;

Richard fitz Gilbert, c.1030 – 1091. Son of Gilbert; ally of William of Normandy; fought at the Battle of Hastings; later Chief Justiciar of England; founded the de Clare family;

Grimoald de Plessis, Haimo de Creully, Ranulf de Bessin, Rannulf de Avranches, Roger de Tosny, Raoul de Gacé, Ralph de Wacy, Robert de Vitot, rebel barons of Normandy;

Walter Giffard, William de Warenne, Roger Bigod, Robert de Eu, Roger de Montgomery, Roger de Mortemer, Hugh de Gournay, Pierre de Valognes; loyal barons of Normandy.

Other French Noble Houses

Anjou

Fulk, 972 – 1040. Count of Anjou; called the 'Black,'; known for a nature by turns violently reckless and violently pious; caused endless mischief; died on the last of his four pilgrimages to the Holy Land, leaving Anjou to his son Geoffrey;

Geoffrey Martel, c.1010 – 1060. Son of Fulk; became Count of Anjou in 1040; made alliance with Henry Capet; enemy of William of Normandy; captured the castles of Domfront and Alençon in 1052-53; joined Henry on his invasions of Normandy in 1054 and 1057, but was defeated; died childless and was succeeded by his nephew;

Boulogne

Eustace, c.1015 – c.1087. Husband of Goda of England; stepfather of Ralph; brother-in-law of Edward the Confessor; his visit to England in 1051 sparked the crisis that led to the rebellion of Godwin of Wessex; fought with William at the Battle of Hastings.

Brittany

Alan, 997 – 1040. Father of Conan II; fought against his cousin Robert of Normandy until peace was made in 1030; named one of the wardens of Robert's son William, but was poisoned;

Berthe, ? – ? Wife of Alan; mother of Conan; after Alan's death she married Hugh of Maine and had Herbert and Marguerite;

Conan II, c.1033 – 1066. Son of Alan and Berthe; became Duke of Brittany around the age of eight after his father's death; had to depose his uncle Eudes in order to claim his title; fought against William of Normandy and Harold Godwinson in 1064, but lost; died in December 1066 after being poisoned, likely by William;

Eudes de Penthièvre, 999 – 1079. Brother of Alan; became regent for his nephew Conan, but refused to give up his authority and was eventually imprisoned;

Flanders

Baldwin IV, c.980 – 1035. Count of Flanders; called 'the Bearded,' father of Baldwin V by his first wife, Ogive of Luxembourg; father of Judith by his second, Eleanor of Normandy; his son briefly rebelled against him at the instigation of his daughter-in-law, but peace was soon restored;

Baldwin V, c.1012 – 1067. Son of Baldwin IV and Ogive; became Count of Flanders at his father's death; husband of Adela Capet; father of Baldwin VI, Matilda of Flanders, Robert the Frisian, Richard, and Henry; allied with his eventual son-in-law William of Normandy; became co-regent for his nephew Philip Capet in 1060;

Maine

Hugh IV, ? – 1051. Count of Maine; married Berthe of Brittany after she was widowed; had two children, Herbert and Marguerite; on his death, Geoffrey Martel and William of Normandy began to squabble for ownership of the county;

Herbert, c. 1046 – 1062. Son of Hugh and Berthe; became Count of Maine around the age of five; became a pawn between William of Normandy and Geoffrey Martel; took refuge in the Norman court and swore fealty to William, but died young;

Marguerite, c.1048 – 1063. Daughter of Hugh and Berthe; was betrothed to Robert Curthose, son of William of Normandy, but died before they could be wed;

Ponthieu

Enguerrand, ? – 1053. Son of Hugh de Ponthieu; brother of Guy and Bertha; married Adelaide of Normandy in about 1048, but was excommunicated at the council of Rheims in 1049; became Count of Ponthieu in 1052; turned against his brother-in-law William and attempted to assist his other brother-in-law, Guy of Talou, by relieving the siege of Arques, but was killed;

Guy, c.1025 – 1100. Brother of Enguerrand and Bertha; became count of Ponthieu at the death of Enguerrand; joined the French forces pillaging Normandy in 1054, but was captured at the Battle of Mortemer and spent several years as a prisoner; apprehended Harold Godwinson in 1064 before being forced to turn him over to William;

Bertha, ? – ? Sister of Enguerrand and Guy; wife of Guy of Talou;

ABOUT THE AUTHOR

Hilary Rhodes is a scholar, author, blogger, and history geek. She has published six historical novels about William the Conqueror, Richard the Lionheart, and their lives and reigns. She holds a B.A. in English and M.A. in history, and is currently studying for her PhD in medieval history. She lives in England.

STAY CONNECTED!

Follow me on Facebook:
https://www.facebook.com/hilaryrhodesauthor
Follow me on Tumblr: http:///www.thedeadkings.tumblr.com
Favorite my author page:
https://www.smashwords.com/profile/view/hilarymrhodes

Made in the USA
Middletown, DE
30 April 2017